STONE AND SHADOW

ALSO BY BURHAN SÖNMEZ

Labyrinth

Istanbul Istanbul

Sins and Innocents

STONE AND SHADOW

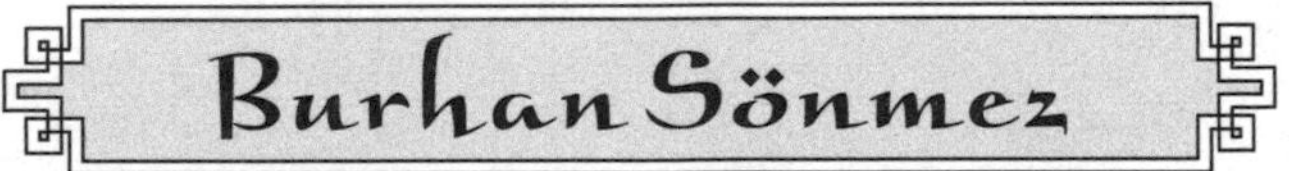

TRANSLATED FROM THE TURKISH
BY ALEXANDER DAWE

OTHER PRESS
New York

Originally published in Turkish as *Taş ve Gölge* in 2021
by İletişim Yayınları, Istanbul

Line art on page ii from Shutterstock.

Production editor: Yvonne E. Cárdenas
Text designer: Patrice Sheridan
This book was set in Chaparral Pro
by Alpha Design & Composition of Pittsfield, NH

1 3 5 7 9 10 8 6 4 2

Printed in the United States of America on acid-free paper. For information write to Other Press LLC, 267 Fifth Avenue, 6th Floor, New York, NY 10016.
Or visit our Web site: www.otherpress.com

Library of Congress Cataloging-in-Publication Data
Names: Sönmez, Burhan, author. | Dawe, Alexander, translator.
Title: Stone and shadow / Burhan Sönmez ; translated from the Turkish
by Alexander Dawe.
Other titles: Taş ve gölge. English
Description: New York : Other Press, 2023.
Identifiers: LCCN 2022042528 (print) | LCCN 2022042529 (ebook) |
ISBN 9781635422771 (paperback) | ISBN 9781635422788 (ebook)
Subjects: LCGFT: Novels.
Classification: LCC PL248.S565 T3713 2023 (print) |
LCC PL248.S565 (ebook) | DDC 894/.3534—dc23/eng/20230208
LC record available at https://lccn.loc.gov/2022042528
LC ebook record available at https://lccn.loc.gov/2022042529

Of the many things hidden from the knowledge of men, nothing is more unintelligible than the human heart.

Homer

Death is a mystery and must always remain such.

The Epic of Gilgamesh

Merkez Efendi Cemetery

Istanbul, 1984

Avdo considered the gravestone he would make for the dead Man with Seven Names whom they had buried today. He drew on his cigarette, took a sip of tea, and thrusting forward the fingers of his hand that held the cigarette as if he were talking to someone, he thought to himself, the gravestone would have to be black and with a hole in the center. You should be able to see the emptiness on the other side. The void should grow and deepen the more you looked. The dead man had been a soldier. When they found him stretched out on the bank of the Euphrates during the Dersim military operation, he was unconscious, his memory gone. They told him his name was Haydar and that he had been wounded by a band of Kurdish Zazas and had to rejoin his unit. Soon he was armed and made good use of his whip as the enemy was rounded up and driven barefoot into exile. The journey was long and Haydar sometimes felt light-headed, as if he might fall, but he was convinced of who he was and what he was doing. When they stopped at a camp, an old blind man among the prisoners, half of whom had already perished, recognized his voice and said they came from the same village. What happened to him, the blind man asked, and he told Haydar his past. His real name was Ali. During the roundup, he must have been shot on the riverbank while fleeing from the soldiers. Realizing he had lost his memory when they found him and telling him that he was a soldier, they had given him a new past, and a new future. After listening to the man, Haydar fled to the Mesopotamian Plain in the south, where he came to believe he had no one identity. There the plain spoke to him: You are neither Haydar nor Ali, as you have no memory of childhood, and with no memory of those years, you will never know who you really are. He walked the earth, following the stars. He took refuge in God and read every book he found in search of an answer. From Jerusalem to Cairo, Crete to Athens, Rome to Istanbul, he wandered for forty years, finding a new name and a new religion in every city where he made his home. Today he had been brought to the Merkez Efendi Cemetery in a coffin draped in faded muslin, his seven names written on a piece of paper: Ali, Haydar, İsa, Musa, Muhammed, Yunus, Adem. He had spent his last week in bed. In his crowded room, he kept a letter and a bag for his neighbor who came to see him; when he died, they were to be delivered to the gravestone master Avdo.

After everyone had left and the cemetery was silent and a fog was falling over Istanbul, Avdo opened the letter:

> Avdo, I am entrusting you with the work of my gravestone. I have gone by many names; I have adopted many

religions. In the end I have no one faith. And with so many names, I have none. I met you when you were a child and when you sang so beautifully. Your name has been on my mind, Avdo, I don't even remember what mine was then. Maybe you do. Last year I happened to learn that you lived at this cemetery. I heard what happened. I couldn't come. Surely you were already busy enough with all the dead around you. They told me that your gravestones always fit the spirit of the dead. Make one for me. Let my gravestone say to the universe: The only evil of God is that he does not exist. Make a gravestone for this. I am including some money with this letter to cover expenses and for those songs you sang when you were little. I am also leaving a few other things in my bag that may be of use to you.

With a sigh, Avdo put the letter in its envelope after reading it twice. Looking at the fog falling over the graves, he wondered what voices would come tonight. On these foggy nights he sometimes heard the voices of his childhood, sometimes the wailing of the dead. Reading the letter, he had felt as if his barefooted childhood was watching him through the fog. There stood that little boy several feet away like a patient cypress. Softly stirring and with every step the crackling of dry branches. With every rustle, his childhood came to life in sound. Laughing, singing, and shouting unraveled in threads that paid no heed to the wailing dead. Once again Avdo heard these voices and he was content. Leaning back, he lent his ear to the night. He remembered his past, he knew who he was, for he knew his name. He was not like the Man with Seven Names. In the guarded trunks of his mind, he kept all he had endured over the years. He remembered even the oldest melodies; the words were still fresh in his mind. He thought of a song he used to sing in the markets and squares, a song that fed him. He murmured the melody then softly he began to sing so as not to wake the dog that was sleeping at his feet.

Oh beloved, don't squander my day,
One day lasts as long as a lifetime.
Oh beloved, don't throw my gleaming life in the cave,
A lifetime lasts as long as one day.

When he sang at the base of those cold walls, the women would come out from their houses and caress the head of the child who sang with such passion. They gave him bread, warm milk, sometimes a bed. He was glad, and like every other orphan, he took refuge in their compassion, in their hands and breath. He experienced the most beautiful sleep in their homes. Dreaming the woman was his mother, he closed his eyes with the hope of waking up in the morning to find out that his dream had come true. Those nights were as long as a lifetime. In the morning he opened his eyes and looked lovingly on the mother of the household and told her his dream: An old man in a graveyard was chiseling a stone, keeping him safe from the cold, letting him play with his dog. The old man missed his mother, too, a mother he had never seen.

Who was dreaming? Was old Avdo dreaming of his childhood or was young Avdo dreaming of his older self?

On the radio they announced this was going to be the longest night of the year. The fog would lift at midnight and toward dawn it was going to snow. The city would fall asleep in the storm and wake up in white. Surviving the wet north wind that swept over the sea was no easy task, and the cold seeped into your bones. Avdo had a home with a strong roof and sturdy walls and he had his fire. On nights like these he left his outside light on. This was a lighthouse for the homeless. If only his dog Toteve could give some kind of signal to the street dogs, howling them over. But the old beast now lay under the table, stretched out in a world of peace. For the last hour he had not budged. He was getting on in years and took every opportunity to rest, climbing into the little den he had dug behind the house where he passed the daytime hours. Lately he had lost his appetite, he often left his favorite mash unfinished.

Avdo was getting older, too. His beard had gone gray and he was losing his teeth; he knew it from the chill that often took hold of his back. His arms were still strong and he worked throughout the day on his feet, hauling marble and stone. His large body gave him no complaints, save the icy spot in the middle of his back. He felt it in the fall winds and in December he avoided the cold. The fire from the little grill beside his table warmed his tea but it no longer kept him warm. He had taken to wrapping a blanket around his back whenever he sat down. The coldest time of the year, the *zemheri*, had a hold on him.

He stirred three spoonfuls of sugar into his tea and lent his ear to the sounds in the pale darkness. Somewhere over the shrine in the western side of the cemetery he heard the cry of an owl. He stared out into empty space as he struggled to pinpoint exactly where she was. Night was not silence but rather distilled sound. The many different sounds of day turned into clamor, but the sounds of night emerged distinctly. The songs of childhood, the wailing of souls, the crying of an owl. None of it was clear in the chaos of day. The same went for longing and pain. Alone you could feel pure pain at night. The water that now ran from the fountain by the redbud tree in the darkness conjured up those old laments, the sadness of a lover lost years ago twisted around the heart. In the day, it was easy to carry the burden; at night you truly believed that you were alone.

The souls also believed they were alone in the world, their wailing now slowly drifting through the fog. Every morning they rose thinking the sun was rising for them, they found consolation in a thousand and one dreams and in the footsteps of visitors who went among the graves. They lingered in the tumult of the world, losing track of time, until evening fell again. They trembled in the twilight, and as the dwindling light mingled with the gathering dusk, they came to understand their lack of fate. There was sadness and fear. Who could help them? An owl, an old dog, and Avdo. The only ones listening to them as they prayed to the sky.

Avdo looked across at the souls wailing in the cemetery. Our God, they cried, if You are not, then how have we found hope? Our God! You have left us in this world with a fleck of hope but staring into the face of despair.

Avdo smiled. The poor dead, he said under his breath.

You can't choose your place of birth, but you can choose where you will die. Yet those in the cemetery only understood this once they had died. Chasing desires all their lives, not one of them had ever stopped to think where they might like to die. Now suddenly finding themselves down in the earth, they let out terrible cries. Avdo had thought about it before. In a dark abyss that was as long as a night. It was years ago that he had settled here with the decision that this was where his life would end. He dug his grave beside the grave under the redbud tree, placed a nameless gravestone above it. His smooth, long-suffering stone. On that day he would lie down beside the woman who was waiting for him. On that peaceful night a silver star would shoot across the sky. On that long, dark night. Our God!

He turned on the radio. A woman was chatting with a man about the ferryboats that had been canceled due to the heavy fog and the snow clouds approaching from the Balkans. Saying that everyone should stay at home tonight and tomorrow, kick back in a warm chair and enjoy the winter weather. Choose a film from among your collection or a book from the library and have some downtime. *Picoleurs* should have a little white cheese, nuts, open a small bottle of *rakı*. Spend the evening with some easy music. The Istanbulites who had been working so very hard deserved so much. Relaxation was a God-given right, as much as hard work was a responsibility, considering the tough times the country was facing. The first song was dedicated to those citizens of Istanbul who deserved a rest. A citizen himself, Avdo turned up the volume. When they asked him where he came from, Avdo would say he considered himself from Istanbul as that's where he was going to die. From a visitor in the cemetery, he had heard that the trees were the true masters of the city. Cypresses born in Byzantine times were still standing, alive and well; Avdo felt he was one of them.

When the song ended, the presenter read the news bulletin. The value of the American dollar had exceeded four hundred and thirty Turkish lira; seven separatists had been captured in an armed conflict in the province of Eruh; the Ministry of Education had officially announced they would build a place of worship at their head office; members of a gang that had formed a ghost company to deceive hundreds of workers with the promise of sending them abroad for work had been arrested; New Year national lottery tickets had sold out so quickly many of them had ended up in the black market; a Yoncaspor footballer nearly strangled the referee who red-carded him during a match with Beşiktaş; in his first interview from his prison cell in Italy, the terrorist Mehmet Ali Ağca, who had been charged with the murder of the journalist Abdi İpekçi in Istanbul five years ago and who later attempted to assassinate Pope John Paul II after breaking out of prison, claimed he was a Turkish nationalist but had nothing to say when he was asked who was operating behind the scenes. On the debate on whether girls and boys should study together a new poll showed more than ninety percent of students preferred a coeducational system. When the bulletin finished, the male presenter made a dirty joke and he and the woman broke out laughing, which was followed by a rousing local dance number.

Avdo warmed his fingers over the fire. He touched the hot brick on the grill. With a pair of tongs, he stirred the fire. He lifted the teapot and filled his glass.

He looked at the bag that had belonged to the Man with Seven Names then pulled it off the table and held it in his lap. His gravestone should be veined, black marble, he thought, thin lines on the surface like stars streaming across the night sky. It was difficult to work with veined marble, but it was the right choice. White streaks on the dark surface, like those vanishing stars.

The black leather of the bag was worn, cracked, covered in scratches. Avdo ran his calloused fingers over its surface and thought it had to be the color of the bag that made him think of black marble. The bag was about a foot wide and the flap that stretched over the front had a lock in the middle. He pushed on the bolt of the lock and it suddenly popped open without a key. He pulled open the flap and stopped to breathe in the strong scent of mold before reaching inside. There was a notebook and a fountain pen and a flute in the inner pocket.

He turned the leather notebook over in his hands, flipped through the pages. The edges were worn, the ink faded. The last few pages were blank. This was a journal. Some lines had been crossed out and rewritten, afterthoughts dashed off in the margins. In the dim light, it was difficult to make out the words penned in cramped letters. Trying to make out a sentence on a random page, Avdo heard something crackle in the fog, raised his head, and looked into the open space.

What was it? Maybe the uneasy whispers of souls or the wild fantasies of his childhood. Or perhaps the branch of an old Byzantine tree had fallen on a fresh grave after waiting all those years. Avdo listened but heard only the sound of water running from the fountain. He mustn't forget the fountain. Toward morning there would be frost, which meant the water pipes might freeze and burst. He had to turn off the valve before he went to bed, and with weather like this he might have to keep it off for several days. It would do the fountain good to have a break from running every day of the year. It had a right to rest as well. "It is a citizen of Istanbul, too," he said, looking gravely at the radio, as if the presenters were listening.

The sound of fountain stopped for a moment and then started. Either an animal had passed under the running water, which was unlikely in this weather, or someone had drunk from the tap.

Toteve raised his head and growled several times. The dog would never wake up from a sleep this deep for no apparent reason. Someone was at the fountain.

Avdo turned off the radio, waited a little for a sound, and then called out into the fog.

"Hey! Who's there?"

There was no answer.

He put the journal back in the bag with the feeling that he would never know how to make the gravestone of the Man with Seven Names until he read what was in it. Maybe not black marble, not a hole in the center, maybe this dead man would need an entirely different kind of stone. Avdo would not rush. He would take everything he could from the pages of the journal, and in the dreams he would have on those long nights he would conjure up a spirit and then a gravestone.

Toteve rose to his feet and barked sharply several times, baring his teeth. Avdo touched the back of his neck. "Okay," he said, "calm down, it's only a homeless person who has come to visit."

He tried to make his voice carry to whoever was waiting in the fog, making his location clear. He called out again.

"Hey! You at the fountain! I can't see you, but I know you're out there. Come over, you'll freeze in this cold. My dog won't harm you. Come and warm up by the fire."

As he waited for another sound, Avdo opened his cigarette case and rolled two cigarettes. He pressed the end of one against an ember in the fire, and it caught. His first drag was deep.

"I have a cigarette, and I rolled one for you, too!"

As the silence drew out Avdo almost thought he was mistaken.

Or were these treasure hunters? Last year they haunted the cemetery, digging up random graves with strange maps in their search for treasure. The imam of the mosque caught a few of them, but the more ambitious ones started using plastic shovels, even sifted through the dirt with bare hands. More of them came when rumors went around that golden cups and coins had been buried in some graves. In the end they set their sights on the fountain. Avdo had also heard the rumors that the fountain had been built by a Christian saint who had lived in the neighborhood before Ottoman times, that its waters had been blessed by the apostles and that a hoard of emeralds and precious jewels lay beneath its marble slabs. On a moonless night two months ago Toteve scared off two hunters that had come for the fountain. Avdo had raced after them, shouting at the top of his lungs.

Were they back?

When Avdo sat up, a pale shadow appeared in the fog. This seemed like someone from among the dead, who could barely stand and who had suffered a thousand and one hardships to get up out of her grave and walk this far. A shroud of a dress fell down over her knees, her long bony arms hung at her sides. She was dragging her feet, one foot was bare. The young girl's body was covered in mud, her hair tangled, her lips cracked.

She took a few halting steps then stopped before coming any closer. She waited with her head tilted to one side. Maybe she felt guilty for coming uninvited or she didn't have the strength to take another step. Avdo went over and wrapped his blanket around her shoulders. He took her by the arm and slowly they limped to the fire. He had her sit down on the divan and took off her shoe. He knelt down beside her and wiped her feet and ankles with a cloth. Her feet were too numb to feel anything. Noiselessly she trembled, her arms clasped across her chest. How long had she been wandering like this in the cold?

"This won't do," said Avdo. Taking her by the arm again, he tried to help her up. She was lifeless. In one swift motion, he had her in his arms and carried her inside. There was a bed on one side of the room and a divan across from it. He lay her down on the bed and covered her with a blanket. He picked up a towel at the foot of the bed and left the room. Pulling the brick out from the grill, he wrapped it in the towel. He could feel the heat through the towel. He went back inside, placed the brick under the girl's knees, and drew the blanket back over her.

"When the weather is cold I warm this brick up in the fire and put it in my bed. It stays warm until morning."

He went to the woodstove in the corner and threw in a couple logs. The embers flared and the fire sprang back to life.

"In a little while it'll be as hot as a hammam in here."

He picked a pot up off the floor, placed it on the stove. This was the hearth of his home, his kitchen nothing but this corner of the room. On a shelf were several glasses, plates, pots, and pans. Lined up on a chest to one side were small bags of food. He took a spoon off the shelf, lifted the lid of a pot, and looked inside.

"I made it this evening. Tarhana. Dried vegetable soup. Really warms you up. I have soup when I'm cold, it revives you. It'll help you get your strength back. I wish you had come earlier instead of waiting out there in the cold..."

He glanced at the fire in the stove then stirred it with a pair of tongs. When he turned, he saw the girl curled up in a ball with her knees on her chest. She had the brick pressed against her stomach. It wasn't her legs then, she wanted to warm up her stomach first. Her wide-open eyes were taking in the room: a photograph on the wall, the chest in the corner, pots and pans on the shelf. Her eyes were so big. Or her face was so thin. She lightly coughed.

"Are you okay?" he asked.

"Yes," she said faintly.

"You'll feel better," he said. "Have something to eat, rest. Until your voice is stronger. My soup has put many people back up on their feet. For now, just enjoy it..."

He helped her sit up and put a pillow behind her back as she leaned against the wall. He went back to the stove and watched the steam rising from the open pot. Filled a bowl with soup and sat down on the side of the bed. Handed her a spoon that slipped from her grasp.

Avdo had hosted many homeless people before but this was the first time he was faced with someone so thin and so sick.

"When did you last eat?" he asked.

Her eyes rose and she looked at him. "I haven't counted the days," she said.

Avdo took the spoon. Filling it with soup, he brought it to her mouth. Half went in and the rest dribbled over her lips. He wiped her chin with a towel. This time he took half a spoonful and poured it slowly through her lips. "There we go."

Soon her face seemed more relaxed. Her skin, which was still cold, softened. If she could eat and rest like this for a couple of days she would get back on her feet. But she would need more time for the bruises on her neck and the cuts on her arms to heal. He wondered when all this had happened; the wounds would leave scars even after they healed.

"When was the last time you slept in a warm bed?"

She answered without looking at him. "I haven't counted the weeks."

Avdo couldn't help but laugh. He collected himself when he met her gaze. "Oh, it's just the way I laugh," he said, "think nothing of it."

She looked away.

He spooned more soup for her.

The essence of life was in the spoon, in the roaring fire, in the soft bed. It was everything those people who lived hungry on the street would dream of, and yet it was still too much. They wandered aimlessly, hardly dreamed, and were wounded along the way. They might share their dreams, but never would they ask each other about their wounds. Neither would Avdo. Right now, the hot soup was precious, spicy, and rich with butter.

"Did you like the soup?"

"Yes."

"Finish this, and I'll give you some more."

Her breathing was returning to normal. She brought her hand to her brow and fixed her hair, a hopeful sign, maybe she could now hold her spoon.

"No one is going to hurt you here," said Avdo. "Do you understand? You don't know me, you happened on this place in the dark, but everyone around here knows me, they trust me. You can trust me, too. You can sleep after you finish your soup. I'll lie down on the divan. If you need anything, just let me know."

She nodded. What if she didn't trust him. With a body so battered, what worse could become of her.

"I'll just have a little water," she said, struggling to sit up.

"I'll bring you some," said Avdo. He poured a glass of water from the pitcher on the chest.

"I keep the pitcher near the stove. It's warm."

She tried to take a few little sips. Then pushed away Avdo's hand holding the glass up for her.

"Thank you."

"Let's have some more soup then."

"Maybe later? It's hard to eat after so long."

"All right, you catch your breath then."

He straightened the pillow behind her.

"I'm Avdo," he said and went on before she could speak, "I made tea on the grill outside, would you like a glass?"

"Okay."

As he walked over to the kitchen he pointed to the dog stretched out beside the stove. "The one who is always sleeping is Toteve. He'll only wake up if he catches a strange scent. See, he's accepted you already."

He took a large mug off the shelf, put a teaspoon in it, and being careful not to disturb Toteve, he opened the front door. As he stepped outside he heard her whisper: "Reyhan."

He stopped and looked into her eyes, which seemed even larger now. Outside the water still ran over the fountain's white marble, soothing the restless dead who were now finally drifting back to sleep. The cold night wind slipped through the open door and filled the room. All night Avdo had felt the cold, but now it felt good. "Reyhan, hmm..." he said.

Embers were flickering in the grill. Standing on his porch, Avdo spoke to the fire, something he had learned in childhood. What happened to the idea that the old have a long past and the young a long future? What happened to the long future of youth? He thought, even I was always grasping at the thread of time on my way to this old age, and still the present and the future of the youth today is uncertain. As if the thread of time has already slipped out from their fingers, they are already dead, and soon more young than old will come to rest in this cemetery.

He put his hands around the body of the teapot to feel its warmth. Filled the mug with tea, added three spoonfuls of sugar, and stirred. Thinking it would do her good, he added one more.

When he went back inside, he could see that she had drifted off to sleep, her head to one side, the blanket freed from her grip. Deeply breathing. A thin strip of blood ran from the right side of her mouth. He wiped away the blood with a cloth. She felt nothing, not an eyelash fluttered. Taking the pillow out from behind her back, he gently slid it under her head. He brushed the hair off her brow, placed her hands under the blanket, put the brick back under her knees, and tucked her in tightly.

It was midnight when he went outside to tend to the empty teapot. He threw dirt over the fire. He took the bag off the table and went inside. Still dressed, he switched off the light and lay down on the divan with a blanket. The light of the fire was flickering on the ceiling. He listened to the crackling fire, Toteve snoring beside it, and the calm breathing of the girl only a few feet away who seemed to have slipped into a dream. He was content. The light of the fire on the ceiling flashed and trembled as if one by one new stars were coming out in the sky of the room. Night was falling on one side, dawn approaching on the other.

Avdo pulled the blanket up over his chest. Listening to her calm breathing, he drifted off to sleep.

When they were both asleep the sound of the fountain circled the cemetery seven times. The wind blew in over the sea, rustling the tall cypresses. In the deepest corners of the cemetery, the worms hibernating through the winter stirred to life. The last birds took shelter in the nooks of red-tiled roofs. The rising chimney smoke was thin and faint;

stones were covered in frost. As the sky slowly turned the cemetery and the city outside and the sea beyond turned from blue to white and from white to black. The fire in the stove went dark. Toteve raised his head and looked.

Avdo opened his eyes the moment he heard the growling. Sitting up, he saw that Reyhan was still asleep. Her pale face was childlike in the porch light cast into the room.

"Shush, Toteve," said Avdo, "you're going to wake her up."

Toteve continued to growl.

Avdo put on his shoes, opened the door, and went outside. Toteve followed him.

The fog had lifted, he could see the fountain. Listening to the running water, he remembered he had forgotten to turn off the valve. Mumbling to himself, he went around the side of the house, lifted the lid off the ground, reached in, and turned off the valve. He came back to the porch.

"Look, Toteve, it's quiet out here."

Then from the distance, near the sea, came the sound of another dog. Toteve growled again.

"Is that it?" said Avdo. "You woke me up because a friend of yours was barking?"

Toteve barked a couple times in quick succession. In response came barking from the same dog.

"Okay, that's enough, you're going to wake her up already."

The sound of her voice came from the doorstep.

"They are here."

"What?" said Avdo, startled to see her standing there. "It's freezing out here, get back to bed."

He pushed her inside and sat her down on the bed. She wasn't trembling from the cold, this was fear.

"Why did you get out of bed? You need to rest," he said.

"They're coming, that's their dog, they've tracked me here," said the girl.

"Who's coming?"

"Soldiers, police..." Her lips trembled, her eyes filled with tears.

Avdo paused for a moment to consider what to say. "Why? Did you steal something? Did you kill someone?"

"Nothing like that."

"Then what do they want?"

"To ask me about people I don't know, about things I don't know."

Avdo ran the possibilities through his head and found nothing that might put her at ease.

"Reyhan," he said, using her name for the first time. "Don't lose hope so quickly. There is law and order. If you did something wrong, you'll go to jail. Life there is hardly any different than life out here."

"I can't bear it any longer."

"If these people are the people you say, I mean, if they are men of the law, then they won't hurt you."

"No, they won't take me alive."

"Why are you so afraid?"

"I'm better off dead—"

"Wait, calm down."

"I've been in their custody for days, weeks, but when the fog fell this evening I found the chance to escape. I managed to get this far."

"I'll speak with them, find a way."

"Where was that knife?" she said as she rose to her feet and walked to the kitchen.

"What knife?" said Avdo, stopping her.

"Give me a knife."

"How will a knife protect you from them?"

"I'll take my own life, give me a knife."

"How could you even think that?"

"They won't take me alive."

"Maybe you're wrong, maybe no one's coming for you. That could have been any street dog."

"That was their hunting dog, coming closer."

They strained their ears. The dog was indeed slowly coming closer, winding around the trees and rocks in the cemetery that bore her scent.

"I don't know you, dear," said Avdo. "But I'll help you. You keep on running. For now, I'll distract them, buy you time so you can get away."

"They'll catch up with me."

"Cross over to the asphalt road on the other side of the cemetery and you'll be at the old city walls. No one can find you in the tunnels there."

"The dog will catch my scent. And I won't get far in the state I am in. Give me a knife."

Reyhan moved to find a knife in the kitchen. Avdo took her by the shoulders.

"Stop," he said, "wait, let's think about this."

Hopeless, she stopped. She could taste salt on her lips. Her voice quivering, she said, "Avdo . . . Avdo . . ."

Narrowing his eyes, he was thinking, trying to come up with a plan. She had said his name twice and he hadn't even noticed. Now he was muttering under his breath, "There's a way, yes, it could be . . ."

"Avdo," said Reyhan again, "I came here because I know you."

"Know me? What do you mean?"

"I came here once before to visit Elif under the redbud. I know your name, but this is the first time I'm meeting you in person."

"Elif?" said Avdo, squinting his eyes.

"I had no choice but to come here," she said, "I had nowhere else to go. Otherwise I wouldn't have disturbed you like this."

"How do you know Elif?"

"She's my aunt."

Avdo couldn't move his lips. The names and faces of years ago raced through his mind, some nearly lost from memory altogether. "If Elif is your aunt..." he said.

"I'm telling you the truth."

"Your mother... yes, I remember."

"I have no one left in this city."

"I understand... it's good you came, but—"

"I had no choice."

Suddenly Toteve was barking violently outside.

Reyhan grabbed his hands. "Please," she said, "don't let them take me alive, I'm begging you."

Avdo spoke with conviction. "The men are coming. We don't have time to talk. I'll hide you in the back."

"Hide? How?"

"I know a place, come on."

"The dog will sniff me out."

"No, it won't, believe me."

"How?"

"Come on, I'll show you, hurry."

Reyhan could hardly speak as she sobbed. "Just give me a knife, I'll use it if they find me."

"On one condition: You have to stay calm and do whatever I tell you."

"Okay."

He brought her a bread knife, placed it in her palm, covering her long fingers with his hand.

"I want you to promise me," he said, "that you are going to wait to the very end, you won't use the knife?"

"I promise," said Reyhan, her eyes now bloodshot.

He wrapped a blanket around her and quickly led her outside, turning off the porch light. As they hurried around to the back of the house, he called to Toteve in a low voice. "Toteve, come! Toteve!"

They passed the stones waiting to be carved, half-finished gravestones, and then the workshop. Soon he stopped at a slight bump in the ground and pointed to a little den to one side.

"This is Toteve's den. Only a dog can fit inside, but you're thin, you can get in there."

Reyhan looked at him doubtfully. "They'll find me there," she said.

"No, they won't. Once you go in I'll have Toteve sit at the front. They'll assume their dog has come for Toteve. All you have to do is quietly wait."

"Isn't it really small?"

"It turns in the back, don't worry, it's deep enough."

"There's no other way."

"Come on, quick."

Reyhan sat down and put her feet in the hole, leaned back and slowly slid inside. When everything but her head and the knife she held were hidden, she said, "Avdo, I have to tell you something."

"You can tell me later, there's no time to talk now."

"I have to, just in case."

"Is this about Elif?"

"No, it's about me."

"Tell me, I'm listening."

"I think," said Reyhan, and she paused, "I think I'm pregnant."

His hands hung in the air as he narrowed his eyes. Should he speak or keep silent. He smoothed her hair, took her shoulders, and slowly pushed her down into the den. He watched her moist eyes disappear in the small mouth of the den.

Then he turned to Toteve and took him by the scruff of the neck. "Come on, boy," he said, "it's your turn now, get down there."

This was one of his favorite rituals and Toteve happily crawled in and lay down, his long tongue hanging over his paws.

"Bravo, now you wait here, don't leave that spot." He pulled some cured beef out of his pocket and left some for Toteve.

Snow was now swirling in the sky. The city would be covered in white by morning.

Avdo went back to his house and bolted the door. He fixed the divan he had been sleeping on and put away the blanket. He took off his sweater and his pants and in his long underwear he got into bed. He took the brick Reyhan had left there and placed it on his stomach—it was still warm.

Through the night the cemetery was normally quiet save the sound of the running fountain, but now and at this late hour it was filled with the sound of a dog barking and people shouting. They were almost here, training lights on the trees, checking every grave the dog had sniffed.

"Commander! There's a cabin over here, it looks like a house!" a voice cried out.

"Release the dog!" snapped a voice. "Have two people go around the back."

The dog circled the fountain then moved decisively to the house. Up on the porch, it sniffed patterns on the floor. It stopped outside the front door, running its nose along the threshold. Avdo could hear the damp, rapid inhalations as he waited, clutching the edge of the blanket. Not for some time had he felt this afraid, and he wondered if he should have taken a knife as well.

The bolt snapped with one strong kick and the door flew off its hinges.

"What's going on," said Avdo, rising to his feet. He stood motionless in the light of the torches, facing rifles and pistols. They poured inside.

"Hands up!"

"Stay right there!"

"Don't move!"

"I'm not moving."

They switched on the lights and quickly searched the room.

"Who is in the back?"

"No one, it's a bathroom."

"Check it!"

The bathroom door opened and closed. They looked under the bed and in the chest, rifled through quilts and blankets.

There were more than ten. Most were soldiers, three were dressed in civilian clothes. The soldiers bore rifles; the others carried handguns. Orders rained down from one of the plainclothes officers they called the commander. He had to be a high-ranking police officer or even an agent.

The commander went outside and checked the divan on the porch, the grill, and the table. When he noticed that his dog was still busy sniffing around the house, he came back inside and went over to the chest in the corner. He looked over the bags of food and then noticed broken glass on the floor. Leaning over, he picked up a shard.

Tilting his head, he turned his eyes to Avdo and asked, "Was this a teacup?"

"Yes."

"It was full? There's tea everywhere."

Avdo hesitated for a moment, looking down, he didn't know what to say. Finally, he said, "Yes."

"It is 'Commander' when speaking with me."

"Yes, Commander."

"They call me Commander Cobra. Remember that."

"I understand, Commander."

"This glass you filled with tea and left here, is that right?"

"I thought I might as well have the last of the steeped tea. I poured myself a glass, but it was far too bitter, so I left it, I already had too much tonight."

Twisting his dark red mustache, the commander poked at the broken shards with the tip of his boot. "I saw a glass on the table outside. How many people were here tonight?"

Caught off guard, Avdo gave the closest version of the truth. “Sometimes the homeless come and ask for bread. One came for a tea and then left.”

“Left in this cold? When there’s a stove inside and a grill outside?”

“You never know what they might do, Commander, coming or going. Maybe he had friends waiting for him at the walls. They stay at the walls on the other side of the road. Some often come over here for a brief visit.”

Avdo was now putting on his pants and his shoes.

“There’s an unwashed bowl here,” said the commander.

“For soup.”

“I didn’t see another one. Didn’t you offer this homeless guy some soup?”

“I did. That was his bowl. I’d washed the one I used before he came and put it away.”

“The man ate his fill, drank his tea, and left.”

“And he took a little bread with him.”

“Who was he?”

“I don’t know. They don’t tell me their names. And even if they did I wouldn’t remember.”

The commander grabbed Avdo by the arm. Through clenched teeth, he said, “You are not to forget! If I ask, you will not forget the answer.”

“All right.”

“You got it?”

“I got it.”

“What was my name?”

“Commander Cobra.”

“Just like that, you are not to forget names.”

“I won’t, Commander.”

"What's your name?"

"Avdo."

"Avdo, I'm going to ask you again then, who was here?"

"It was someone who goes by the name of Broke, Commander, he never told me his real name. They all have nicknames. Why wouldn't I tell you his name if I knew it?"

"Who's Broke?"

"One of the homeless who lives out there on the walls."

"He comes here often?"

"He does, others do, too. They all know my place here."

"You call this shed a home?"

"A poor man's home—"

"Did anyone else come here tonight?"

A soldier called out from the door and everyone turned.

"Commander! Slowy is going around back."

After sniffing every inch of the floor, all the pots and the pans, their dog Slowy had moved back out onto the porch, his nose to the ground, and was now making his way around back, no less distracted by the falling snow than the fog that had covered the city earlier in the evening.

"Come on," said the commander, knocking Avdo's arm, "fall in line."

Avdo took his coat and went outside.

With Slowy leading the way the soldiers followed, then the plainclothes officers, Avdo, and finally the commander. They passed the stones and then the workshop and came to the darkest section of the cemetery. Slowy stopped and they held up their lights.

Slowy was a few meters from the mouth of the den, facing Toteve.

The old dog looked like chiseled stone. His steady gaze took in the people standing across from him as he sized up Slowy's intentions. Both dogs were baring their teeth. Testing each other as they growled. If this went on any longer Toteve's grayish-brown head and Slowy's cinnamon-colored coat would be covered in snow. Slowy could wait no longer. He approached the den, sniffing the ground, and stopped a foot away.

"Stupid animal!" said the commander. "You followed the scent of this rabid dog. Is that why you came out here?"

In the standoff they heard the distant cry of an owl. Avdo turned and looked at the shrine. The great master of the night was unfolding her wings as she released her damp cry. The fountain was no longer running, the ground was covered in a blanket of snow. The little house in the cemetery was steeped in a bitter silence. The owl was mistress of that house, too. Long nights, the seasons, the ages, it all fell under her wings; traces of time were but stains on her feathers; the living or the dead had no sway over this time. When there was none, she was there, and after everyone had gone she would remain. Her cry was long and mournful, hanging on the white cloth of the sky.

Slowy craned his neck, growling nervously. His back-right leg scraped at a thin layer of snow. He was hesitant but poised to attack, his tail taut, saliva dripping to the ground. He scraped at the snow again. Sensing the danger, Toteve could wait no longer. With one savage bark, he sprang onto his front paws. As the full bulk of his body loomed his jaws snapped like a flash of lightning. Startled by the sudden attack, Slowy lost a piece of his nose and Toteve circled around with a speed that defied his age, biting Slowy's throat and the back of his neck. Pushed back away from the hole, Slowy was forced to retreat. In silence he turned and lowered his tail, whimpering in pain, licking the blood that ran from his nose.

Avdo laughed, then covered his mouth with his hand as he looked around, an embarrassed expression on his face. "That's just how I laugh, Commander, don't mind me," he said.

The commander's eyes shimmered in the torchlight, the corner of his mouth twitching. Suddenly he turned and struck Avdo in the face with the back of his hand. Avdo stumbled backward, struggling to keep his balance. His eyes went dark as he raised a hand in the air to ward off another blow, his other hand clutching his forehead. He stood there until the pain had passed then ran his fingers over his eyes and his nose. As he looked up he wiped away the blood with the sleeve of his coat.

"Commander," he said, "that's just how I laugh, I can't help it."

"Good," the commander said, twisting his mustache, "Slowy's blood for your blood."

"Yes," said Avdo, who was willing to shed his own blood for Toteve.

The commander wrapped his woolen scarf tightly around his neck and pulled up the collar of his coat. He was feeling the cold. He put a hand in his coat pocket. "So, I will ask you again," he said with frustration in his voice, "who came here tonight?"

"The man I told you about, Commander, the one they call Broke was here. If you like I can go over to the city walls and find him."

"I don't need him."

The soldiers had now given up hope on Slowy and were searching the surroundings. Their lights flashed through the snow now falling in heavy flakes over uncarved marble slabs. They were merely making a final round of checks before the night was over.

The commander went on, "I am looking for someone else."

"One of the homeless from around here?" asked Avdo.

"I'm looking for a young girl," said the commander, "who got away from us this evening."

"A girl?"

"Did you see anyone?"

"Here? Commander, why would a girl be here in the middle of the night?"

"She might be hiding somewhere in the cemetery. Maybe you saw someone in the distance, if nothing else."

"It's been foggy all night, impossible to see a thing."

"And your dog didn't pick up a scent, didn't start barking for no apparent reason?"

"No, Commander, I didn't even see him, he's been sleeping in that hole all night."

"What are you doing in this cemetery? Seeing you were asleep, you can't be the night watchman. Are you a gardener?"

"I carve gravestones, for the people buried here. That's my workshop."

When they heard the growling, they turned suddenly and saw Toteve lunging at the commander's hand. He pulled back just in time. Avdo quickly intervened, throwing out his arms. "Get back," he shouted to Toteve. "Back!"

There was fear in his voice. He knelt down and put his arm around the dog's neck, caressed his head, and waited for his breathing to settle. He led him back to the den. He had him sit at the opening and blew softly through his lips, *vouu vouu*. These were sounds Toteve had loved ever since he was small. Avdo stroked his nose and his neck. He scratched his brow and stayed with him until he was sure the dog was settled there. When he came back, he tried to mask his anxiety in the darkness.

"My dog grew up on the streets, Commander," he said. "He's a little aggressive. That's why he attacked your dog. Yours is well-behaved and doesn't know how to fight."

"He doesn't know how to fight?" There was both hostility and surprise in the commander's voice.

"What I meant is, when he retreated like that..." Avdo already regretted his words and knew whatever more he said would come out wrong and he stopped. The commander's unblinking eyes were fixed on him. He shivered.

"What did you say?"

"I meant to say that my dog is aggressive, he has a bad temperament—"

"My dog doesn't need to know how to fight," said the commander. "He only has to take me to the person I am looking for. I can fight in his place."

"Of course, that's what a real dog should do, track the scent, show the way..." Avdo stuttered.

The commander stepped closer. "I can fight in his place," he said, emphasizing every word this time.

"Of course, Commander."

The commander bared his teeth. Avdo could feel his breath on his face. It seemed the ends of his teeth were sharpening, his tongue growing longer. Slowly the commander drew his gun.

"Do you see this?" he said, holding up the firearm.

Looking at the gun in disbelief, Avdo said, "Yes."

Training the barrel of the gun on Toteve, the commander asked again, "And now?"

"Of course, Commander, I do, but—"

"Then watch closely."

Avdo stepped in front of the gun. He looked at the commander, his eyes imploring. "Please, no..."

The commander threw a punch and Avdo's feet left the ground. He fell like a log. For a moment he lost consciousness and when he came to he had no idea what had happened. Though he felt he might not be able to stand, he struggled to his feet. The commander put his foot on his head and slid the jagged bottom of his boot over his neck, nearly suffocating him.

The commander turned to look at Toteve and seeing that the dog was poised to pounce he fired instantly, pulling the trigger several times. Sparks from the barrel flared in the darkness, crackling like bolts of lightning in the sky. The snow seemed to swirl even faster in the air. With every shot, he seemed to pull the trigger harder. As if a vast and savage army stood before him, he was full of hatred. Into the dead body of the animal, he unloaded his rage and exhaustion, emptying the magazine of his gun.

Toteve's blood ran like the fountain's water, spreading over the earth until Avdo's cold fingers felt the warm blood. He turned and strained to see Toteve but couldn't. His mouth was full of snow. When the warm blood touched his wrist, Avdo could feel the dead dog in his pulse. Flowing through his veins and to his eyes that filled with tears.

The commander clicked out the empty magazine, reloaded, cocked a bullet into the chamber. He lifted his foot and knelt down beside Avdo. Through his teeth, he said something, but Avdo's ears were ringing and he couldn't make out the words. He could only hear the sound Toteve had made when the first bullet struck him in the brow. When he found Toteve twelve years ago, he was nothing but skin and bones, so little he could sit in the palm of his hand. Back then he let out the same thin, pleading sound. *Vouu.*

When the commander left with his men and his dog the snow was falling even more heavily, and now the cemetery was a garden draped in white. Earth and sky were one. The branches of the trees were heavy with snow. Toteve's blood lay under a white blanket as the time of the living and the dead turned white. There was a humming in Avdo's ears, the ringing of his distant childhood. Where was he now, how old was he? What was the season? What loneliness was he feeling and in which city? The sliding past fell over him, slowly covering his body. He gave himself up to the silence of another time until the cry of the owl came to him again from some corner of the night, the last sign of life. He lifted his head and wiped the snow from his face, and in the dim cemetery he looked at the shape of his lifeless dog that lay only a few feet away from him. This was the longest night of the year. Now Avdo could remember the time and where he lay.

Paris Gazino

Istanbul, 1965

The Paris Gazino was full on Saturday night. Under the light of crystal chandeliers the white tablecloths, red vases, and fresh flowers were all shimmering. The players had taken their places on the stage two steps behind a microphone mounted on a stand for the singers. First a woman, then a man would warm up the audience with sparkling pop and folk songs before a dance group would come to liven the crowd with dance numbers. Straight after came a group that played rock and pop, and now the drinks were flowing faster and faster, and as soon as the stage lights were switched back on, the belly dancer of the night would appear to set the place on fire, shaking her hips, jingling bells on her fingers. Toward midnight, after everyone had had their fill of drink and entertainment, the crowd would begin to long for tenderness and a quieter mood, and it was then that the headline singer, Perihan Sultan, would arrive in her glimmering, silvery dress to glide from one end of the stage to the other as if walking on water. From the very first ballad she had the crowd mesmerized, and as they handed her flowers, she placed them along the edge of the stage and blew kisses to every table, winning over the hearts of her fans whose names she knew by heart.

There was still some time before she would take the stage as she sat, one floor above her audience, chatting with her assistant, Yüksel, describing her day as they ate wrapped kebabs and drank ayran.

"So I said to Seyrani, you're strong, you're tough, you can squeeze water from a stone. But me? I'm nothing without you, the world would end if you didn't come to the gazino every other day and show your face. It might not mean the end of the world for the others, but it would for me. They'd all keep on living, lights would still be shining, laughter rising, but my world would go dark and disappear. You understand? I'd float off like this smoke from my cigarette. You have many friends, Seyrani, and even more enemies. I know why you have so many enemies, we're surrounded by a bunch of scoundrels and they're jealous, they can't stand the sight of you, they get up to no good behind your back. You're right to look after yourself, and it's good to be cautious. You're busy, I've heard what you have been up to, but you need to think about me, too. When I miss you like this I'm a wreck, and I throw back drinks until morning, waiting for you to come. The more I wait, the more I long to see you, my heart burning like a candle, melting like one, too—that was a good one, wasn't it, melting like a candle? Last time I saw you was two weeks ago, and then you were gone. Every day you send someone to ask after me, it helps to hear your name and know you're well. They said you stormed a venue in Yenikapı last week, that's bold but what if something happens to you, Seyrani, I'm begging you, what would I do without you. They say Perihan Sultan sings such passionate songs. What else can I do? I sing them out of longing, I sing in sad lament. Yesterday Canip the Junkie came to the gazino with five men, but the bodyguards wouldn't let him in. They screamed and shouted and said they would find Seyrani to settle the score. They said they would see to it that I'd never be with my man again. On their way out they smashed the glass signboard with the picture of the Eiffel Tower. You broke up their drug ring, and if that venue in Yenikapı is really theirs, like they say, you did a good thing, and if not the rumor's enough to shake up the scene. Look after yourself, Seyrani, but don't leave me alone. And you know you're going to have to look after yourself even more from now on. I said this and stopped, looking wearily into his eyes. As I looked at him like that, he sat up in his chair, glanced at the men waiting at the door. They weren't looking, they were busy keeping watch. Seyrani snubbed out his cigarette. He took my hand and said, dear Sultan—oh Yüksel Abla, my heart was about to leap out of my chest—he said, my Sultan, I am in this world to look after you, not me. I won't let anyone touch even a hair on your head, he said, last night I watched Canip the Junkie getting kicked out the front door of the gazino, and when he slipped into the back streets I went after him, spraying bullets, I got one of his men. Oh, Yüksel Abla, have you heard about it? I said, Seyrani, that's what they didn't tell me. I cried and he wiped the tears off my cheeks. Don't worry, dear Sultan, he said, these are everyday affairs, soon enough everything will be back on track, don't think about it, he said. I said, I think about you now more than ever. My voice was trembling. He looked into my eyes and asked me if there was something else I had to say. Yüksel Abla, I was about to faint and fall to the floor. So I gathered my courage and said, There is something. I took it slow and heavy, like one of those girls in the movies, you know how Türkan Şoray glowers in the movie *The Black Eyes* that came out last week. He struggled to hold back a smile. Then I felt better. I said, Seyrani, I'm carrying your child. He stopped. You never know what men from worlds like his will do, and just when I was thinking that he didn't believe me, he brought my hands to his lips and kissed them. I couldn't help but throw myself around him and drown his black jacket in my tears. I said, Seyrani, when I'm not with you my tears flow like fountains, deadly rivers flow into my heart. Didn't I put that well, Abla? Fountains of tears, deadly rivers in my heart, as if I were singing, with the same feeling. So he stroked my hair, he kissed my brow, and then he said, You have to look after yourself, you can't stay out too much, don't take the stage too often, I'll talk to Kalender Bey about your work here. As you wish, I said. He said, From now on Yüksel Abla shouldn't go to hers at night, she should stay with you. As you wish, I said. He said, If it's a boy we'll name him after my father. Now I didn't say, As you wish, I told him to speak to Kalender Bey about it. Raising an eyebrow, he looked at me. So I told him the moment Yüksel Abla learned I was pregnant today she raced off to Kalender Bey, but I was really angry because I wanted you to know first. That's just what I said, sister, what else could I have said? And then I told him that Kalender Bey came racing over to ask me if there was anything I needed. When he heard I was going to see you today he smiled and sent his greetings, he said, tell Seyrani if it's a boy he should have my name. He said it twice. I said it was up to Seyrani. You know, Seyrani, my brave man and the father of my child. Then Seyrani smiled even more. Are we going to upset Kalender Bey, he said, he was like a father to us, he got us up on our feet. First he saved me from this swamp and then he saved you. Yüksel Abla, I'm so very happy but there's still one thing I couldn't ask him. What if it's a girl? Can I name her after my mother? Then I would call her Reyhan. What do you think, sister, isn't Reyhan a beautiful name?"

"It is," said Yüksel Abla. "Hey, slow down, girl, you're going to choke on that."

"I just can't get enough, you know most of this is going straight to the little one inside, there's nothing left for me. I say order us two more of these."

"You're about to go onstage, if you eat that much you'll just feel bloated, wait for the end of the show."

"Oh, sister, you want me to faint and fall up there? I swear my stomach is still grumbling."

"Okay, I know you haven't felt full for the last week, but if you go on like this you'll hit a hundred kilos."

"No, I won't, the baby eats most of it."

Yüksel Abla went to the door and called, "Fadime! Fadime, come over here!"

A young girl hurried up to the top of the stairs and said, "Go ahead, sister."

Fadime was a twelve-year-old girl who sold flowers in the club at night and on the street during the day. She also looked after her little brother and her father who was ill. In the afternoon she would come from Tarlabaşı with a basket of flowers and work until midnight. Customers who knew her story paid far more than the normal price for her flowers. Many of the stories of the girls who sold flowers in Beyoğlu were the same. Customers liked paying for stories. In her songs, Perihan Sultan sang of the hardship of these girls and the sorrow of their tenderhearted patrons.

"Fadime, take this money and run down and grab us a couple more kebabs. And get one for yourself."

"But I just ate, sister."

"So be it, you can take it home."

"Thanks, sister."

"And take an ayran, too."

Before returning to her chair, Yüksel Abla stopped in front of a mirror and sized up her appearance. She fixed her hair. Then turning a leg to the side, she pulled her skirt up over her calf. "Girl, am I gaining weight?" she said.

"What are you talking about, sister, you're thin as a pole. They couldn't find a girl like you if they combed all of Beyoğlu with a bag of gold."

"You're the only one who knows that but for some reason no one else can see it. I am almost over thirty."

"What's this? Something's happened? Come on and tell me."

"What's there to tell, dear, we're still counting the days until the shy men can find the courage, or more like weeks or months. So I left the house today on my way to the minibus stop and I was about to get on the next one when I look up to see Muzaffer from your village waiting there for his yellow minibus and I thought I'd pretend I hadn't seen him, but you just can't not see that bright yellow and his minibus was the only yellow one. Once he noticed me looking he came right over. He took my bag and before I could say a word he brought me to his line. So I got in and sat down next to him, but the line was hardly moving, the morning crowd was gone, three minibuses were still idling ahead of us. The man has the courage to come and take my bag but then he's got nothing to say. If I hadn't said something we would've just sat there in silence. So I asked him about his mother, the old woman is all alone. Same old same old, said Muzaffer, she's doing the best she can to manage her rheumatism. Now I know Muzaffer has a good heart but that's not enough. Am I supposed to come out and say, marry me and I will look after her, am I supposed to put the words in his mouth? Then he asked me what was happening with my house and finally we started chatting. It seems he heard I was getting roughed up again by my ex over the deed, oh dear, how quickly word spreads. After I got ownership in the last case the guy wouldn't give up, filed a case in the higher courts. So I took the reins and I said, Muzaffer, time flies and has no mercy, I'm thirty years old and I'm still tied up in trials over deeds. I didn't tell him I was thirty-two, but I did remind him of his age, I said, you're over thirty, too. I'm thirty-four, he said. Oh, I thought to myself, he's two years older than me. Girl, of course I know his age, there's ten years between you two. He said that, too, that he was exactly ten years older than

Perihan Sultan. I remember when she was born, he said, I was carrying milk from the sheep yard when they called out to me through the garden, but her name wasn't Perihan Sultan back in the village, it was İpek. There I cut him off, all right, I said, the name was different in the village but it's Perihan Sultan here, İpek from the village is dead, I said, she lives as a singer here—now that was a good one, right? He's already so shy and then he blushed and went completely quiet, sadness filling his green eyes. Why do you villagers love to talk about your villages so much anyway? You have a village and you think the world revolves around it, that's what I told Muzaffer. There's only one memorable thing about your village, I said, the people there are warm-hearted. I know this from Perihan Sultan, I said, not to be too open about everything, but I hope he understood I had meant him, too. Backing me up, he said, that's why her voice is beautiful, it comes from the heart, everyone used to gather around when she sang folk songs as a child. So after we got to talking about the village, he said he was going there next week to sell his last plot of land, he had found a buyer, then he'll come straight back. Can you check in on my mother when I'm not here, he said. Okay, I said, all you need to do is ask, Muzaffer. By that point we were at the head of the line so we got inside and left with all the other passengers. As if they were family members who might gossip about us later, he stopped talking to me altogether. He just mumbled along to the songs playing on his tape player the whole way, turning to look at me now and then with a smile. Now I'm fine with this, girl. Sitting there with him, listening to the same song, traveling along the same road in silence, I swear the man has a place in my heart. But it's like there's no one else in the world for him but his minibus and his mother and he'll pass on to the next one knowing nothing more. It can't go on like this. I'll pay his mother a visit next week and plant the idea in her head. I don't think she can find a better daughter-in-law than me."

"How is she ever going to find anyone better than you?" said Perihan Sultan. "Sister, why don't you invite Muzaffer here? Have him come to the gazino one night as our guest. It's been so long since I've seen him."

"Really? Forget the gazino, he's too shy to even walk the streets of Beyoğlu."

"Don't push him too much, he was like that in the village, his own special bumbling self. He got this old without ever getting married because he's shy. You call him and have him come in, tell him Perihan Sultan needs to speak with him."

"Speak with him about what?"

"Tell him to come in before he goes to the village."

"Are you going to talk about me?"

"If you give me permission I will, but you never do, how many times have I told you."

"No, please don't. I'm going to handle this myself. If it comes to it, I'll sit down with his mother and just settle into their home."

"Now that would be best." Perihan Sultan broke out laughing, paused, and tilted her head to listen to the music coming from below. "Ah," she said. "The boys have started. Is this pop or rock? I just can't understand what the public finds in these songs."

"I like them, they're good kids, harmless even when they're a little drunk. They really like you. They say the gazino fills up because of Perihan Sultan, and we get part of the share."

"I like them, too, but those songs are something else altogether. I swear they're going to bring the house down."

"You didn't finish, girl, what are you going to say to Muzaffer?"

"I was thinking about it today, I thought, what if I send word to the village, ask my older sister, Elif, to come. I don't know if she has the courage, but she needs to know just where I live now, and she should know she can come if she wants to. I'm going to have a baby and if she comes we can all live together."

"It's a beautiful idea but I really don't know if your sister would consider coming here after all this time."

"I don't know either, so I'll just send word. You tell Muzaffer that Perihan Sultan wants to talk about Elif. I'll write a letter he can quietly pass on to her when he goes to the village."

Village of Konak Görmez

Haymana Plain, 1958

It was forty days after the passing of Kara Agha. The earth of his grave had taken plenty of rain when they called on the stonemason Avdo who had been wandering the villages on the plain making gravestones for the past year. Kara Agha's two sons put state-minted gold in Master Avdo's hand and promised him three more if his gravestone was more glorious than the one that had been made for the father of their family's rival. They took Avdo to the local rivers and hills to choose from the stones. On the southern slopes he was struck by the sight of bright marble that had slid down in the rainwater and said he hadn't seen such a wonderful piece in a very long time. As he fastened six ropes around the stone, six horses dragged it to the village with men patiently replacing the ropes that snapped along the way. There the elderly, young men, and children were all curious to see the marble as they gathered around. The elders said that such pure and unadulterated marble was abundant in the past and that members of the tribes would bring pieces one by one to homes, mosques, and fountains of the villages where they would be used as foundation stones. There were many stones on the plain back then but no marble beds. Refined stones were leftovers from Ottoman times, but the marble was even older. When they ruled, the Byzantines brought them from distant lands to use in their buildings. Most likely this piece of marble had been carved and set by Byzantines, who had made it as round as a wheel, but strangely there was no script on it. Figuring there had to be something on the other side, they managed to pull it upright with horses and washed off the mud, moss, and worms with plenty of water. When the deep mark of the cross, which surely had not seen the sun for ages, appeared they looked upon the sign with amazement and fear. Around the cross were words of an unremembered alphabet. Some then hoped they might find buried treasure near such a beautiful stone, but when no such treasure was found they were left to believe that the stone was cursed. The elders told the sons of Kara Agha to take it back where it came from to keep any trouble out of the village. Never before had anyone seen a Christian cross in a Muslim cemetery.

Master Avdo protested. He turned to those villagers who'd had the chance to go to distant lands for their military service and asked if anyone among them had served in Istanbul. Fine then, so was there anyone who had served in Trabzon. One man stepped forward and said that he had served there, which he said was the most beautiful city in the world—he had seen no other. When Avdo asked him if he knew the Ortahisar Fatih Mosque, he said that naturally he had gone there for afternoon prayers on one of his leaves. Avdo went on to explain that it was first built as a church, not a mosque. And that there used to be coronation ceremonies of Christian kings in that church and that kings were buried there. When Fatih Sultan Mehmet took the city, he converted the church into a mosque, the very same thing he had done to the Hagia Sophia in Istanbul. Citing examples in other cities, Avdo went on to say he had seen countless mihrabs that had been made from Christian marble. The villagers listened to him, curious and envious of this man who had been to so many distant places. That was until Avdo told them that their village was in fact a Christian village. From the name it was all too clear. When their tribe came from the east to settle in this village two hundred years ago they adopted the old name of the village—as was the case with many other tribes—but the meaning was turned around. How was it that a village bore a name like Konak Görmez, which literally meant "the one who cannot see a mansion"? Indeed, the word *konakormas* came from one of the Byzantine languages and had changed over time. Avdo told them he had come across a mountain with the same name—Konak Görmez—when he was on the peaks of Palandöken in Erzurum.

With some discomfort, the elders attempted to give an explanation, saying the official village name of Konak Görmez had been recorded in archives that dated back to Ottoman times, but that everyone in the plain knew the village by the Kurdish name of their tribe, Şêxan Village, and that was enough to satisfy them. Avdo was unrelenting and went on to say that the name of the Haymana Plain came from Armenians and that the Armenians called themselves "Hay." Then the patience of the crowd wore thin. They jumped in and abruptly made it clear that Avdo had to stop denigrating them like this and that he should look to his own roots before questioning theirs. They put it that they had no idea where this man, who had come to the plain only a year ago, lived before and where he actually came from. Why had this stonemason been to so many different places and why did he speak so many different languages? Avdo told them that he had no home or homeland and that he had grown up as an orphan and that from a very young age he was introduced to a new language in every other city: Kurdish, Turkish, Arabic, Armenian, Syriac, and Greek.

In the following days children often came to watch Avdo smoothing out the marble in the cemetery. The best way to polish marble was with marble. When it was polished with patience it shone like a mirror. When it came to this the old stone masters used to tell their apprentices: Polish until you see your own face in the marble! Following Avdo's patient hand, the children entertained themselves with the riddles he would put to them. But the elders kept their distance, telling people to doubt the faith of this stranger who never came to Friday prayers in the mosque, as he might very well carry heathen blood, for he himself admitted that he never knew his mother or his father. They allowed Avdo to rub out the Christian cross and give the marble new shape before he mounted the stone at the head of Kara Agha's grave. They would hear no more unsettling stories from this tall young man who had far too much to say. The women in the village watched him from a distance, and when they drifted off to sleep at night they listened to the songs he would sing from the rooftop where he slept.

When the sun set Avdo would go to the fountain to wash the dust from his face and hair, and the young girls would stand back and wait for him to finish before they filled their jugs with water. As they watched him slowly walk away they could feel that the spell of this stranger was stronger than all the village secrets. Under that spell every girl pictured a journey and dreamed that when this stranger left the village he might take her with him.

Despite the many glances from unmarried girls, Avdo fell for the one who was already engaged. Every day he waited for Elif to come to the fountain, and there he learned that she lived in the house covered in indigo plaster, so at night he began to sing only after the lights in that house went out. It was the time of dreams and a loneliness that flowed between wakefulness and sleep. After her mother, her father, and her sister had fallen asleep, Elif would sit up in bed and tend to the blue beads in her hair for a while and then lose herself in those songs that drifted through the village like a gentle wind. Ever since she noticed the way he looked at her, she knew the songs that Avdo sang at night were sung for her.

What if I were to come at dawn to give you a red rose, oh beloved,
A rose lasts as long as a lifetime,
What if I were to say the red of this rose was your blood,
A lifetime lasts as long as a rose.

In every song Elif felt this stranger might leave the village with more than a golden coin, she feared he might cover her too in his enchanting shadow. Then he would take her to his horse after the village had gone to sleep and together they would ride off into the distance.

Village of Konak Görmez

Haymana Plain, 1958

Kara Agha had three flocks, three shepherds, and a house with three floors. His manor rose majestically above its large courtyard while the shepherds lived in houses beside the hayloft. After Baki, who was the ten-year-old son of the head shepherd, finished his work at the sheep pen he spent his time with Avdo, who was making a gravestone for Kara Agha. Avdo would teach Baki how to read and write and how to hold the chisel and how every piece of marble had a soul. In return Baki brought him cold drinking water from the fountain when the sun was high in the sky and green plums from the trees at the head of the road. As Avdo's work on the gravestone drew on from day to day the villagers praised the patience of his craft and the subtlety of his art, but it was only Baki who came to know the essence of his work, and because he brought his letters to Elif, he also knew the master would be staying for a while, and this made him happy.

The next day he would take Elif's reply to Avdo and carefully study the changing expressions on his face. The sun was not yet high in the sky and the earth not yet scorched when Avdo sent Baki to the fountain, saying, "Bring me some cold water." After drinking and pouring what was left in the cup over his head, he shared the contents of the letter with his only friend in the village. I'm engaged, said Elif. Stop loving me and find someone else. If you want someone like me consider my sister, İpek, she's sixteen and she is free. Many are asking for her hand, but she hasn't accepted an offer yet. She will say yes to you if you want. I'll convince her, and when you leave the village, she will leave with you. Her voice is as beautiful and as passionate as yours, you will be happy together. Don't love me, love her.

"Baki," said Avdo, "who is Elif engaged to?"

"To our young agha."

"Who is that?"

"You know Kara Agha's two sons; they have a younger brother who's now serving in the army."

"So her fiancé is a soldier."

"Elif is waiting for him to return, his name is Mikail. He's crazy, and everyone in the village is afraid of him. He beats us."

"Even you?"

"Once he even beat my dad."

"So he's that kind of person . . ."

"My dad did nothing wrong. One night a wolf attacked our flock, made off with one of the sheep. He hit my dad for that. If Kara Agha hadn't gotten angry with him and stopped him, he would have done even more." Baki's voice trembled with sadness and fear as he spoke of this.

"So you're afraid of him, too, is that right?" said Avdo.

"Not that he'll hit me, I'm afraid he might hit my dad."

Avdo put his hand on the boy's shoulder. "Don't worry about it," he said, "things like this can happen to us all in life, and they will pass if only we can be a little patient. I grew up as an orphan, and I was often beaten, but look, here I am now, sitting on this marble with you, having a friendly chat. So things do pass and move on."

"Mikail will be even angrier when he comes back from his service."

"Why is that?"

"He still doesn't know his father is dead. They didn't tell him to keep him from grieving away from home. His father loved him the most and he loved his father, always heeded his word. But now no one is left to rein in his temper."

"When is he coming back from his service?"

"I don't know."

Avdo waited a few days before he wrote another letter. Baki stuffed it in his undershirt and went over to Elif's house on the other side of the ravine. There he saw Elif and her sister, İpek, making gözleme at the clay oven. When he was turning to go before they saw him, Elif caught sight of him and called out. She said she wanted to give him something to eat. Lifting one of the gözleme off the hot pan, she brushed it with butter and set it down before him.

"So you caught the scent of fresh gözleme, didn't you, you clever child," she said.

Baki nodded his head with no intention of opening his mouth, which was already full of the first bite.

How difficult it was to understand grown-ups, Baki thought, and he wondered if he was going to turn out like them. Elif was beautiful and İpek too, so there was no difference between them. If Master Avdo loved one why wouldn't he love the other one, too? With İpek he would have what he desired and live happily for the rest of his life. İpek was tough, and she turned away suitors who sent messages with the excuse that her older sister was to be married first. If she really loved someone, she would have long since run off with him. Seeing she hadn't done that, she must be waiting for her good fortune to arrive, and so Elif took to praising Avdo. Women were probably smarter than men. Baki thought he could love either Elif or İpek, but grown men were certainly hard to understand.

"Girls, one of you come over here and help me," called their mother, Reyhan.

"İpek," Elif said, "you go, I'll take care of this."

Now it was just the two of them, Baki took the letter from his shirt and handed it to Elif. Keeping one eye on the door, she quickly read the letter and threw it in the fire when she was done. Then she stirred the fire with a pair of tongs. She turned and looked at Baki, who had finished his gözleme. She gave him another.

"Now you eat your fill," she said.

"Thanks, Elif Abla," said Baki.

"I guess this guy's crazy," said Elif.

"My master is a good man," replied Baki.

"Your master? How is he your master?"

"He is teaching me how to carve stone, how to read and write. When he heard the aghas weren't sending me to school, he said, don't worry, I will be your teacher. I help him in return."

"So you help each other then, and that includes carrying his letters," said Elif, who was now vigorously stirring the fire, scattering the ashes of the letter into the air.

"What did my master say?" asked Baki.

"You don't need to know that," said Elif, "besides, there won't be any more letters after this."

"Why?"

"What business do I have with a stranger, my fiancé is coming back soon, and there will be a wedding. You tell this man, your master, that he mustn't send you here again."

"Aren't you going to write him back?"

"No, I will not, and like I said, don't come here again."

"Never again?"

"Of course, you can come to see us, just don't come here with that man's letters, all right?"

Baki was silent as he watched Elif pull the flowery head scarf off her neck and spread it on the ground before she wrapped up several gözlemes.

"Take these," said Elif, "take them to your master, he's a stranger, have him put something hot in his mouth."

Baki looked pleased as he picked up the cloth and made for the door. He stopped on the threshold. Thrusting his hand in his pocket, he pulled out a handkerchief sealed with a double knot. "I almost forgot, my master also told me to give you this," he said.

"What's that?" asked Elif.

"I don't know," said Baki, "my master put something inside without showing me, then he tied it up."

There was a voice from outside.

Elif took the knotted handkerchief and stuffed it in her shirt. Then she gestured for Baki to go.

Baki left the clay oven and ran to the ravine, passing the fountain and the cemetery, with the hope that when he reached his master the gözlemes would still be hot.

Taking the hot cloth in his hands, Avdo said, "What's this?"

"Elif Abla said she won't write you another letter, and that she is waiting for her fiancé. She sent you this in place of a letter."

Avdo put down the cloth, opened it, and looked at the buttery gözlemes that were still steaming.

Merkez Efendi Cemetery

Istanbul, 1985

After the first cold snap of winter had passed and people had pulled through New Year's Eve, the ice in Istanbul was beginning to thaw and a dark mood was lifting. They hoped the new year would open new doors. They all knew the optimism on the radios and on the streets wouldn't last for long, but they also knew that hope was an addiction that was hard to give up. And Commander Cobra, coming to the cemetery in the middle of the day, still had hope.

Visitors were scattered across the grounds trying to keep their balance on the ice as they slowly made their way around the graves. They had come to pour water on the grave of a loved one who had come to mind at the start of the new year with the hope that they might spend the rest of the year with her spirit. Noticing a man walking over to his workshop, Avdo assumed he was coming to order a gravestone for the recently departed. When he narrowed his eyes, he recognized Commander Cobra, surprised to see him without all his soldiers and his dog. This time he had come alone.

"Hey there, Master Avdo," said the commander excitedly, "it seems we had no idea who you really are."

Avdo glanced at the trees in the distance and for a moment he thought that soldiers might be on their way or scouring the surroundings. But everything was still.

The commander held a packet in one hand and was fixing his hair with the other.

"So I said to myself I should pay a visit to the master, as we had a bit of an unfortunate meeting the first time around. I figured I should come back to win you over."

Avdo put his chisel down next to his mallet on the stone he had been carving and waited for the commander to come over.

"Go ahead, Commander," he said.

"I said, Master Avdo must be hungry so we should have lunch together. I brought these."

He put the packet down on the middle of the marble desk and pulled out two ayrans and unwrapped two lamb sandwiches. He handed one to Avdo and took one for himself.

A fire was burning in a large can set on the middle of the desk. This was Avdo's daytime stove, and when his hands went numb from the cold he would throw in another log and warm them over the fire. He added two more logs and looked up at the commander.

"You have a tough job, too, master," said the commander, "slaving away all day with your hammer and chisel."

“It’s not a hammer, we call that a mallet,” said Avdo, looking down at the mallet made from mulberry wood.

“Whatever it’s called, the job requires craftsmanship. That is not in everyone’s blood, good on you! But our job’s no walk in the park either, we face an entirely different set of challenges, and sometimes we make mistakes doing everything we can to protect the state and this nation. We don’t always act in the right way. We can’t always know. Sometimes we end up hurting people we don’t want to hurt. Like when I hit you here that night. It stayed with me, and I thought, what a terrible mistake, how rude I was to a blameless man. You see I have a sister who is paralyzed. I live with her and look after her. I told her that I had been rough with a purehearted man, damn this profession, may God break my wrist.”

The commander bit into his sandwich and took a sip of his ayran. Seeing Avdo just standing there, staring into space, he said, “Come on, the food won’t eat itself, you need the strength, come on.”

“Thanks,” Avdo said in a low voice before taking a bite.

“What was I saying, my sister said, go and win back his heart, no matter what it was you did. My sister’s a religious woman, like you, with a pure face. She said, if someone can do wrong, then someone can make right. My sister knows the hardships that come with this profession, she raised me from when I was little, helped me with my homework, got me to where I am today. She said, your work isn’t easy and not everyone knows that, it’s hard and it’s sacred, so you go and see this man the first chance you get, and you tell him about the conditions of your work. If he’s a citizen of this nation, he'll understand you, he'll understand your sleepless nights, how you sacrificed your youth so that the people of this country can live in peace."

Avdo waited in silence as he wondered where the commander was going with this.

"But there isn't a scratch on your face," the commander said, "that makes me feel a little better. I'd like you to understand me. When I came into the cemetery, I heard the call to prayer, so I took my ablutions straightaway and then I went into the mosque. I knelt down to pray, I prayed for Merkez Efendi, the protector of this mosque, I prayed for your forgiveness, I prayed for my sin to not be etched in my book in the afterlife. I'm really busy so I don't have the time to pray. Would you believe that I can't even get to that beloved mosque in Ortaköy and we live only a couple of minutes away. I just went to the mosque over there and prayed, see how sad I was about what I did to you. I prayed for God's forgiveness and for you to—"

"Don't worry about it," said Avdo, cutting him off. "I'm a human being, I'll forgive you, I just hope that my dog will forgive you, too."

"What's this have to do with the dog?"

"He's a living being, too, he was old, and he was going to die soon anyway but he suffered so I hope that he will forgive you, too, he also has the right to choose."

"A dog has rights, too?" said the commander with a snort. "What's done is done, I'm not concerned with the dog, but I am with you, do you understand? When I get home tonight I'm going to tell my sister about it. I'm going to tell her that I came here and saw that you were a good person when I saw your face in the daylight."

"Best wishes to your sister, Commander, I hope they find a cure for her."

"Unfortunately, there's no cure for what she has. She's been in bed for three years. When you go to the mosque you can pray for her."

Avdo stopped and thought about his answer and then said what was already on his tongue. "I don't go to the mosque, but I will pray for your sister."

The commander put his ayran down on the desk and wiped the wet ends of his mustache with the back of his hand. Somewhat surprised, he said, "You don't go to the mosque, at your age and with that beard, amazing, and when the mosque is right there."

"I don't know why either," said Avdo, "it started out this way and goes on like this."

"But you're not Alevi so I really don't see why you don't go to the mosque."

"I'm not Alevi," said Avdo and then hesitated. "In fact, I don't know what I am as I grew up without a mother or a father."

"Ah yes, that," the commander said, nodding his head meaningfully.

"And if I were Alevi, they wouldn't let me work in a cemetery."

"You're right, it wouldn't be right to have an Alevi making gravestones for Sunnis."

"Is that what you think, too?"

"That's how it is. You know what they say, you can't eat Alevi bread."

"So Sunnis only eat Sunni bread? Did you know that many of the mosques built in this city were actually made by Christian architects, including the mosque you mentioned in Ortaköy? People pray in those mosques, but then they don't accept gravestones carved by Alevi masters—"

"I don't think about that sort of stuff," said the commander with self-confidence. "I sure enough don't want my gravestone made by some Alevi, the nation's number-one enemy. If only you knew the kind of people we meet and have to deal with... But if you were an Alevi we would have seen that in your file, and I didn't see anything like that."

"What file?"

The commander paused, perhaps thinking he had jumped into the matter a little too soon, before he went on. "I was curious about you before I came, I wondered what sort of man you were, so I went to the head office and I looked over your file. I'd be lying if I said I wasn't surprised. You've been through quite a lot as well..."

Avdo studied his face as he tried to understand how much this man knew about him.

"Commander," he said, feigning indifference, "I've been through as much as anyone else."

"No, not like everyone else, Master Avdo. I was saddened when I read your file. Being torn away from your loved ones like that, getting involved with the dead, spending all those years in prison, it's not a small thing, not at all."

Why had this man been sifting through his file, and why had he come here to make that so clear? Was he a cop or was he from an intelligence agency? Avdo felt he couldn't openly ask him why he had come to remind him of his past.

"It's all in the past now," he said faintly.

"I was curious about your name, Avdo, a strange name. I've never heard it before, there's nothing about it in your file."

"I also don't know why they gave me the name or who gave it to me," said Avdo. He paused then tried to change the subject. "Commander, you were looking for someone, tracking someone, did you manage to find her?"

The commander moved his hands closer to the fire. He put his head over the can as if trying to see something in the flames. "This really warms you up," he said, "without it you wouldn't be able to stay out here all day."

"Yes, it's a real savior. I have plenty of wood and kindling I collect from dried-up trees, lasts me the whole winter."

The commander pulled out a pack of cigarettes, tapped one out, and gave it to Avdo. "Marlboro, filtered cigarettes," he said, "from the goods we confiscate on raids. I'll leave this pack with you, I have enough of these as you have firewood stored up for the winter."

He left the packet on the desk.

"Thanks," said Avdo.

"She got away," said the commander, "the girl we were looking for that night, evaporated like steam, leaving no trace behind."

"In a city like Istanbul, Commander, someone can slip inside and disappear. How could you ever find someone here who doesn't want to be found."

"Well said, someone who doesn't want to be found, so my job is to find those who don't want to be found, to save the state from the trouble they cause."

"May God help you, your work is hard."

"When I leave the house every morning, my sister prays for me to come back alive. I have lived with those prayers all my life, and a couple of times I came back from the dead. Many of my friends died at my side, but my fate has tended to me."

"Was that girl someone like that, I mean was she very dangerous, involved in major crimes?"

"When it's a matter of the security of the state every crime is major, but this girl isn't like the others. Think about it, she was clever enough to slip away from the police the way she did."

"Seeing she managed to get away from you, she must really be dangerous."

"We checked all the addresses, brought in and questioned people who know her, and still found no trace. It's like she's buried in one of these graves here."

"Commander, was she wounded, maybe she died tucked away in some corner—"

"God forbid," said the commander suddenly and with some concern in his voice. "I mean, we need her alive, she has information we need. Somehow we can't get to the root of these people. For many years the military rule managed to infiltrate countless dens, capture countless traitors, many of whom were executed, thousands thrown in jail, but somehow new ones keep coming, it's complicated, they are manipulated by foreign powers. They know they can't win, they couldn't care less about winning, they only want to disturb the national peace." He spoke like a radio presenter, emphasizing every word.

Avdo responded to these opinions positively. "Commander, thanks to young people like yourself, we are able to live in peace."

The commander looked at him with a satisfied smile. "If only all the young ones were like me, someone who has dedicated himself to this nation. You see I should be married but I can't find the time to make a life for myself with all my work."

"You're still young, one day you will fulfill those desires and find someone like that girl who is on the run, I mean you'll find someone who is young."

"I see, of course, someone who is—" The commander stopped and came closer to the fire. His eyes were blank; a sadness fell over his face as he stared at crackling blue flames.

"Destiny," said Avdo, "you never know when and where she'll turn up."

"You're right, you're a man who has seen a lot."

"Your destiny now watches you from a distance waiting for the time that was written for you."

The commander nodded his head. The sadness on his face seemed like it might never leave, and it spread to his eyes and then his voice. "That girl," he said, "she's hiding somewhere, but where, I mean the one who is running. Master Avdo, she didn't come here after we left, did she? If she did you would let us know."

"Of course, I would, Commander, I don't want to have anything to do with someone like that."

"I thought," said the commander, now with a persuasive look on his face, "that maybe you were angry with us that night over that somewhat unfortunate incident, or maybe you were scared so you might be reluctant to share information with us."

"That's one thing, Commander, protecting a fugitive is something else, I have enough of a head on my shoulders not to confuse the two. You know I was in prison for years and I'm in no state to go back at this age."

"That's what I thought when I read your file this morning, I thought this guy has common sense, someone who will see where I am coming from."

Avdo threw another log into the can and put his hands over the fire.

"Doesn't the girl have a family?" he said. "Haven't they looked after her, stopped her from going down the wrong path?"

"Her mother and father died when she was very young, actually they were killed. She was orphaned. It's not surprising that someone like that lost her way and got wrapped up in dark dealings."

"I'm sad to hear it," said Avdo.

"Yes, it's sad. If I find the girl I'm going to help her make a new life for herself, I mean as a state we are going to help her."

"Commander, I grew up without a mother and father. If I'd had a family, I would have had a more stable life, and I would have stayed away from all kinds of trouble. It isn't easy being alone."

"I understand, of course it's hard, but it doesn't seem like this girl was alone, she joined an anarchist organization, adopted them as her family."

"What a shame," said Avdo with regret. "The lives people lead out there. What was her name? I mean if it isn't a problem asking..."

"Why would there be, she's even listed in the papers, her name is Reyhan."

"Reyhan," said Avdo, feigning curiosity.

"Does it sound familiar?"

"Never knew anyone by that name."

"Her mother was the Arabesk singer Perihan Sultan, who worked in the *pavyons*, and moved on to the gazinos when she became famous. She's seen it all, but she was eventually killed in a shoot-out. Years ago they killed the girl's maternal aunt. I saw it in the archive, newspapers wrote all about it. Do you remember?"

Avdo tried to avoid his gaze. "I haven't had much of a chance to read the papers while I am here in the cemetery. I have a radio that keeps me informed. But I have no memory of that. Wouldn't it be easier to find the girl if you posted pictures of her on the streets?"

"She's changed a lot, looks nothing like the photos we have of her," said the commander. "She doesn't look her age, she's twenty but you'd think she was fifteen."

"She looks younger than her age."

"She's lost weight, she's much smaller now, looks like a child."

"Really?" said Avdo, turning to look at him.

"What's odd about that?"

"Oh, I don't know," said Avdo in an increasingly agitated tone of voice. "I just had a thought."

The commander lowered his hands, bringing them even

closer to the fire in the can. “Or is there something I should know?”

“Maybe I have it wrong, but when you say she still looks like a child...”

“Come out with it,” he said, his eyes rounding.

“Talking about her and how she’s running from the law, someone so dangerous, with a troop of soldiers after her, all chasing this one girl, I just pictured someone big and strong. Someone this dangerous has to be robust, I don’t know, that’s just how you see it in your mind. But your description is of someone else altogether.”

“Like what? Or did you see her?” He seemed on the brink of losing his patience.

“No. But there are groups of adolescent street kids that live near the city walls. If the girl you mentioned looks that young maybe she went and joined one of them.”

“Master,” cried the commander, “you’re right. We searched those walls that night but those homeless people beat it the moment they saw us and we found no one.”

“Well I could be wrong, Commander...”

“But if I go over there on my own this time, and without those soldiers in uniform, they won’t run away, I could get information from a few of them. I could find out if someone new slipped into their group.”

“Do you want me to come with you?” said Avdo reluctantly. “There are many different tunnels where they hide and take shelter along the city walls, I know their hideouts.”

“You took the words right out of my mouth, Master Avdo, I was going to ask you the very same. You’re a man of the world, the state needs people like you. Reading your file this morning, I felt like I knew you already, I could feel your smarts among the lines. I had this strange feeling today. I don't know what, but look at my good fortune now, it seems my prayers have been answered. It's a good thing I listened to my sister, a good thing I came here. Come on, let's not waste any more time."

As he turned to go, Avdo pointed in the opposite direction. "Let's go this way," he said, "there's a crack in the cemetery wall that takes you to the asphalt road, we can cross there. But let me put out this fire first. I don't want a sudden wind to blow these flames into the trees. Just in case."

"Be quick about it."

Avdo threw a couple of handfuls of snow on the fire to douse the flames. Then he tightened the laces on his boots and wrapped a scarf around his neck and tightly fastened the front of his coat.

"Let's go, Commander," he said.

Mardin

Mesopotamian Plain, 1939

Among the coppersmiths and roasted-chickpea sellers and the craftsmen of Shahmaran mirrors, who were all lined up in the street market, stood a thin-faced boy who was singing. So small and so thin you might miss him if not for his voice, which was as piercing as the hammers of the coppersmiths who labored beside him. For two days he had come to sing in the same spot and now was singing on the third day as the morning chill was breaking over the plain of Mesopotamia. In his lap he kept a loaf of the holy bread that tasted of the first grains that were planted here thousands of years ago and that somehow were replenished every day, and when he took a break from singing, he tore a piece of bread from its end and popped it in his mouth and watched the passing rubber shoes and the dusty hooves of the donkeys while he ate.

The bronze-faced villagers who had come early to the city from their villages to explore the street market would pass the young boy and hear his voice as if it were the breath of a blessed angel, and if the day finished as gloriously as it had begun they made a promise to themselves that they would give alms to the boy. Soon the streets were packed with people and the sound of bargaining was ringing in their ears and the rising sun was crossing the ancient plain before sinking into the sand of history and before long the villagers were hastening back to their villages. They had forgotten all about the boy who watched the sky change its cover of day to night and who sang poignant songs in several different languages, his voice taking flight on the wings of a bird that coasted above the heads of the children, the elderly, and a wild young man in tattered pants. When the young man in tattered pants—a man who passed this spot every morning—stood in front of the boy, the boy stopped singing. A satchel was slung over the young man's shoulder and he held a flute in his hand, in his other a handful of roasted chickpeas. He sat down beside the boy and held out some for him.

"What a beautiful voice you have, kid, you have a voice that feeds you. I've been watching you for three days now and I know that whenever you start singing they switch off the radio in that shop there and everyone listens. I play the flute on the back streets where it's busier, but I don't collect as much money as you do. Are you alone?"

"I am, I just came to Mardin."

"You are very young to be all alone, how old are you?"

"Ten, maybe eleven."

"You don't know your true age because you've been on the street as long as you can remember, is that so?"

"I don't know when I was born."

"Well then, do you know where you come from?"

"I don't know that either. The first place I remember was Urfa, I was lost in a crowd, crying on my own."

"Like you, I don't know my place of birth or the year I was born. See, both of us have fallen into this world from the sky."

They looked up at the sun that was rising in the sky. Summer was gone but autumn had not yet rounded the corner, the Mesopotamian sky a bright glimmering blue.

"We couldn't have fallen from the sky, it's too high, we would have died if we'd fallen from way up there."

"Oh, kid, maybe we had wings and when we hit the ground they snapped from our backs and disappeared. Lean over and I'll check." In one swift movement he had the boy leaning over and he pulled up the back of his shirt. "Yes, it seems I was right, there are traces of the roots right here on your back."

"Are you crazy?"

"Is that how I look to you, too?" He laughed. "Don't worry, I have all my wits about me."

"Why should I believe you?"

"Of course, you should. My name is İsa, after blessed Jesus, believe me. What's yours?"

"Avdo."

"Avdo, what a beautiful name."

"Is a name ever beautiful? What is beautiful about the name İsa?"

"If a name makes me happy then I say it's a beautiful name. I had two other names before, Haydar and Ali.

Because of them I lost my head, I forgot everything I knew. I took the name İsa."

"İsa isn't your real name? You tell me to believe you and then—"

"İsa may not have been my first name, but it's my real name."

"You are crazy, aren't you. Tell me the truth."

He laughed again. "I swear that I am completely sane, smarter than the people who work in those shops, smarter than the craftsmen who hammer pictures into their copper platters. I have traveled to more places than all of them combined, I have met more people, the world's much bigger than they know, and I'm bound for other places, too."

"Why? Are you looking for your mother, too?"

"I'm not looking for anyone. But I take it you are looking for yours."

"I remember her being in a market, holding my hand. Then I was alone in the crowd, I suppose she lost track of me. Since then I have wandered with the hope of finding her, maybe I am going from city to city because she's looking for me the same way."

"You're going to come around to what I'm saying, kid, and one day you'll come to believe in the beauty of names. When you find your mother, her name will seem like the most beautiful word in the world. Do you understand? These are the words of a wise man."

"I'm trying to understand."

"With your mother you'll find the most beautiful word in the world."

"But I already know it..."

İsa looked at the face of the young boy who spoke to him with confidence. "And what is that?" he asked in a mildly condescending air.

"Mother."

"Is that so? I thought you might give me a name. But that isn't one."

"But it's beautiful. Say it, too, and you'll understand."

"Am I a kid?"

"If you aren't crazy, you'll say it, come on and say it."

Looking down at the barefooted boy, İsa smiled and said, "Mother."

"Say it again," said the boy, joy spreading over his face. "Say it in every language: *anne, dayê, emo, umm, mayrig, mama.*"

İsa repeated what the child had said in Turkish, Kurdish, Syriac, Arabic, Armenian, and Greek. "*Anne, dayê, emo, umm, mayrig, mama.*"

"So you aren't crazy then."

"I am happy to hear you say that, kid, so now we can be friends. Tell me, how did you come to learn so many languages at your age?"

"Wandering through so many different places and speaking to everyone."

"Avdo, where do you stay, where do you sleep at night?"

"I don't have a place. I curl up in a quiet corner. Do you have one?"

"I do. Would you like to come with me? It's not my place, I stay with the gravestone mason Master Josef, come along and we'll make room for you."

"Sure."

"Have some more chickpeas."

"Have some bread, it's fresh."

"Give me a bit of the crust."

As the young boy popped freshly roasted chickpeas in his mouth and İsa ate a piece of bread, they listened to the state news headlines playing on the radio in the nearby shop. Gone were the softly sung songs and now a full-throated male presenter was talking of a war brewing between Germany and Poland, England and France had just declared war on Germany. Avdo had never heard of these countries before, and had never met anyone who had come from such faraway places.

"I suppose those countries are a very long way away," he said.

İsa was silent, his eyes fixed on nothing as he squeezed what was left of the bread in his hand.

Sensing something was wrong, Avdo leaned over to him. "What's happened, do you see someone?"

In a voice that was steeped in despair, İsa said, "War has broken out, kid. I need to go."

"What's that got to do with you? People fight with each other all the time and everywhere you go."

"In a fight you're up against people you know, but in war you kill people you don't know."

"Why is that?"

"I don't know. It's one thing if someone came down from the top of this street and opened fire on the crowd, and even if he went on and killed the people on the street below, that is not enough, and if he killed the whole city and went to their houses and took their gold and their women and felt good about it, well, that's what war is like."

"It seems hard."

"It is very hard."

"Did you ever go to war?"

"Once and I have never left. Don't be fooled by seeing me here like this, the person who went to war was a different person altogether."

"You're crazy," said Avdo hesitantly, "but you're not telling me."

"Don't worry about that," said İsa with a concerned look on his face. "Just listen to the radio, they are always speaking of war, as if there's no other news to report. This is a disaster. I need to go. Come to the Şeyh Zırrar Cemetery at sunset. Do you know where it is?"

"I know a few cemeteries, but I don't know their names."

"Go down this street and when you come to the mosque you'll see the cemetery on the other side. Don't go in, go around it, passing to the far side where you will find Master Josef's cabin. See you there in the evening."

İsa got up and almost ran off into the crowd.

Night fell early. And as Avdo made his way through the narrow streets of the city, he looked at the terraced houses that swept up the mountain, their flat rooftops that drew out the stars, the garden walls soaked in yellow limestone, and the castle that sat like a crown on the hilltop. They were all letting go of another weary day in Mardin. Every street seemed to delicately unravel, every window seemed to pull in the sky, and in the flickering starlight every dwelling seemed even more beautiful. Without noticing such beauty—for Avdo it had to be the same all over the world—he found the mosque, the cemetery, and then the cabin of Master Josef.

İsa and Master Josef were seated at a stone table in front of the cabin, deep in conversation. Food and a bottle of wine were on the table. They were waiting for Avdo to arrive.

"Avdo," said Master Josef, "İsa will not stop praising your voice. Come then and let us get to know you through a song."

As Avdo had been singing for as long as he could remember, he began without hesitation. He was so hungry that he chose a short song so he wouldn't have to wait any longer. It was a joyful song about reunion, not a song about love and separation and rivers of tears that ran like blood.

"I wish you would sing one of the heart-wrenching songs you sang in the market—" İsa was saying when Master Josef interrupted him.

"And what will you do with so much pain," he said. "How beautifully the kid has sung. Well done, boy, your voice is a jewel, well done."

Avdo saw no trace of the joy İsa wore on his face that morning; his expression had been strained ever since he had heard the news on the radio and there was no sign of it letting up.

"Master Josef," said İsa, "if only you could see how Avdo attracts the crowd in the market when he sings, it's as if he takes the passing souls like the reins of a horse and pulls them in. His is a powerful voice. I hope it does not go to waste."

"What?" said Master Josef. "Why would that be—"

"I play the flute for money as I wander near and far, but if this kid lives alone as I did—"

"Oh İsa, your soul has been turned into a dark lake today."

İsa fell silent, lowered his head and stared at the ground between his feet. Then he looked up.

"You're right, Master Josef," he said, "a darkness has fallen over my heart. Listening to the news on the radio today the misfortune of this kid was hammered into my head."

"Don't fret over that, look, the kid met you today, and he is meeting me tonight, there is some good in this, let's see what happens next."

"I can't stay here for very long," said İsa. "According to the news this will be a great war, and it will spread quickly, I must go before it gets here. The only person to leave behind was you, but with this kid there are two."

"First let's light this fire and warm our hands, then we can talk about his plight and your journey."

"I'll light the wood," said İsa. Striking a match, he lit a dry piece of kindling and placed it among the others.

"Where are you going?" Avdo asked intently.

"To Jerusalem."

"Which way is that, is it very far?"

"It is a faraway city, where you can find whatever it is you seek. The city of prophets."

"If you want that, then go to Urfa."

"Urfa is close, I must go far away where the war will not reach me."

"Are you going tonight?"

"I didn't say I would be that quick, kid, I have a few things to do first. I will set out in a couple of days once they are settled. I need to put together some money and find something to wear, as the weather will be cold soon, winter is upon us, and I can't set out half dressed."

"I..." said Avdo reluctantly, "I can give you the money I have collected, it'll help."

"See, Master Josef, the kid has a heart of gold."

In silence Master Josef held his hands over the blazing fire, his gaze fixed on the flames.

"Meanwhile," İsa said, "I need to write a letter before I set out, and send it to Istanbul, sealed at the Mardin post office."

"To Istanbul?" said Avdo.

"Yes. I have been putting it off, but seeing that war has broken out I have to hurry. War will come to Istanbul before it comes here, I have to warn them."

"The city of the fairy tales, amazing, so you know someone there?"

"I don't know anyone yet, but I will."

"Then who are you writing to?"

"Someone I don't know."

Avdo's eyes opened wide. "You're crazy," he said, "but you're not telling me."

Master Josef laughed. "Now this I like," he said. "Avdo, you don't have to worry about İsa, listen to me, I'm an old man, and I need help. Would you like to be my apprentice?"

Taken aback, Avdo looked at İsa. He could see a trace of the joy of that morning returning to his face.

"Be your apprentice? Really?" Avdo said, surprised.

"You heard me, that's what I am saying," said Master Josef.

"Well what I am to do?"

"You will make graves for the dead, you will carve their gravestones."

"Is it easy? Can I learn how to do it?"

"When I started out as an apprentice I was your age, and as big as you are. If I could do it then so can you. It will be a little hard in the beginning, but you'll get used to it."

"I'll do the best I can," said Avdo, enthusiastically.

"You will look after the dead. For this you will have to look to the sky and follow the signs there, you will have to read the stars and carve reflections of the stars on gravestones."

"How will I read the stars?"

"You are a smart kid, you will learn quickly. It's like reading the alphabet."

"But I don't know the alphabet."

"You will learn that, too, I will help you."

"All right then, can I quickly learn how to build a house?"

"Whose house?"

"A house for me..."

Master Josef paused and set his eyes on Avdo. He looked at İsa and then the dead who lay in rest side by side in the cemetery. "Now listen to me, Avdo," he said. "If you are to receive my help there are conditions."

"Sure, master, I'll do whatever you say."

Master Josef looked into eyes that were full of hope. "Listen to me carefully," he said, "you will carve gravestones, but you will not build houses. That's the first condition, a gravestone mason does not build houses."

"Why is that?"

"Everything we do is for the dead, if we build a house it will become a grave for those who live there. We don't build houses, and the builders of houses do not make graves, then our art form would be cursed. Do you understand?"

"I can't build a house for myself then?"

"If you want you can build a house for yourself, as your master I can grant you permission for this alone. But you must swear to me that you will only build a house for yourself and none other."

"If you say so, master, I will build a house for only myself, but I swear to you that I won't set a single stone in the wall of anyone else's home."

"It is understood then, and with you as our witness, İsa. Now let us come to the other conditions—"

"There are other conditions?"

"Naturally you cannot learn an art form without conditions. You will take money from those who give it, and you will not ask for money from those who do not have it, and you will make their gravestones just as beautiful."

"So it's like singing, those with money will give me alms and those who cannot will listen to me without sparing a penny and I sing just as beautifully for them."

"Bravo, you have understood precisely what I'm saying. Another condition, your own home must be either in the cemetery or beside it and you will keep your door open to the homeless who come to the cemetery to sleep and you will share your food with them."

"I already do that. I share my bread with the other beggars and any money that comes my way."

“Then you are going to pick this up fast, you will become an excellent master. Let us celebrate our agreement. To my apprentice Avdo.”

“The kid will drink wine?” İsa protested.

“Why not?” said Master Josef. “Anyone who drinks water can drink Zamzam water or wine.”

İsa relented and raised his glass with Master Josef and Avdo.

“To honor.”

“To honor.”

Avdo scrunched his face as he struggled to swallow the wine.

“In my youth,” said Master Josef, “I lived in both Syriac and Muslim cemeteries. But when I saw the perils I moved my cabin off the grounds. When I lived in a Syriac cemetery the Muslims wouldn’t let me make their gravestones, and in a Muslim cemetery the Syriacs never gave me any work. Now I’m no longer on the grounds of a cemetery. See, at the top of this cemetery is the Şeyh Zırrar Mosque, and below is the Mor Mihayel Church. With my cabin between the two, people of both religions can come to me. And here no one bothers me about my wine. That is important.”

“Wine is important,” said İsa.

“Avdo,” said Master Josef, “we have listened to you sing, and we will hear much more. But have you ever heard İsa play his flute? Did you hear him play in the market?”

“He never played on the street where I sing, so no.”

“İsa is a now little world-weary as he has heard news of war. So let him take his flute and play for us some of his beautiful melodies.”

İsa reached into his bag and took out his flute. With his fingers he wiped his lips and then placed the flute on the corner of his mouth, closed his eyes, and began. Stars trembled in the quilt of the sky. Flames in the fire flickered from blue to yellow. Blending with the flavors of the Syriac wine, the music of the flute drifted back to ancient times and there it gathered laments from when the city was called Izala and songs from when the city was called Mardia, songs that were sung in forgotten languages now cast over the red earth of the cemetery. Avdo turned and looked at İsa and thought, this man isn't crazy, he can make music as magical as the fairies of Istanbul.

Mardin

Mesopotamian Plain, 1939

Leveling and shaping the corners of a stone with his chisel, Avdo was pleased to have finally finished a stone without it cracking. It was the first time he had succeeded after several days of trying. Blowing away the dust on its surface he walked around the stone that now resembled a blank tablet from ancient times. He gave it one last look then called out to his master.

Watching him from a distance, Master Josef came over to the stone, touched the corners, ran his fingers over the surface, then he picked up the stone and placed it upright on the ground.

"Avdo," he said, "this time it is good. Don't worry about the dozen you cracked over the past week. Look, you have done a fine job, it took me a month to make my first smooth stone. This is enough for today. You can start crafting the motifs on top tomorrow."

"Master," said Avdo, "I was thinking I might not work

tomorrow and instead go to the market to sing to collect a little money to give to İsa. As he'll be traveling..."

"Don't worry too much about İsa, I'll give him some money. But of course you can sing in the market if you'd like to give him something yourself."

"Thank you, master."

"Now go and wash your hands and rinse the dust from your hair. We have a guest coming tonight and we have to set the table."

"Who's coming?"

"Master Dikran is coming from Urfa. He'll be staying with us for a few days. I am praised for my skills in making gravestones, but you will see that Master Dikran is the master with true skill. This is the beauty of our art, there is always a fine artist whom you can respect. In our work a fee is calculated on the size and the hardness of a stone—whether it is a male or female—but Master Dikran's fee depends on his ornamentation. He does the hardest designs so beautifully you would think he painted them on a mirror with a brush, not carved them in stone: the scales of the Shahmaran, its eyes, its rosy lips. You have talent, too, Avdo, there is the beauty of your voice and to know more languages than I do at your age is priceless. And once you become a gravestone master you will be in a league of your own."

Master Dikran arrived as the full moon was rising over the constellations in the east. They cooked meat over the fire and made many other side dishes, too. They filled their glasses with red wine, and the first sip came with a toast to Master Dikran.

"I have known Master Dikran for forty years," said Master Josef, looking at Avdo and İsa. "In this world we come to know many people, some we like less and others more. And then there are the good friends, who are different from our acquaintances. In this life my only good friend is Master Dikran. In a lifetime I have succeeded in making one friend, how happy I am."

"How happy I am," said Master Dikran.

"I hope to have a good friend in the future," said İsa.

"You are still young," said Master Dikran. "If you are to live in Jerusalem then you will make friends there. But I am surprised by your sudden decision to go. The last time I was here I remember you saying you would be staying."

"I would stay," said İsa, "if not for the war."

"I have relatives in Jerusalem you can see there, they can help you."

"Thank you, I will pass along your greetings. But how will I speak with them? I don't know any Syriac."

"They know all the languages spoken on these lands. The other day I received a letter from a cousin that began in Syriac, switched to Turkish, and then ended in Kurdish. It seems they really miss these parts. They miss the past. Three thousand years ago our forefathers founded the city of Nineveh. God sent the prophet Jonah to Nineveh to warn its people. While many believe that the holy prophet spoke Syriac or Aramaic or Akkadian, the great Ottoman traveler Saint Çelebi had another idea; he claimed the holy prophet Jonah spoke Kurdish with the people of Nineveh. Perhaps what he says is true. You, too, can speak Kurdish with my relatives if you like."

"Just like the prophet Jonah, or Yunus as we say in our tongue."

"Yes," said Master Dikran with a soft smile.

Curious as a child, Avdo joined the conversation, saying, "Master Dikran, did you also live in Jerusalem?"

"No, I have never seen the city of Jerusalem, but when my relatives escaped from these lands and fled to the four corners of the world, some of them ended up there."

"Why were they fleeing?"

"That isn't important," said Master Dikran, as if speaking to the child of nothing unusual, "there was a war here in the past, and, well, lives are uprooted in a war. Families, cities, states, they break apart. Then the day comes when the war is over and nothing is as it was in the past."

"If war is on the way then why don't we flee? Why not gather up our things when we have the time, we can go to Jerusalem as well."

Everyone turned to look at Avdo who seemed to be speaking of some unknown monster. As a child who had lived on the street Avdo was accustomed to all kinds of horrors, but now he had the sense of a horror like none other and he held his breath and waited.

"The fault is ours," said Master Dikran, "we have caused concern with all this needless talk. Don't worry, war will not come here. What business do we have with a war going on at the far end of Europe? İsa was looking for an excuse to leave, his plan to wander near and far until he wins back his memory. Is that not so, İsa?"

Avoiding the question, İsa said, "Master Dikran, I am pleased that you came this week, it would have saddened me to leave without having kissed your hand."

"There will be many who will kiss yours. On your way to Jerusalem you will travel on the road to Damascus, like Saint Paul. Everyone finds their own inner light on that road, and I hope that you will find yours, comfort for your mind and peace in your heart."

They raised their glasses as if in reverence to the wine and they listened to the stories Master Dikran had to tell of Saint Paul and the cities of Damascus and Jerusalem. More than a stonemason, Master Dikran now seemed like a priest giving a spirited sermon in the open air. His voice rising and falling, he was always pointing out the stars. In his voice were traces older than the lines in his face. That voice was one thousand years old, two thousand years old, as old as those settlers who first planted wheat on the Mesopotamian Plain who knows how many thousands of years ago.

"Master Dikran," said İsa when there was a lull in the conversation, "Avdo finished his first stone today, he'll grow up to be like you, speaking with fire, stars, and stones."

Master Dikran looked at the stone standing not far from them and in the light of the fire.

"Well done, Master Avdo," he said, honoring the boy, "ambition is the key to the lock. I see that you have that key and that you will open the door and enter the courtyard in which we have whiled away a life. Can I say a few words on the matter of your first stone?"

"Please do, master," said Avdo, delighted to see that he had been accepted.

"I don't know what kind of motifs you will give the stone tomorrow, but surely your master will tell you. Master Josef is the master of motifs and lettering. I will tell you of those stones that have neither. Have you heard of them?"

"No, my master hasn't told me about that yet."

"In this world we all have a right to a grave, every grave has the right to a gravestone, and every gravestone has the right to a word and motif. The only exceptions are the gravestones of executioners. They are given no funeral and are secretly buried at night, a rectangular gravestone set above their grave. The stone is painted black and left blank so that no one will know who is there. Lying beneath a black gravestone with no word or motif shows the kind of life they once led."

"Should I not leave the stone overnight without words?" asked Avdo anxiously, and then he added, "I'll put a notch on it so it won't be blank."

"There is no need to hurry, the stone has yet to be set at a grave, it can wait like this."

His gaze drifting among the red, yellow, and blue of the flames, Avdo thought for a moment. Although Master Dikran had said the stone could wait, he wanted to be quick about it. He would get up with Toteve and get to work. He could go to the market the following day to collect alms.

"Master Dikran," he said like a student paying close attention, "I will do the motif on this stone tomorrow. I won't let it wait. And my stone is white like mother's milk, it's not black."

"I can see, Master Avdo, I see that your stone is white. Nahit limestone would still be so if left out in the sun and rain for a thousand years. I didn't tell you this to worry you, I only hope the knowledge of this will prove useful to you in your long life. Do not fear if a black stone comes along, you are a master and with a motif it will suddenly become the most beautiful gravestone."

The full moon slowly made its way to the height of the sky, like an old man hauling a nahit stone on his back, as they continued their conversation over wine.

Village of Konak Görmez

Haymana Plain, 1958

The gas lamps had been put out and everyone was drifting off to sleep. There were more stars in the sky than straw on the threshing floor. Was the evening star also waiting in the sky or had she long since slipped into the darkness behind the hills in search of the sun? Elif was in bed undoing the braids in her hair, pulling out every strand with her comb that was decorated with a Shahmaran. Now and then she glanced at the mirror she had placed on her pillow as if she might actually see a reflection of herself in the dark room. What are you doing, Elif, said the mirror, who are you undoing these braids for, who are you preparing these blue beads for? At the sound of the voice Elif turned away from the mirror and looked at her younger sister who was sleeping at her side, listened to the sound of her mother and father breathing through the open door of the adjacent room.

A state-minted gold coin, a loaf of moldy bread, and a knife sat before the mirror. Elif would return the gold to its rightful owner, she would eat some of the moldy bread every day, and if she did not die from food poisoning at the end of three days, she would place the knife on her wrist and cut her veins. She had considered the bread because she was afraid of dying by a blade, and if it worked she might end her life without suffering.

When she was a little child she found the dead body of her auntie beside the firepit, blood running from her wrist. Her auntie was a beautiful woman, and Elif was now her age. The villagers said that when she came as a bride from the neighboring village the djinns came after her and took hold of her mind for a year before dragging her to her death. Once Elif had seen her auntie secretly crying and noticed the purple bruises on her neck and arms, but she never would have thought this was the work of djinns. Elif assumed her uncle was oppressing her auntie. When she saw her uncle's wife crying all the time, she knew that the djinns had never left, they had settled in the village, in this house. Now they were coming for Elif. They were confusing her, keeping her awake, and telling her to take her own life instead of waiting for her fiancé who was soon to return from the army.

Elif moistened her comb with some lavender oil and passed its teeth through the length of her hair. Slowly she pulled. How could she bear the sharp tip of a knife when even a comb hurt? Two tears fell from her eyes. She wiped them away with her fingers. In the silence of the night, she bit her lips to stop herself from sobbing. Once these were Elif's favorite hours, when everyone had gone to bed and even the dogs had abandoned the night. She would rise at dawn, and working in the stable or at the firepit or in the fields she would anticipate the moment of solitude that came with the night. When she was alone in the darkness, she would dream, slipping into a world as colorful as her embroidered dress. She would wander through that world in a flurry and stretch out on the grass, drenched in sweat, and when she woke the next day with the sun she would calmly set out for work. And so the time of night she once loved dearly was now a time she feared. Thoughts raced through her mind, the questions piled up, and there were knots impossible to untangle. She simply could not sleep and in the morning she would get up feeling exhausted. She neglected to comb İpek's hair. Who knew what wonderful dreams she was having in her sleep? She hoped that her sister would have another life altogether, one that was long and full of love. She would leave her comb for her, which was made from the horns of a ram so maybe she would find the man she loved and comb her hair in a mirror he brought her.

When Elif eagerly listened to those love stories that came here after they had drifted through the other villages on the plain, she used to think those sad endings only ever happened to girls in faraway villages, she never for a moment thought that one day she would stumble into that same sadness. Back then she would look up in the sky at the stars whose names she did not know and drift off to sleep along with everyone else. But those peaceful days now seemed far away. Who could she confide in, who could understand her pain? She picked up the loaf of bread, she smelled it, she kissed it, hoping for a way out. Bread was holy and even when it was moldy, it was still the source of miracles. Kissing it again she tore off a piece. She held it in her fingers, closed her eyes, then brought it to her lips. The taste was not bad, it tasted like fresh sheep cheese. As she chewed another bite of the bread the scent of mold filled her mouth. Opening her eyes, she looked down at the bread, and the knife, and the state-minted gold coin. Should she curse or nurture a piece of hope? She placed the gold coin in the palm of her hand and kissed it as if it were a holy relic then pressed it to her chest. The tears fell again in fine drops.

She had run out of prayers. In the middle of the night and when the homes in the village were awash with dreams, she was all alone with a mirror and a knife. Her neck and her back were drenched in sweat. Looking through her misty eyes her gaze fell on the mirror. In the dark she could see nothing more than a vast abyss. Her heart was racing and she felt as if she might fall into the mirror if she leaned closer. Her mind was reeling and she was not sure if it was morning or evening coming to an end. The djinns were there, from the deep dark of the mirror her auntie's djinns were watching her. Elif knew that she had been overtaken by their magic and accepted hopelessly the fact that she could not struggle against their power. She lacked the courage to turn over the mirror that bore the silver traces of the evening star on its back. They were one and the same, the evening star and the djinn, the source of the same fear, leaving Elif breathless in the loneliest hour of the night.

Village of Konak Görmez

Haymana Plain, 1958

Out of breath Baki hurried back with the news. He stood beside Avdo, who was working on the gravestone. "Master," he said, "my young agha has sent a letter, he sent a letter to his father, as he thinks he is still alive, in the letter he said that his days in military service are almost up and that God willing he will be home at the start of the month to kiss the hand of his father. His two brothers were delighted and they are preparing for his arrival, they ordered the shepherds to select the lambs to be sacrificed and instructed the women to make fresh cream and yogurt every day and to clean and organize the top floor of the mansion."

What was the date that day? As days were not counted in the village, Avdo had to think long and hard about it for a moment then finally understood there was one week left till the start of the month. The young agha could show up any day now. His two older brothers were anticipating his arrival, his horse and his servants, too, but what about Elif? Avdo threw his mallet and chisel aside and sat down. He took out the flowery head scarf Elif had used when she sent him gözleme. He squeezed the scarf, which he had washed days ago and dried over purple crocuses. Until then it had been easy, dreaming as he waited, there was nothing he could do but wait. And yet he felt he might remain like this in the village for nearly all his life, he would work on the same gravestone every day with his eye on Elif as she made her way down to the fountain from her home across from him, her furtive glances filling him with hope, and the river that he called life would flow like this forever.

Avdo raised his head. "Kindhearted Baki," he said, "you know how the elders were angry with me when I spoke of how the village name of Konak Görmez has nothing to do with either of those Turkish words, and that the name in fact comes down to us from Byzantine times. In fact the roots go even deeper than the Byzantines but they didn't give me the chance to say so. The actual meaning is 'the People at the Peak of Mother Goddess Country.' How beautiful, isn't it? Your tribe came here from distant lands with a thousand and one hopes, but do you know that only two among them have embraced the spirit of the Mother Goddess who has been waiting for centuries, only two have assumed her greatness. One of them is you and the other is Elif. Those elders who were angry with me would never understand this, they have nothing but their belief in wheat and prayer. I want to take Elif away from here, that's my dream, and if you did not have a family I would take you with me, too, and be a father to you. But you are fortunate, Baki, you have a father, and when the day comes for me to leave this place you must take good care of yourself and him, too, don't lose hope in the face of hardships, don't close your eyes to the future, do you understand?"

At a loss for words, Baki looked at him with a blank expression on his face as he wondered if he should be happy to have a father or sad that his master would be leaving him.

"Are you going to leave before you finish your gravestone?" he asked.

"I finished it long ago, I am now merely biding my time," said Avdo.

The time had come for Avdo to finish dawdling over these details, refining minor motifs on the gravestone. Equally majestic and alluring, the gravestone had long since been ready for the dead man who was lying impatiently in the uncultivated earth. It was waiting for Avdo's moment of decision. And the day had come for that. Avdo would go and tell Kara Agha's two sons that the gravestone would be set tomorrow and that they should make ready the three state-minted gold coins they had promised him. He had come as a stranger, worked as a stranger, and tomorrow he would leave as one.

"Baki," said Avdo, "you have done so many good deeds for me, but would you do one more?"

"I will do whatever you ask of me."

"Go to Elif now and bring her my final word."

"You want me to bring a letter?"

"No, I won't write a letter, it'll suffice if you simply tell her what I have to say. The rest is up to her. It isn't important if she has nothing to say in reply, just give her these words and then come back to me, okay?"

"Okay, master."

Avdo gave Baki his message in no more than a few words. He told Baki to go and come back with haste. It brought a smile to his face when he saw that the boy was equally anxious.

"When you come back I will tell you a fairy tale, what do you say to that?"

"Really? Which one?"

"The tale of the fox."

"I'll go straight to Elif Abla."

Village of Konak Görmez

Haymana Plain, 1958

TODAY, NOON

Avdo bid farewell to the sons of Kara Agha and gratefully accepted the three new state-minted gold coins they provided him. When he embraced Baki, he discreetly slipped a coin into his pocket. "Don't say a word, you are my apprentice, and this is your right," Avdo said softly. He went to the fountain for the last time and drank from the cool water and wet his hair and he glanced at the house with indigo plaster on the other side of the ravine. There was no one around, not a sign of either Elif or her sister or the dogs. The empty space seemed a reflection of the cloudless sky. Avdo mounted his horse, and as he slowly made his way out of the village he turned to see if anyone was bidding him farewell from among the trees or behind a wall. There was only Baki, who had climbed onto a roof and narrowed his eyes to watch his master ride to the farthest point on the horizon, like a mournful falcon.

YESTERDAY

Baki went to see Elif to give her the news from Avdo. "Master Avdo will leave the village tomorrow, but he won't go very far, he will turn back at nightfall and go into the almond-tree grove and wait for you there until dawn. He said that you mustn't be afraid, that you can come to the grove, he asked me to tell you this." At the time Elif was putting the laundry out to dry. She said nothing in reply as she continued to pick up the freshly washed clothes that lay on the white stone. Shaking every item of clothing, she took her time to work out the wrinkles before carefully pinning them to the line. It was as if in that moment in the village, in that moment all around the world, there was nothing more important and more beautiful to her than the bright colors and fresh scent of those clothes. She didn't turn to look at Baki's face.

TODAY, AFTERNOON

After he left the village Avdo went south to the reedbed that ran along the shore of the stream. There he let his horse out to graze on the pasture, undressed, and waded into the water. Listening to the frogs and the meadowlarks, he bathed in the stream. When he came out of the water, he saw the sun sinking over the soft-headed hills. Beyond the reedbed, bright green fields stretched into the distance with the good news of an approaching harvest to the villages on the lower plain—it would be bountiful. Avdo was also anticipating good news. Thrilled at the thought, he dressed, and after evening had fallen he gently rode his horse to the almond grove below the village. He tied his horse to a tree among those rustling in the wind and he watched the stars flutter in the night sky like the pollen of flowers.

TODAY, NIGHT

After having grown accustomed to hearing Avdo singing from his rooftop after the evening call to prayer in April and May, the villagers now went to bed in silence. Although they had adapted quickly to his presence in the village, they returned just as quickly to their old way of life after the sound of Avdo chipping marble by day and singing by night was gone. They thought of the health of their rams and cows, they dreamed of reaping a great harvest on the threshing floor. But tonight there was someone who could not return to the old way of life. After the dogs had ceased barking and drifted off to sleep and the fairies of the night were idling in the gardens, a shadow slipped out of the house with indigo plaster. A shawl the color of the night on its shoulders, a scarf the color of the night on its head, and softly treading the kind earth it forded the stream. Leaving behind the fountain and the mosque and the cemetery. From a distance one might have thought it was a fairy of the night as it moved with such resolve and grace.

TODAY, MORNING

With the aid of horses Avdo hauled the gravestone he had made for Kara Agha and put it in its place. Stepping back he looked at the gravestone with admiration, the elders standing around him. "I have not made one as beautiful for some time now," he said. "In this stone there is a spirit to befit the bounty of the saints and mother goddesses in every prayer and every dream; a spirit that carries the winds of the mountains in its heart even after it has come down to the plain, as a farmer was once a nomad."

TODAY, NIGHT

Avdo had been waiting for hours with his ears tuned to the many subtle sounds of the night when Elif appeared in the darkness. He hurried over and took her in his arms. She was so anxious she might have fallen but he held her there for a while. She held on to his arms then slowly wrapped her arms around his waist, rested her head on his chest. She took a deep breath. He tried to calm her fitful breathing. "Don't be afraid, everything will be fine, we'll go far away, don't be scared." But he had no idea his voice was breaking, too, and his hands were shaking. He took her hands and warmed them in his. The nights were still cool as the summer season had not yet blossomed. He pulled a blanket off the saddlebag and wrapped it around her shoulders. "Warm up a little and settle down before we set off," he said. Elif finally managed to speak. "No, let's not wait, let's go right away." They embraced again. Felt their beating hearts. As they were mounting their horse, they startled at the sound of a branch that cracked among the almond trees. Avdo pulled a gun from his hip and aimed at the darkness. As he steadied himself to fire a voice slowly rang out: "Master Avdo!"

Mardin

Mesopotamian Plain, 1939

As the sun fell over the horizon the crowds that had been wandering the streets of the marketplace were breaking up. Soon the city would be covered in a blanket of fear. From his first day in Mardin, Avdo noticed the change: The same people who met his gaze during the day would avoid his gaze at night. A hidden mask fell over their faces, their footsteps quickened as they made ready for a night that concealed that which no one knew. From the Byzantines to the Sasanians, the Artuqids to the Mongols, the people of Mardin had fallen to countless tribes over the ages and now spoke with each other in many different languages, and although they laughed and joked they sometimes were taken by the devil and came to blows, shedding blood on these ancient lands. After the bodies were buried and the hatred that had raged like a disease had subsided, they began to live together once again. When those travelers who came from the deserts in the south on horses clad with iron hooves saw those little, bare, boxlike houses in the distance at the end of a journey that lasted days, they took the city for a vast cemetery that had housed the dead for a thousand years. But after sleeping through the night they arose and looked upon the city in a new light, marveling at the intricate designs on its walls, its elegant doors and radiant windows that opened to the sky like silver mirrors, and they were suddenly bound by the magic of the city.

Master Josef was passionately speaking with Avdo at the fire, the subject of their conversation changing with every fresh glass of wine.

"You know how the people who in those houses up there are afraid of the dead, well I'm not afraid of them. I'm afraid of the people in those houses. Sometimes there are such funerals: a brother shoots his brother, a bride is beaten to death by her husband only three months into marriage, a baby is the victim of a blood feud. The heart can hardly bear it. Then they say, 'Master Josef, why don't you ever come to town, why do you stay so far away from us?' I have all I need here, Avdo, and you know how that is yourself, this is how you came into this world, and you can be sure that it is fine this way, you'll understand this later on. In the evening I light a fire and speak with the flames. I always have my wine, and my dog Toteve beside me, and now you are here, what more could I want. Don't worry, there will always be people visiting us. Yesterday we sent İsa on his way to Jerusalem, and before that we saw Master Dikran off to Urfa. Other guests will come and take their place."

"I am very grateful that you took me on—"

"This isn't something to be grateful about, it is something to be toasted. Come then and raise your glass."

Swept away in Master Josef's joy, Avdo raised his glass and with his master's encouragement took a small sip. They had agreed that one should drink a measure to match his size.

"Do you know why we light the fires in the evening?"

"To get warm."

"There is that, too, of course, the coolness of autumn is in the air. Avdo, when we look into the fire and speak we never lie. Fire is the home of truth. You know I didn't tell İsa this but he felt it, and when we sat down at the fire one evening he began speaking to himself. He spoke of how he had been wounded, how he had lost his memory, how he became a soldier and then escaped. He doesn't remember his life before that, he doesn't know his real name. If he hadn't said all this at the fire I wouldn't have believed him, I would have taken him for a madman."

"So then what do I need to do here?" asked Avdo.

"I am not telling you this to have you do anything in particular. It is enough to get used to spending time at the fire. If you don't speak with the fire, it will speak with you. You will learn this as you get older. Do you remember the evening you first came here, and how we lit the fire again? I looked at the fire and lost myself in the flames, and when I knew that you were a good kid I asked you to be my apprentice. The fire did not deceive me, Avdo, you are good."

"Do you think İsa will return?"

"Crazy İsa?"

"Don't call him crazy."

Master Josef responded with laughter to the emotion in Avdo's voice. "What's the matter, kid, you were calling him crazy before, or has your opinion on the matter changed?"

"İsa isn't crazy, he's a good man."

"Of course, his heart is clean, our great, holy İsa, or Jesus as we call him in our tongue." Master Josef made the sign of the cross.

"When İsa saw me on the street he spoke to me so nicely that I knew right away I could trust him."

"He's a *gavsono*. He feels the people who are like him."

"What's a *gavsono*?" said Avdo.

"It's a word in Syriac."

"I never heard it before."

"Maybe that is better," said Master Josef. "*Gavsono* means migrant. It is someone who has been torn from his land and blown to another. Like a leaf at the head of the wind. To lose your land is to lose your memory. But İsa experienced just the opposite, he first lost his memory and then he lost his land, swept away in the wind, he is now wandering near and far."

"Am I also a *gavsono*, master?"

"You have been until now, but I hope this will change and that you will have ties to this land."

"If *gavsonos* can change maybe İsa can change, too, and connect to one place."

"Of course, why not. The truth is Master Dikran says we all are born as *gavsonos* and we only get back home when we die. For him our true land is our little grave."

"Maybe İsa won't find the place he's looking for but will come back here."

"İsa loved you very much. Once I heard him speaking by the fire, honoring the names of all the prophets, pleading to Jesus, Moses, and Muhammed, asking them to protect the child, praying to them to keep you from turning into a shadow like himself. When a person is left hopeless in this world he loses his self, he turns into a shadow. İsa believes he is a shadow. A shadow with nothing but a heart. That suffers, that hopes, that pines. He didn't want you to turn out like that. Pleading to the fire, he entrusted you to the many prophets and I suppose that one of them will keep an eye on you."

"Master," said Avdo faintly, "which prophets should I believe in? Everyone has one, some say Jesus, and others Muhammed, which one should be mine?"

Master Josef turned from the fire and looked at Avdo, he caressed his hair with the silence of a father.

"Look," he said, "we can see the lights of the Mor Mihayel Church below and from the Şeyh Zırrar Mosque above us comes the sound of the call to prayer. You are now right between the two. There is no hurry, you will come to know and choose a prophet that is right for you, or maybe you won't and you will live that way."

"Can one live without a prophet?"

"Of course, don't worry about those who already have their prophet, most of them believe only in themselves, but they keep that a secret from everyone else. Let yourself get a little older and then you can make the decision yourself. I will ask only two things of you: to be good and to work hard. This is what befits a human being."

"You believe in the holy Jesus, but you make gravestones for the dead that believe in other prophets. How can that be?"

"Avdo, the living are sometimes good but the dead are good for all eternity, this is what I believe when I make gravestones. This will come to you in the future, too, the time when they ask you to make graves and gravestones for people whose religions you have never even heard of. For the sake of the dead you won't turn them away."

"I don't understand what you're saying," said Avdo. "Am I too young to understand?"

"This is the way I speak, in a jumble, but you'll get used to it in time. Look how you are getting used to the wine, to the fire, and to the dead in their graves that listen to us at night."

"İsa also spoke in a jumble but I had no problem getting used to him."

"But he's crazy, that's why, it'll take you a little more time to get used to me."

Master Josef laughed so heartily that the dead sat up in their graves to listen to the old man and the child speaking through the crackling of the flames.

Village of Konak Görmez

Haymana Plain, 1958

TODAY, MORNING

Baki rose early. When it was time for milking he rounded up the sheep whose characters he knew so well and lined them up for the young girls who were waiting with their copper buckets. When the milking was done, he saddled his father's donkey and filled the saddlebags with provisions. Then he went to the firepit to see his father. "We will overnight on the meadow," said his father, Heyran. "Let the herd graze and have their fill. We'll return in the morning. You like sleeping in the meadow, Baki, will you come with us?" Baki was feasting on the buttery bread his mother had prepared. "I have work today," he said to his father. "I will clean the stables and fix one of the troughs that is broken, and Master Avdo is leaving the village today so I will go and say goodbye to him." His father said, "Ah yes, so your master is leaving, give him my regards, he is an honorable man who taught you how to read and write, may his journey be light." There were times when Kara Agha's head shepherd Heyran would go early to the mosque and it was then that he would overhear ill rumors about Master Avdo, which made him uncomfortable because Master Avdo had taught his son how to read and write, and so Heyran would leave without saying a word, saddened by the lies these men were spreading.

YESTERDAY

While Avdo was polishing the gravestone, he told Baki what he had told him for the past two months. "Baki, I am leaving tomorrow. Don't forget what I have told you, you must keep reading and writing to make progress, borrow books from your friends who are going to school and read them. As for stone masonry, you only need more practice, take every stone you can find and give it shape with your chisel. Marble like this will be hard for you, and you won't find examples like this around here, we call these male stones, as they are hard. You've seen how hard I have struggled with this for the past two months, shaping it with the steel comb from top to bottom and from side to side. The stones around your village are easy to work with, this plain is full of sedimentary rock. These rocks known as female stones are softer than marble. You must truly know the stone that you choose, understand it from the moment you set your eyes on it, know if it is right for your hand. When you are working on a female stone with your comb you must only work from top to bottom, as if you are combing long hair, never ever from side to side or you will end up with a crack and then a break in the most unexpected place. Do you see the stone above that crumbling grave, that is argillite, choose those, there are many in these parts and they are easy to work with. They call the rocks above it sandstone, that is good, too. Love your stone and work on it with patience, and the more you do the more your skill will grow. A skillful master needs three things: patience, passion, and imagination. And he must have good equipment. I have extras with me, look, I will leave these with you. A comb—which is usually made of iron but opt for one made of steel—a miter, a plummet, an engraving stylet, a water level, a chisel, and of course a mallet. This mallet was once called a *külüng* by our ancient masters, the word refers to the sledgehammer that can pierce a mountain, the name comes from the same sledgehammer that Ferhat—of the legend of Ferhat and Şirin—used to break through the mountain to reach his beloved. And yet it seems the strength of my mountain-breaking sledgehammer was not enough for Elif's heart. My master from Mardin, who taught me the craft—Mardin? It was the city of my Master Josef. Josef? Syriac name. Syriac? It is another religious belief—but anyway, so my master had a close friend, Master Dikran, they were good men back then, and when they gathered they looked at stones strangely, they touched them strangely, and they worked with them strangely. Do you know what they would do? They would open up a hole in a great stone and place a poplar sprout inside. Then drawing on patience and time they would wait. The poplar put out roots that spread and eventually cracked the stone into pieces. Master Josef called this the law of life, in which the hardest thing was broken by the softest touch. I have been in your village for two months and if I stayed longer maybe I could plant a sprout in Elif's heart, and the great power of its roots might crack her heart, and I would have the chance to watch it open. But that did not happen, fate would not bestow it, and so we have come to the final day."

TODAY, AFTERNOON

Through his wet eyes Baki watched Avdo slowly make his way out of the village on his Arab steed that everyone so admired, turning to look over his shoulder now and then as he carried away with him a magical world. Baki went up on the tips of his toes and when his master was finally gone he fell to his knees and wept. He was all alone, his village and the great world around him felt completely empty. The girls had already come to the fountain for water, leaving it desolate in the afternoon heat, the men had gone to the mosque to pray. There was no one here to send off his master, no one to wave a friendly goodbye. Why was the village like this? What sort of people were they? Had they no sense of goodness? They did not send Baki to school. They beat his father before his very eyes. Every day they gossiped about his master behind his back. Baki put his hand in his pocket and pulled out the smooth, state-minted gold coin. He rubbed it with some spit and held it up to the sunlight. He rubbed it in the palm of his hand, he felt its warmth, he rubbed it again. If he tried a little harder he wondered if a great genie would emerge from that piece of gold that glittered like a magic lamp to grant him whatever he desired, to save him from this village.

TODAY, NIGHT

For the past two months the villagers had grown accustomed to dreaming and then finally falling asleep to the songs of Avdo that wound into their hearts. But how could they comfortably leave it all behind and return to sleeping as if nothing had changed at all? It was hard to understand the elders, hard to understand the aghas, hard to understand the women. Unable to sleep, Baki stepped through the door, and as he looked at the houses that resembled the village graves, he thought about how he understood the women least of all. Why didn't Elif Abla love Master Avdo? Maybe he would learn the reason why when he grew up, but no, this had nothing to do with age, seeing that even Master Avdo didn't know. He wondered if Elif Abla has suddenly forgotten all about those songs his master would sing, and if she drifted off to sleep like all the other villagers. Baki had to know right away. Without thinking a second longer, he put on his rubber shoes and left the courtyard, making his way around the other houses before he came to Elif's. He stepped over to the dog stretched out in the garden and rubbed the back of his neck to keep the dog from barking. Then taking cover behind the trees, he looked up at her window. Maybe he would see a light, a shadow by the window, and then he would know that Elif Abla was not asleep, he would know that she was thinking of Master Avdo.

TODAY, MORNING

While Avdo was putting in place the gravestone he had made for Kara Agha and the villagers around him were murmuring their praise, the happiness in the air was palpable. They were not happy about the beauty of his gravestone; it was the thought that this stranger who had finished his work would finally be leaving. They were unresponsive to the anger in Avdo's voice as he made his speech at the head of the grave, and they were silent when he spoke of nomadic life, which they frowned upon, along with his talk of more mysterious matters such as the Mother Goddess. This time they held back the words they had said to his face when he first came to the village. This stranger they had adopted with such ease and who made them feel such unease was about to go away.

TODAY, NIGHT

Baki watched a shadow at the window. A little later the front door opened and the same shadow left the garden on soft footsteps, turning south. When he recognized Elif, who was wrapped from head to toe, he understood where she was going and he swiftly followed her. It seemed that only Elif and Baki were awake as they slipped out of the village without the sleep fairies ever knowing, even the village dogs were asleep. But it wasn't long before Baki understood that they weren't alone. Watching Elif from the other side of the ravine were two harbingers of doom in dark cloaks. He could clearly see the rifles in their hands. He quickened his step, keeping his eye on Elif and the two shadows. He knew where they were going, and his heart beat faster than his footsteps. When he reached the almond grove, he peered out through the trees, scampering left and right, and then he heard their voices. Slowly he approached. Shivering from the cold wind and fear. If he had seen these two—his master and Elif Abla—at any other time, he would have been as happy as a fool, but now his voice came in a whisper. “Master Avdo,” he said, stepping closer, “two men are following Elif Abla. They were hiding in the ravine. They may have lost her in the dark, but they could be here any moment.”

Merkez Efendi Cemetery

Istanbul, 1965

A cemetery is the home of trees. Spruce, cypress, and pine greening together, bringing life to a garden suspended between life and death. If not for the trees the dead would not know the ground above them, they would not feel the sun, wind, or snow. They could all leave the cemetery, those mourners and birds, leaving only the trees. Like stars guarding the sky. As Avdo made his way among the spruce, cypress, and pine he wished he were one of them so that he might achieve the peace that comes with standing guard for a lifetime beside a grave. It would have made him happy to guard the grave below the single redbud farther ahead. They described it like that, they said Elif's grave was under a redbud in the north of the cemetery. During all the years he had spent in prison, Avdo had seen no other tree but that great poplar. And when he saw the redbud in the distance, alone among the crumbling gravestones, he slowed down.

There was no other in the cemetery, it was the only one. How simple was this single grave among hundreds of other ancient graves, and the redbud seemed as simple among hundreds of other trees. Only Elif's grave was adorned with redbud in the same way that only the Byzantine emperors of ancient Constantinople could wear its noble color of royal purple on their capes, the redbud purple reserved for nobility. The grave was blanketed by its gentle shadow and shedding flowers. Avdo stepped into its shadow and stood at the head of the grave. He had found her at last. Not a soul around them, not a thing. Only a tree, its shadow, and the earth, nothing more. The soil on her grave had not yet settled, it was still fresh, which meant there had been little rain this spring. The earth was still waiting to settle down in peace. Avdo leaned over and took a handful of the soil. Slowly he walked around the grave. He circled it seven times, stopping every time to take a breath as the earth kept turning around him. When he finished his final turn, he stopped at the head of the grave. While the earth brought to mind death, the redbud made him forget it. He sat down and crossed his legs. He realized this was the first time he was sitting on bare earth since he had been in prison.

People think, why has all this happened to me, when they should really think just the opposite: Why has all this not happened to me. Avdo wondered why he was living when he should have died in the almond grove, why he was here when he should have been executed, and why Elif, who was lying under the earth, was not sitting beside him. His heart in turmoil, he thought about why what had happened to her had not befallen him and he knew he would find no answer. He was not someone who believed everything in life happened for a reason, there was simply no reason for this, life was like this.

Avdo turned and looked at the old cabin a little farther ahead, its broken roof. He got up and walked over, he studied its walls, he went around to the back. When he came to several rocks and stones that seemed to be waiting to be carved in an open area that was covered in weeds he thought of that other man, who was like him, who had once lived here. From among the stones he chose a smooth one of medium size. It wasn't that heavy. Without having to strain too much, he brought the stone to the grave and placed it under the redbud. He hadn't chosen it for Elif, he had chosen this one for himself. He made out the space beside Elif's grave, a space that would be large enough for his grave, he threw fresh soil over the ground and made a mound so that no one else could claim it. Then he placed the stone at the top to give the impression that there was now a dead man lying in the ground. There was no writing on the stone, but those looking wouldn't think anything of that, they'd wander on without a second thought.

Avdo lay down on the earth and closed his eyes. The day was long. It was warm in the spring season. As visitors wept above the graves of loved ones he slept with a silent peace whose source he did not know. It was as if he had waited all his life to sleep here. His breath softened, his body let go. The pain that he had been gathering in his chest for the last month slowly faded, melted, slipped through his skin, and poured into the earth. As the sky darkened he opened his eyes, he felt as light as a shadow. The sun was sinking over the horizon, the earth was cool. Stars shone in the sky like night-lights. When the spring breeze blew in from over the sea, Avdo understood the silent peace that was in him. He had found the place where he would die. After a lifetime of wandering near and far to find a place to live, he now understood that he was actually looking for the place to die. He had never thought about it before, and now sleeping by this grave and waking with a peace of mind, he knew that all his life he was looking for this place, he was sure of it. This was where he wanted to die, he would spend the rest of his life here. The knots in his mind were untangling. His mind was now as light as his body and he began to laugh. He let out great rolls of laughter until the tears fell from his eyes. At least it was evening now and everyone had left the dead, he was alone in the cemetery. There was nothing but the sound of a crying owl.

Then he heard footsteps. He turned and looked at the dark shape moving through the cemetery.

"Hello, there," said the approaching man.

"Hello," said Avdo.

"I am the imam of the mosque, they call me Eşref Hodja. In the evenings I take a stroll through the cemetery after my evening prayers. I heard your voice, or rather your laughter, and I thought I should come and say hello."

"When an old memory came to mind I couldn't help but laugh."

"A memory about those who are resting here? My condolences, two fresh graves sides by side."

"Thank you for your kindness. One is the woman I love and the other one I set aside for myself."

"Why the hurry? You're younger than I am, one shouldn't turn his gaze to the earth so soon."

"I just wanted my place to be known. Who do I need to see about buying this grave? Does the mosque look after such affairs? Some cemeteries are like that, or is it a matter for the municipality?"

"Even if this were a cemetery mosque it still would not have such connections to the cemetery. You have to go to the municipality," said Eşref Hodja as he sat down on the ground. "But tell me, why the hurry?"

Avdo shared enough of his background to introduce himself to the imam. He said he was recently released from prison and had come here from Ankara two days ago, and that he did not have the chance to attend the funeral of the woman he loved. When he told Eşref Hodja the first thing he was going to do was to make a beautiful gravestone for the grave, the imam said, "Do you know how to make gravestones?"

"Not counting the time I was in prison, carving gravestones was the only thing I ever did since I was ten. I have been all over the country working on stones I would then set at the head of graves in various cemeteries. I have seen many beautiful gravestones while I was wandering through this one."

"Well then I should call you a master, is that all right, Master Avdo?"

"Of course, Eşref Hodja."

"Where are you staying? Do you know anyone in Istanbul?"

"Nobody. I am staying in a hotel. I have enough money to keep me going for a while. Then I have to find a way to get back into my old line of work, I can't live without making gravestones."

"I know a few workshops on the other side of the neighborhood where they make gravestones for this cemetery, you could work in one of those."

"Hodja, I had a look behind that cabin there and saw many stones waiting to be carved, it seems as if someone who did this kind of work lived there."

"Before I came to this mosque there was an old man there, he made the gravestones, but I never saw him myself, that was his cabin. It was left empty after he died, and then it fell to ruin."

"What would you say if I fixed it up, Eşref Hodja? Could I stay here?" Avdo went on before he received an answer. "One of the conditions that was given to me by my master in Mardin, who taught me this craft, was that I had to live in a cemetery or near one."

"Are you from Mardin?"

"I grew up there."

"I have heard wonderful things about Mardin. The churches are beautiful. God willing, I will see them before I die."

"Hodja, it isn't only the churches but the homes, the market, the plain, all of it is stunning. Every living being should see it. If the woman I love was not resting here I would go back, I would choose to die there."

"Well, seeing that you want to live here now and that you want to be buried in that grave you have set aside, let me talk to them about that cabin."

"Who will you talk to?"

"I'll ask our mufti about its legal status, and if they don't know I'll go to the municipality. I hope I can handle it, and then you can get to work on it."

"Thank you very much, Eşref Hodja. When I came to this cemetery I carried in me the sadness of the woman I love, but now I suddenly feel content, thanks to you."

"Wait, don't rush. Let me see them tomorrow."

"And if I need to pay anything—"

"Pay for what? You are just out of prison, and now you're supposed to hand out money? Keep your money in your pocket. Maybe later, when things have settled, I might ask you for something."

"Of course, please do."

In the darkness Eşref Hodja pointed to the western side of the cemetery and said, "Don't be deceived by the size of our mosque, in the past it was an important Sufi lodge. Do you know about the *çilehane*, the penitence chambers where Sufis would go for forty days all by themselves, there's one here, but it's been locked for years. The inside must be falling apart. It needs a helping hand, it needs repair."

Avdo's face went stiff. "Hodja," he said, "nobody lives in a çilehane, I mean they are not to be lived in, no? It could never be someone's home?"

"Nobody could live in such a small place. Sufis wouldn't go there to live, they would go there to die, to purify their souls, to self-interrogate, and after all those days they would come back to life. That one has been like that for years ever since they were shut down by law. Have I asked something difficult of you?"

"The work isn't hard for me. I am asking because of the conditions my master in Mardin set out for me. One of those conditions was to never build a house. If one who digs graves and makes gravestones builds a house it will become a grave for anyone who lives there. It is not right for us to build houses. That is why I asked."

"I understand. But a çilehane is not a house, nobody lives there, don't worry. And those who do go there are only ever there for forty days, and that was in the past. But tell me this, if building a house is forbidden then how can you repair the cabin?"

"The only home my master allowed me to build was my own."

Merkez Efendi Cemetery

Istanbul, 1965

TODAY, MORNING

After Avdo settled into the old cabin in the north part of the cemetery, which he had repaired himself, he set up a workshop in the empty space in the back. There he placed an enormous stone that he would use as a counter, and he made an awning of wood that would protect him from the sun and rain. The stonemasons of beautiful Mardin would sleep through the heat of the day and work in the cool hours of the evening and morning, but Avdo preferred to work in the day no matter what the weather was and in the evenings he would sit and lose himself in thought. The season was spring, and he spread fresh branches over his wooden awning—you could find everything in Istanbul except for reeds.

TODAY, NOON

The imam of the Merkez Efendi Mosque, Eşref Hodja, unlocked the chains to the çilehane and pushed open the door.

The light of his torch lit up the dark room and he led Avdo inside. Looking at the mold on the walls and the cobwebs in the corners, Eşref Hodja was gripped with a sadness and asked what could be done as he stepped on a broken stone. For Avdo it was easy, he would replace the broken stones on the floor, complete those missing on the walls, and fix the leaks in the roof. He only needed a few days. As he relayed all this to the hodja an expression of delight fell over the imam's face. This in itself was payment for Avdo's debt to Eşref Hodja who had arranged for him to stay in the old cabin on the cemetery grounds and who came to chat with him every night.

FOUR HUNDRED AND SEVENTY YEARS AGO

After fifteen years of an education in the former Ottoman capital of Bursa, Merkez Efendi traveled to Istanbul to visit those hodjas whose names were known all across the land. He planned to participate in their lectures. As he did not hold a favorable opinion of Sünbül Efendi's custom of *devran dönme*, Sufi whirling, and his belief in a unity of existence—Sünbül Efendi held a key position within the social complex of Koca Mustafa Pasha—he kept his distance from him despite his fame and influence. So Merkez Efendi joined the Lodge of Mirza Baba in Fatih and married Mirza Baba's daughter. It was then that he had a dream, but when he asked religious leaders about its meaning no one knew. He then closed in upon himself, he stopped eating and drinking altogether. In another dream, he saw Sünbül Efendi forcing open the door to his room and interpreting his mysterious dream. The next morning Merkez Efendi awoke in a sweat and raced over to Koca Mustafa Pasha, a nine-hundred-year-old holy monastery that had recently been turned into a social complex. He was nearly out of breath. Sünbül Efendi greeted him graciously and had the bright young man—of whom he already had heard—sit down and join the discussion of the day. The talk dealt with how pilgrims circled the Kaaba in the same way all the stars circled the North Star, and in the same way that all the angels circled the world. Existence was a circle that circled around a center. The truth was both the circle and the center—in other words, everything and the singular. In this whirling or *devran* human beings slowly approached the creator as they circled, becoming one with the creator. The center merging with the circle. One day blessed Rumi was passing through a jewelry market when he heard the sound of the hammers and he stopped in his tracks and began to whirl. It made no difference if the zealot condemned him and named him a sinner. For Rumi has shown that the truth can be found in any moment and everywhere. At the end of the gathering, Sünbül Efendi looked into the eyes of the young man who sat beside him and praised him before all the others, saying, "You are the center of our circle here." And from then on the young man whose name had been Musa Efendi was known as Center Efendi or Merkez Efendi.

TODAY, AFTERNOON

Avdo wandered through the cemetery and to the opposing city walls where stones had been set aside in a corner, looking for those he might use for gravestones and his restoration of the çilehane. Then he returned to his new home and sat at the table outside his front door. On a blank piece of paper, he wrote down the kinds of stone he would need, colors, shapes, numbers. He made a list of the items he would need for carving stone, something he had desperately missed during the seven years he had spent in prison. At the end of his list, he wrote the word "mallet" and next to it: the sledgehammer Ferhat used to pierce the mountain.

TODAY, EVENING

After Eşref Hodja recited his evening call to prayer and swiftly performed the five motions of his salat, he went to Avdo's home with his arms full of food. He laid everything out on the table outside the front door. He told Avdo that this place they once called a cabin had become a home. He tasted the bread, cheese, tomatoes, and halvah in small bites. After taking some tea with plenty of sugar, as Avdo liked to take it too, he felt his tongue loosening. "Avdo, my brother, it has been exactly a month since you came. You left prison and began a new life for yourself here. When the Sufis went into that room of penitence in the past they had the hope of being spared the suffering of this world. Existence itself was *çile,* or suffering, and the Sufis knew this, they knew that the çilehane, the city outside of it, prisons, they were all the same. There are only the distances between, the world is one. Time in the çilehane lasts forty days, the cold of the *zemheri* lasts for forty days. The forty-first day is the day of departing the çilehane, and the day of leaving behind the *zemheri*. Which is why they speak of forty-one doors in fairy tales, doors opening and closing with hope and disappointment, but the forty-first opens onto the truth. The way to understand the world is to leave it behind for a çilehane, and to understand the çilehane you must leave it behind for the world. The only difference is the distance that lies between. You remember how you told me you could repair the room quickly, I don't think you should hurry at all. Keep a tally and work for forty days, see the infinite world contained in that little room. Merkez Efendi spoke to his disciples of four kinds of death that elevated humankind: a green death for those who made do with it, red for those who fought against their own selves, white for those who stayed away from worldly possessions. And the black death which was about patience and always keeping hope in the face of any disaster. My dear brother, the black death is your test, you have lived in this world with patience, and you will continue to do so. Your soul is close to those in our community. Come join us, twirl with us in our circle. I have never seen you come to pray, your faith may be faint or lost altogether, that doesn't matter, you can come and join our whirling whenever you like."

Village of Konak Görmez

Haymana Plain, 1958

When Avdo learned that Elif was being followed by two men, he reached into the saddlebag hanging from his horse, pulled out a handful of bullets, and put them in his pocket. He had told Baki to go home right away, taking the road up the steep path to keep out of sight, but it was already too late. Holding their breath, the men approached their target. In the silence of the night, they took cover under the trees on the outskirts of the grove and were quick to fire. The first bullet hit the darkness like lightning, finding neither the large body of Avdo nor his Arabian steed nor Elif in her slender height, but catching ten-year-old Baki in the neck and knocking him to the ground. The boy did not let out a sound. He lay on the cool earth like a branch, his blood running into the earth.

Avdo pulled Elif to the ground then lay down beside her. He crawled over to Baki and took the boy's hand, touched his face. There was nothing he could do. Right then he wanted to drive his fingers into the earth and bury the entire village. He was furious with himself and with his fate that gave him this life. He turned back to Elif and told her to stay still and wait. He told her not to look up no matter what happened, he told her to hold her breath. The sound of gunfire kept ringing in the air. Bullets flew past branches above them, some striking the trunks of trees a little farther away. The men could not pinpoint their location and were firing broadly. And yet the first shot had struck Baki. Avdo was living on the streets, hungry and bare, motherless, when he was Baki's age. Baki was not hungry, he was not unclothed, he was not motherless, and he did not deserve to die no matter what fate had in store for him. Avdo racked his brain: He could not understand what fate wanted of him. Would he please fate if he were to die? If he were to put his gun to his head and shoot himself? When Elif took hold of his hand he turned to her. "Wait for me, Elif," he said, "don't be afraid." Then he took his gun, rose to his feet, and hurried off through the trees, breathing like an angry dog.

There was no moon above them. The sky was streaked with a few clouds, a scattering of stars, and the countless leaves of almond trees. Nothing was clear in the darkness, but Avdo could make out his two enemies from the light that flashed from the barrels of their guns. To shoot more freely Avdo took shelter behind a tree. He fired again and again. His strong wrist holding firm. When his gun was empty he stopped to breathe, and he reloaded his magazine. The men were also breaking to reload their weapons. When the shooting started up again it became clear these men had no intention of leaving anyone alive that night. Branches snapped, leaves went spiraling. Now there were more clouds in the sky and the stars seemed to be racing for cover. The bullets were coming closer, the men had figured out where Avdo was. He paused, waited for the men to unload their weapons, and then he fired his last two shots. He thought he heard someone moaning but he couldn't be sure over the clamor. He reloaded. His hand in his pocket, he realized his bullets were running low. Coming out from behind the cover of a tree, he took aim and began firing. Now there was only the sound of a single gun firing back. Then he knew he had struck one of them. Leaving only two opposing men. Thinking only of avenging Baki and overwhelmed with courage, Avdo shuttled to another tree, coming even closer to his target. Just then he felt what he thought was the sharp beak of a bird strike his chest, then a warm feeling. His hand on his chest, he felt running blood. He went behind a tree, breathing heavily. The wound was serious, but fate would have to come up with more to stop him. He rose to his feet and changed course. Walking to one side without firing and keeping low to the ground, he made for his target. The man was still firing from the same spot, and after he had emptied his rifle he pulled out his pistol. Avdo could sense his rising anger, shooting even more violently. The moment Avdo came upon the figure and noticed the dark shape loom before him, the man spun around. Eye to eye, the two men fired at the same time. The man took a bullet in the forehead and died instantly. His last round struck Avdo in the shoulder. This time he felt the pain of the bullet, and he fell to the ground, stretched out on his back. It was like a gravestone had fallen on his chest.

Avdo felt as if it wasn't Baki who lay stretched out on the cold earth under the almond trees, lifeless, it was Avdo. The young boy had left this world without having enjoyed life, without having achieved but the smallest dream. Would his mother be devastated to lose him? Would she think of her lost son for the rest of her life? Would she see him in her dreams? When she came across a beggar on the street would she hand the boy alms and say, "Take this for the sake of my rosy-faced boy"? Does anyone still remember Avdo? Maybe an old woman is still searching for him in a crowded street market. In her dreams he is never any older, she will forever see him as the same age. Sometimes she hears his voice in her dreams, she is running to his voice in the white void, trying to track down the sound of her son's voice. Holding out her hand, she says, "Avdo you have my heart, I am here Avdo."

Opening his eyes Avdo looked up at Elif who was standing over him.

"Avdo, are you all right?" said Elif with tears in her eyes. "Don't you dare die! My God. How are you feeling? Are you in pain? Do you hear the dogs? Everyone in the village is on the way. Come, get up, Avdo, let's get out of here right away." Softly Avdo said that he was badly wounded and that he would not be able to stand. He was having trouble breathing. He listened for the sounds of the dogs, then took Elif by the hand. "You get out of here," he said. "Leave before they get here, don't let anyone see you, go home." Elif protested, her voice quavering, she said that she wouldn't leave him. Gathering all his strength, he said, "I am dying, Elif, you go." His head fell to the side and he heard neither Elif's voice nor the dogs nor the shots fired in the air as the villagers hurried through the almond grove.

Village of Konak Görmez

Haymana Plain, 1958

The dead had left this world to find peace. The almond grove was silent when the dogs and the villagers arrived. Faced with an impenetrable riddle, the villagers scoured every corner of the grove. The light of their kerosene lamps shining through the trees. With every step they mumbled their discontent. What possible grievance could Master Avdo have with the sons of Kara Agha? Just today he had finished his work for them. The gravestone was finely done and in return for it he received his full payment of state-minted gold. They had shaken hands and gone their separate ways, contented. So how was it that they met here in grove and in the middle of the night?

What was Baki, the son of the head shepherd, doing there? With whom had he come? The two aghas or his gravestone master? Seeing they had killed such a poor boy, they assumed these men were blinded by their anger. And the Arabian steed that everyone had so much admired since

Avdo first came to the village had fallen to a bullet, too. Its chestnut fur darkened with blood, it seemed like the depiction of a horse in a tapestry.

There were countless almond trees around the dead and just one question. Wandering from tree to tree, the villagers looked for the answer. Inspecting the trunks of trees that had been torn apart by bullets and peering under the stones that had come loose and into the faces of the dead, they could find nothing. Cigarettes were handed out as they drove back the dogs that were sniffing the blood. The villagers had seen many a blood feud play out in the villages on the plain before and yet they had never come across a case of bad blood this mysterious. None of them were capable of coming up with a logical explanation among the bodies that lay dead. Hostility was a fire covered with skill, hidden with patience, until the time came for it to flare—the villagers were masters of this. However they had to confess that never before had they seen or heard of a feud so well concealed and so embittered that it ended with the death of a young boy and those formidable young men.

One of the villagers called out to the others and they all came and gathered around Avdo. The light of their kerosene lamps illuminating his face, they came close to have a look and saw that he was still alive. His body was covered in blood, it was clear that he was seriously injured. They discussed putting him on the horse cart and taking him to the health clinic in Deveci Pınarı village at the top of the hill. The only health clinic and the only gendarmerie station on the plain were in Deveci Pınarı. If they went quickly they could be there in an hour, they could wake up the doctor who could save Avdo's life. They could also inform the gendarmerie, leaving the matter to them and the doctor.

Some of them spoke in hushed tones, others were silent. When one of the elders came forward and said that perhaps this man was innocent, that perhaps any ill intent came from the sons of Kara Agha, they were stirred into action, saying only God could know the truth. Two horses drew a cart into the grove, and then slowly Avdo was set down on the bedding they had placed in the cart. With a dozen armed horsemen, they drove the cart to the base of the hill in the east. As they listened to the wind howling in the cold of the night, they wondered if this gravestone master who in their minds had brought nothing but misfortune to their village might die on the way. Though his death would scarcely have saddened them after all this, they were also considering how the secret of the night depended on whether this man lived or died. Hoping he might recover and tell them everything, they drove their horses on into the night.

Village of Konak Görmez

Haymana Plain, 1958

Elif heard voices in her head. Frightening and confusing voices that echoed from one ear to the other. Why are you running straight home across the ravine, said the voices, go back, go to the meadows, run to the wilderness where nobody can find you—they went on and on. What good would come if she went home on such an accursed night when so many had died? It would be better for her to scream, pull out her hair, run away, lose her mind altogether. She could survive on the roots of thistles, hide among the reeds by the stream, following the voices in her head she might disappear without a trace.

The sound of dogs barking and the familiar cries of the villagers from above the ravine were far away. They had now reached the almond trees. Surely they were stunned to find the bodies among the trees. Master Avdo had already left and so why had he come back here? What grievance could the sons of Kara Agha have had with him? And the young boy? The villagers must have looked at one another in shock and disbelief.

Elif spoke with herself as her mind considered questions. The frightened voices in her head had no answers. Why had Kara Agha's sons been following her? How did they know she was planning to run away when no one else knew? What about Avdo? Did he really die after he said those words to her, his head resting on the ground, or had he just lost consciousness? Elif had put her ear on his chest and waited to hear the sound of his heart but heard only her own heartbeat and the sound of the villagers rapidly approaching. Then the voices in her head had begun to speak, telling her to get out of there right away.

When she reached the middle of the ravine, she was exhausted. Her foot slipped on a rock and she fell facefirst onto the earth. Thinking she'd be caught any second, she sprang to her feet and ran. The voices in her head told her to run the other way, but she followed another instinct, setting out for her home along the same path the two cows took every day when they came back from the pasture. Keeping a safe distance from the women who were draped across their windowsills talking, she moved quietly through the darkness. Her face was wrapped tightly in her scarf. She made it to her house unseen and slipped into the garden. She stopped by the trees before she approached the door to see if anybody was home. Her mother, Reyhan, and her sister, İpek, were huddled by the door in fear, peering into the distance. There was no sign of her father, perhaps the only thing to be happy about on this wretched night. Elif stepped out of the darkness and in her miserable state she slid over to her mother and her sister. Her knees gave out and she fell into their arms.

They brought her inside before the neighbors noticed. They washed her face with water and rubbed her wrists. They told her that her father didn't know anything and had no idea that she was ever gone with the hope that this would calm her down. When they'd heard the first gunshots, her father flew out of the house with his rifle and joined the other neighbors who were already on their way to the almond grove. But once he was gone, İpek went to tell her mother that Elif wasn't in her bed.

Elif drank a glass of water and told them her secret, her eyes pleading. She spoke of her auntie who took her life at the firepit when Elif was little, and how she was haunted by the same djinns that tortured her and led her to her death, driving her insane, filling her heart with fear. For days Elif had been beside herself, she didn't know what she was doing. After everyone else had gone to bed she would sit up waiting until morning. Speaking to herself in the darkness. Feelings she had never had before would flutter through her heart, thoughts she had never had before were racing through her brain. Even now she felt she might be dreaming. She didn't know how to drive back the djinns. She was so tired, she only wanted to sleep. But if she went to bed now only to wake in the morning to find that she was still locked in this horrible dream, she would have no other choice but to take her own life just like her auntie had done, it would be the only way to free herself from the djinns.

Elif's mother gave her a strong slap across the face and then another a glass of water. She told her two daughters to listen to her closely. This was a secret that would be kept between mother and daughters. No one knew that the tragedy tonight had anything to do with Elif. Anyone who could have spoken on the matter was now lying dead in the almond grove. The only thing for them to do was keep quiet and carry on with their lives as before. Neither their father nor their neighbors would ever suspect anything. As for driving away the djinns, she would take Elif to three shrines in different villages where she would have prayers recited and a talisman made on her behalf.

Merkez Efendi Cemetery

Istanbul, 1985

It was a sunny day. Avdo took a break from his work in the afternoon and sat down at his table on the porch to some bread, cheese, and yogurt. When he noticed the two men in sunglasses walking over to him, he assumed they were mourners at a funeral, accompanied by Imam Muhittin, whose blank expression was the look he wore to express his sadness for the deceased. They passed the fountain and greeted Avdo at his porch.

"Master Avdo," said Imam Muhittin, "these officers have been asking after you, they would like to speak with you on a personal matter." His voice was as formal as the faces of the officers.

Avdo put down his bread and stood up. "Please," he said, "what's the issue? An urgent gravestone?"

Both officers had short hair and were clean-shaven and looked like special agents right out of a movie. With fedoras on their heads. One wore a black overcoat and the other a gray one.

"No," said the man in the black overcoat, "we are looking for a friend, the person in this photograph. You know him, right?"

Avdo took the photograph and looked at it carefully. "This is Commander Cobra," he said. "I don't know his real name, he came here two weeks ago searching for a fugitive with a team of around ten other men."

"Yes, that's him. Two weeks ago. Did you ever see him again after that?"

"I did," said Avdo with a composed expression on his face, "three days ago."

The officers glanced at each other.

Avdo went on to explain. "We had an unfortunate episode a couple of weeks ago when he was first here. He felt bad about it, or so he said, so he decided to come and open up to me, this time alone."

"Around what time?"

"It was after noon prayers. Because he told me he had just prayed in our mosque."

"Our commander?" said the officer, a little surprised. "He went to pray? He told you that himself?"

"Yes, it was just three days ago, I remember it well. May I ask what's going on?"

"Avdo Bey," said the man in the black overcoat and then he paused.

Avdo wasn't used to hearing himself addressed with the formal "bey," especially from police officers—or were these intelligence officers?—this kind of formality was alien to him.

"Forgive me," said Avdo, "I've kept you standing, do sit down, or come inside if you like."

"There's no need for that, this is fine right here."

The two officers took the chairs and Imam Muhittin and Avdo sat on the divan.

"Would you like tea? I'll put some on the stove, it'll steep while we talk."

"No, thank you, we'll just finish here and get going. We have other places we need to check. We won't be bothering you."

With their sunglasses, their hats, formality, and stock phrases like "We won't be bothering you," these officers were truly straight out of a mob flick.

"Please go ahead, I'm listening," said Avdo, adjusting his tone to match theirs.

"Avdo Bey, our commander, whom you know by the name Cobra, has been missing for the past three days. We have no idea where he is. He left the office on New Year's Day to check on several locations and he was never seen again. We checked those places and learned that he was never there. And we have no idea why he went to work when everyone else was on a holiday that day."

"He was feeling heartsick," said Avdo.

"Heartsick?"

"I mean he was frustrated, he needed someone to talk to, to relax."

"He needed to talk to you?"

"Sometimes a bad episode can bring two people together."

"What do you mean when you say a bad episode?"

Flicking through his prayer beads, Imam Muhittin looked down at the photo on the table. "Could I have a look at the photograph? If that is okay?" he asked.

The officers nodded.

The imam took the photograph and quickly looked it over.

"I also saw this man," he said, "he was praying in the mosque. This time of winter only a handful of elderly men come to pray so it was impossible not to notice this gentleman, tall with a thick mustache. I assumed he was coming to visit a grave."

"You're sure it was him?"

"I am," said the imam, "I saw him put money in the donation box beside the door. Our mosque is small, and we have few donations, so I notice when people give."

Avdo was surprised to hear that a donation box had been placed in the mosque six months ago after Imam Muhittin took his post. In his twenty years at Merkez Efendi Cemetery he had never heard about anything like this.

"And did you speak with him?"

"No," said the imam, "he seemed in a hurry, he put money in the box once he finished praying, then he put on his shoes and left. He had a package with him, yes, now I remember, he was carrying something."

"He was in a hurry because he was coming to see me," said Avdo and he started to laugh. Unable to stop he put his hand over his mouth.

Frowning, the officers looked at Avdo and then at the imam.

Not sure what to say, Avdo nervously looked the other way. The imam spoke on his behalf.

"Don't get the wrong idea, gentlemen, Master Avdo has a disorder of a kind, sometimes he can't keep himself from laughing. Happens all of a sudden. But this has nothing to do with the topic at hand, he just can't stop himself."

"It seems hard not to take it the wrong way," said the officer in black, the other nodding in agreement.

"I know," said Avdo, trying to explain, "I can't understand it either, it is a tic I have had for some twenty years. Forgive me. In fact this was why Commander Cobra was angry with me two weeks ago."

"Would you tell us what happened?"

"They came here with a scout dog, Slowy, in the middle of the night. They were searching for someone who was running from the law, or so they said. That night the fog was so thick you couldn't see a thing, and then it started to snow, but they were still looking everywhere, checking every grave, looking behind every tree. Then their dog tried to pick a fight with my dog. And at the worst possible moment my damn laughing kicked in. I couldn't stop it. The commander was angry with me about it so he drew his gun and shot my dog. He made my dog pay for that laugh."

Avdo fell silent and no one said a word. They looked over at the trees and the graves covered in snow. The bright reflection of the sun on the pure white snow dazzled their eyes. The officers were comfortably shielded behind their glasses, but Avdo and Imam Muhittin had to squint in the light.

"That's a shame about your dog," said the officer in black. "The commander must have been sad about that, seeing that he wanted to come back here and—"

"About my dog?" said Avdo. "I wish he was but no, he was sad about what he had done to me, he came back here to win me over."

"What he did to you, I mean about killing your dog..."

"You know when I laughed that night the commander was furious, he didn't know what he was doing, and that's when he hit me. He gave me a bloody nose. They left me like that. But it wouldn't leave his mind for days after that, it ate him up, so he decided to come and see me."

"We are truly sorry, we apologize on his behalf," said the officer. "This is a tough job, Avdo Bey, you're out there putting your life on the line to do the best you can and suddenly you find yourself making a mistake."

"No need for you to apologize, the commander already felt sad about it, he couldn't sleep at night. He came here with the intention of making friends with me, of forgetting the hard feelings, he brought me lunch. Lamb sandwiches and ayran. I suppose that was the package the imam saw."

"Can you tell us what you talked about, maybe that would help us find him."

"He was so sad I tried to console him. I told him the unfortunate episode that we had was nothing in comparison to the extreme nature of his line of work. It was a little like a father-son conversation. We talked about how he still wasn't married, and then—"

"Is that so? The commander brought up with you the fact that he wasn't married?" said the officer.

"Yes, how else would I know if he was married or not. It seems the difficulty of the job has prevented him from starting a family. He was complaining about that."

"The commander never talks to anyone about his personal life or his feelings. Seeing that he opened up to you like that he must hold you in some esteem."

"Sir, I was talking about how unfortunate episodes can bring people together, and this was the case here. You must have read my file, and learned about my past. I lost my family, grew up an orphan, I spent time in prison. If I were to learn years later that I had a daughter or a son, I would press them to my chest, and that's exactly what I felt toward the commander, I saw him as my own child. This happened three days ago, he stayed for a couple of hours, two hours that felt like two years."

Silence fell over the table. Imam Muhittin bowed his head and drifted into thinking over what had just been said. He felt they were on the brink of serious trouble but he also felt relieved by the natural rhythms of Avdo's speech. Praying for the conversation to end as soon as possible, he softly recited the names of God as he counted the beads on his *misbaha*.

"I hope the commander turns up as soon as possible," said Avdo, picking up the thread. "Maybe he went to see someone he knew so he could shut down for a few days. Like I said, he seemed troubled."

"Let's hope that's it, let's pray he turns up as soon as possible. But we can't just sit here and wait for him to come back. We are exploring every avenue, even the possibility of his abduction."

"Abduction?"

"Anarchists, terrorists, separatists, our list of enemies is long. If they had taken him and killed him, we would have already heard about it, they would have used it as propaganda. If they wanted to trade him for a terrorist in prison they would have already made contact, and we would know the score."

"And nobody has been in contact with you?"

"Unfortunately, no. We say unfortunately because we're worried, we would be happier to know for sure that he had been abducted."

"What a shame," said Avdo and he sighed. "It was also sad to hear about his sister. The poor woman must be dying to know what's happened to him."

"His sister?" said an officer with a note of surprise in his voice.

"His sister?" echoed the other officer.

"Is there a problem?" asked Avdo, looking at them, confused.

"You said his sister . . ." The officer in black faltered as he struggled to find the words, then collecting himself he said, "Please, go on, what did the commander tell you? What did he say about his sister?"

Avdo spoke slowly. "He told me how he had spoken with her about what had happened here. He told her how he hit me. Seeing how upset he was about it she told him to come here, she said he should try to win me back. In a way the commander came here for her sake."

"Are you sure he said his sister?"

"Of course. It seems like he really loves her, looking after her, as she's sick, she has no one else."

The officers glanced at each other and came to an understanding without saying a word.

"Avdo Bey," said the officer in black, "it seems there's some confusion here, and I really don't know why. The commander had a sister, but she died last year. He's been living alone ever since."

Now Avdo and the imam exchanged looks.

"Almighty God!" cried the imam, his face going pale. "You do both good and evil, oh God, and you the only one among us to know."

Avdo tried to explain. "The commander said his sister was religious. That she would pray for him when he left in the morning and when he came home in the evening, pray for God to protect him and keep him safe. He said she was paralyzed and bedridden for the last three years."

"That's all true," said the officer, "his sister was bedridden for three years, and she was a pious woman, but then she died of a heart attack. We also attended her funeral at the cemetery in Eyüp."

"I don't understand," said Avdo.

"Oh God, you are great, look over your subjects, you are both creator and the destroyer," said the imam, his voice tearful.

"I don't know," said the officer, "I wonder if he started seeing things? Speaking to his dead sister he thought she was still alive, thinking he was saying all that to her when he was only speaking to himself? His sister was the only person close to him before she died, and we know how shook up he was when he lost her, but for it to come this far..."

"I'm sorry to hear it," said Avdo, his voice unsteady. Rubbing his eyes, he turned to the imam and asked, "Do you see what happens to people when they lose the only person they have? You must pray for us all, for God to forgive us our sins."

Suddenly it seemed as if they were sitting in front of the holy mihrab in the mosque redolent of rosewater, not on Avdo's porch.

"Oh the great Almighty," said the imam.

"Who would have thought?" mused the officer. "The commander speaking to his imaginary sister. We never picked up on anything like that."

"I wonder if he went somewhere assuming he could hear his sister's voice?" asked Avdo.

"We'll have to look into that possibility now."

"If so, then he'll be back."

"Maybe."

"What else could it be? Seeing terrorists haven't got him, he'll be back."

"Let's hope that's the case. Avdo Bey, what did the commander say before he left you? Did he tell you what he was doing or where he was going?"

"He told me that he was going to go back to his sister early to tell her about our talk and come back to see me in a few days. I wonder if he went to her grave to pour out his feelings?"

"We need to look into that. Yes, so we'll be going then. Avdo Bey, this is our number, if you remember anything you'll call us straightaway?"

"Of course," said Avdo, looking down at the number on the card.

The officers stood up and left the same way they had come in through the cemetery, walking gingerly on the icy ground. Lost in thought, they stopped at the fountain then pulled out packs of cigarettes and lit up. During the conversation they had chosen not to smoke as this was the official protocol. It was rare to see officers like this in times like these.

Imam Muhittin called after them: “Sir, I was curious, that fugitive, the one the commander was pursuing that night, was she apprehended?”

Pulling his cigarette from his lips, the man in black answered: “No, she is still out there.”

Merkez Efendi Cemetery

Istanbul, 1984

TODAY, NIGHT

The lights of the mosque went out not long after three old men who had come for evening prayers despite the *zemheri* cold slowly stepped out of the mosque and headed home. Then the lights in the house beside the mosque went on. Avdo was waiting for the moment and he quickly walked over to the house and stuck his head through the open door. Imam Muhittin saw him and gestured with his long, bony hand for him to come in, silently fluttering his lips as if to say there might be others around.

TODAY, MORNING

Since Imam Muhittin was posted to the Merkez Efendi Mosque he had shown himself to be a different kind of imam: He wrote talismanic prayers for elderly women and young girls who came to the mosque for prayers and wishes, on the condition that they donated to the mosque;

and he would meet with people in the municipality to arrange for the acquisition of a grave site, providing that a donation was involved. In the past there had been plenty of space in the cemetery, but people were now following a trend set by celebrities and choosing this side of the city, and Merkez Efendi himself was held in high esteem. Grave prices were on the rise. Mourners who wanted their deceased ones to be buried close to the famous composer Sadettin Kaynak or the famed author Halide Edip Adıvar were easily convinced to give the money that was requested. Once Imam Muhittin had asked Avdo to make an urgent and very special gravestone. Avdo assumed he was doing a good deed for someone, but later he would learn how things were operating in the background. But he never would have thought that this gravestone would end up helping him. That morning he went to see the imam and told him he needed to hide his daughter. If the imam would provide a place for her for a little while he would agree to make a donation to the mosque, and, as Avdo had expected, the imam's initial fear of the state was lessened by the idea of five hundred American dollars. When Avdo promised him another five hundred the following week, the imam softened even more. The imam said he would do that only for the sake of helping Avdo's daughter and that Avdo had to think about finding a suitable place for her. With little time to consider the options, Avdo suggested they unlock the door to the çilehane located under the mosque complex and use it after a cleaning. The imam was curious to know how Avdo had learned that such a place was even there. He reminded the imam that he had only lived in the Merkez Efendi Cemetery for six months while Avdo had been living there for twenty years, and he explained how the former imams used to open up the room every year for a cleaning and that he would help them.

FOUR HUNDRED AND SEVENTY-ONE YEARS AGO

At the time that Merkez Efendi decided to build his Sufi lodge in Istanbul the population had swelled considerably since the conquest sixty years ago and so he deemed it fit to move beyond the city walls. He chose the site of a holy spring that dated back to Byzantine times and had recently fallen out of use. Christians had said the water of the spring was holy and once took it as a cure for a wide range of woes and maladies related to magic spells, fear, and longing as well as physical ailments, but now it had almost no visitors. Merkez Efendi considered building a dervish lodge around his çilehane, a main kiosk, a fountain, and a hammam. Although he was over fifty years of age he worked side by side with his laborers and disciples. In the making of the çilehane in particular he gave the sweat of his brow. He went down to the base of the spring, which was seven meters deep, put up the walls of the çilehane, and dug a well in the neighboring garden to replenish the water in the spring. The darkness of his penitence room and the holy waters of the spring would bring him one step closer to God. If Sheik Sünbül Efendi of the Halveti Order would grant him permission—for he was on his path—he would stay in the room not for forty days but for forty years. This is what he desired, he desired to have an endless conversation with God during which he would forget himself in silence, solitude, and darkness and feel in his jugular vein that there was no other God in this universe but his own self.

TODAY, NIGHT

When the sky filled with thick clouds and was steeped in darkness, Avdo left the cemetery for the city walls. Moving through the caverns and tunnels, he eventually found Reyhan, who had been waiting all day in a cold, secluded corner, wrapped up in two blankets. Beside her was a knife and some bread. The place was deserted and the fog was settling again. Taking her by the arm, Avdo brought her to the asphalt road and back to the cemetery that was covered in a quilt of white snow.

FOUR HUNDRED AND FORTY-SEVEN YEARS AGO

An esteemed Sufi sheik, Merkez Efendi was also an excellent physician. He once concocted a paste of forty-one different herbs and spices as a cure for a malady that had been plaguing Ayşe Hafsa Sultan, the mother of Sultan Süleyman the Magnificent, and soon many others had adopted the paste and its application, calling it *mesir macunu* and eventually using it as a cure for nearly every ailment one might imagine. But now as the Kanuni—as Süleyman the Magnificent was known—was making ready for a new war campaign, he decided to take Merkez Efendi with him as his sheik of war and not his chief physician. Merkez Efendi was more than seventy years old when he took this new position, he was a graybeard and the army needed wise men like him. The sultan's goal was to cross the Adriatic and take the city of Otranto before moving on to conquer all of Italy. Fifty years after his great-grandfather Fatih Sultan Mehmet withdrew from Otranto, the Ottoman dream for those lands burned as lively as the kindling in a fire. The sultan's army had already taken Baghdad in the east and the Hungarian Kingdom in the west, and after a great deal of preparation they set off on this new campaign. The armada was now at sea and waiting for the arrival of the ground troops when their plans were dashed by a conflict between a Venetian fleet that had previously promised to remain impartial, and the campaign changed its course for the island of Corfu, which was under Venetian control. This ended in a stalemate and six months later the sultan returned to Istanbul empty-handed, drained, and disappointed. Christian states in Europe feared this sultan who bore the title of Magnificent, a sultan who desired to rule them with a power that came only with the standing of a Caesar. His great-grandfather Fatih had conquered Istanbul, ending the Byzantine Empire, which earned him the title of the Roman Caesar that had been passed down to him from the city's history. And when his father, Yavuz Sultan Selim, took Cairo and the Kaaba, and earned the title of caliphate, the title of Caesar was forgotten in the Ottoman palace. If the sultan could have conquered Italy he would undoubtedly have established the title of Caesar absolutely and become Caesar the Magnificent of Europe. Merkez Efendi tried to lessen the sadness of the sultan, whom he had known since he was young and still a prince and heir to the throne, and stayed with him at Topkapı Palace for a month after they returned from the war campaign, but soon he asked the sultan for his permission to return to this humble life. At his dervish lodge outside the city walls, he spoke with his disciples, returned to the Sufi way of life, and closed himself up in his çilehane under the weight of his gathering woes. For forty days he would stay there seeing nothing but the four walls of the little room, hearing nothing but the sound of darkness.

TODAY, NIGHT

Reyhan went down the steps to the door of the çilehane, which was narrow even for her small body, lowering her head as she stepped into the room. Since the founding of the Turkish Republic sixty years ago, this little room had been locked, along with Merkez Efendi's Sufi lodge and all the other dervish lodges. The room was damp and smelled hundreds of years old. Although it had been washed with bleach Reyhan caught the sharp scent of mold in her nostrils. She shuddered at the thought of those Sufis who used to turn their backs on the world, shutting themselves in a place like this for forty days. She turned and looked at Avdo. "Dad," she said. On the way over to the cemetery, Avdo had told her about where she would be staying, and how the word *çile* came from the Persian and meant "forty," and how Sufis would come to a place like this to free themselves from the suffering of the world, to find solace, a balm, and how he hoped this room would bring her this. And how he had only managed to arrange for such a place by telling the imam she was his daughter who had come to him after so many years, and that only with such a lie would life be easier. Leaving Reyhan alone in the room, he hugged her and said, "My dear daughter."

Haymana Plain, 1959

The wedding of Mikail Agha was put off until this year's harvest as he was still mourning the loss of his two older brothers and his father. It was a long period of mourning and they were still waiting to hear of the fate of the gravestone mason who had slain his brothers. Two seasons passed. The gravestone mason was sentenced to death for murder. Two more seasons passed. The villagers harvested the crops while they all began making preparations and at the end of the month of August it seemed that everyone on the plain was on their way to the wedding. Forming a crowd larger than the one that had gathered at the funeral a year ago, people poured into the village of Konak Görmez with the hope of sharing in this young man's happiness and helping him set aside his grief. From the village of Abdal came three drummers and three horn players, a folk group of friends of the same political party in Ankara; men on horseback raced about the village, children's laughter rose above all the other cries, and girls and boys dancing the Halay had their share of the wedding that would last for seven days and seven nights.

DAY ONE

After lunch the imam read a prayer and when the sound of the drum and horn filled the air the young boys and girls made ready for the Halay. Peers of the young agha were first in line, and they gave their joy to their friend's new life. The sun was now at its wildest. Adolescent boys and girls moved about with trays, handing out ayran to the young who danced drenched in sweat. The first day of the wedding started late and the evening came quickly. When it was dark the playful young boys and girls joined the Halay line under the light of kerosene lamps and then began a game of "steal the hat." Here a youngster would swipe the hat of someone from another village and race off at top speed. The entire village was the playing field. On one side were the villagers from the same village as the young man who had stolen the hat, facing off against the villagers on the other side, who were hunting down their team's stolen hat, it was a great game of chase in which they struggled to trip up their opponents in the darkness.

DAY TWO

The next day someone stole the hat of one of the musicians from Ankara. As the youngsters of the village made off with the hat, Kutlu the musician and his friends went after them, joining the village tradition. Taking the risk of the challenges that came with tracking down the hat in a dark and strange village, the musicians split up for the chase. Anyone who came close to the hat would whistle to give word they were closing in. As they raced about, the drum and horn continued playing, the dancers continued dancing in the house of the groom. Following the shadows in the dark, Kutlu stepped into a garden where he saw a girl sitting on a wall. From a distance she was watching the house of the groom. Kutlu asked her if she had seen any of the young men who had made off with his hat. She said she had seen no one come this way. Kutlu was curious and asked her why she was sitting here alone and not with her friends at the wedding. Because of course everyone else in the village had gone to the agha's wedding, all the houses were dark. Avoiding his question, the girl asked him which village he came from. Kutlu told her that he came from Ankara. Now this sparked her interest. "This is the house of the bride," she said, "the family of the bride doesn't attend the groom's family wedding. Isn't it the same in Ankara?" Kutlu smiled. "We have the same custom," he said. "Is Ankara big?" she asked. "Oh, it's really big, and it's completely lit up at night," said Kutlu. She was staring at him now and Kutlu asked what was running through her head. "I hope you aren't the bride sitting alone outside her house," he said. "No, I'm her sister."

DAY THREE

İpek combed Elif's hair with some lavender oil while Elif sat in silence, she had been this way since the start of the wedding. İpek braided her sister's hair and lined every braid with red, yellow, and green beads. When she was done she sat down in front of Elif and let her sister do the same. Elif combed her sister's hair with lavender oil. As light as a feather she ran the comb through her hair. "İpek," she said, "after I am married come see me often, don't be shy because it is the agha's house, come and sing to me with your beautiful voice." Assuming there were tears of sadness in her sister's voice, İpek turned to look. But her sister's eyes were all dried out: She had shed a lifetime of tears over the last year alone. İpek looked down to avoid her sister's gaze, she was now crying on her sister's behalf for the bride was expected to cry every day of her wedding. Now the words were tumbling out of Elif, this was the first time in days she was talking like this. "When I leave this house, I'll leave you my comb. It's the only thing of value I have. I have spoken to this comb while daydreaming at this mirror, pouring myself out to it. It made me happy to see the Shahmaran on it and its smile. But only lately have I come to realize it wasn't smiling at me. My fate has played tricks on me. Now my wish is that the Shahmaran will smile at you."

DAY FOUR

But there was one other family in the village that did not attend the wedding party, along with the family of the bride. From their house on the hill the former head shepherd Heyran and his wife were now watching the wedding party that lit up the center of the dark village like a full moon. Heyran didn't blame Master Avdo after the murder of his son, indeed he insisted that Avdo loved his son and that he would never hurt him, and he even went so far as to say that the young aghas had treated his child badly. His words spread quickly through the village and finally fell upon the ear of Mikail Agha, who gave the head shepherd a slap before he banished him from his work and home. Heyran took his wife with him and built this one-room house on top of the hill that faced the village. When the day came Heyran went to see Avdo tried in court and despite the countless stories the villagers told against him, he still insisted the gravestone mason was a good man and that he should not be held accountable for the death of his son. The villagers following the trial were hardly interested in hearing what Heyran had to say, they wanted to hear Avdo's defense. Steeped in sadness, Avdo told how he had stopped in the almond grove to rest after he had left the village and woke after nightfall to noises. He said that he had no idea why the sons of Kara Agha would try to take his life, and no idea why young Baki was there, and so the villagers were left in the dark. When the judge declared that Avdo was to receive the death penalty, snapping the pencil in his hands, only Heyran cried out, "No! God!" No longer able to find work in the village, Heyran had gone to the neighboring village of Deveci Pınarı. One day a month he would come back to the village to see his wife. It would go on like this until it snowed, and the animals were stabled. Today he had come home with his donkey, carrying cheese, butter, sugar, and tea, and leading a cow. His wife, Mihrinaz, was especially pleased to see the cow after the five chickens that Heyran had brought her last month. What more could she want in life.

But of course, they prayed for a healthy child. A year after Baki's death Mihrinaz was pregnant again. In the villages on the plain it was common for children to join old blood feuds from the names that they were given, becoming part of a past they knew nothing about. If Mihrinaz gave birth to a girl, Heyran would have no part in naming her and if she gave birth to a boy he would be named İsmet. For the past six months the name of İsmet Pasha, who had founded the republic with Atatürk and who was now leading the opposition party in the current government, had been fixed in his mind.

SIX MONTHS AGO

When everything was buried under snow in February the village was shaken by news over the radio of a plane crash. The voice of the state broadcaster who relayed the details of the accident was as cold as ice. "The plane of Prime Minister Adnan Menderes has crashed in the capital city of London, killing most of the passengers." The speaker went on to say that they still did not have any information on the state of the prime minister. The village was up all night, but they heaved a sigh of relief when they heard the following morning that the prime minister was among the ten people who had survived. Only Heyran was displeased with the news, openly saying that it would have been better if the prime minister had died in place of all the others. He stubbornly pointed this out to Mikail Agha, whose family supported the party of Adnan Menderes, and on election day they pushed the villagers to vote for the same party. But the villagers would cast their votes for Adnan Menderes despite the pressure to do so. For they said that during İsmet Pasha's time in government the nation was torn apart from its religion. In the not so distant past, it was customary for village children to be named after İsmet but now many were being named Adnan. After the murder of his son and losing his job as head shepherd, Heyran channeled his animosity for Mikail Agha into politics, voicing ideas one would never expect from a shepherd. He said the country was being poorly managed, playing to the tune of those with the money, following orders from America, providing villages with nothing but the comfort of prayer; in fact he was repeating what he was hearing from Blacksmith Mamet from the village of Deveci Pınarı. Not ten years had passed since the village was established. In the wake of the Second World War the communists came to power in Bulgaria and a population of three hundred thousand Turks who had been living there for centuries migrated to Turkey. The government made the decision to place the incoming population in various spots across the country and a seventy-household village was made beside an old spring on a hilltop in the middle of the plain where camel caravans once rested on their long journeys. During the two-year period of population exchange, Turkey and Bulgaria were challenged with a diplomatic crisis when it was reported that Gypsies were migrating with the Turkish community, and, blaming the Bulgarian government for deliberately allowing this to happen, Turkey shut down its border several times. Although the government had done everything it could to restrict the Gypsy population from coming it was rumored that there was a Gypsy family among the tribe that had settled in the village of Deveci Pınarı. Blacksmith Mamet denied such rumors, saying his family was as Turkish as any other and that they spoke Turkish like everybody else. Although Mamet had indeed fled a country ruled by communists, his thinking was no different than theirs. He spoke of the inequality that was rife in Turkey and how the government deceived its citizens, mentioning the high cost of living and the atrocity of the gendarmerie who favored the aghas while they oppressed the poor villagers. He treated Heyran, who was working for him and tended his flock as well, to extra provisions. He said a shepherd should have sufficient means to better his lot in life and that this was the government's responsibility, and so he did what the government should do. He gave Heyran extra chickens, a cow, and a dog. In light of how he was now being treated, Heyran loathed his former agha even more, and the villagers were puzzled by the strange words this ordinary shepherd was now using to talk about politics and the government.

DAY FIVE

When night fell the saz player Kutlu came to the garden and sat down on the wall beside İpek, who had been waiting for him. He took her hand and told her that he was in love with her and that he wanted to take her away with him when he left. First he and his friends had to play at a wedding in another village, and he couldn't let them down, but when he finished there he would come back for her. İpek agreed at once and they decided to meet the following week in the almond grove on the outskirts of the village on Friday night. When they parted İpek looked long and hard at Kutlu and said, "Don't leave me here."

DAY SIX

Since the start of the wedding Elif had waited with her eyes fixed on the wall. During the day she wished the night would never come and at night she wished the new day would never dawn. Fearing the sight of blood, she no longer contemplated using the knife to cut her wrist. The hodjas of three villages had made her *muska* amulets and one by one she would take them out of her bosom and kiss them. As she did not have the courage to die she knew that she would be a slave to her fate and destined to live a life like the others, all this she hopelessly accepted.

DAY SEVEN

When the bright face of the sun was ablaze above the village they put Elif on a white horse. Holding the reins, they slowly led her through. The girls who were single watched the bride with envy, her neck and arms shimmering with gold. Beneath a red shawl, her head was bowed. Everyone there assumed that tears were running from her eyes but they were empty pools whose water had run dry.

THE FOLLOWING WEEK, FRIDAY

İpek managed to do what Elif could not. In the middle of the night she met Kutlu in the almond grove, and climbing into his car that smelled of cigarettes, drink, and gasoline, she left behind the village she had lived in for all seventeen years of her life. On her flight she took with her a little *bohça*—a cloth bundle that held her clothes and her sister's comb with the Shahmaran that looked out at the future with empty eyes.

Merkez Efendi Cemetery

Istanbul, 1985

Paying his respects to Avdo and Imam Muhittin, Selim Bey, the head of the Registry Office, left them alone on the porch.

Selim Bey's daughter had been diagnosed with cancer at the age of two and last week her frail body had hopelessly succumbed to the illness. A large group of people attended the funeral and both men and women wept for the only child of Selim Bey and his wife. When they read the date of birth and death on the nearby gravestones the mourners were devastated to think this poor little girl was the youngest of the dead, and the greenest sapling in the cemetery.

Earlier that morning Selim Bey and Imam Muhittin had come to see Avdo to ask him to make a truly beautiful gravestone for his daughter. The voice of Selim Bey had those refined tones of an Istanbul gentleman but also the pain of a devastated father. Avdo shared his grief and told him that he would make a gravestone not for the father who lost a child but for the innocence of this young girl, who was taken from this world before her time, and said that those who set their eyes upon the beauty of her gravestone would see the delicacy of her soul. Taking him by the hand, Selim Bey thanked him, and kindly said that he would pay Avdo whatever he desired in return for his work. But the imam intervened. He said that money was not an issue and that he would speak to Master Avdo himself. After presenting them with his gratitude, the head of the Registry Office left the two men on their own.

The imam felt the need to explain. "Master Avdo," he said, "I thought there was no need to speak of money so soon with such an important person. You know, his father's a prominent man, too, the assistant to the mayor. You can start working on that gravestone and one day next week I will go to see Selim Bey in his office for a chat and bring up the matter of your fee, what you deserve for your labor, I'll take care of it then."

"Yes," said Avdo, mulling something over as he ran his fingers through his hair. "Yes, yes," he repeated softly.

"I hope this doesn't give you the wrong idea..."

"Oh no, not at all," said Avdo.

"This is an important man with many connections, maybe one day we'll need his favor so we need to keep him in ours."

"You're right, you have matters to handle, and so do I. Maybe he'll turn out to be helpful."

"What do you mean?"

"Imam Efendi, you are young enough to be my child, and seeing that we are supporting each other, let us speak openly, let us set matters straight."

"What exactly are you talking about?"

"I'm talking about my daughter who has been tucked away in that room for three weeks, I keep thinking about what can be done for her."

"I'm going to ask you something, and I have asked you this before, but you didn't give me a proper answer. You are quite sure that your daughter isn't the young woman who is running from the law?"

"How could you think that, Imam Efendi," said Avdo, forcing a smile. "Does she look like someone who is on the run? She's nothing but skin and bones, a frail little girl, how could that be?"

"That's what I thought when I first saw her but with all this coming together I started to wonder if there really could be so many coincidences."

"You're right to wonder, but the police are searching for a savage terrorist, someone capable of threatening the entire state on her own, who knows what terror camp that girl is in right now."

"You're right, these are strange people, that much is clear from their faces on those Wanted pictures they put up. They look like creatures that have escaped from the jungle more than anything else. Even the military couldn't pull out the roots. May God help us, who knows when they will leave this country in peace."

"Who knows . . ."

"Master Avdo, I don't know your daughter's problem. I just hope they don't find her and get me in trouble."

"Don't worry about that, Imam Efendi, we've already talked about this. If anything happens you know what to say. You don't know her, and you never unlocked the door of the çilehane. As far as you know it has been locked for the last sixty years. You don't have the key, I do. The imam before you gave it to me to clean the place when it was necessary, you have no idea where the key is, right?"

"Of course, we spoke about it, I know. If you don't want to tell me about your daughter then there is nothing that I can say."

"This is something that belongs to the past, something I nearly forgot altogether. If you really want I can tell you about it."

Imam Muhittin couldn't restrain the curious expression on his face. Leaning back his chair, he indicated that he was ready for the story.

"All right," said Avdo, and he took a deep breath. "You know the homeless that live over on the city walls, the beggars. They often come to the cemetery and the mosque to ask for help. When I first settled here twenty years ago, there was a young beggar who was quite beautiful. But first things first, I was just out of prison, I didn't know who I was and... I slept with her one night. That's it, and then she disappeared. I never saw her again. How was I to know that she was pregnant and gave birth to the child somewhere else in the city and raised her in some secluded corner. The moment I learned all this I went looking for her, I asked all the vagabonds that I knew. But I couldn't find a trace of her. So I stopped. Then last month the ship of fate finally dropped anchor, ravished by storms. I got word from some people on the wall and I went over and found her there. And what do I see: this poor, disheveled girl. Her mother had recently passed away, but she had mentioned me before she died, telling her that the man in the cemetery was her father. So far so good, but the rest is not so good. It turns out her mother got her wrapped up in stealing. Now she has a record with the police, and she is wanted for several different crimes. When her mother died, she fell ill and couldn't look after herself. That's when she decided to let me know. They came and told me that I had a daughter, she is so-and-so and staying in so-and-so. I went to Cankurtaran and I found her in some den on the coast. What would you do if you were me, Imam Efendi, tell me, what would you do if a daughter of yours whom you had never known or looked after suddenly showed up? What would you do?"

"Good God, Master Avdo, what a fate!"

"Meanwhile I hear she has made several enemies among the other drifters, some who were hostile toward her mother and are now going after her. I took her out of there right away and brought her here. Now I'm doing what any other father would do, I am struggling to get her out of that swamp and keep her safe from her enemies and doing all I can to get her healthy again. Thank you, I will never forget what you have done."

"Please, there is no need for that," said Imam Muhittin with a proud smile on his face. "But how long can the poor girl stay down there in that narrow little room, have you thought about that? If someone does see her and goes to the police, she would be taken in and we, I mean you, would be in trouble."

"I have been thinking that over, too, looking for a solution for days. She has other problems, too."

"What other problem could she have?"

"On top of all this she is pregnant."

"What? That little girl is pregnant? Oh, Almighty God, what is this?"

"I couldn't believe it either."

"Well then where is he, I mean the father of the child?"

Avdo's brow went tense as he hardened his gaze. "That place is full of wastrels and bums. What do you think would happen to a poor girl in those secluded corners, living in garbage dumps . . ."

Avdo didn't want to say any more and Imam Muhittin saw that it would be best to console him.

"Don't fret over it, what has happened has happened, the great Almighty of the universe has written different paths of fate for us all, and so it is for that poor one, too. You pull yourself together, see what can be done from now on."

Pleased with his story, Avdo brought the subject back to his initial idea.

"You're right, I need to see what can be done from now on. Do you know what I was thinking?"

"What was that, Master Avdo?"

"You know how you said that you were going to see Selim Bey, I think you shouldn't wait until next week. Go tomorrow and chat with him for a while."

"Why is that necessary? For the gravestone fee?"

"As I understand it," said Avdo, "you want to get close to the head of the Registry Office so you can ask him to handle some of your personal business, ask him to have you posted to a larger mosque, and if necessary you can seek help from his father, who is the assistant to the mayor no less."

"Yes, I thought about that, but not with bad intentions. In this age you can't get anything done without such connections."

"I am going to recommend something else. Before you talk to Selim Bey about your affairs why not bring up the topic of my daughter, ask him to handle that. Would that be possible?"

"Your daughter's matter is a matter of a police record. She is being pursued for crimes of theft. What can the head of the Registry Office do here? Why not call those two plainclothes officers who were here last week? They are the ones who can help."

"I don't want that kind of help," said Avdo. "A police file is tricky, and no doubt my daughter's file is overwhelming, she could never get out from under that."

"Then what are we going to do?"

"I was thinking if I could only get her registered under my name then everything would be solved. But I can't go to the courts and open a file of custody as her father, she would go straight to jail. Instead she could be registered as an official family member, then there wouldn't be a problem."

"That's impossible."

"It's not that difficult, it really isn't."

"How can this be done? I can't get my head around it."

"You can be sure that it's much easier than it seems. I remember when I was issued my own identification card. I was ten years old when they took me to the Registry Office in Mardin and asked them, there was a good man there and within a day my card was ready. All you have to do is make them see the need for it to be done and they take care of it right away."

"You grew up in Mardin?"

"Yes."

"You were raised by Muslims or heathens?"

"You mean the Syriacs?"

"It seems there are many Christians there."

"Imam Efendi," said Avdo, his voice now strained, "Mardin is the most beautiful city in the world and you can believe me that its people have good hearts."

"I meant no offense. We're just chatting. How did the subject come to this?"

"Oh no, no offense, we were only chatting."

"So what were we saying?"

"I was saying that you should go pay Selim Bey a visit tomorrow. You have a sweet tongue, and you only need to speak with him openly about the matter, tell him my life story if you like, or simply the story of my daughter, do this in the right way and he will understand."

"What about going and speaking to him yourself? He would be just as impressed with you."

"It would be better for you to go and when you do you can give him an envelope with my greetings."

"What envelope?"

"An envelope full of American dollars."

The imam sat up in his chair. He placed his hand on the table, his prayer beads hanging from his fingers.

"Master Avdo," he said, "do you really think this sort of thing can be sorted with a couple of hundred dollars?"

The ease in Avdo's voice inspired confidence. "You're

right, that amount wouldn't do. I'll give you an envelope with two thousand dollars."

"Two thousand? You have that much?"

"I've been working here for years. Where else can I spend the money I make? At most I can help those homeless who live out there on the city walls. Don't worry about me, when you visit him tell him that there will be more."

"More?"

"Bring him the envelope tomorrow and tell him that you will give him another envelope when the ID card comes through."

"Really? You mean four thousand dollars? Master Avdo, for that money you can adopt ten vagabonds."

"So you're saying it's possible then?"

"Bring me the money straightaway."

"But there's something else I was going to ask you. And this might seem a little strange."

"What's that?"

"Tell Selim Bey that this doesn't include my work on the gravestone I will make for his daughter."

"What does that mean? You're going to give him four thousand dollars then turn around and ask him for a few pennies to cover the stone?"

"Not a few, it would suffice to give me just one, providing that he pays me something for the gravestone."

"I don't see how I am supposed to explain that to the man."

"I was at his daughter's funeral, it was nothing like the many others we see here every day. I will never forget the painful look on her mother's face, I have seen that face for days now. When Selim Bey came this morning and asked after her gravestone, it made me happy, thank God, I thought, I now have a stone to make for the poor little girl, a stone that lives in my spirit. Yes, put it like that, I don't want the dollars in the envelope to be mixed up with the value of a gravestone I will make for a girl who has left this world far too soon."

Merkez Efendi Cemetery

Istanbul, 1985

It was midnight when Avdo opened the door to the çilehane. The room was dark, starless and moonless. Reyhan got up and came over to the door and looked up at the clear sky that seemed to open onto a garden of dreams. The winter clouds were gone for today and a shimmering blue quilt was thrown over the night. Reyhan had spent forty days in this room of penitence, in a darkness she knew from those two months she had spent in a prison cell; as if drawing in the darkness that changed even the color of the light in her eyes, she took a deep breath. She put her hand on her belly that now filled her palm, it was growing every day. She turned to look at Avdo when she saw him gathering up her things. Every night he had come with a dish of food he had prepared, taken away the dirty dishes, filled her bottle of water, emptied the chamber pot, and left the door open for a little while to let in some air, but this time he had neither food nor water, and he was holding only the large bag that contained her things. “This is as far as we go,” he said, “we’re going home now, the seclusion of the çilehane is over.”

With consent but still full of fear, Reyhan took Avdo by the arm and together they crossed over the ice and snow, passing the graves and the cypress trees. She went through the little door of his home. A bountiful fire in the wood-stove made the room especially hot, two pots of food were steaming on top of it. He led Reyhan into the bathroom and showed her the water heater and gave her green soap and clean clothes before shutting the door behind him. Soaking in the bath, Reyhan slipped out of the dirt and grime that had seeped into her skin for months like she was a dark snake, tears running from her eyes. She believed hot water and soap alone could remake a human being. When she came out of the bathroom in the flowery dress Avdo had bought, her face beaming, she stopped at the doorway thinking she must now look like someone else altogether. She hardly managed to force a smile. Putting the teapot on the stovetop, Avdo came over and sat her down on the bed. He said, “I have something to tell you.”

Reyhan laid her eyes on him, they looked darker against her flushed skin. Listening carefully to his words, she struggled to understand and then believe. Avdo went over everything he was saying twice. “There’s no longer any need for you to be afraid, no reason for you to hide. I did something without asking for your permission. I know that you have no mother and no father, and neither do I, so I had you registered as my own daughter at the Registry Office. I told them I had a lost daughter and that I had searched for years until I finally found her. I had them give you my last name. The police and the army cannot find you now. The Reyhan they are looking for has another surname, different parents. How did I do it? Well I had a little help from the imam who knew someone in the Registry Office, and we managed to get it done. In fact they finished with the paperwork three days ago but the imam waited until today to bring me your ID. He wanted you to finish the forty days so that the seclusion of the çilehane would be complete; he felt that you should come back only after you had been purged of all your worldly troubles. He believes that this will count as a good deed he has done. I told him about the history of the çilehane, he knew nothing about it. When I came here twenty years ago a very special imam was here, Eşref Hodja, who told me about the çilehane and the traditions of the dervish lodge. In that old world, now completely forgotten, time went by in numbers, anxiety, and absolution. Life was measured by these. Yesterday the forty days of *zemheri* ended and today your forty days of penitence has ended, too. This day forty-one is the beginning of your new life. All the days before are dead. Now you are officially my daughter, no one can deny that. This ID is the proof. The imam provided me with the photograph, his niece has your thin face and your big eyes, so he used one of her pictures. Don't you think she looks just like you?"

Reyhan took her new identity card. Name: Reyhan. Surname: Demir. A stamped photograph. As if from a mirror the thin-faced girl with big eyes looked back at Reyhan. Tears welled up in her eyes and ran down her cheeks. Unable to contain herself any longer, she threw her arms around

Avdo. They cried together. But letting themselves go. Someone outside the house might have thought the news of a sudden death in the family had shaken an otherwise peaceful home. If not startled by the sound of the metal lid rattling on the teapot they might have stayed like this until morning. They let go of each other and breathed. As she lay her trembling fingers on his palm, she spoke in a quavering voice. "So they won't be coming after me anymore. Those two officers won't come back here asking for me? The man they call the commander won't hunt me down?"

Avdo smiled to show her there really was no need to be afraid. "Those two officers will never come back again. And Commander Cobra has gone missing. He can't bother you anymore. You are completely safe. I am so sure of it I didn't feel it was necessary to change your first name on your ID despite changing everything else. Your name is a gift from your mother, I couldn't take that away from you."

"But I'm still afraid, I can't overcome the fear," said Reyhan.

"I know what it's like," said Avdo, "but it will slowly pass. Believe me."

For a moment Reyhan caught a familiar look in his eyes: This look was the essence of love in a body that spreads from one body to another. Passed down from generation to generation, the look not only gave them a future but also opened a door to a new past. They would believe in each other. They would find each other in the past and look upon people they once knew with fresh eyes, and live in the footsteps of a longing that was passed on from one heart to another.

Merkez Efendi Cemetery

Istanbul, 1985

Avdo lay down on the divan like a tree freshly cut on a hot summer night and gently closed his eyes as the sleep fairy came to sprinkle her stardust over him. The voices in his head fell silent, his thoughts went pale, and he slipped into a misty dream. In the dream he had lost his way. With the sound of water from the fountain circling around the cemetery seven times, Avdo awoke with a thirst that burned his mouth. He lifted his head from his pillow. He looked at the fountain across from his porch and the trees and the gravestones, as if for the first time. He rubbed the back of his neck, drenched in sweat. He could not remember where he was. Was this a dream or real life? He got up and staggered to the fountain where he put his mouth under the running water and drank his fill. He washed his face and neck. He wet his hair. Listening to a voice in his head, he walked toward his workshop. He felt the weeds brush against his ankles, which he would not have noticed during the day. So weeds grew quickly in dreams. Was time measured here in weeds? Measured against their height, their colors that changed from season to season, or with the time it took for them to green and then die? It was hard enough to grasp time in real life, impossible to understand it in a dream. Avdo came to the workshop and stopped in front of the nahit stone at the entrance. He ran his eyes from the top to the bottom—the blue stone was as tall as he was. He walked around it, then picked up his mallet and chisel. The first blow to the neck of the stone was at shoulder height. Failing to decide how he would make the gravestone for the Man with Seven Names, he had put off the task for months. If this was a dream, he would listen to the voice in his head and give the blue nahit stone the shape of a long leaf. How did this nahit stone, which he knew was from Mardin, get here? It must have come in a dream. The color of the stone was the blue of a leaf that had been blown near and far like the man who would lie beneath it. Where had he seen this blue leaf before? It must have been in another dream. The blue was light, softly blending into the darkness, bearing the burden of many ages. Again he used his mallet to drive the sharp tip of the chisel into the stone. How the sound rang out in his dream.

Do you hear that ringing, said Avdo, as if it were not the nahit stone he was speaking to but the Man with Seven Names. The sound is echoing in my head, he said. When I was small, I could not see how I resembled you. Master Josef said that you saw yourself as nothing but a shadow and that you carried only a heart, not a body, which is why you suffered. I am a shadow, too, and this I only came to understand when I was older. I am a shadow made up of nothing more than a heart that has been gripped by a whirlpool of longing and pain. Now this stone before me is lit up by the moon. My shadow is falling on the stone. This is a dream, there is no stone, there is no I, there is only a shadow. My hand holds the shadow of the mallet I bring down upon the shadow of the chisel. In the darkness the shadows ring mournfully.

The inhabitants of the cemetery weren't used to hearing the sound of his mallet at night. Swallows, hedgehogs, ants, and human souls were roused. As they looked at one another, they wondered: Avdo carved his gravestones during the day, what was the meaning of this clamor in the dark? Paying no heed to the stars shooting across the sky they followed the sounds and gathered around his workshop where Avdo stood in front of the tall stone like a stone himself. As he swung his mallet, at times with the softness of water, at times with the speed of lightning, his chisel slid over the surface. It was unclear if he knew what he was doing. His wrist was tense. His face drenched in sweat. At one point he raised his head and looked up at the full moon. He wished for even more light. He paused to catch his breath. With the back of his hand he wiped his brow. He looked for a hole in the stone that would take his chisel. He ran his fingers over the stone, patiently searching. Touching the grooves, he found one and checked, it was good enough, he placed the tip of the chisel in the hole. He held the chisel tightly in his hand. Then raising his mallet, he brought it down swiftly, as if it were the sledgehammer of Ferhat who had bored through a mountain. The startled swallows, hedgehogs, ants, and human souls looked upon the stone split down the middle. In his dream Avdo failed in making the gravestone for the Man with Seven Names. He put his mallet on the ground.

Sirkeci Bus Station

Istanbul, 1965

Looking out the window of the bus that had set off early that morning from Ankara, Elif was still afraid. Though Muzaffer was sitting beside her, the fear in her heart had not subsided. Traveling from her village and now from Ankara, she knew that every moment she was coming closer to Istanbul and her sister, İpek. And yet she felt like everyone on the bus was watching her. On breaks she devoured bread and cheese, which was a good sign, and now and then she even managed to smile. When she reminisced about her sister, Muzaffer would remind her that her name in Istanbul was now Perihan Sultan, not İpek, and this always made them laugh.

Muzaffer was not the kind of man who would normally have the courage to bring the wife of Mikail Agha to Istanbul. He was not doing this for Perihan Sultan, he was doing it for Yüksel because he had found no other way to confess his love for her. Once they arrived in Istanbul, he would open up to Yüksel at the first chance and tell her that he had not married all these years because he was keeping his heart for her. He would tell her about the mountains and the rivers he had seen during the journey and how every time he looked out the window he would see her in the shadow of a mountain, he would hear her voice in every river. He might find the right words to say to her in books, or he might learn the words of a beautiful song by heart.

Eventually Elif drifted off into sleep. The letter she had been holding since morning slipped out of her hand and fell to the floor. This was the letter Perihan Sultan had asked Muzaffer to bring to her sister. Leaning over he picked up the letter and glanced at the first few lines in which Perihan Sultan encouraged her sister to leave behind her unhappy life and come live with her in Istanbul. He put the letter back in her hand and didn't wake her until they were in Istanbul. When Elif opened her eyes, the bus was on a car ferry crossing the Bosphorus. She thought this might be a dream. It was not the Maiden's Tower or tall buildings on the far shore that caught her eye but the shimmering sea as vast as a plain, as blue as the sky, and with waves that rippled like the human heart. Her thought was that everyone must see the sea at least once before they die. Meeting her own reflection in the window, she studied the happiness on her face with a joy she had not felt for years.

Soon the ferry had sidled against the shore and five minutes later the bus pulled up to the company storefronts on the street beside the Sirkeci bus station. For Muzaffer this seemed a narrow street but not for Elif. They collected their bags and got off the bus and walked toward the end of the street to hail a taxi. The sky was clear, but the ground was wet with rain, an April shower had gently fallen on the city earlier in the day. The sound of music wafted over from a record store on a side street. The narrow sidewalks were full of traveling street salesmen selling hot lahmacuns, musk perfumes, handheld mirrors. Elif was now thinking that the defining feature of Istanbul—after the sea—had to be the noise. The car horns, the cries of the traveling salesmen, and the rising clamor of the trains in the nearby station. Among the din it was hard to make out the distinct sound of gunfire. The rising screams. People scattered in every direction, cars sped off. The street was nearly empty when Elif and Muzaffer fell onto the sidewalk, drenched in blood. Her scarf had fallen from her neck and into the rainwater that had gathered on the roadside. Walking tall through the crowd, Mikail Agha came over and stopped above Elif and Muzaffer. He looked down at their lifeless bodies. Leaning over, he spat in their faces. Then putting his gun in his pocket, he walked slowly through the crowd without paying attention to anyone, as if wandering over an open plain.

Paris Gazino

Istanbul, 1965

In her room on the top floor of the Paris Gazino, Perihan Sultan sobbed as she dabbed lemon cologne on her neck and brow. She handed the bottle back to her patron, Kalender Bey.

"My sister, my unfortunate sister, you left this world before seeing the dawning day. The vile beast shot you in the back, cutting you off from this world, let his soul rot, let his eyes run dry. Just wait till Seyrani gets out of prison, he'll go after you, Mikail Agha, and then we'll see how far you will go as a village agha. Oh, my sister, my dear sister."

"I sent a lawyer to the prison," said Kalender Bey, "he spoke with Seyrani this morning. The witnesses have withdrawn their statements. Now there is no viable evidence against him, they can only charge him for an unregistered gun, he should be released in two months."

"Let him come then, let the brave Seyrani come and take revenge."

Kalender Bey poured water from a pitcher and handed the glass to Perihan Sultan. He had taken her out of those second-rate bars and put her name up in lights outside the Paris Gazino, and although he had seen her cry on countless occasions he knew this time was different.

"I am very sorry, Perihan Sultan, sorry that it fell to me to bring you the painful news."

The police had called Kalender Bey the night before and told him that they had come across the name of the Paris Gazino in a letter found on the body of a woman who had been killed in Sirkeci.

"When I got the call from them I assumed that we were dealing with a complete stranger. All the same I got up and went over to see them. First they showed me the letter, which you had signed with your old name. Then they took me to see her, and the moment I set eyes on her face I knew she was your sister. She has the same eyebrows, the same nose, the same lips. If only she could have had a fate like yours."

"Fate, Kalender Bey? You call this fate?"

He had nothing to say. He'd had a long day, too. Early that morning he had gone to the Merkez Efendi Cemetery to arrange for a burial plot that would befit the sister of the prima donna Perihan Sultan, handing out large sums to acquire the most suitable spot. He told his men to send word to the papers, and while photos were taken at the mosque and the cemetery, he never for a moment left Perihan Sultan's side. He had some idea how the papers might run the story the next day. Having started out in the fringe neighborhoods and now in the limelight in the gazinos of Beyoğlu, she would only now achieve stardom.

"You lie down and get some rest, Perihan Sultan."

"How can I sleep..."

"I'll go down to have a look, the show is about to start. I'll have them bring you something to eat."

"I'm not hungry."

"Don't you go and drink, think about your baby."

"I'm in no mood for food or drink."

"Try eating something, and then sleep. No one will bother you. The reporters are downstairs, but I won't let them come up here."

"I have no strength to talk to them, they saw what they had to see in the cemetery, learned what they could."

"I'll tell them you won't be performing for a while as you grieve."

"Thank you, Kalender Bey."

"Come on, try to rest a little, you and your baby are both tired after a long day."

After Kalender Bey left the room Perihan Sultan waited several moments before taking some whiskey out of the glass cabinet. The bottle was already open. She took a deep drink from it. She thought of her childhood, her adolescence, and the days she spent with her sister in their village. Her memories seemed to belong to another person's life. Losing the most precious part of a life that she had erased from her mind years ago, she now wanted to burn all those memories down to ash. She took another sip of whiskey. She murmured a melody under her breath. Now she was the one shedding tears to her song that made wretched lovers cry.

Çapa State Hospital

Istanbul, 1965

When she came into Muzaffer's room, Yüksel was happy to see through her red eyes that he had come back to his senses. She went and sat down in a chair across from his bed.

"My deepest condolences, my dear Muzaffer," she said, "how are you?"

"I am in pain," he said slowly through his dry lips. "The doctors tell me the IV drip helps relieve the pain, otherwise I'd be feeling a lot worse."

Yüksel took a handkerchief from her bag and wiped the sweat off his brow.

"I spoke with the doctor. He said the operation went well, they took out the bullets in your lungs and your leg. Now you need rest and good care. When the doctor saw me crying he said, don't be sad, Muzaffer Bey is going to live, God has spared his life for you. That's right, I said, God spared his life."

Yüksel wiped away her tears with her handkerchief.

"I am still alive," said Muzaffer in despair, "but they couldn't save Elif."

"The poor thing, what an unfortunate woman."

"She was so happy on the way here, it was the first time Elif had ever left her village, the first time she was ever in Ankara, the first time she saw those forests, those mountains. So many trees all in one place, she said when she saw the forest, how sublime are those sheer cliffs, she said when she saw the mountains, after all she was a woman of the plains, and so she was most surprised when she set her eyes on the sea, staring out over the water without saying a word. Who could have known what was going to happen to her. Getting off the bus, I thought I saw a familiar face in the crowd, but I couldn't be sure, then I said to myself, you're confusing him with someone else. But no, Mikail Agha followed us and . . . I don't know how . . . maybe in a car . . . First he shot Elif and turning at the sound of the gunshot I looked straight into his face—there was such fury in his eyes—then he leveled his gun at me and pulled the trigger. How strange, I thought, as I fell to the ground and lost consciousness, and I knew that she was dead."

"That miserable man is going to pay for this, just wait till Seyrani gets out of prison—"

"I've heard about this Seyrani before."

"He is a brave man, and on top of that, he's the father of the little one Perihan Sultan carries in her womb."

"She's pregnant?"

"Don't ask, before the poor girl could be happy about it her man was sent to prison and then her sister was murdered. Such is life, we can never know what will happen tomorrow. Muzaffer, here we are living out our days without knowing the value of each and every one of them."

"Do you have a sweetheart?" Muzaffer surprised himself by asking a question like that. Struggling to explain, "Well, don't get me wrong, but . . ." he said.

Quickly she pulled herself together, picking up where he left off, "What's wrong about asking, Muzaffer, no, I don't have anyone like that, your mother asked me the very same thing and I told her, too."

Muzaffer tried to sit up in his bed and Yüksel took him by the shoulders and placed a pillow behind his back.

"Thanks, that's better. Look, here I am going on and on about my troubles, forgetting all about my mother. How is she? You went to see her?"

"Of course I went to see her, Muzaffer. I hardly ever left her side. I've been over to see her every morning, helping her with whatever she needed, cooking something for her before I went to work."

"Did you stop by this morning? Did you mention me?"

"I saw her but I didn't tell her, she's old and I didn't want to upset her so I told her your work in the village would last a few more days. She didn't wonder why I knew so much. Because I left the house in a hurry saying I had something urgent, I didn't cook for her, and that's when she fixed her eyes on me. Still she didn't say a word."

"Our house is not far from here, what if she comes over and sees me like this . . ."

"But aren't you in bad shape?"

"I don't know, Yüksel. You're a smart woman, you know better than I do. Right now I'm just thankful to be alive.

How did you hear about it? I mean how did you and Perihan Sultan hear?"

Yüksel took a deep breath. She mopped Muzaffer's face and then slowly told him what happened.

"Our patron at the gazino got word from the police last night. We were there when he called and said we should come. Perihan Sultan and I raced over to the police station, but we still had no idea it was you two. You see Seyrani is trouble, he has a beef with everyone so we figured this had to have something to do with him. We couldn't be sure. The guy's locked up in prison but his influence goes a long way. So we were pretty scared on the way over, but then what do we find, Perihan's sister is lying there dead, in a cold little room, covered with a cloth. Perihan Sultan was devastated, thrashing and wailing. We could hardly calm her down. I assumed you were dead, too, and I cried out for you, thinking your dead body had to be in another room. But the police and our patron assured me you hadn't died, they said you were in the hospital. Now, was I supposed to hug Perihan Sultan and console her or was I going to leave her there and come running over here? But Perihan Sultan let me go, bless her, she said, you go and see Muzaffer. She was also shaken when she heard about you. I came here to see you last night, but they were operating and wouldn't let me see you so I waited until you came out, but even then they wouldn't let me see you. They put you here in this room, the doctors said that your operation went well and that you were sleeping. So I went back to Perihan Sultan. We cried together till morning. When I came over to see you again, you were fast asleep and you looked so tired that when I saw your face I thought, he's going to look like his mother when he gets old. So I left to go do your mother's shopping like I always do or else she would have worried about me, but she did ask me all these questions when she saw my red eyes. I told her I didn't sleep a wink last night because of the work in the gazino and she pretended to believe me. Then I took Perihan Sultan to the cemetery. The patron had arranged a plot for her sister that was garlanded by lush plants and flowers, bless his soul. But what a crowd, Muzaffer, if you only could have seen it, Perihan was shocked to see how many people love her so deeply. You would think all the shops of Beyoğlu had closed and everyone dropped whatever they were doing to come over. Reporters, too, I'd say around twenty, you'd say thirty, taking pictures all over the place, asking questions, digging for more details of the story. I'll bring you the papers tomorrow, most probably the event will be reported with loads of photographs. They will write it up as 'Perihan Sultan's Older Sister's Flight from the Village.' And I'm curious to see what they will say about you."

"Does it matter what they say?"

"I mean, Muzaffer—"

Muzaffer held out his weary hand and dropped it into Yüksel's palm. Now he looked into her eyes without any reservation or shame.

"Yüksel," he said, "I get so happy when you go on and on like that. Every time it happens I say to myself, if only she could be with me for all my life, forever talking to me like that. I think, she makes me happy and I would do everything I could to make her happy, too, tend to her every desire. It's easy to think to myself but when it comes to saying so much to you openly I lose all my courage. Gazing out the bus window yesterday while Elif was daydreaming, I got lost in my own dreams. You know, you are the only one I dream about. If I dream in the morning, it's you, if I dream at night, it's you. As I looked out over those plains while we were making our way here I thought of all the beautiful words I could say to you. But if you were to ask me now I wouldn't remember a single one, but I swear, they were beautiful."

Yüksel pressed Muzaffer's hand in hers and looked at him with tears in her eyes.

"Muzaffer," she said, "you can say all you want to me or say almost nothing at all, I will always be happy with you."

Central Prison

Ankara, 1965

"Bitter News for the Beloved Lead Singer of the Istanbul Gazinos!" *The Işıltı Daily*.

"Murder in Istanbul! Sister of Singer Killed!" *The Seher Post*.

"Young Singer Cannot Bear the Pain! Faints at her Sister's Grave!" *Serbest News*.

While reading one of the papers, Avdo stopped at a familiar face among the photographs and quickly read the story of the murder. Then he gathered up all the papers on the table and studied all the photographs that had been taken at the cemetery. When he finished, he raised his weary head that was drenched in sweat. His breathing was now a low rasp and then he slowly started to cough. This brought tears to his eyes and he looked blankly around the room as if he had just woken up in some strange place. Without responding to his cellmates who had gathered around him, he sat up in his chair and climbed onto his bunk and lay down, his eyes locked on the ceiling. Realizing the situation was grave, his friends lowered their voices and left him alone in silence, smoking cigarette after cigarette, losing himself in his memories. Every evening they waited for him to climb down from his bunk while his same sadness swept through the ward. As the only inmate who had been sentenced to death, Avdo was respected, and as he had traveled much and spoke many languages, people felt they could trust him, but now he had closed down like a newly sentenced convict who was beside himself, grappling with the impact of the news story he had read. This was his seventh year in prison. After his death sentence was issued, Avdo's trial was awaiting approval from the high courts when the military overthrew the sitting government in a coup, issuing pardons to many convicts. Later another pardon reduced his sentence to seven years. Now the time had come, there was just one month left until he was to be released. He had been eagerly awaiting the moment he would leave this place and return to his old life. He spoke a lot, and laughed more than usual. He was thinking about seeing Elif, how he would take her to some faraway place. He was planning. Not just one plan, he was drawing up different scenarios. But at the end of every one, he was reunited with Elif: They would settle down and have children. For years he had saved his most beautiful songs for her. Every convict lived with such dreams, dreams that adorned the day and night and that gave resilience over the years, that safeguarded mental health. Now in a moment the dream that Avdo had nurtured for seven years was dashed. His mind was reeling. He knew this place, he could stay here.

There was no need to leave now, he could spend the rest of his life here, indeed he could even die here. In the forty-year history of the prison, nine had been executed; tonight Avdo wished they would take him from his ward as the tenth convict and lead him into the courtyard to read him his death sentence, his face feeling the soft breeze of dawn, and, after hearing those final words, they would take him to the gallows.

THIRTY-NINE YEARS AGO

The idea came from the German architect Carl Christoph Lörcher, who had drawn up the first city plan for Ankara. To turn this building, which had once been an armory and a stable, into a prison. The War of Independence had come to end, the Ottoman Empire had collapsed, and the Republic of Turkey was newly founded. The founder of the republic, Atatürk, had declared Ankara as the new capital city instead of the old capital of Istanbul. With a new capital on the Anatolian steppes, his aim was to cut ties with the recent past. Over the course of history Ankara had fallen to the Phrygian king Midas, the Macedonian king Alexander the Great, and the Roman emperor Augustus, but now under the leadership of Atatürk the hope was to return the city to its former days. To bring this dream to fruition, the architect Lörcher was invited to come from Germany to put forward a suitable plan for the new city. While Lörcher busied himself with designing the roads, squares, hospitals, schools, and government buildings necessary to turn a town with a population of twenty thousand into a modern city, he did not forget one institution. He suggested transforming an armory to the east of the city into a prison and in his report noted that convicts could be engaged in reform work in the surrounding fields. Soon the prison opened, convicts were sent to the fields, the first execution took place. The prominent religious figure Atıf Hodja of İskilip was not expecting a death sentence. During the War of Independence, he had published pamphlets denouncing Atatürk's army, and although he had preached on this matter as well, this was not the subject of his trial: that was a matter of his protest against the clothing reformation. The fate of the young republic was barreling forward as it struggled to catch up with Western civilization. With the abolishment of the caliphate, they were now on the road to offering women the right to vote and hold public office, there was even a new Hat Decree. The customary hat in society had been the fez but now it was forbidden, along with other religious headgear like the turban, and Western-style hats were encouraged. A year before the decree was officially announced, Atıf Hodja of İskilip had put forward the idea that this idealization of Western-style clothing was not in line with Islamic beliefs. Muslims should adopt the techniques and discoveries of the heathens in the West, but they were to abstain from alcohol, dance, theater, and similar cultural values espoused in the West, and that included dress. Indeed, Atıf Hodja was a reflection of hundred-year-old divisions in society. While Atatürk was still a young lieutenant in the Ottoman army, he joined discussions in which he was reported to have said that society had to be changed from the top down, pointing out that this could not happen slowly but swiftly. Now as he was bringing to fruition those same ideas that he had defended in his youth, he made no hesitation. The resistance to the Hat Decree that flared up in many different provinces only showed how important the issue was. In the province of Erzurum, thirteen people were executed, in Rize eight, in Maraş five, and in Ankara, Atıf Hodja of İskilip might have been issued a lighter sentence. The prosecutor was satisfied with sentencing him to three years in prison, but the following day Atıf Hodja appeared in court and said that he would give up his right to defend himself—he provided no reason or justification—and the judge issued him with the most severe punishment. Atıf Hodja was taken from the prison and brought to a small square in Ankara where he was allowed to say his final words before he was hanged in front of a crowd. "We will no doubt settle our score with the oppressors and killers on Judgment Day," he cried.

TODAY, EVENING

Avdo didn't come down from his bunk, nor did he eat, nor did he speak with his friends who now and then came to see him. But he always took a glass of tea whenever they handed him one. So he rolled cigarettes and drank countless glasses of sugary tea. He was the only person in the prison who had been there for so many years without a sole visitor, even the famous Ankara ruffians in the seventh ward would be moved when they heard that Avdo was sentenced to death and taking no visitors and with due respect they would send their greetings and gifts. So when whispers about Avdo having received dark news that day had made its way to the seventh ward, that ward fell silent, too.

Everyone had taken to their bunks. The evening clamor of the neighborhood had stopped, too, as if someone had been executed. Over the years, a shantytown had grown in the fields around the prison, turning the entire area into a poor neighborhood. There was the constant sound of children banging on pots and dogs barking, exhaust pipes popping. The neighborhood only ever went quiet when a man was executed, and then even the dogs were put into the coal sheds while the neighborhood mourned.

EIGHT MONTHS AGO

The last person who was executed in the Ankara Central Prison was a fearless officer whom both convicts and guardians addressed as Colonel. Colonel Talat Aydemir was a reflection of the chaos the country was going through at the time. Five years ago he had supported the military coup that had ousted the government of Adnan Menderes, stepping into action with the other young officers. He defended the need to firmly block any challenges to Atatürk's revolutions, and agreed with the decision to execute Adnan Menderes. After having survived a plane crash in London with only minor injuries, Adnan Menderes would not survive the hand of his own army. Then matters changed course. When a new government was established and the young officers who had organized the coup were shunned, the first reaction came from Colonel Talat Aydemir, who was known for being outspoken. With the intention of bringing Atatürk's revolutions along even further, the colonel orchestrated another coup, which failed, and he was forced into retirement. But he would not stop there and within a year he had organized yet another coup, which in turn failed again. Now there was no option of forced retirement, and after a swift trial the colonel was sentenced to death. Missing his last chance of legal absolution three months earlier, he could no longer avail himself of such an opportunity. In line with new implementations after the coup, conspirators were to be executed in prison courtyards instead of city squares. So now one of those who had started this custom of private executions with the execution of Prime Minister Adnan Menderes in a prison courtyard was himself going to be executed in the same way. One night they came to wake the colonel. They brought him to the large poplar tree that stood in the prison courtyard. No one knew how many years the poplar had been there. Its thick trunks stretched up into the sky, indeed it was so impressive that they called it "the mighty poplar." It was as if it had stood there since the lands were bare and people tilled the fields around it and then came the prison walls and finally the gallows in the courtyard. As the colonel stepped onto the plank, he looked at the great poplar and not at the executioner. He repeated his last words, which he had firmly put down in a letter to his wife: "Nothing has come to an end."

TODAY, MIDNIGHT

For years Avdo saw that poplar in his dreams. For him they had not set up a gallows, only a noose hanging from a poplar branch. In his dream he is walking to the rope when Master Josef of Mardin comes over to remind him how rocks are broken into pieces. "Listen, child," he says, "you open up a hole in the rock and place the sprout of a poplar inside. The green sapling will slowly and gently work its way into the rock, putting out roots. Don't be afraid, it's your turn now for you will be planted in the great poplar where you will grow roots. Do you think you will become a stone just because you chisel them? Don't be afraid because from now on you will live inside the poplar tree." Avdo kept having the same dream, even after he was pardoned, and he would wake up at night in fear. But tonight he wasn't afraid. He wished he might have the same dream again and stay there. He said to himself, let me be the tenth convict to be hanged in this prison. Everyone leaves behind a letter, a farewell note, but what should I leave and to whom? I have no mother, Master Josef is dead, Elif was murdered. Seeing I have no one left, I will bid myself goodbye. And then I will laugh at myself. What makes me laugh has no importance. Let those who are watching my execution look at my face in bewilderment. As I burst out laughing let me rouse those sleeping in the wards. Let them all wonder why I'm laughing, and I shall wonder, too.

Paris Gazino

Istanbul, 1965

While people were under the sway of music and drink as they danced under the shimmering lights of the chandeliers in the Paris Gazino, Avdo was sitting at a table in the back of the hall. He put down his glass and trained his gaze on the stage. The dim lights in the gazino went out, leaving nothing but a blue spotlight onstage. When the long figure of Perihan Sultan appeared in the light, her misty voice soared through the room as if blown by a sea wind, and then it was calm. No one made a sound. She moved with fairylike footsteps. With a microphone in one hand, she threw colorful petals with the other. They fell around the tables in the front row. Other lights in the room flicked on as she stepped across the stage. She was returning to the stage after forty days of mourning, and most of her fans had flocked to the venue to throw flowers at her feet. Perihan Sultan's voice was even more sorrowful, or it seemed that way to her audience—for them tears fell from the chandeliers, not light. No one knew when the song had started or when it was finished. When Perihan Sultan greeted her guests with a nod, the hall was filled with a flood of applause.

Despite her extravagant clothes, her makeup, and her hair, Avdo thought this woman looked no different than the girl he knew so many years ago when he was in the village of Konak Görmez. In the same way he had recognized her tearful face in the papers, he would also spot her in a crowd in Beyoğlu. He had not expected her voice to be this good. When Elif would praise the voice of her sister, he assumed she was exaggerating in order to turn his favor. So all these fans had a very good reason for coming. Avdo almost failed to find a table as they told him that the hall had been fully booked for days but eventually they set one aside for a price. Clearly Perihan Sultan deserved her fame and so much more. She was beautiful, she was smart, and her voice was like no other. Avdo put her smarts down not just to the fact that she had left her village for the city but that she had changed her name. Leaving her name, she was leaving her past, and it was wise to cut off all her ties to such an accursed place.

Tonight Avdo hadn't come to listen to Perihan Sultan; he wanted to speak with her. He was careful not to drink too much. With every song, he drifted back into the past, as if in a dream. Dreams that had to do with the past, as he felt that he had no future, unable to give room to the future in his dreams. After Perihan Sultan had finished and flowers were thrown onto the stage and she had left the applause and clamor to the night, Avdo paid his bill then went outside.

Pleased with his tip, the waiter had told him about a back door entrance but Avdo found it locked. A group of reporters with cameras in their hands were wandering about the street. Outside the door a young girl was selling flowers. As he pressed the buzzer beside the door, she looked at him.

"Why are you ringing the bell? What are you trying to do?" she asked.

"I want to see Perihan Sultan."

"She doesn't speak with everyone, look at all those reporters waiting here."

"Do you know Perihan Sultan? I mean, do you ever have the chance to speak with her?"

"I always speak with her, she likes me," said the girl.

"Okay then, would you help me?"

"Why should I?"

Avdo put his hand in his pocket and pulled out his wallet.

"Tell me," he said to the girl, "how much for all the flowers in your basket? I'll buy them all if you go and tell Perihan Sultan that someone wants to meet with her."

The girl stood over her basket. "Brother, I'll go and ask her, but will she want to speak with you?"

"Tell her Avdo has come to see her." Then he paused, thinking maybe that was a mistake. "Say Master Avdo, yes, then she'll know who I am."

"Master Avdo, is that it?"

"Yes, go on then, I'll wait here with your flowers."

"Your flowers," she said, smiling, "as you're going to buy them all—"

"What am I going to do with all those flowers? I'll give you the money, and you can keep them."

The girl's face lit up with joy. Instead of ringing the bell on the gray door, she turned for the front door, passing the guards without a problem.

Waiting by the flowers, Avdo took in the street life. Although it was after midnight, it was as crowded as it would be during the day. Avdo had seen many different cities but none of them were anything like Istanbul where day and night blended into one. Wondering if this was good or bad, he turned at the sound of a door opening.

The flower girl came out of the gray door, followed by a woman.

Looking at Avdo's face, she said with doubt in her voice, "Are you Avdo? You said so. Is that right?"

"Yes, I came to see Perihan Sultan."

"I'm her assistant," said the woman. "She said the person she knows as Master Avdo is doing time in prison."

"True, but I received a pardon, and just got out."

"Perihan Sultan told me to ask you a couple of questions, if you know the answers you can come in."

"Questions?"

"Yes, she told me to ask you how many state-minted gold coins you received in return for the gravestone you made in our village."

"Four," said Avdo with no hesitation.

"Then how many did you leave in the village?"

"Two."

The woman looked at him suspiciously from the door. "That isn't correct," she said, "the real Master Avdo left one state-minted coin in the village and now he is doing time in prison. Who are you?"

"Look, I sent one coin to the person you know, but I also left one with the boy who was my apprentice. No one knows that."

"Wait," said the woman, "I'll come back."

"Tell her the name of the apprentice, his name was Baki."

After the woman left Avdo took out his wallet and said to the girl, "Thank you for taking care of this for me."

"Wait up, you haven't gone in yet, they might not let you in."

"Don't worry, they will. Look at me, kid, you don't have anyone, right? And here you are working out on the street at this hour."

"I have my dad and my brother, and we don't live far from here."

"Wouldn't it be better if you worked during the day."

"Sometimes I do but work's better at night."

"It doesn't seem that way. Look, your basket's still full."

"This is my third basket tonight and it was the first time Perihan Sultan was performing after a long break. I made good money."

"All right then, take this and go earn even more."

The girl happily took the money and said, "Thanks, brother."

"So now you know my name, but I still don't know yours."

"Fadime."

"What does your dad do, Fadime? Why does he make you work like this?"

"He did construction work, but he fell and broke his hip so now I'm looking after him and my brother."

"Is your brother little?"

"Latif just started primary school. He really likes it."

"Do you go to school?"

"I'm in the first grade of middle school. I go in the morning and come home in the afternoon to cook for my dad and then I come here."

"Well done, you're a smart girl."

Avdo pulled a small case from his pocket, took out a rolled cigarette, and lit it.

Fadime came very close to him and said, "You seem strange."

"How so?" said Avdo.

"You didn't ask about my mother. When I tell people my story everyone asks about her."

"Ah . . ." said Avdo, losing the confidence in his voice, "I just assumed she had died, and I didn't want to upset you by asking about her."

"It's not like that, my mom disappeared two years ago. I guess she didn't want to have to look after her two kids and my sick dad. One day she just left the house and she never came back. Someone saw her in Kadıköy on the other side of the city."

"Do you think about her a lot?"

"I feel bad when I think about her living somewhere else in the same city, it'd be better if she was dead."

"Don't say that, she must have her own problems. Don't say that about your mother."

"You're strange."

"Do I really seem strange to you?"

The door opened and the woman called out to Avdo with a softer expression on her face. "Come, let's go upstairs."

"Goodbye, Fadime," said Avdo.

"Goodbye, brother, I am always here, don't forget."

"I won't."

When they went upstairs the door to Perihan Sultan's room was open.

Slowly stepping inside Avdo saw the painful expression on Perihan Sultan's face. She was standing there, waiting for him, and he stopped. Like two opposing mirrors, they stood across from each other, looking at the agony on their faces. Perihan Sultan gestured to a chair beside her.

"Welcome, please, sit down," she said, sitting on the opposite couch.

"Sorry to disturb you at such a late hour," said Avdo.

"You didn't. This is when we come to work. Yüksel Abla, could you bring us a couple of lemonades, I feel so thirsty and overheated."

Yüksel Abla filled two glasses from a pitcher and Avdo drank his in one go before putting the empty glass down on the coffee table. Unsure of how to begin the conversation, he looked at the walls of the room and the cupboards. Bottles and thin-necked glasses everywhere. Embroidered lace covered the shelves.

"Brother Avdo," said Perihan Sultan, "I didn't know that you had left prison, I hope you are okay."

"Thank you, Perihan..." He realized how difficult it was to address her by her stage name. He went on. "Perihan Sultan, I was released from prison three days ago and came straight here. I went to the cemetery, too, and I looked for Elif's grave among all the others, but I couldn't find it. I figured I should come to ask you and offer my condolences. Forgive me, as I don't know where you live I came to the gazino. My condolences."

"Thank you. This apartment is home. It's easier living here on the top floor of the gazino. I suppose you got the news from the papers."

"I was counting the days I had left in prison when I saw your picture in the paper. Your name had changed but I knew your face, and then I read Elif's name."

"My poor sister. We didn't get the news about you. You were on death row so we assumed you would either be hanged or left to rot in jail."

"I suppose you know what happened in the village that night, Elif must have told you."

"She told me, and she told my mother. There was nothing my sister could do after that catastrophe, she fell silent, she shut herself in. She married Mikail Agha, but when she failed to get pregnant she was devastated, and they all looked down on her. Last month I said enough was enough and I called for her. If I knew you were getting out I would have waited, she would have waited, too."

"She never had children then . . ." Avdo's eyes were misty.

Perihan Sultan unwittingly put her hand on her stomach. When she noticed Avdo looking at her, she felt the need to explain. "I'm pregnant, four months now but I dressed tonight so as not to let on."

"May God let the child be raised by a mother and a father."

"The mother certainly will and God willing my child will have the fortune to be raised by a father, too, if only he gets out of prison."

"Prison? Is the sentence long?"

"My fiancé," said Perihan Sultan, weighing her words, "we are keeping an eye on when he'll be getting out. Our lawyer says he could be released any day now so we are waiting. Of course, if he gets out there's no guarantee he won't go right back in again."

Yüksel Abla stepped in to explain. "Seyrani is one of the famous ruffians in Istanbul, with as many enemies as friends," she said with some pride.

"May it pass quickly for brother Seyrani," said Avdo, who knew the common parlance of a convict.

"Brother," said Perihan Sultan. "If I knew you were still alive, I would have learned where you were, I would have written to you, my sister couldn't but I would have written in her place."

"Perihan Sultan, I was a little reluctant coming here to see you, I thought you might be angry with me, if nothing else I am the reason all this happened, if only I had never set my eyes on her and loved her, then none of this would have happened."

"You loved each other. So my sister lost and you won?"

"None of us can know what's in store tomorrow. I waited seven years for this day to come and then it all changes in the last moment and I am faced with an entirely different vision."

"What's past is past, now you will wake up to a new tomorrow." She stopped when she realized she was repeating the words of a beloved song. "What will you do now?"

"I can't think of anything since I heard about Elif's murder. I only want to see her grave. The papers wrote about it. I went yesterday and spent hours trying to find it. So here I am disturbing you like this."

"It's easy to find. There's a redbud in the north of the cemetery, the grave is under that tree. If you like we can go there tomorrow. Yüksel Abla and I can show you where she is."

"Thank you but I should be able to find it on my own, no need for you to go to the trouble."

"I still haven't had her gravestone made. They told me to wait a couple of months for the earth to settle and then I can have it done."

"So she waited for me after all," said Avdo. Through blank eyes, he looked at a wall and tried to imagine the trees in the cemetery. In a map he was drawing in his mind he tried to place the redbud. "Don't worry, I'll find it. And I will make her a beautiful gravestone."

Perihan Sultan could no longer hold back her tears. Dark lines of mascara ran down her face.

"What happened to the man?" said Avdo, changing the subject. "In the papers I read that there was a man with Elif, who was seriously injured. How is he?"

"Muzaffer survived, and he is receiving care in the hospital. They found several bullets in him. He'll be released this week. He's engaged to Yüksel Abla."

"May he recover quickly," said Avdo, turning to Yüksel Abla.

"Thank you," she answered.

"He was from your village?" asked Avdo. "I remember there was someone called Muzaffer."

"Yes," said Perihan Sultan, wiping away her tears with a handkerchief, "he was from our village but he's been living in Istanbul for some time. He went back to the village to look after some business to do with his farmland and I had asked him to come back with my sister. How was I supposed to know that this would happen?"

"I see," said Avdo, coming to the last question that was still on his mind. "But what about the agha? I read that he fled the scene, and that they still haven't apprehended him."

"They haven't. We just heard that he paid someone who was registered as a laborer in Germany and left the country under his name. But Seyrani will show him just how small the world is, he'll track him down in Germany. Seyrani sent me word from prison that he's going to handle him, he won't get away."

Avdo laughed. Unable to stop himself, he blushed. "I just can't stop laughing at that agha," he said, "for his fate is now written, and yet he thinks he can escape it by running far away."

Perihan Sultan looked at him with empty eyes then got up and went into the other room. She came back with a folded handkerchief in her hands.

As she sat down she said, "My sister had packed a travel bag that contained her clothes. After the police gave it to me I found this inside.She had shown this to me years ago. Take it, it's yours."

Avdo recognized the handkerchief and took it in his hands. After patiently unfolding the corners, he looked down at the state-minted gold coin. He stuttered as he spoke.

"I asked my apprentice to bring this to Elif. I wanted her to know that I was loyal to her, and that I had nothing else to give her. She was angry and waited for my apprentice to come back so she could send it to me. On my last day in the village I sent him back to her and told him to tell her to meet me in the almond grove at midnight, that I wanted her to go away with me. But he came back to me full of sadness. When I asked him why, he said Elif had not said a word to him, that she didn't even look him in the eye as she was putting the laundry out to dry. That's when I knew there was a chance she might run away with me. Otherwise she would have sent back the coin when she heard that I was leaving the village for good. But she didn't, so either she forgot about it or she was planning to come away with me. That night I waited for her in the almond grove with this hope in mind."

Village of Konak Görmez

Haymana Plain, 1965

TODAY, NOON

Mikail Agha's funeral was more crowded than his wedding of six years ago. On the plains the sowing season had just begun when everyone dropped what they were doing and left behind mounds of wheat seeds to be harvested and the newborn calves to their mothers in their pens. All the tribes of the plain set out for the village of Konak Görmez on horse and carriage, tractor, automobile, and some even came on foot. The death of Mikail Agha was like a dark veil. Elders talked of how the roots of this great family were drying up while women feverishly whispered to each other at the fountain. Mikail's father passed and then his two brothers were killed, and when his wife finally fled to Istanbul years later, he committed murder to protect his family honor. On the steppes, tradition meant fate. Mikail Agha had blood on his hands, living the life of a fugitive in Ankara until he was caught one cold autumn night by the cold hand of executioners. That night he was in a club with his friends and members of the same political party, and, after drinking copious amounts of his beloved *rakı*, he stepped outside at the late hour. He was alone on a deserted street taking some fresh air when the two men approached and fired on him and he fell to the ground. No one knew who they were, maybe strangers he had fought with in the club, maybe relatives of his wife. Elif's famous sister in Istanbul came to mind. No one ever thought of her mother or father, they were an old couple that had lost contact with the world as they waited for the angel of death to come knocking on their door. As for the family of Mikail Agha, there was no one left behind to wait for death at the door. Neither he nor his brothers left any children before saying goodbye to this world and so all of their wealth had gone to an uncle and two boys who lived in a southern village on the plain. The boys swore to avenge Mikail Agha as he was lowered into the grave, and while laments were sung at home they vowed again before everyone there that they would have their revenge. Their anger and pain burned like the sun high above the steppes. Now they only needed a name for their enemy. Which would come sooner or later.

TODAY, EVENING

Two families in the village did not come to the funeral or join the procession at the cemetery: Elif's mother and father, and the former head shepherd Heyran and his wife. Heyran no longer worked for anyone, over the years he had accumulated a flock of fifty sheep and that was all he needed. During the day he would go to pasture with his flock and after he had put his sheep back in the pen in the evening he would spend time with his wife, Mihrinaz, and their six-year-old boy, İsmet. Heyran and Mihrinaz likened İsmet to their deceased son, Baki—maybe it seemed that way to them alone—and sometimes they even called him Baki. Now Mihrinaz was pregnant with another child. She was close to the time of birth. This time they would not name their child after an old politician. Since Heyran had joined the newly formed Labor Party, he had taken to criticizing the republican regime, too. He insisted that changes had to be made at the roots, and he was busy working for the general election that was due in a few months with Blacksmith Mamet and a few other young men on the plain. Heyran's interest in politics was born out of his anger toward the aghas whom he held responsible for the death of his son. But now that Mikail Agha was dead Heyran no longer had a person on whom to place his fury. Keeping a level head, Mihrinaz had been looking for ways to overcome the grudge, biding her time. Now the time had come. She put the matter to her husband. The best thing to do, she told him, would be to go to the house of Mikail Agha and offer their condolences. If people could not make peace at a funeral when could they, she said. And since there was no one else to make peace with, perpetuating this animosity on their own was meaningless.

THE FOLLOWING DAY

At the house of mourning Heyran received a warm welcome from the sons of the uncle of Mikail Agha. It was clear that they wanted to leave behind hard feelings in the village to honor the dead. They led Heyran to a respectable corner of the house where he was seated. Villagers who had not seen him for some time greeted him with the same respect they greeted all the others, placing a hand over their hearts.

Çapa State Hospital

Istanbul, 1965

After hours of painful childbirth Perihan Sultan took her daughter in her arms and shed tears that came from joy and sadness, not pain. For in her daughter's face she saw the face of her mother and her sister, not her own. Her first instinct was to name her daughter after her mother but that was when her sister was still alive. Now she didn't know what to do.

"Yüksel Abla, what do you think? Whose name should I give my daughter?"

"Your first intuition was the right one. Give her your mother's name and call her Reyhan."

"Shouldn't I name her after Elif?"

Yüksel Abla felt that if Perihan Sultan named the child after her murdered sister she would entangle their fates and pave the way for a curse, but she kept the thought to herself. She realized Perihan Sultan was already aware of this and that she was only confused now by the sadness of losing her sister.

"When the baby was still in your womb you said you would name her after your mother, if indeed she was a girl. Reyhan is the woman who gave birth to you and your sister. The four of you are present in the name of Reyhan: your mother, your sister, you, and now your baby."

Perihan Sultan was easily convinced. "Reyhan," she said as she kissed the eyelids of her daughter.

Six other women who had also just given birth were sharing the same room and they could hardly hear each other over the crying of the babies and the chatter of the other visitors. Yüksel sat down on the side of the bed and took the baby in her arms. The moment the little girl was born she knew that she would be even more beautiful than her mother and her aunt Elif. "Let her fortune be as beautiful as her face," she said. She gently swayed her arms as if rocking the child in a cradle. Touching the wisps of hair on the baby's head, she combed them back with her fingers. She breathed in the smell of her neck. Her head still buried in the child, she looked up at Perihan Sultan and said, "What a good thing you did."

"Sister," said Perihan Sultan, forcing herself to smile despite her weariness, "you and Muzaffer need to get moving and have a child so they can grow up together."

Yüksel Abla looked out the corner of her eye as if she were afraid that someone might have overheard them.

"What are you saying, girl? We got married just two months ago. Are babies supposed to come like urgent telegrams?"

"And why not, just be quick about it."

Yüksel Abla placed the baby on the pillow beside her mother. "She's had her mother's milk so she should sleep comfortably now. You need to sleep a little, you're exhausted."

"I want to sleep and I don't."

"I know why you don't want to sleep. I'll be here with you tonight so you have nothing to worry about, I'll wake you up if there is any news."

"Do that, Yüksel Abla, I want to hear from Seyrani."

"Nothing will happen to him, and there's no need to worry about that as if you don't already know it. Muzaffer is waiting outside, he'll let us know if he hears anything."

"I wish I could be happy like you are, Yüksel Abla, look, I don't even get to see Seyrani in person. He's out of prison, but he's gone and hurt someone and they're already looking for him. As if that isn't enough he even raided a venue."

"Slow down, girl," said Yüksel Abla. "Can't you see this room's full of people, someone will hear."

"What will happen to me or my baby then? Seyrani isn't thinking about us. It's as if he came to this world for the sake of his enemies. The last thing on his mind is getting married or settling down with a family. Is this precious little child going to have to grow up without ever having the chance to see her mother and father together?"

"Don't let yourself go like that," said Yüksel Abla, whispering, "we're talking about Seyrani here, once he gets his mind on something he'll take it to the very end. Don't forget your old man, saz player Mutlu or Kutlu, what happened to him when he wouldn't let you go. Just let it be, let Seyrani get his things in order, get back on track then everything will be just fine, after all he's racing around in a patch of thorns."

"Yüksel Abla, you're talking just like Kalender Bey, too. You either really think everything is going to be all right or you're just trying to drive away my fears. Seyrani didn't even come to your wedding ceremony. Have you forgotten?"

"How could he with enemies all around him? But he's thoughtful, he sent a gift. I'm telling you, be patient, don't let your heart worry. How was Seyrani supposed to know you would give birth today? Kalender Bey sent word when we were on our way here but they couldn't find him. The talk is that he's going after someone out of town."

"Yüksel Abla, I keep telling myself to be patient but for some reason the voice in my head changed during labor. Seyrani was never in my life, said the voice, I've been alone all my life. Gripped in that pain, I thought of my sister and how I was so very much alone now that she is gone. I was in such pain, and my baby wouldn't come, maybe because she was unsure of her future in this world, she didn't trust me. That's what the voice in my head was saying, now there's no longer anyone in this world I can trust."

"What kind of talk is that, girl, you're the great and wonderful Perihan Sultan, surrounded by her adoring fans, and let's say there really is no one else left, I'm here at your side."

"Sister, you're the only one I can trust. I thought about it during labor, I have you and I have my baby. Don't tell Seyrani, he's in some other home in some other neighborhood, some other city, sometimes in hiding, sometimes in prison, we've never spent two days together. May God protect him, for if something happens to him who's going to look after my baby? During the birth the doctors thought

I was weeping out of pain, but for the first time I realized I was alone and that's what I was crying for."

"Slow down and speak more softly."

"Oh, sister—" Perihan Sultan's strained voice was interrupted by the baby crying. "My little Reyhan, are you up? What's wrong?" Taking the baby in her arms, she placed her little head on her left breast, and she gently rocked her back to sleep. As she looked down on her child, a smile fell over her face.

Merkez Efendi Cemetery

Istanbul, 1968

It was an ordinary day when the blond sailor first came to the cemetery to kneel down beside a grave. The same birds and trees and the light of day streaming through branches. Not only convicts were unable to attend the funerals of their loved ones; sailors would set foot on land after the soil had been overturned and the dead were of the earth and they would hasten to the cemetery with the scent of salty wind in their hair. This blond sailor had been coming to the cemetery every day of the week to wander the graves from morning until night, and so indeed it became clear that he was more than an ordinary visitor.

After a week he took Avdo to his father's grave and asked him to make a gravestone for his father who was once a sailor. Tears welled up in his eyes as he described the shape of the stone and he wiped the tears with the scarf around his neck. Aware of the fact that fewer and fewer men shed tears, Avdo said some consoling words and returned half of the money he had been offered. But the sailor insisted. "I will be heading back out to sea and when I return in three months I would very much like to see my father's beautiful gravestone. This amount is too modest a sum for him so please accept it." Then he added, "When you write his name on the stone give him the epithet 'the Old Sailor,' what his friends used to call him."

To be born on land and die on the sea was not a choice but a fate for sailors. Their breed embraced their fate and never fled from it or cursed it. The way they died was different, the way they loved was different, and their songs were all different, too. Their cries of *heyamola* that rang out in their songs over the sea filled them with joy and were a balm to their sadness. In his final years the blond sailor's father's sadness was born of his knowledge that he would not die at sea but would return to the earth like those who dwelled on land, or so the blond sailor thought. Of late he learned that he was wrong. For even if his father had not died at sea, he assumed that he would want to be buried in a cemetery that overlooked one, such as the Aşiyan Cemetery on the Bosphorus or the Eyüp Cemetery above the Golden Horn. Fathers wanted their sons to be like them and yet they didn't know their sons, and what of the sons, how much did they know of their fathers? The blond sailor loved his father but he now understood he didn't know him.

Every sailor has a secret treasure, and his father's lay in this cemetery. His first love, who died of an illness at a tender age, lay here. Now the blond sailor knew that the grave of his mother, whom he had lost when he was still young, was in Cyprus, but he didn't know that his father had loved someone before her. In his youth his father was engaged to her, but when the Ottoman Empire sided with the Germans and entered the First World War, he was sent to the front lines and forced to leave her behind. One year later while he was fighting on the front in Gallipoli his fiancée died of tuberculosis. Returning to Istanbul after the war had ended, he asked around and finally found the grave of his lover in this cemetery. He came regularly to visit her grave and before he died asked his friends to arrange for him to be buried here. Having learned all this from his father's friends, the blond sailor was now looking for the young girl's grave.

Avdo was the same age as the blond sailor and together they sat on his porch and pieced together the story as if they were old friends. Avdo asked him if he knew the girl's name. "My dad used to talk about a Madlen," said the sailor. Seeing that she perished during the Battle of Gallipoli, the year must have been 1915. At that time they were still using Ottoman script and so they had to check the stones with old Ottoman inscriptions for the girl's name, which no doubt was Armenian. During the Battle of Gallipoli, the Armenian population was torn from these lands, exiled to the deserts in Syria. So maybe the girl's family had been exiled and she died on the hard journey. And not to upset his father, they may have told him that she had died of tuberculosis. No, it couldn't have been that, seeing that his father had found her grave here, she must have died in Istanbul. Then there was another question. This was a Muslim cemetery, so why would they bury an Armenian girl here? They went over the various possibilities. Maybe if her mother was Armenian and her father a Turk, she could very well have been buried here as a Muslim. Or was it that she was sheltered by Muslim friends when her family was exiled, and since they'd registered her as a Muslim, she was buried here when she died. Or maybe both her mother and her father were Muslim, and it was simply that they had named her after her Armenian midwife. The speculation went on and on.

Avdo consoled the blond sailor and told him he would finish the gravestone for his father while he was at sea and search for the girl's grave, which should not prove too difficult as he was familiar with the old script. Avdo promised the blond sailor that when he came back, he would sit down with him for a drink. He knew that sailors liked to drink and that they longed for the land and the trees when they were out to sea. And there were many trees in this cemetery. When Avdo pointed this out to him, the blond sailor told him that it was not the land or the trees he longed for the most when he was at sea but ever-flowing, clean drinking water. In the salt of the waves blown by the wind and the salt in the fish, even the salt of the dead in the middle of the sea, he always longed the most for clear spring water. In his dream, he would see himself place his mouth at the tap of a fountain to drink his fill and wash his hair with the spring waters.

"I think this has to be what the dead miss the most," said the blond sailor. "The dead want to hear running spring water and want to taste it seeping into the earth as they sleep."

Three months went by quickly and the blond sailor came to visit the cemetery once he had returned from his sojourn at sea and to be welcomed at Avdo's table.

The night sky was made lucid in the sharp north wind and it seemed like the stars were falling all around like drops of water as Avdo and the blond sailor sat down to *rakı* and *meze* and listened to the songs on the radio, their melodies blending with the sound of water running from the fountain, twisting and turning as it flowed into the darkness.

"So that's how it is then, Master Avdo, you thought of making the fountain after speaking with me..."

"Let me tell you how it happened, but first you tell me how I should address you."

"Well you call me Blond Sailor, isn't that enough? Would you rather address me by my name, Levent?"

"You grew up in this neighborhood and everybody knows you, but I have never heard of anyone calling you by your name."

"True, my friends in the neighborhood call me 'Blond,' the elderly would call me 'Sailor,' those on my ship call me 'Captain,' and so it goes."

"I have had few friends in life, but never one that was either blond or a sailor so it seems best for me to keep on calling you Blond Sailor."

They clinked their glasses and when the sharp taste of *rakı* stung their mouths, they both took a sip of water.

"Master Avdo, don't they say anything about you drinking in this cemetery?"

"I always drink here on my own. When the cemetery empties out in the evening. Eşref Hodja never says anything about it, he simply tells me not to let anyone see. I've been here for three years now and this is the first time I am hosting someone at this table. You are my first *rakı* guest in this cemetery."

"It is a great honor for me then. From now on I hope to be your guest every time I come to Istanbul. You can go ahead and drink the foreign whiskey I brought you on your own, but we can steep in the *rakı* together at this table. And I would be pleased if you could give one of these boxes of chocolate to Eşref Hodja, for his children."

"Of course, let us not forget Eşref Hodja. He is the one who took me in and made it possible for me to settle here. And he was helpful to you as well."

"My father's funeral—"

"No, I mean that he helped me find Madlen's grave, he spent days wandering the graves, reading the gravestones. When we finally found it he was delighted."

"I really am surprised at how you found that grave."

"We read all the graves that were marked 1915, some had names, some didn't. On one marked 1915 there was only a single letter and the image of a broken rose. The Arabic letter *mim*, which in the old language was used for M, the first letter of Madlen. I suppose they made do with that so as not to write out her full Armenian name. And they used to make those images of a broken rose to show the dark fortune that had befallen a young, unmarried girl. Among all the others this grave could belong to no other girl."

"I think so, too. For sailors, there's something known as the sense of a storm. On the vast ocean old sailors can sense a coming storm even before they feel it in the wind or see it in the clouds on the horizon, they get the indication of a storm not from the sky but from the depths of the ocean. They, too, cannot explain how it happens, it's something they feel when the waves are still and the bed of the ocean is stretched out before them in peace and when you would otherwise think that everything is going well. I felt it today when I came to the cemetery to visit my father and the girl whom he spoke to here after her death and whom he missed so dearly. Perhaps her soul lying there under the earth opened up to me because she found flakes of my father's soul in my soul. For a moment I felt like him, I felt his pain."

The full moon was hiding behind the trees and the color of the night was changing with every glass. The cemetery seemed like an ocean swept by a cool breeze, and no one knew what lay beyond the horizon forever gazed upon. Swaying in the blue north wind, the sky was gently dropping with the stars.

Avdo spoke. "While I was looking for the girl's grave, I thought about what you had said about sailors at sea and how they do not long for land or tree but for pure spring water. I couldn't forget what you said about how the dead would listen to the sound of water from a fountain and fall asleep to the taste of that same water as it seeps into the earth. Later I understood the reason why. Years ago gazing upon a young woman at a fountain, I fell in love. Elif would be pleased if I made a fountain here, she would sleep more peacefully. When I understood this I gathered those old stones and piled them up in that empty spot across from us. There are so many stones left over from Byzantine times that you only need put your hand among the grass to find an old piece of marble. I couldn't use those with old Ottoman script as they might think I was defaming a holy stone. I laid a water pipe connected to my system here at home, and connected that to my water meter. The fountain in that village where I once worked was between Elif's home and the place where I was staying. Now I have made a fountain between my home and her grave. At night, when everyone in her village had gone to bed and a silence fell over the village, you could only hear the sound of spring water falling across the fountain stones. Now I can fall asleep to the same sound here. Sometimes I open my eyes in the middle of the night and slip into a happy dream when I remember that Elif is lying there only a little way away from me, listening to the same sound of running water."

Paris Gazino

Istanbul, 1972

"Kalender Bey, how could this be my fault?" said Perihan Sultan. "Some come and give me flowers, some hand me requests for a song on a little slip of paper, and some come all the way up to my room to congratulate me in person, emboldened by the money in their pockets or the flashy convertible they have parked out front. It's out in the open for everyone to see. Over all these years have I ever done anything wrong? Yüksel Abla is with me day and night, let her tell you. Did I ever encourage even one of them? So my name comes out in the papers, printed beside I don't know whose picture. I am to blame for this? All the other musicians are covered in the news, and we know that they make this stuff up. Kalender Bey, you tell me, what I am supposed to do? What is it now? So the high-and-mighty industrialist Koçsanlı has fallen for me, and I am secretly meeting with him. What a story. I saw the man twice. Once when he came here to see me perform, and once when I was invited to sing for his birthday celebration at his home. I went with the other players, Yüksel Abla was with me, too, I sang a few songs and left once the show was over. There were other singers there, too, singing classical Turkish music, pop, foreign music. But now they are saying the man has a picture of me in his bedroom. Who's going to believe that. Turkey's greatest industrialist, who has the whole world in the palm of his hand, is supposedly interested in me? Some reporter got into his room and saw my picture there, it stinks of a lie right from the start. These papers are eating up and spitting out everyone who works in this industry and now they have me in the mix, making up stories with my good name. No one else believes this stuff so why does Seyrani buy it? Now he's telling me that I need to watch my step. Can you believe this, Kalender Bey? Our daughter has started primary school this year and she hasn't seen her father since. Why doesn't Seyrani think about that? I want my daughter to be with her dad, that's my right. I love him and wait for him, but he lives on the run like this, does time in jail and forgets all about his little girl and then sends word to threaten me. I'm okay even with this, believe me, but if he's going to threaten me then at least he has to come and do it in person, so that I get to see him. He doesn't even know where Reyhan goes to school. She's just a little girl, she wakes up in the middle of the night in tears, asking for her daddy. We're people, too. With hearts and desires. If Seyrani's going back to prison let him go but then he needs to come back and hold my hand and take up some other line of work. Here you are Kalender Bey, he can take you as an example so he can turn over a new leaf in life. If you talk to him, he'll listen to you, Kalender Bey. You took us by the hand and brought us here, help us again, Seyrani can't say no to you."

As Perihan Sultan paced up and down the room with just an hour before she would take the stage, there were tears in her eyes and her fingers were trembling. Kalender Bey was worried. He knew she would sing most of her songs through tears tonight and that the audience would be even more moved. But that was not his concern, his concern was that Seyrani was getting more wrapped up in these strange ideas, letting himself go, and that he was neglecting Perihan Sultan. Three months ago, he met with him and offered his advice, telling him to try and pull himself together. If he kept this up he would only lose his good reputation in his world. Now everyone still feared him, but respect in the underworld was something entirely different. In the past Seyrani would arouse both fear and respect. But these days the fear he spread was at its breaking point and he was losing respect. Seyrani had listened to Kalender Bey carefully and had promised that he would get his affairs in order soon and pull himself together. But he doubted Seyrani would really do it and decided not to tell Perihan Sultan about the meeting.

"Calm down, Perihan Sultan," he said, "I'll speak with him. Don't think anything of him threatening you like this. Who knows, maybe he was drunk or lost himself in a fit of anger when he told his men to come over here. I've known him for years. I know that he loves you and that he trusts you. The relationship you have is nothing like the passions that sweep through this world of ours. You have been together for ten years, and look, Seyrani is still thinking about you, he can't let this gossip about you go. If he didn't love you why would he bother with something like this. He has all different kinds of trouble in the maelstrom and now the courts just won't leave him alone. He can't settle into a routine and he can't adapt to yours. Like you said, he needs to take a step in a different direction. This world is a cruel one, what heedless men have come and gone, and we don't even remember their names. I nearly lost myself in the same way. I like Seyrani, he reminds me of myself, but he's in a strange state of mind right now. He knows his harbor, but the storm won't let him through, and now he's out on the high seas searching for a way in. Think about it like this, you're his harbor in the storm, there is no other shelter for him, believe me."

"Kalender Bey, I swear you talk like someone right out of a Turkish movie. It gives me some comfort to listen to you. I believe you, and I know that you are going to find a solution for this. Not for me or Seyrani but for the sake of our little girl. Give me your hands so I can kiss them."

Smiling, Kalender Bey pulled back his hands and hid them.

"What's this about kissing my hands, Perihan Sultan, hold on, your fans are crowded around the tables downstairs, waiting to kiss your hands. Come on, you need to get ready. I'm going down there."

After Kalender Bey left the room Perihan Sultan fell into Yüksel Abla's arms, and the tears poured from her eyes.

"Go ahead and cry, dear Perihan Sultan, cry and let the pain out. If it weren't Seyrani but someone else who was giving you all this trouble, I would know what to tell you. The word 'love' falls short, he is such a fan of yours, he is such an adoring fan. You should never doubt that."

Slowly looking up, Perihan Sultan wiped her eyes with a handkerchief. Yüksel Abla handed her some water and after she had some she was able to settle down.

"Yüksel Abla, you always take the side of that wild card. Seyrani's good like this and good like that, but what I am doing here, has he no pity for me?"

Yüksel Abla looked at her like a mother, not a friend. "Would I ever speak ill of you? Girl, you're the person I love the most in this world, I love you more than Muzaffer, but I would never tell him that."

They looked at each other and laughed.

Mısır Apartment Building

Istanbul, 1972

Sitting by a window on the top floor of the Mısır Apartment Building in Beyoğlu overlooking the sea, the industrialist Vahit Koçsanlı was sipping red wine and listening to a Charles Aznavour record he had purchased on his last visit to Paris. Too tired after a long day at work to return to his waterfront mansion on the other side of the Bosphorus, he had come to this apartment, which he often used as a pied-à-terre, telling his chauffeur, who doubled as a bodyguard, that there was no need for him to wait at the front door and that he could pick him up late in the morning as he was going to sleep in a little on Saturday. When the record stopped, he leaned over to the record player, picked up the needle, and placed it at the start without getting up from his seat. Koçsanlı had seen Charles Aznavour onstage in Paris, meeting the star through some mutual friends. His voice suited the city of Paris. As Koçsanlı watched the lights of the ferries and the freight ships gliding up and down the Bosphorus, he thought this man's voice suited Istanbul, too, for if nothing else a part of him from his mother's side of the family hailed from these lands.

He had just finished his second glass of wine when the doorbell rang. Who could it be? He wasn't expecting anyone this evening, it was either one of the women who knew this place or his driver had come back with something he had forgotten. Putting his glass down on the coffee table, he walked slowly to the door. When he opened it, he found himself standing across from a man he had never seen before, and suddenly three or four other men rushed inside. Drawing guns from their waists, they leveled them on Koçsanlı and forced him into an armchair. One man stood over him while the others checked the rooms in the apartment and soon came back with the report.

"Brother Seyrani, the house is empty, there's no one here."

Seyrani sat down in the armchair next to Koçsanlı.

"Vahit Koçsanlı Bey, you have a nice place."

"No one knows about it. How did you find out?"

"Thanks to these boys, who were keeping an eye on you."

"Who are you, what do you want?"

"We don't want your money. Let's make it clear in the first place."

Koçsanlı looked confused, as if what surprised him wasn't these men raiding his home but what this one man was now saying.

"If you don't want my money then what business do you have with me? You must be confusing me with someone else."

"You can be sure that's not the case. You're one of the richest men in this country, you have ten bodyguards in your company, and ten at your white waterfront residence so we couldn't have gotten in there, but you only keep one at the entrance here and for whatever reason he wasn't around tonight. So where did you send him? To bring over one of your lady friends for tonight?"

"What friend are you talking about? Who are you? Tell me that first."

"Now there's no need to hurry. We have plenty of time here."

"Are you one of Deniz Gezmiş's friends? Taking me hostage to stop his execution?"

"Deniz Gezmiş? Oho, these days it seems everyone is trying to save the kid. You thought we were one of them? I like him, he's a tough guy, but I know nothing about the anarchy they are in for. They are playing with the world, that's not for me, Istanbul is all I need."

"Sorry but I really don't understand anything you are saying."

Seyrani smiled out of the corner of his mouth. "You really are quite the courteous man. Are the women into the way you talk, or is it the money that turns them on?"

"You still haven't told me who you are or what you want from me."

"Fine then, we'll get to that soon enough. They call our scene the underground, and there they know me as the number one."

"The number one of the underground scene? You mean someone like Al Capone?"

"You know I saw Al Capone's movie right here in the Atlas Cinema. His luck was going his way at the start then took a bad turn. But you know what? I don't like the guy, I'm not dishonest the way he is. I would never fleece the poor. My strength is right here in my wrist, I race with everyone in being a brave man, not being Al Capone."

"Your style tells me you're one of those famous ruffians. So if you don't want money from me, and you're not an anarchist, what exactly are we talking about?"

"You are going to leave my woman alone. That's what we're talking about."

Seyrani lifted his gun off his knee and pressed the tip of the barrel into Koçsanlı's cheek. As Koçsanlı inched back in fear, he tried to figure out which woman Seyrani was here for. He was seeing many, but none would be a match for a man like this.

"If you could only be a little more clear—"

"About what, you heard what I said."

"I mean if you could only tell me who it is that we are talking about..."

For some time Seyrani kept his unblinking eyes on Koçsanlı, then he lowered his gun and stuffed it in his belt. Crossed his hands in his lap.

"Koçsanlı Bey, you are a great man who was born and raised in Paris, in other words, you are not a match for this world of ours, and our people don't match with you, do you understand me?"

"I'm doing my best."

"You see your name has come up in connection with my woman, and I couldn't believe it when I heard it because I have no doubts about her, but then they tell me that you are falling for her. At first I didn't believe that bit, too, but then the news came out in the papers. So I decided to come and see you. I set the boys on the fox and when the fox came back into his den I said it was high time for a visit."

Following every word, Koçsanlı searched for a clue as to who this man was talking about, his eyes wide open.

"So then your name is Seyrani, is that right? Seyrani Bey, I really don't know what you are saying. Would you just tell me who you are talking about? I believe there has to be some kind of misunderstanding here."

"Seeing you're so comfortable talking about it why not just spit it all out then? What do you want with Perihan Sultan? Why are you after her?"

Koçsanlı held his breath as he combed through the names and the images that fluttered through his mind, bringing up certain memories again and again, and when he finally had everything settled and he could be sure, he laughed. It was a hearty laugh that underscored the baseless fear that had overwhelmed him and the absurdity of what he had just heard. When he had collected himself, he began to speak, breathing rapidly.

"Seyrani Bey, please forgive my laughter, it's just that I really can't believe what I am hearing. So you have come here chasing after a lie? I was afraid that you might have come for a serious matter."

"Koçsanlı Bey, is this not serious? Are you taking me lightly?"

"How could I be? I'm not taking you lightly but the lie they printed in the *Işıltı Daily*. In any event I have taken them to court, and they will pay for it soon enough."

"You took them to court? Why didn't I hear about it?"

"You didn't because none of that was covered, but I will release the story once the trial is over and the paper is issued their fine."

"I have no business with the courts, so you need to account for this yourself. If you deny it then why the smoke but no fire?"

"It's one of the many absurdities of a reporter coming up with a story at his desk, there's no other explanation for it."

"Then let's talk seriously. What was Perihan Sultan doing in your house?"

"I don't remember anything like that."

"What do you mean you don't remember? Didn't she come to sing on your birthday?"

"You mean that? How should I know? I assumed you meant she came to my house on her own for some personal affair. We organized a big party for my fortieth, and I invited several different musicians. Perihan Sultan was one of them. When she came I was hosting my guests, so I didn't have the opportunity to welcome her. My assistants took care of her. It was such a big event that even Aznavour was going to come, but he fell ill at the last minute and couldn't make it."

"Who's Aznavour?"

"You don't know then, he is the musician who is singing right now on the record, he is from Paris, where I met him."

"Which Paris?"

"Which other one is there, Seyrani Bey? I am speaking of the capital of France."

As Koçsanlı looked at the man sitting across from him, who was ten years younger than he was, he pitied his lack of knowledge.

"I see," said Seyrani, narrowing his eyes.

"Seyrani Bey, even Aznavour himself was going to come all the way from Paris to attend my birthday party. It was in the wake of such a celebration that a meddlesome reporter mixed my name up into some sensational story. Truth is they regret it now, the head of the paper came to see me twice to tell me that they had fired the reporter but I won't let this go, I'm going ahead with the trial."

"If that's the case then why is Perihan Sultan's picture hanging in your room. Tell me that."

"That's where the fabrication begins, Seyrani Bey. Come to my home tomorrow and see with your own eyes. The walls are covered with the photographs of my ancestors and famous paintings I have collected over the years. I'm serious, you and your friends should come tomorrow evening and be my guests, please, and of course you already know the address."

"So if you listen to musicians from Paris and you collect the paintings of those famous painters then what is a gazino singer like Perihan Sultan doing at one of your celebrations?"

"It wasn't my idea. While my assistants were organizing the event they thought it was right to invite musicians of all different genres and said that I had to invite someone who was famous in the gazinos. I suggested Perihan Sultan."

"Aha, so now we have it," said Seyrani, sitting up in his chair. "How do you know her, why her among so many others?"

"Seyrani Bey, there's an explanation for this, too. Now I'm not the type to go to those kinds of places, and I have absolutely no interest in this new music coming out that they are calling Arabesk. Some time ago I had several guests from abroad who said they wanted to see the different sides of Istanbul and they told me that they wanted to go to a gazino. My assistants brought me a list. It was full of so many strange names but when I saw the name Paris I was intrigued so I chose that one. I went to the Paris Gazino with my guests and they absolutely loved Perihan Sultan's voice, and considering how much they did, I assumed she would be just as loved at my party. Apart from that, I know nothing about her nor had I seen her before."

"You're saying you went to the Paris Gazino and you knew nothing about Perihan Sultan?"

"I had never even heard her name before, I only chose the name from the list for my love of Paris."

Now Seyrani erupted in laughter. He laughed so hard his gun fell from his waist, which was not the most becoming sight for a ruffian, and quickly composing himself he picked up the weapon and stuffed it in his belt.

"Koçsanlı Bey, now you can pity my ignorance, fair enough, I only went to primary school and I can't pronounce the names of the schools you went to. But look, there are some things you still don't know, that gazino isn't named after the Paris you know, it's named after my Paris."

"Now you are speaking to me in riddles again, Seyrani Bey." Koçsanlı leaned back comfortably and put his hand in his vest pocket as if he was speaking to an assistant in his office. With no trace of the mood he wore when he first arrived, Seyrani let a shoulder drop as if he were now having a casual chat.

"It's the name of my village, Paris," he said. "No one believes it and when I told it to these kids here, they thought

I was joking. Do you know Eruh, in the province of Siirt, it's there."

Koçsanlı blinked to show that he really had no idea what he was hearing and Seyrani picked up on it.

"I'm talking about my village, the village of Paris in Eruh."

Koçsanlı tried to smile. "Seyrani Bey, you're serious, that much I can tell from the look on your face," he said.

"Of course I'm serious. Here, see for yourself."

Seyrani held out his ID card he had pulled from his pocket and pointed at the name of his village.

Koçsanlı took the card and looked at it closely. "This is real?" he said.

"That's my real ID," said Seyrani, putting it back in his pocket, and he went on, "The owner of the Paris Gazino, Kalender Bey, is from our village. A childhood friend of my late father. He named the gazino after his village when he first opened it. But Kalender Bey knows how to run a business so he put a picture of the Eiffel Tower on the sign so that people like you would think it had been named after Paris in France."

"Then I have learned something from you, Seyrani Bey. I'm curious, one day I'd like to go and see your Paris."

"Don't bother, it's a little village with only fifty homes and no electricity."

"A Paris without electricity, that's even more interesting."

"If you are so interested you should go and see it with your own eyes." And with that Seyrani rose to his feet. "So our time is up, we need to go."

Rising to his feet as well, Koçsanlı said, "Seyrani Bey, I have no problem with you, and I am assuming that you no longer have a problem with me. Let us end this evening as friends."

"True, Koçsanlı Bey, I no longer have an issue with you, somehow you have come to understand my grievance. So we'll be going now with no trouble caused to either of our lives or families."

"I am glad that we can agree on that," said Koçsanlı.

Koçsanlı shook hands with Seyrani and his men. After they had left, he locked and bolted the door. He thought of calling his assistants then decided against the idea: He was sure that Seyrani would not be back. He poured himself another glass of wine, turned up the volume on the record player and sat down in his chair. Looking out at the lights of the ships passing into the sea, he took a sip. *J'aime Paris au mois de mai*, he murmured along with Aznavour.

I love Paris in the month of May
When the buds are newly opening.
A new youth
Seizes the old city,
The city whose lights start to shimmer.

Merkez Efendi Cemetery

Istanbul, 1972

Master Josef would say that the true master of life is not light or darkness, earth or air, and certainly not bread or water, the true master of life is fire. Master Josef had once said that if he did not believe in Christ who died on the cross he would believe in fire, and he had shown Avdo the beauty of fire. With his eyes on the fire, Avdo could see the changing patterns of his fate reflected in the flames, and struggling to see his future, he finally understood that fire was indeed the hardest language. As he grew older he came to accept the fact that he would never come to know the secret that was tomorrow and that losing oneself in dreams at the foot of a fire was enough.

During discussions in prison when everyone spoke of what they wished for most, Avdo used to say that his wish was to light a great fire and sit beside it through the night. Looking into the flames he would hear the sound of his mallet falling on the marble and in the distance he would see the woman he loved approaching. His plan was to request a roaring fire in the center of the prison courtyard so he could slip into such dreams before he was executed—indeed he had the right to one last wish. Looking at the fire would bring to his mind those days that are now gone, and reaching for a piece of happiness he might grasp from among those days, he would stretch his neck out for the rope. When Avdo spoke like this his cellmates would be saddened and they whispered to each other, "Number Ten is troubled again." It was Avdo who named himself Number Ten, for he was next in line following the ninth man who had already been executed at the Ankara Central Prison. After the pardon laws had been passed, he did not forget his place in line, saying that he believed in pardons no more than he believed in fate and that indeed one night he would be woken from his deep sleep and taken into the courtyard. So Number Ten knew his place in dying, he was ready and waiting in the wings.

The spirits in the Merkez Efendi Cemetery were accustomed to the fire that Avdo would light every month. Looking into the flames, he would speak with spirits, listen to their secrets and tell them of his own. Last night he lit the fire for Hıdırellez to celebrate the advent of spring, and it wasn't customary to light a fire the following night. Building such tremendous fires two nights in a row had never been seen before, and the spirits gathered around, full of curiosity, waiting for the words to fall from Avdo's face that glowed in the light of the flames. He threw a little more wood on the fire, and surrendering to the enthusiasm of a fire with flames that leapt up over his head, he cried out,

Come spirits, come! The dead have no troubles, so come and hear the troubles of the living! Watching the flames twist into fantastic shapes, he struggled to gather his thoughts. It was clear enough what was running through his mind, but how could he know what to say, how could he know the right words. The only thing he knew in life was longing, and death was a part of that. You must all come, he said, tonight we will talk about me, let not one spirit stay in the grave. Come to the head of the fire!

Curious, the stars came down, and the cypress trees, the pines, the spruce, and the only redbud in the cemetery all stretched out their branches to better hear the talk around the fire. The fountain was gently flowing, silently releasing its water in rivulets. Following the spirits snakes, mice, and worms under the earth came up above ground, coming closer to the fire. Only the owl's cry broke the silence. Long and mournful, her misty voice cast a bleak night blanket over the flames.

Hey fire, said Avdo, I'm no longer Number Ten. For years I counted the days leading up to my turn, remembering those who were executed before me, giving each one the name of a planet. The first man executed was Mercury, the closest planet to the sun, and the last one was Pluto, the farthest from the sun. My cellmates said that there was no tenth planet, that the ninth was the last, that I would be spared and sent home. I didn't listen to them, I patiently waited for my turn. Looking out at the sky through my cell window, I tried to find the tenth planet among the stars. When I was a child, Master Josef taught me how to see the twelve zodiacal constellations in the sky and how they guided the caravans; he also taught me the nine planets, honoring the maps that showed the forty-eight constellations made by the first wise men. But he did not show me what lay beyond the nine planets. What came after nine, was it death?

Fire, listen to me! I was once Number Ten. One night they were going to rouse me from my sleep and take me into the courtyard to hang me beside the mighty poplar tree. Beyond number nine was death, and there I would find peace, I would be reunited with the soul of my beloved. I, who always think about this same thing whenever I am standing over a fire, I thought about it last night, too. How could I have known that while I was sitting here by the fire last night a young man in the same prison would be woken from his sleep. How could I know that they would say, you are Number Ten, wake up. Then they led him into the courtyard, they put the noose around his neck. While I lost myself in the fire, they hanged Number Ten and left me here alone, an ordinary stonemason, with you. Hey, fire! O gracious fire!

LAST NIGHT

The Ankara Central Prison was moving ahead with executions. For the tenth execution they took Deniz Gezmiş from his cell in the middle of the night. Four years earlier the '68 protests were set in motion in Paris and the youth in Istanbul were ready, waiting under the leadership of Deniz Gezmiş. They took control of the universities in clashes with the police and right-wing groups. When a group of right-wing students met the arrival of the Sixth

Fleet of the US Navy in Istanbul on their knees in prayer, Deniz Gezmiş and his friends rounded up every US soldier and threw them in the sea. He was a legend, he was danger, frequently in and out of prison. Soon his name was mentioned in even the smallest villages in the country as if he were a saint; when people saw him they felt they had come upon a saint. Newborn girls and boys were named after him. With every passing day he was widening his reach, soon crossing the border into Palestine, taking up his struggle there. The CIA began their pursuit of him, and when one of their most famous agents in the history of the CIA, Aldrich Ames, was assigned to Turkey, he gained the confidence of Deniz's housemate and they were able to surveil him even more closely. The politics of the time now revolved around this young man who was of the opinion that the Turkish Republic, founded fifty years ago, had to evolve into a new stage, and that now the poor needed more, they needed the equality of socialism. In the wake of the '71 military coup, it wasn't surprising that Deniz Gezmiş became a prime target. Posters of him were put up all around the country and a bounty was put on his head. The moment he was captured he was sentenced to death, although he had never committed murder. Deniz Gezmiş told his friends his last wish before execution was to listen to Rodrigo's Concierto de Aranjuez with a glass of tea and he waited for that moment until the end. They woke him in his cell and took him to the head guardian's room where they gave him pen and paper. Writing a letter to his father, Deniz Gezmiş turned to look out the window. In the courtyard was the gallows and beside it the mighty poplar that bore witness to all. In his goodbye letter, Deniz wrote, “Father, it now falls to you to console mother,” and then added, “The important thing is not to live a long life but to do as much as you can with the time you have. And so I find it normal to go so soon.” He was twenty-five years old.

Merkez Efendi Cemetery

Istanbul, 1972

Over the weekend the city surrendered to the rain and the southwesterly wind. Poor neighborhoods on the outskirts of town were flooded, trees uprooted, rooftops torn from houses. After spending two days inside Avdo finally stepped out onto his porch to look at the muddy cemetery that was strewn with broken branches, the sky still covered in cloud. The cemetery was shrouded in a darkness that hid the unknown in its far reaches. From among the distant humming of the city came the faint whimpering of a dog. Avdo pricked up his ears but he couldn't be sure if this was a puppy or an older dog. Stepping into the mud, he went around to the back of the house, flashing his light to either side as he checked his workshop. It sounded as if the dog were in pain, maybe trapped beneath a broken branch. Soon he found them by an old grave. The mother had died giving birth to eight puppies. Six had died in the rain that had fallen throughout the day, but two little ones had managed to stay alive with their mouths attached to their mother's teat and no idea what had happened to her. Avdo took them in his arms and brought them home where he wrapped them both in a blanket. While they warmed up, he prepared some gruel, mixing flour and water, and then he sat the dogs down in front of him and fed them with a spoon. This was not as sweet as mother's milk but after supping on the gruel they drifted off to sleep.

The next morning the sky cleared and the sun generously warmed the world as if avenging herself of the two-day storm. Avdo found an unvisited grave where he buried the mother and her six whelps. Men had forgotten the tradition of the ancient Egyptians who shared their graves with dogs. Taking the two pups in his arms, Avdo carried them to the fountain where he washed away the dust and grime with water. He sang to them.

A mother and her daughter who had been waiting for Avdo to leave the fountain stepped up and let the water run to wash away the dirt that might have been left behind from the dogs. They filled their cupped hands with water and recited a prayer before turning to face Mecca with the consecrated water and drinking it. With the dogs in his lap, Avdo watched them and realized for the first time that people considered the water from this fountain to be holy. When he asked them what they were doing, the woman spoke of the holiness of the spring with a ring of hope in her voice. Since time immemorial the waters of the spring had drawn on the tears of those people with good hearts and ran clear with the strength of spirits that lay in the earth. You could tell from the taste, no other waters in

Istanbul were so flavorful. Indeed, the fountain was made by the disciples of Jesus, and when Fatih Sultan Mehmet conquered Istanbul, he'd had its broken stones repaired. Although the Redbud Fountain had been languishing for years, they had decided to come visit after an elderly neighbor from the area had told them about it. According to her the waters from the Redbud Fountain could take away the grief of those in mourning and lessen the pain of those suffering and shine fortune on the young women who were in fear of becoming spinsters.

Forgetting he had never before argued with anyone in a cemetery, Avdo raised his voice, telling them not to come back to the fountain, and that if it was healing they sought they should go to Merkez Efendi's tomb where they could pray and ask him for succor. The woman and her daughter then raised their voices. They spoke ill of his shabby clothes and scolded him angrily for sullying holy water by washing those filthy dogs in it. Avdo then laughed. Fearful of the strange and sudden change, they raced off in a panic. Now convinced of the madness of this man who wandered the cemetery, they would probably not come back to the Redbud Fountain again.

When the Blond Sailor turned up in the evening Avdo embraced him and made ready the provisions the sailor had brought with him for a lively meal together, he had not seen his friend in months. They had known each other for four years and met whenever his friend came to Istanbul. Over the seven years Avdo had spent night and day in prison, he had not made a single friend among the many inmates, and he didn't know why he was so fond of the sailor.

"What do people look for in a friend? Now and then I think about it but I have yet to find an answer."

"Perhaps," said the Blond Sailor, "we don't know the reasons behind such things, we only experience them. Like loving the sea, drinking *rakı*, or falling in love."

"And do you have all those?"

"What do you mean?"

"You mentioned those three things, that's what I mean, you love the sea, you drink rakı, and falling in love?"

"Ah, the same matter again. There are women I like and even long for in various ports of call, but this time around I have yet to find someone to whom I can dedicate my whole life. At this late hour I don't think someone like that will turn up. I am alone like you, Master Avdo, but you have someone you have loved and to whom you have dedicated your life after death. You are on the road to a happy life. My father wanted to be buried in the same cemetery as his fiancée who had died young, you are like him. If fortune had gone my way I might have been like you two."

"Oh the way you talk, like an old man who has run out of hope. You just wait, there are many more seas for you to cross, and many more hearts for you to steal, but sure enough someone will race away with yours. Now don't drink too much *rakı*, finish that water first, I filled that up with water from the spring, it will bring you good fortune."

"Water and good fortune?"

"It has healing powers."

"Master, what are you saying?"

"Don't ask," said Avdo with broad smile on his face, "a mother and daughter came to the fountain today and they were reciting prayers over the water. Apparently it is holy water that heals and brings good fortune to those young women who are still unmarried at home. The apostles of none other than Jesus found the spring. Now it's not a habit of mine to lose my temper, but when I heard all this nonsense I got quite angry and shouted at them. And it seems there is a name, the Redbud Fountain. Can you believe that?"

"What if you had told them that you made it—"

"Do you think they would believe it?"

"You're right. Indeed if they were to accept that you made the spring yourself they might even believe that you were one of Jesus's apostles who popped in now and then to speak with both the living and the dead, and then the rumor would spread."

"An apostle who pays the water bill, is that right? You know the water pipe to the spring is connected to my water valve at home, and I pay the municipality for it. Apostles don't get a discount."

They broke out laughing, and then clinking their glasses filled with spring water, they drank water and not *rakı*.

"Apostle Avdo!" said the Blond Sailor. "It's not a bad name, it suits you."

"I was actually angry with the women for disparaging the dogs. Just once I was over there washing those puppies and they looked at me in disgust for supposedly sullying the water. How can you sully running water? People who don't like animals are ugly. Even Eşref Hodja treated me with more kindness."

"What happened with him?"

"He was happy to see puppies and brought them fresh milk, even fed them with his own hands. Before I could tell him that I buried their mother and six siblings in the cemetery, he shushed me. He had seen me do it that morning. He warned me to keep those sorts of matters to myself and let no one know about it, saying they wouldn't approve for religious reasons."

"Where did you bury them?"

"I found an old grave with an overturned tombstone and weeds all around it, the ground sunken, I buried them there, put fresh soil over them and then sprinkled a little seed. Is it so bad for people to be buried with dogs?"

"Although it is a tradition no longer followed on many ships, I carry the spirit of the past with me so I give the dead to the sea and the fish. In the earth our bodies become one with worms, bugs, insects, other creatures, so why not with a dog? A dog is perhaps the most suitable animal for a cemetery. According to old Greek legend dogs wait at the entrance to the land of the dead, so the dead won't escape. You are taking after them by having dogs at the gates of the land of the dead, so no one can run away and so that you can sleep in peace."

"Enough joking and raise your glass, you've had some of the healing water now it is the time for *rakı*."

"To the honor of those two dogs that survived."

"To their honor! Blond Sailor, you are a dear friend, shall I share something else with you?"

"Of course. What is it that we are sharing?"

"One of these two dogs will stay with me and I think

that I will give the other one to someone who would like to have her. You came to mind. Would you like her?"

"Really?"

"Yes."

"Right away, I'll take her with me. She'll get seasick at first but will get used to it in time."

"Wonderful. This evening is getting better and better."

"But on one condition, Master Avdo, I won't take her without a name. Have you found one for yours?"

"Oh that was clear. My master in Mardin looked after me but he also looked after a dog. I'm going to name this one after Toteve."

"Toteve, an unusual name. What does it mean?"

"I don't know. I asked Master Josef about it, but he didn't know either. Although I speak many languages I never figured out where the name comes from. Does it mean anything to you?"

"Well, no, it's not a name I ever heard before."

"How different are the languages of a sailor compared to someone of these lands. While you speak Italian, Spanish, Portuguese, French, and English, I speak Arabic, Armenian, Kurdish, Greek, and Syriac. If you were to travel through Anatolia on your way to Mesopotamia not a soul would know the languages that you speak, and if I were to sail across the seas not a soul would know mine. We complete each other."

"Master Avdo, today you are both talkative and yet quietly troubled, or does it just seem that way to me?"

"On the contrary, I feel quite joyful, I have a dog and here you are in Istanbul."

"Well if you are joyful then give my dog a joyful name."

"Oh," said Avdo, raising his arms up at the sky, "that has been ready for some time now."

"Well?"

"Apostle."

On hearing the name, the Blond Sailor let out a laugh, and Avdo laughed along with him.

Merkez Efendi Cemetery

Istanbul, 1973

One year had passed when the Blond Sailor returned from his long journey. Who knew what seas he had crossed, which continents he had traveled. But he had clearly changed. His hair that once fell down over his shoulders was cut short, his mustache glistened with almond oil, his face was freshly shaven, and gone was the dirty scarf that he always wore around his neck. A golden ring had joined the silver rings he wore on his fingers.

"Look what you have done, Master Avdo!" he said, showing him his new ring. "That spring water really must be holy for it unlocks our fortunes. Last year neither of us believed the rumors about its holy powers and we laughed, but several glasses changed my fate. That night I was given a dog whom you named Apostle and she truly became a companion of mine worthy of a disciple. We had traveled to Venice to pick up cargo on our first journey together and while our ship was moored in port I went out to walk the streets one evening. Winding through streets that all looked the same, I lost Apostle and soon I was wandering about and calling out her name. It wasn't long before I heard her barking and I followed the sound into a garden where Apostle was sitting at the feet of a woman and looking up at me. She had found the most beautiful woman. Now this dog is mine, said the woman and she smiled so beautifully I felt ready to give her the rest of my life along with Apostle. She offered me fresh tea and told me that her name was Roberta. I told her the name sounded more beautiful than Dante's Beatrice. I was so keen to tell her everything that was running through my head that by the time I had finished my tea it felt like someone else was talking. Although I expected my boldness could very well end in her showing me and my dog the door, Roberta looked kindly on me. Levent, she said, your name is like a letter that has come to me with beautiful words. After so many years Roberta was the first person to address me with my real name. I gave up my name to her right there. We had tea that night in her garden and the night after that. Soon my ship would set out and I didn't know what to do. The Black Sea, the Mediterranean, indeed all the oceans of the world were done. Roberta, I said, my ship is waiting for me but I don't want to go. Levent, she said, if you go will you return? I have no other place to return to, I said. Her head turning to the sky, she pointed to the southeast. Do you see Sirius? she said. You are a sailor, so you know they also call that star the Dog Star. I will let you go on one condition, that you leave your dog with me. Waiting for you here with Apostle I will follow that star. And with that Roberta pulled Apostle close and stroked her neck. Above all she brought you to me, she said. And with the same passion I said that she was the one who found you for me."

When the Blond Sailor finished he was out breath and Avdo raised his glass and said, "Your lips are dry so take a sip."

Picking up the thread of his story the Blond Sailor did not notice the tears gathering in Avdo's eyes.

"Now I understand you, Master Avdo, and I understand my father who wanted to be buried beside his fiancée whom he had not seen for fifty years. I envied you spending what remains of your life here beside the grave of the woman you love but I also thought that you could make another kind of life for yourself. I thought if I were to bring you out to sea with me, your horizons would change, that you might stake out a new life for yourself. Now I realize that there was a room inside me but the door was shut, it was locked, I did not know how to look on life as you do. When I went back to Roberta, I told her about you. I told her how you were waiting to be buried beside the woman you love in a city you know nothing about. Now this was what I wanted, too. I wanted to live with Roberta and to be buried in the same cemetery when I died. When I told her she looked at me with curiosity in her eyes. I thought sailors wanted to be buried at sea, she said. I had forgotten all about it, I had no idea that my burning desire to be buried at sea was gone. For a moment I was afraid, the fear of seeing what love is capable of doing to us. But Roberta showed mercy on me. I would like to be buried at sea with you, she said, in the same sea. Now I knew that there was no such place as land or sea, that in the world there was only a place beside the woman I loved. Do you know how sailors like to tell these kinds of stories that are all dressed up and full of exaggeration? Whenever I hear such a tale I feel as if it has moved beyond the truth, that most are but reflections of a dream, and now look what has happened to me, I have ended up in the kind of story I would have doubted. Sometimes I wonder if all of this is real. In the end I have turned out like you, Master Avdo."

It was then that the Blond Sailor noticed the tears in Avdo's eyes. He put his hand on his friend's wrist.

"I have opened up an old wound of yours with all my heedless talk."

"No," said Avdo, "it is joy that is making me so emotional. Seeing you like this only makes me happy. The good-hearted Blond Sailor!"

They clinked glasses and took the meat off the grill, and then realizing they had neglected their grumbling stomachs they tasted some of the side dishes.

The weather was cool. They would feel the chill if they were not sitting so close to the fire.

"When a person loves he perceives what he knows in a new light," said the Blond Sailor. "I enjoy the different aspects of the languages I know and I speak them all with pleasure. Now Italian seems to me the most beautiful language in the world. There is a saying in Italian: *Perdere la trebisonda*. Losing your Trabzon. Once the Trabzon port on the Black Sea was the meeting point for ships and caravans that shuttled from Europe to the East. The expression was first used when a ship or caravan was lost on a perilous journey, but eventually it came to be used for a person who had lost his way in life. Throughout a life traveling by ship to every harbor on the map it turns out I was lost and looking for my Trabzon. Even stranger is how you only know what it was you were seeking when you find it."

"True," said Avdo approvingly, "you don't know until you find it."

"This time I have come alone but next time I will come with Roberta so that you can meet her. Or maybe you could come visit us in Venice. What do you think?"

"No," said Avdo, turning to look at the redbud in the darkness and the grave beneath the tree. "I can't leave Elif."

"It won't be for long, we'll be back in a couple of months."

"I would rather die."

"Well then how about a week? We could go by plane not ship."

"She's restless even when I go shopping in the neighborhood market, and I come racing back. A week is too long."

"Think it over. I really want you to see our home in Venice. And Apostle will be so happy to see you."

"Really," said Avdo, "what sort of dog did she turn out to be? Mischievous? Calm?"

"She has a gentle soul, she lets everyone pat her on the head. She loves to eat, she's never full, much bigger than her brother." The Blond Sailor looked over at Toteve who was sitting at the end of the porch. "How is Toteve? He also seems like a gentle dog."

"Oho!" said Avdo. "Don't be fooled by the way he is around you, he's actually quite rough, I hear people in the cemetery shooing him away, even scolding him. He won't let a cat or another dog in the cemetery and chases them off once he catches the scent."

"Master Avdo, I left my dog in Roberta's care when I came here. You can leave Toteve to look after Elif, then you won't have to worry about her. If only for a few days you'll be able to see Venice. Let's say three days?"

"You are like those men of legend, the man who leaves his dog with the woman he loves before setting out on his journey. Blond Sailor, you are a man of legend, not me."

Merkez Efendi Cemetery

Istanbul, 1965

One orange summer morning Avdo began making the gravestone for Elif. The first letter in the Arabic alphabet, *elif*, is but a single upright line whose top is slightly curved. Simple, absolute, a beginning. Working all day under the sun, Avdo engraved the single letter *elif* on the stone. That night he fell asleep with the grief of bygone days. The next day he got up and worked on another letter *elif* again until evening came. For days he did the same. The summer was long, the sun was hot, and as Avdo filled the stones with *elif* his grief slowly began to wane. Autumn came, the days grew shorter. One day under a sky covered in red cloud, Avdo finished engraving the letters on the stone. He put down his mallet and wiped the sweat off his brow. Kneeling at the stone, he counted the letters, there were ninety-nine *elif*s in total. That evening Avdo fell asleep with a lightened heart and drifted into a white dream. In the dream the cemetery had become an infinite void and there he saw the gravestone standing alone. Elif was one and only, a beginning and an end. Carved into the shape of an *elif*, the gravestone stretched up into the void like a dark cypress tree:

ا

Paris Gazino

Istanbul, 1976

After being caught in the act of wounding a man and spending a year in prison, Seyrani came out with a new state of mind and decided to make a regular life for himself as Kalender Bey had done. Since his friend had urged him to keep his distance from the dark corners of society, Seyrani suggested they open a nice venue on the Bosphorus that they could run together. Perihan Sultan loved the idea more than anyone. At first it all seemed like a dream—Seyrani coming home every night to spend time with his daughter and taking them on outings to Çamlıca Hill or the Princes' Islands—but soon she came to believe this was a gift granted for all the tears she had shed over the years. Spring was more colorful and fragrant than ever before with the mimosa flowers bursting along the streets. The days were growing longer but even then they were never long enough for Perihan Sultan. For the first time in her life she was truly happy and for the first time since her closest friend Yüksel Abla had left she was able to laugh.

After Muzaffer's mother passed away last year Yüksel Abla and Muzaffer decided to join the growing trend and sign up for work in Germany where they planned to set up a new life for themselves. They had applied for their passports, packed their bags, and said goodbye to Perihan Sultan with tears in their eyes. They were still having problems conceiving and this was one reason for going to Germany. The latest therapy offered there was proving successful, so they set off with the hope that in Europe they would find the solution to all their problems.

"I can't say this enough," said Perihan Sultan one evening when she was talking on the phone with Yüksel Abla. "I don't know how to put it, Yüksel Abla, you'd think that the old Seyrani had died and God sent him back to me with the soul of an angel. I go to bed at night and there he is at my side, I wake up in the morning and he's still there. Some nights I wake up and he's gone and I don't know where he is but it turns out he has tiptoed into our daughter's room and there he is stretched out beside her. So you tell me, is this the Seyrani you know? This much joy is too much, it scares me. The other day I told Seyrani I could quit the gazino if he wanted me to and just record, in fact I could stop doing that, too. I'm serious, and you know what he said? Dear Perihan Sultan, you love music, why would you give up the thing you love most? I was about to faint and fall to the floor. Even now I can feel my heart pounding as I say the words. When are you coming back for a holiday... Oh well then you'll be able to see it all with your own eyes, you won't believe it. You'll want to pluck out three strands of my hair and put them among yours to get a piece of my joy."

But Yüksel Abla never got the chance to pluck out those three strands.

While the garden of the Bosphorus restaurant was being organized, Seyrani wanted Perihan Sultan to see it, too. They left home early in the morning. As they drove past Ortaköy and then Emirgan in their convertible, they took in the warm air that blew around them and looked out over the strait on their right through sunglasses before they finally pulled into Tarabya. They parked in an empty lot to one side of the restaurant. The ground was still covered in dust, they would have to start work on this area once they were finished with work in the restaurant. They dusted themselves off after getting out of the car and took off their hats as they walked arm in arm. The parking lot was no more than twenty meters from the restaurant but Seyrani and Perihan Sultan would not make the trip. An approaching black car rolled down a window and suddenly they were under fire. Seyrani was quick to draw but the bullets came faster, he fell to his knee then collapsed in the ongoing blaze. Perihan Sultan could only scream before she rolled onto the ground, her bloody head bent over Seyrani's arm. As their muscles went slack they shut their eyes at the same time and gave up spirits that had borne weariness and love.

There was a police station nearby and officers were the first to arrive on the scene, recording the names of the deceased and running the announcement through their radio set that all black vehicles in the vicinity should be stopped. Soon a doctor arrived but he could only confirm the time of death. Kalender Bey was the last to arrive; he had wept beside his men all the way from Beyoğlu to Tarabya. He got out of his car and, pushing through the crowd, he wiped away his tears to keep them from the public eye.

The following day the newspapers ran the story in the headlines:

"The Queen of Arabesk Victim to a Bloody Trap!"
"Perihan Sultan and Her Husband Murdered!"
"Istanbul Loses a Poignant Voice in Bloody Attack!"

In a photograph that all the papers were pleased to print Perihan Sultan seemed to be sleeping, her head on Seyrani's arm.

Once again the crowds at the funeral seemed as magnificent as they appeared on the front pages of the papers. Groups of men from the underground attended in the largest numbers, paying their respects to Seyrani, whom they described as a legend to young gangsters. Far larger in numbers than the gazino regulars, who had come in droves, were leading artists of the music world, fashionistas, soccer players, minibus drivers, and porters. Of late there was little drama an Arabesk singer had not already been up against: Some had been slashed in the face by a former lover, some shot in the leg while performing onstage. In life and death Perihan Sultan resembled those songs on her records, those poignant, grief-stricken laments that longed for happiness. In those songs joy was brief, sadness was long, and grief was eternal.

Kalender Bey arranged for the funeral and handled the reporters and the police. Standing in front of a crowd of journalists, he announced that he had lost two of his own children. He spent the following days searching for that black car. He sent his men everywhere to figure out who was behind the hit. He made a list that stretched back over the years, Seyrani's enemies and Perihan Sultan's obsessive fans, looking into everyone. He handed over his business in the gazino to some of his men while he returned to many of those dark dens he hadn't seen in years, asking old acquaintances for clues. There were many suspicions. Maybe they were members of a hashish gang, maybe relatives of Mikail Agha, who had been killed in Ankara eleven years ago, or maybe they were men hired by the industrialist Vahit Koçsanlı who had been biding his time for four years before extracting his revenge on the hoodlum. One day smoke would rise and Kalender Bey would pick up the trail. But as he patiently continued his pursuit, he never neglected Reyhan. He looked into where he should send her for an education, coming to the conclusion that the best solution was a boarding school. He had to keep his distance because if she were to ever catch the scent of these streets she might never leave them.

Çamlıca High School for Girls

Istanbul, 1976

Autumn came early. Yellow leaves were strewn over the ground and clothes hung out to dry on balconies were fluttering in the wind. Holding Muzaffer's arm, Yüksel was unusually quiet as they waited nervously in the large garden of the Çamlıca High School for Girls. When she finally saw Reyhan coming down the stairs among all the other girls, Yüksel realized how quickly she had grown since last year. Now it was not just her face that resembled her mother's but the slight curve of her neck and the way she walked.

"My God," cried Yüksel, squeezing Muzaffer's arm, "if only she wasn't the spitting image of her mother."

Reyhan raced over and threw her arms around Yüksel's neck and buried her head in her chest. She stayed like that for a while so that none of the other students would see her crying. They shed many tears together before sitting down on a bench, and after drying their eyes and noses they waited to catch their breath.

"My dear Reyhan," said Yüksel, "how are you? Are you comfortable at school?"

"I am, Aunt Yüksel."

"It's much bigger than I expected. We had a look around while we were waiting. It's a beautiful place. How is the dorm?"

"Fine."

"Were you able to make friends with any of the other boarders?"

"I made a few friends."

"And the older girls? Do they help you?"

"The high-school girls sleep in a different dorm. We middle schoolers sleep together."

"Are they nice?"

"They're nice girls, and helpful. They have a fun time in the dorm at night, singing together."

"Do you sing, too? Do you have fun with them?"

"No, I only watch."

"That will come. We asked everyone we knew about this place and heard that this was one of the best schools in Istanbul. How is the food?"

"It's good, if you want you can buy something from the cafeteria, too."

"Do you have enough money?"

"I do, Aunt Yüksel. When I need some I ask the principal and he gives me a little spending money. He told me that Uncle Kalender left him with a lot of money."

"I am grateful to have Kalender Bey, he is a good man. Does he come to visit?"

"Yes."

"We paid him a visit as well."

"When did you come to Istanbul?"

"We arrived yesterday and went to see Kalender Bey straightaway, we asked him all about you and here we are with you today."

"When are you going back to Germany?"

"In two weeks, but we can stay longer, it's up to you."

"Up to me?"

Muzaffer, who had been quietly listening to their conversation, took out a card and showed it to Reyhan.

"Look, Reyhan, this is the residence card the German government has given us. Get one of these and your life is saved. Now we both work there, making good money, and we live in a nice home. Yüksel and I were talking about the possibility of bringing you back with us. If you were to come with us, you could be a part of our family and start a brand-new life for yourself."

Muzaffer stopped for a breath, and to be sure that he was choosing the right words, he looked at Reyhan and then Yüksel, waiting for one of them to go on.

Reyhan kept her eyes glued to the ground as she played with her fingernails.

"My dear Reyhan," said Yüksel, "we could adopt you if you like. We would like to live with you, and have a life with you. You don't need to decide right away, think it over and we can talk again some other time. Yesterday we shared our thoughts with Kalender Bey, who was very pleased with the idea. He said that you could have a future growing up in our home, not to mention in Europe. The best schools are in Germany, oh and if you could only see the cars and the underground trains, the subway, that's what they call it. We live near other Turkish families and if you like you can make friends with their children, and with German kids, too."

Realizing she wasn't going to be able to hold back the tears, Reyhan lowered her head, and then she leaned against Yüksel, who took her in her arms.

"I miss my mom," she said without looking up, "I miss my dad. I think of them every night, and every morning I think I am going to see them again. When everyone else in the dorm goes to sleep, I pull my blanket up over my head and cry. It's really hard, Aunt Yüksel…"

Watching Yüksel and Reyhan cry like this, Muzaffer could feel the tears welling up in his eyes. He got up from the bench and took a couple of steps forward. When he saw a man coming over to them with a smile on his face, he knew that he was a teacher. He smiled back at him.

"Hello," said the man, "welcome to the school, my name is Ferruh, I am the principal."

"Pleased to meet you, I'm Muzaffer from the same village as Reyhan's mother. But we live in Germany now. We just arrived, we were excited to see Reyhan."

"You have done a very good thing, sir."

Yüksel stood up and introduced herself to the principal and shook his hand.

"I'm Reyhan's mother's closest friend. We've been working abroad for the past year and finally found the chance to come for a visit."

"I know, Reyhan has told me a lot about you."

"She's like a daughter to me, I was there when she was born. Muzaffer, you remember, you were waiting in the hospital garden."

"How could I not? It feels like yesterday, you came and told me what a beautiful baby she was."

With a pleased expression on his face, the principal looked at Reyhan and then turned to Yüksel and Muzaffer as if he hadn't noticed Reyhan's bloodshot eyes.

"You don't have to worry about Reyhan. My family lives here. She can come and stay with us whenever she wants. I already told her she's now a part of our family and that I am here for her whenever she needs me."

"Thank you, Ferruh Bey," said Muzaffer, "it's good to know that the children here are in the good hands of a teacher like you. As you know the current situation in the country is far from stable, what with children fighting each other in schools, it's a cause for concern."

"So true, Muzaffer Bey. But worry does no good. Which is why we keep a close eye on our children. It's our duty to raise them in an environment that is both safe and illuminating."

"Wonderfully put," said Yüksel. "Living in Europe lets you see this even more clearly. Our country can develop in the same way, too, as long as there is no worry and the minds of our children are untroubled."

"If you have the time," said Ferruh Bey, "why don't you come to my office where we can chat over a glass of tea."

Yüksel placed her hand on Reyhan's shoulder as if she were holding her own daughter and they happily climbed the staircase together.

Çamlıca High School for Girls

Istanbul, 1976

When the dorm lights were switched off the girls were no longer allowed to move about freely and so they would whisper to each other in bed. After the warden had turned off the lights and shut the door behind her, Reyhan slowly climbed out of her bed and went over to her friend Süreyya. She climbed in and lay down beside her.

"You're not asleep, are you?" she said.

"What?" said Süreyya. "Girl, I haven't heard you crying lately, I guess you're getting used to this place."

"I'm getting tired of crying. Is that what it's like?"

Süreyya was a year older than Reyhan, and for girls their age a year was vast in terms of accumulated thought and vital experience.

"Didn't I tell you? We all started out the same way, not liking it at first but then we did. Teachers are important but it's friends that really count. If you get used to everyone else you become part of the place."

"I suppose I have started to become a part of it then."

"Your relatives came to see you again today, I saw you from the window."

"They're going back to Germany tomorrow. Who knows when they'll come again, maybe a year, maybe two . . ."

"Didn't they bring up the idea of taking you back with them today?"

"We talked about it. Again I told them I wanted to stay here. They said the door's always open if I ever change my mind."

"You're sure you aren't going to go?"

"I don't want to. My mom and dad are buried here, I should stay close to them."

"Reyhan, that's what you think now, your wound is still warm, you'll see things differently in the future. Then you can go to Germany. It's better than living here."

Süreyya spoke like a teacher. Although her mother and father often came to visit, she tried to keep in mind what it must feel like for an orphan and how Reyhan's feelings could change over time. When she talked with her friend, she always tried to instill confidence.

"I hope my thinking on this doesn't change," said Reyhan decisively. "I can't think of anything else but staying in Istanbul."

"Okay, so tell me what they brought you this time, more German stuff again?"

"They brought me German clothes the last time, I showed you those. This time they brought me clothes they bought here, and a whole bag of food. Would make your mouth water if you saw it."

"Don't think I even need to see it."

"Tomorrow I'll get you some from the fridge and we can eat together when the lights go out."

"Did they give you money?"

"Even more than last time. What am I going to do with that much money, I gave it to Ferruh Bey."

"You didn't keep any of it?"

"A little."

"Good. We can do something."

"Let's go to the cinema in Kadıköy."

"New movies are out."

"But not this weekend."

"Why?"

"I'm going to the Eyüp Cemetery this weekend to visit Mom and Dad. Ferruh Bey kept saying it was too early to go but I asked Aunt Yüksel about it and she talked to Ferruh Bey. I'll be going for the first time."

"Are you sure about it? I mean do you think it's right to go now?"

"I want to. And Aunt Yüksel said it was okay. Actually if I'd asked her when they first came to visit we all would have gone together."

"You're not going alone, right?"

"Ferruh Bey and his wife are going to take me there."

Çamlıca High School for Girls

Istanbul, 1978

It was a beautiful spring day and the school garden was empty as most of the boarders had gone to stay with their parents for the weekend. Greening poplars stretched up into the sky and the scent of red, white, and yellow blooming roses drifted far and wide. Reyhan and Süreyya couldn't bring themselves to pick them so they had gone out to collect flowers from the gardens of the houses that lined the street.

On both sides of the street running through Acıbadem were detached houses and apartment buildings surrounded by abundant gardens. Flowers draped over their low walls: roses, lilies, trumpet vines, and clusters of mimosa that were in their final days. Being faithful to the flowers, they took no more than two from every garden before they moved on to the next one, and when they were halfway down the street they both had large bouquets in their arms.

Then noticing a garden full of trees whose branches were laden with green apricots, they climbed in over a crumbling wall. Looking through the trees, they didn't see anyone at the front door of the house and the windows were shut. Feeling no need to worry or rush, they gathered fresh apricots. The branches hung so low they nearly touched the ground; they didn't even have to climb. They filled their pockets as they sang. Then they left the garden and carried on down the road, which looked even more beautiful as their joy kept rising.

With all those flowers in their arms, they stopped by a wall draped in wisteria. It would be hard to pass up something as beautiful as this. They started choosing between the racemes when they heard a woman calling out to them from the house in the garden.

"Girls, what are you going to do with all those flowers? Taking them to your boyfriends?"

"Let's get out of here," whispered Reyhan.

Süreyya stopped her. "Auntie," she called out, "you're right."

"How old are you two?" said the woman, squinting her eyes to get a better look at them.

"Auntie," said Süreyya, "it doesn't matter who you bring flowers to but who you pick them with. We're lovers!"

"What are you saying, you shameless creatures," said the woman, now raising her voice. "I can't see how tall you are from over here but God Almighty your tongue is longer than a shoe. I'm coming over there."

In a breath Süreyya and Reyhan were on the street corner. They had dropped a few flowers on the run and turned to look over their shoulders. No one was coming after them so they calmly continued picking flowers as they ambled along the street. The youngsters they were planning to meet in Bahariye were going to love these flowers. Reyhan and Süreyya were convinced that none of the other kids tasked with collecting flowers had picked such a bounty as they pulled fresh apricots out of their pockets and popped them in their mouths.

Tomorrow there would be a May Day celebration. Endless flowers were being brought in for the cortege to be displayed at the demonstration. The grown-ups were preparing large posters and signs while kids were sent out to pick flowers over the weekend. Süreyya and Reyhan had insisted on joining the march but they weren't given permission. The attack on the celebration the year before that led to the death of thirty-three people had made everyone especially cautious.

"Maybe they'll let us join the march when they see how many flowers we picked," said Süreyya.

"Ferruh Bey is going to be angry with us for skipping school tomorrow," said Reyhan.

"Education first! Education first!" cried Süreyya, deepening her voice to imitate Ferruh Bey.

Reyhan was quick to join in. "Education first! Education first!"

Paying no attention to the people who stared, they carried on like this until they got to Bahariye. On a corner at the end of the street was a tea garden and a group of people were sitting around a table with a great pile of flowers. So other kids had already come to drop off their flowers.

With grave expressions on their faces, Süreyya and Reyhan walked over to the group like well-behaved young girls.

Voices rose up from the table.

"Oh, look who's here!"

"So now we can wrap it all up."

"Spring flowers, Süreyya and Reyhan!"

Meaning the flowers they were holding and the girls themselves.

They went over to the table and put their flowers down with all the others and said that this was all they could get for now but that they could pick more if they had to. Süreyya said, reluctantly, "Reyhan and I were just wondering if we could come to the march tomorrow, only to watch from a distance..."

"We already talked about this," said one of the youngsters, "this demonstration is going to be really risky. You know what happened last year, the same could happen again. We already told everyone that nobody your age is coming, if we let you go Ferruh Bey would eat us alive."

"But we were thinking that seeing as we picked all these flowers to help we could also help at the demonstration tomorrow."

"Don't worry, five hundred thousand people are coming and that's surely enough help."

And with that the young boys and girls stood up and collected all the flowers without giving Süreyya or Reyhan another chance to make their case. They said goodbye and left.

"So they're going without us," said Reyhan.

"I just hope nothing happens to them tomorrow," said Süreyya.

"Me, too."

"Reyhan, do you know what we forgot?"

"What?"

"We forgot to give them the green apricots. How could we not have thought of it when our pockets are still stuffed with them?"

"We can bring them the next time we see them and make up for it then."

"Apricots, flowers, and..."

"And?"

"Of course, girl, the cinema."

"Come on, let's go check the posters of the new releases."

Half an hour later they had checked five different cinemas and after studying all the brightly colored posters of local and foreign films and reading right down to the small print, they chose *Star Wars*, which was showing at the Reks Cinema. Sitting down in the back row, they held each other's hands as the credits rolled.

Merkez Efendi Cemetery

Istanbul, 1983

On Saturday students from the Istanbul University Folk Dance Society met for a rehearsal in the gymnasium of the Atatürk Student Dormitory. When a dozen girls walked into the garden of the boys' dormitory that weekend, the boys whistled and called out names and laughed behind their backs. But the girls paid them no attention as they went into the gymnasium where they rehearsed with the boys who had been waiting for them. They were getting ready for a competition that would be held among the universities two months later.

After the rehearsal the students dispersed and Reyhan and Süreyya left the campus together on their way to the bus station on the main road. Both were studying law at the university, Reyhan in her first year and Süreyya in her second. Laughing and carrying on as they wound through the narrow back streets, Reyhan suddenly stopped at a corner and pointed up at a signpost.

"Süreyya, look at this," she said, "the Merkez Efendi Cemetery is over there."

Süreyya remembered the name of the cemetery. It had a place in the stories Reyhan used to tell her. They looked at each other, there was no need to say a word. Following the sign they turned and walked down the street through the warm sunshine. Soon they came to the well-shaded cemetery and went inside. Wandering among the old stones and the graves overcome by weeds they looked up at the trees: Great cypresses, pines, and spruce were scattered across the cemetery, and soon they clapped their eyes on the redbud in the distance. When they came closer they looked down at the gravestone beneath the tree. Once more Reyhan told Süreyya about Avdo and his simple home. "When he dies he dreams of being buried next to my aunt," she said. They sat down on higher ground so they could have a better view of the house below them. Wondering what sort of life was led in such a shack, they waited for a sign.

"Don't you want to meet him?" asked Süreyya.

"No," said Reyhan. "He made a life for himself here and he might not like to meet someone with a connection to his past."

Then they saw him coming around the side of the shack. Tall and with gray hair and a stern gaze, he went up onto his porch, stepped inside, and came out with a bowl. He put it down in front of the dog that was stretched out on the porch. He sat on the divan. Pulled a tobacco case from his pocket and rolled a cigarette. Turned on the radio on his table. From a distance it was silent. The cemetery was cloaked in the sound of cars rumbling on asphalt, visitors milling about the graves murmuring to one another, birds, and the soughing of the trees. Here time flowed to the sounds, not the hour. When the afternoon call to prayer rose from the mosque and into the sky, Avdo stood up. From a pitcher on the table he poured himself a glass of water and drank. Evening was still far off. Soon he walked slowly to his workshop in the back and a little later they heard the sound of his mallet.

Had Reyhan and Süreyya heard the sound of his mallet when they first arrived? The sound was like the stars, mounting as it spread through space. A human being could never know which sound to pluck out from the whole, which one to follow and make meaningful. The spirits knew this best of all. The spirits in cemeteries followed every sound, they made sense of them all: a hedgehog trundling over leaves that crackled, a pinecone that struck the earth with a plop, a foghorn that had wafted to the cemetery over all those houses. Life was here, and as long as the spirits could hear they were part of it, too. The sound of Avdo's mallet falling on the hard marble, making clean cracks. Every letter and every pattern was born of sound, not image, the sound of a pen writing words on paper, the sound of two people sitting side by side, breathing wordlessly together.

Süreyya took Reyhan's hand. "Are you all right?" she asked.

Reyhan looked up as if she had just awoken.

"I miss my mom and dad," she said. "Although I never knew my aunt, I miss her, too. I know her whole life, her hopes, her ill-fortune. If I feel like this then who knows what Avdo carries inside, he shared so much of their pain.

Listen to the sound of his mallet. Coming to us today from a distant past. In those sounds he sees furtive glances, charming faces, carefully combed hair." Reyhan took her comb out of her bag and put it in the palm of Süreyya's hand. "This is the comb left to me by my mother," she said. "Look how old it is. See how the Shahmaran design is fading."

Süreyya took the comb and held it up to the sun, looked at the front and the back as if she were examining a diamond. "You couldn't find something this beautiful today," she said.

"It's actually Aunt Elif's comb. When she was a young girl she used to comb her hair in front of the mirror and lose herself in dreams. She thought the Shahmaran on the back was smiling at her. But when she lost the man she loved and was married off to another man she left the comb with my mother. When my mother fled her village with only a few things, she took this with her. She also thought the Shahmaran was smiling at her. Over time she couldn't be sure what she saw on the comb. Combing my hair with it she would tell me the story of the Shahmaran, who was the sultan of snakes, as beautiful as my aunt, or so my mom used to say. The Shahmaran has the head of a human and the body of a snake. When she dies, her spirit enters another woman. Mom used to say that the spirit of my aunt was left to her along with this comb and that one day her own soul would pass on to me."

Istanbul University

Istanbul, 1984

They were sitting on the bright green spring grass that stretched out over the back garden of the university, celebrating a sovereign sun that drove away the chill in the air and put them both in a pleasant mood. Reyhan pulled Süreyya's hair; Süreyya dabbed a little dirt on her friend's cheek. When Reyhan stood up to shake off her dress a piece of paper fell from her pocket. Süreyya took it and looked at the words.

"What's this?" she said.

"A note from the hospital," said Reyhan. "I called Uncle Kalender this morning, you know how he likes me to check in now and then, and some other man answered. He told me that Uncle Kalender has been in Çapa Hospital for three days now. It wasn't a fight or anything like that, it's just that his headaches were getting worse and then he had a migraine. So they took him to the hospital. I wrote down his room number and I'm planning to visit him today."

"I'll come with you," said Süreyya.

Together they walked to the front yard of the university, passing the old Beyazit Tower before stepping out into Freedom Square. There they jumped on a minibus and set out for the Çapa State Hospital.

In the garden Süreyya sat down on a red bench. "I'll wait here, it's better if you see him on your own."

Reyhan found Kalender Bey's room and when she went inside Şeyhmus, his right-hand man, stepped outside, leaving the two of them alone.

"Uncle Kalender, what's happened to you? I hope you get well soon," said Reyhan after she had kissed his hand.

"Parisienne, there was no need for you to come, but I am happy to see you all the same."

Kalender Bey always liked to call her Parisienne, because it reminded him of her father's village.

"Why didn't they tell me?" said Reyhan. "If I knew I would've come earlier. I called this morning and got the news by chance."

"That's not important, but tell me, how's school going?"

"It's going well, we had midterm exams and I passed them all. In two months we'll have finals and I'm already studying."

"Well done, girl, I'm proud of you."

"Thanks, Uncle Kalender."

"Now tell me, have you ever been here before?"

"To the hospital?" said Reyhan. "No, it's my first time."

"Well then where do you think you were born? In Paris?"

"Oh that's what you mean, I get it now," said Reyhan, laughing. "What do I know, it just slipped my mind. I *was* born here but never ended up coming back."

"I hope you never have to again," said Kalender Bey and then pointed to the flowers in her hand. "Are you going to keep holding those like that?"

Reyhan went over to the window and arranged the flowers in a vase, filling it with some water.

"These flowers will do you good, Uncle Kalender. So what's bothering you? What exactly did the doctors say?"

"I'm as confused as everybody else. I had a constant headache for a month, it was that migraine I get now and then, but it seemed like it was here to stay, and then I lost a lot of weight. I was thinking how good it was to be losing my belly but the doctors didn't seem to be pleased. They ran tests, did X-rays, and they said I would have to stay here for a while and go on medication. Then they planted this IV here above my head. I don't know what it is they're giving me but I always feel sleepy and run-down."

"How nice, that way you'll be able to get some rest. For years you've been working night and day, never really looking after yourself. Have you ever even taken a break? Maybe this will be like a little vacation."

"I hope I can get some rest. Girl, enough worry about me, tell me about yourself. Do you have enough spending money?"

"I do, Uncle Kalender, and I'm grateful to you for that."

"There's no need for that. You know that your mother and father left me your inheritance. I am keeping it for your future. It was actually a good thing that you came because now I can give you a lump sum that you can keep in the bank."

"Why do we need to do that?"

"There are only two places where you can't be sure about your future, and that's in a prison or a hospital. The doctors put me here, but they never told me when I was leaving, they just whisper to each other on the way out. So I need to take care of my affairs, just to be sure."

"Uncle Kalender..." said Reyhan and her voice trailed off.

"There is nothing to worry about, call Şeyhmus in here, he's at the door, tell him to come in."

She did what she was told and Şeyhmus came inside and went over to the bed. "Go ahead, brother, what is it?"

"Şeyhmus, could you take my checkbook out of that bag there, and bring me a pen, too."

Şeyhmus opened the cupboard in the corner of the room and took out a briefcase, and in the front pocket among the wallets, he found a checkbook and put it down beside Kalender Bey.

As he struggled to sit up it seemed Kalender Bey's bones were now as brittle as the hair on his head. With Reyhan's help he was able to sit up straight and, twirling a pen in his fingers, he mulled something over. Then like a student who had just learned how to write, he filled out the check. Reading over his work one more time, he tore off the page, folded it, and put it in Reyhan's pocket.

"These things don't really matter, Parisienne, the important thing is that you study and finish school and grow up to be your own person. Are we clear, assure me of that again."

"Of course, Uncle Kalender, it's always in my mind," said Reyhan.

"Now you should get going, and there's no need for you to come here again. Hospitals are no good. I will make sure you know when they let me out, okay?"

"I'll just pop in and see how you're doing."

"Out of the question, stay away from sadness, this is a sad place. Don't come here again, just wait for me to call. Are we clear?"

"All right then," she said, lowering her head.

"My beautiful girl, may God shed light on your mind. So it's goodbye to you then. I'm going to sleep a little, I'm feeling tired."

She kissed his hand and left the room. She waited for Şeyhmus farther down the corridor.

"Şeyhmus," she said, "what's wrong with him, he's so thin. What do the doctors say?"

"The news isn't good," said Şeyhmus, looking sideways.

"What is it, tell me, please."

He paused for a moment and then said with sorrow in his voice, "Kalender Bey doesn't know yet, and don't tell him, he has cancer."

"What are you saying, Şeyhmus?"

"They say it's pancreatic cancer. The doctors made the diagnosis yesterday, and to keep his spirits up they haven't told him yet. We won't say anything either."

Holding back her tears, Reyhan left the hospital. She went straight over to Süreyya and threw her arms around her friend and cried.

Istanbul University

Istanbul, 1984

The beginning of October was tense. For the first time students had gathered to draw up a petition calling for a change in the examination system at the Faculty of Law, but when the document was submitted to the dean the authorities under martial law claimed the order was issued by a terrorist organization, not a demand for a more democratic model. To expose so-called illegal activities behind the scene, students were rounded up at their dormitories and homes and brought to the Gayrettepe Police Headquarters, the infamous torture center. There was no word from them for days.

A political prisoner had been executed two weeks ago. In the university garden people were nervously milling about, whispering to each other about another prisoner who had been executed the day before. Among the lingering crowd were undercover cops posing as students. In the wake of the execution two weeks ago, the police were unable to round up those students who had been secretly handing out pamphlets; they didn't want to make the same mistake this time. Some of the plainclothes officers were rifling through school books or reading dailies. In newspapers the latest execution was barely given any mention. In other news Coca-Cola's production contract in Turkey had been extended for another three years, an IMF report claimed that price hikes were a cause for concern but necessary, the value of the American dollar to the Turkish lira was at four hundred and ten, *Videosinema* journal was banned by the Martial Law Command Office, and fifty-five million packets of foreign cigarettes would soon arrive in the country. Foreign news ran the story "French Arrogance": A parliamentarian in France had stood in respect for Hıdır Aslan who had been executed in Turkey the day before.

When the signal was given, police officers across the garden raced to the cafeteria steps. At noon the entrance was packed with people. From a distance you could read the sign that had been strung up between two trees. Fearing there might be a bomb attached to the sign everyone kept their distance as two officers circled the trees. They found nothing. The front of the sign read "Capital Punishment Is a Crime Against Humanity," on the back was the drawing of a flower that looked like a daisy. The police spent most of the time looking up at the flower with pursed lips, then they undid the ties on either side of the sign, brought it down, and put it in a plastic bag to be filed as criminal evidence. With a vengeance they looked over the crowd of students watching them as if they were enemies. The officer holding a walkie-talkie and who was now rounding up his men must have been their boss. Then a student went over and told him he had seen the people who had put up the sign. They wore gray duffle coats and their heads were covered but from the way they walked it was clear that they were girls. After putting up the sign, they raced off behind the library, one in red boots and the other in black shoes.

There were plenty of students who wore gray duffle coats and black shoes but hardly anyone wore red boots. Half an hour later undercover police stopped a girl who was coming out of the main gate on Freedom Square. Her name was Reyhan, she was studying law, she wore red boots and had books of poetry in her bag. They took her by the arm and led her to the Beyazit Police Station only a hundred meters away. There they waited for the eyewitness from the university. Reyhan tried to explain that she was innocent, that she had been in class that morning and with no classes in the afternoon she was on her way to the girls' dormitory in Vezneciler that was just minutes away. But when they asked her why she hadn't used the side gate, which was the most direct route, and went out the front gate instead, she told them she was going to stop in at the secondhand book market to buy a book. Now her lips were trembling and when a male student later identified her as the perpetrator her whole body began to shake. Clearly he was an informant on the student body and his statement made it clear that this indeed was the girl who had put up the sign with her friend. He didn't know their names, but he knew they were always together at the school and he only needed to see a picture of the other one to make a positive ID. For the police this was enough proof, and cuffing Reyhan they pushed her into a car that smelled of urine and gasoline. They beat her and split her lip as the car rattled down the road, swore at her and called her a whore, and when they remembered the drawing of the daisy, they laughed and teased her, saying, "You stupid romantic."

Eyüp Cemetery

Istanbul, 1985

Under a blanket of snow, the Eyüp Cemetery looked liked a great weary cloud over a cliff. In the early morning dark forms emerged from the white snow, several people visiting their loved ones and wandering among the graves. But Commander Cobra had come before everyone else and was sitting on a newspaper he had spread over a stone, speaking to the grave before him.

"Sister, I lost her, the girl I was telling you about. Reyhan's gone. It's been ten days now and still no trace of her. I lost her in the fog that night, I thought it was just a game, I thought I would find her right away. But it was like the fog kept growing thicker and she flew up into the sky. She was sick, nothing but skin and bones, hadn't eaten for days, on some kind of hunger strike. Why, I said, why are you tormenting me? I can help, I said. I told her I could clean up her file and let her go right away. A terrorist was executed in prison the other day and in protest the university students put up a sign in the garden. Our guys picked up Reyhan. I was on an operation outside the city and when I got back to Istanbul they wanted me to help with the interrogation. They told me to look after the Beauty Queen, the nickname they had for her; she really was beautiful. So I went into the interrogation room to see what she looked like. There she was sitting on the floor. Naked and blindfolded. When she heard the door creak open and my footsteps, she sat up against the wall. They had really worked her over, you would have had to blow up a police station, not protest an execution, to get that kind of treatment. I went over and undid her blindfold. Sitting across from me was the most beautiful girl in the world. Sister, do you remember how you took to the doctor's daughter who lived in the apartment next door and how you tried to get me to call her. This girl was ten times as beautiful as the doctor's daughter, then add whatever else you can imagine, and you have Reyhan. And think what she would look like when she was in good shape and far away from a place like this. I almost forgot to breathe as all this ran through my mind and she looked at me as if she could sense the strangeness in me. Her connection to leftist groups or her criminal activity or her beauty, I couldn't say anything, but I left the room and told the guys waiting in the corridor that I had an important meeting, I told them not to touch her until I got back. I hurried out into the street. I was a man who had never fallen in love. I felt like someone who had suddenly fallen into the sea without knowing how to swim, thrashing about in the water, struggling against the strong waves. I didn't know what to do. As I wandered the streets the cool autumn air brought me back to myself. Then I went into a tavern and started drinking. I don't know how many hours flew by and I didn't count the number of drinks. When I got up to leave the place it was after midnight and vodka, whiskey, and gin were racing through my blood. I went back to the headquarters and then into the interrogation room. I told my men to leave so I could be alone with her. Blindfolded and sitting on the floor. I pulled her to her feet and cuffed her hands to the table. I remember everything. Even though I was drunk I remember everything I did that night. You know what I want now, sister? No, not for her to get caught. I want what happened that night to never have happened. Seeing that what I did was wrong I want to forget it. I don't want to know what I did, if only I didn't know the evil I did to her when I woke up the next morning with my head pounding. So I find myself at a dead end and came here to talk to you. You remember when I came and told you that I found the girl who was going to fill the void in my life, I went on and on about her, but I couldn't say a single word about what I did to her. I couldn't help but cry and you thought that your little brother was finally experiencing love for the first time, but I was crying for myself. Someone who never cared what other people think, always putting people down. For the first time I was ashamed of myself. But still you gave me good advice that day, you told me to open up to her and talk. I took your advice. When I went back, I didn't go to see her in the interrogation room, I told them to have her get dressed and bring her to see me in my office. I took off her blindfold and asked her to sit down in the chair across from me. I put a glass of tea on the coffee table between us and took a glass for myself, and it was like we were sitting across from each other in a tea garden. I made my unexpected speech. If we were actually in a tea garden, I would have been all twisted up and nervous, tongue-tied in the face of such beauty. But in my office I was used to being in the center of power and I was comfortable speaking with her, as if I were opening up her criminal file. So my words didn't ring true for her. She didn't believe that I loved her, that I was really proposing to her, and that I was prepared to give up my job for her. She looked at me with hostility. In a tearful voice she asked me why I was giving her such a hard time, she said she wasn't that important, she asked me why I was telling her all these lies. And she wouldn't touch her tea. I had to be patient. The next day I spoke to her more tenderly. Every day I brought her to my room and every time she came I tried a different tone to get her to believe me. I talked about you and how you encouraged me to talk to her. I thought if only she could get some rest and was treated well, she might come to have more trust in me. I stayed away for a few days, hoping she would notice a difference between me and the others, and to give her time to think over why I was treating her so well. When I saw her again, she was only digging in her heels even more, she had stopped eating. She said she was on a hunger strike, drinking only water. When I saw her in that state, I really lost it, I couldn't take it anymore and I fell down on my knees. Sister, when you're alone with the one you love there's no shame in lowering yourself so I told her that I couldn't live without her and that if she rejected me, I would kill her and then kill myself. Still she thought this was some kind of interrogation, that I was setting her up. Now I was desperate, I didn't know what to do. Finally I told her that I was going to arrange for her to escape. I said, would you believe me if I let you go and let you to get away? What are you saying, she said, are you going to write up a report saying that I was shot while trying to escape? I read all those stories in the papers, I'm not going to buy that, she said. I told her I was going to convince her. I said I would let her go and find her when she reached a safe space and then we could go wherever she wanted to go together. I opened my bag and took out all the money I had in the bank and two fake passports I'd had made for us. This is enough money for us and with the passports we can go abroad. Then I realized she was beginning to believe me. Her eyes opened wide in surprise. You're serious, she said. More serious than you can imagine, I said. Two days later I set the plan in motion. I got some of the guys in our unit to take Reyhan to infiltrate an underground leftist house close to the boys' dormitory. We went to the location that evening with her and the team. I told the men to stay back and scour the area. Luckily the fog was already falling. When we were in the backstreets, I whispered to Reyhan, I told her to run. By now she believed me, and she raced off knowing we weren't going to shoot. Then I called out to the team who were standing back, saying that she got away, and we started searching for her. I sent them in all different directions, and I went after her myself. I was as thrilled as she must have been. Soon I would catch up to her and take her by the hand and when the fog lifted, we would start a new life together. If I could catch her. I don't know what happened, sister, a tiny little girl vanishing with the mist. We have this tracking dog we brought along. We looked everywhere, searched every street in the area, including the boys' dorm. In the end the dog led us to the Merkez Efendi Cemetery. It was the cold of the *zemheri*, ice was everywhere, and when the fog finally lifted it started to snow. If Reyhan hadn't found shelter somewhere there was no way she could have survived the night in the state she was in. I was beside myself with rage. This guy, Avdo, living in the cemetery shack, I woke him up to question him, but he hadn't seen the girl. At first I had my suspicions about him, but they were ungrounded, the man was asleep and there was only one room in that shack. But our dog had tracked her scent that far and I was really sure we were almost there, but it seems he had picked up the scent of Avdo's dog. He was just a poor old man, but I took my anger out on him. I hit him, and as if that wasn't enough, I killed his dog. I should have killed our useless beast instead. When you lose it, you don't know what you're doing, sister. If only God had broken my wrist to stop me from hitting that man. I haven't been able to sleep for days. What do you say I do, should I go see him and apologize and ask for his forgiveness? My head really hurts, and I can't sleep. Sister, you were alone, and now I am alone. Yes, I am going to see that old man to win him over and ask for his forgiveness."

Çapa State Hospital

Istanbul, 1985

Süreyya had waited for Reyhan on the red bench in the hospital garden when she came to visit Kalender Bey one year ago, and she was sitting alone on the same bench again, watching the milling crowd. It was unfortunate that sick people had to come here and yet they were fortunate to have so many loved ones visiting them. Süreyya was constantly checking her watch, like a worried patient who had been waiting months for a visitor to come and see her. Today was the day she would come. Although Reyhan was much changed, Süreyya picked her out in the crowd. She didn't leap to her feet and race over to her. She was keeping to their plan, she waited for her friend to come over first.

Last year they had decided on a place to meet: If they ever lost each other they would come to this bench every Thursday at two o'clock in the afternoon. They had both agreed to always come here and wait and never to lose hope even after weeks and months had passed. Since the military coup in 1980—how many coups had there been—countless people were disappeared or forced to run, so friends and loved ones had to figure out how to find each other before that ever happened.

Reyhan and Süreyya passionately threw their arms around each other—they had been apart for more than five months. No one was surprised to see the two young women crying. Half of their long friendship was made of laughter; the other half of tears. Now the tears tipped the balance of the scale.

When they sat down it was Reyhan who began. She told her friend everything: how she had been arrested, then escaped, and then became a part of Avdo's life. She could only come to see her friend now as she had been sick, afraid, and confused. Both her body and her mind were weak. She took time to recover in the cemetery, she pulled herself together and eventually reclaimed her health.

"I really missed you," said Reyhan, squeezing her friend's hand.

"I missed you like crazy, too," said Süreyya. "I thought you were dead. When I read in the papers about a terrorist that got away and they gave your name I was actually happy at first, I thought I would find you soon enough. But you didn't call. Our friends were hopeful, too, but you didn't call them either. As time passed, I started to think this might be a ruse the police were playing. Oh, I cried, I cried so much. But I kept coming, week after week, to wait for you."

"Just think about what we have been through, Süreyya, our lives were completely different a year ago."

"After you left, I disappeared, too. They searched my dorm room and my parents' place in the countryside. We worried you might have been killed so we put up pictures of you in many parts of the city. That's when they rounded up a bunch of people and my name was on the list. My picture came out in the papers."

"I didn't know that," said Reyhan, looking at her friend with sadness and shame.

"What we did was not big or dangerous, but the state acts as if this was both big and dangerous. Now they're closing in, our friends say I need to leave the country."

"If you want you can come and stay with us in the cemetery."

"Reyhan, you're a fugitive, they won't let you live if they find you. You need to leave the country or go up to the mountains."

"No, I'm safe here now, I have a new identity and I'm living in place where no one can find me."

"In the cemetery? Until when?"

"It seems strange, right? I'm used to it now. Avdo is like a dad to me. After I've cried so many years he's like a gift that has come to fill a void in my life."

"I understand, stay there a little longer, but in the end..."

"Süreyya," said Reyhan.

"What?"

"Süreyya, I'm pregnant."

It seemed a silence fell over the hospital garden. The sound of footsteps faded, the twittering of the birds, the clamor of the traffic on the main road, and then was gone.

In a void where a thousand possibilities came and were discarded, Süreyya didn't know what to do. Was this a moment to be happy or sad? "What, how?" she stammered.

"It doesn't show, right?" said Reyhan. "I got this baggy dress and my belly isn't all that big yet."

"How many months?" said Süreyya, leaving aside the real question.

"Five months."

As they looked each other in the eye, Süreyya did the math in her head, turning the pages of a calendar as she held her breath. After covering the months and the seasons, she finally stopped at the only possible place.

"I think my heart's going to burst," she said.

"I know this is hard, but I need to tell you."

Reyhan told her what had happened to her while she was kept in custody. Now and then stopping to drift away in thought. When she finally finished her story with a hesitant look on her face, Süreyya leaned over and gave her a hug.

"So you had no other option?" asked Süreyya and quickly answered her own question. "I suppose you didn't."

"Option for what?" said Reyhan wearily looking up.

"The chance for an abortion—"

"No," said Reyhan, "it never crossed my mind."

"You say that because of the police—"

"The baby belongs to no one else," said Reyhan, putting her hand on her belly. "Mine and no other's."

Süreyya could see that she was upsetting her friend, she reached out and put her hand on Reyhan's stomach.

"This baby is yours and will be as beautiful as you are. You can name her after your mother or your father and live happily together for the rest of your life. Okay?"

"All right, but I'm not going to name her after them."

"You have another name in mind?"

"For months now," said Reyhan.

"Really?"

"I'm going to name her Süreyya if she's a girl."

Süreyya leaned back and looked at her, reading the look in her eye. Reyhan was serious, content, and smiling. Süreyya smiled back at her. Now the scale of laughter and tears tipped the other way.

Çapa State Hospital

Istanbul, 1985

When they met the second time in the hospital garden, Süreyya told Reyhan this would be their last meeting.

"Our friends have arranged a passport for me, I'll leave the country in a few days."

"I wanted you to stay with me but then there's the risk of you getting arrested, I'm scared."

"The other day a friend told me about an old man in Diyarbakır Prison and how he lost his touch with reality day by day after being tortured there. Soon he was telling his cellmates that they had all actually died and were now living in hell. This prison is hell, he said, we're dead, and these guards are the hellhounds. The younger cellmates tried to convince him otherwise. Okay, they said, but what about our relatives who come to see us on visiting days. Aren't they real? The old man said they were close relatives who came to cry at our graves and that they had a false impression of really talking to them. Sometime later they released the old man. He couldn't believe it. Since when were you ever let out of hell. He was terrified. And on the day he was to be set free, his heart stopped. I've been thinking about him for days. I have been thinking that what the old man said goes for us, too. This country is a living hell, we've died and gone to hell, and we are now paying for our sins. There's no way out. Just like that man who couldn't get out of prison, I'm not getting out either, I'm not going to be able to make it abroad. When the day comes my heart will stop."

Reyhan looked sadly at her friend and said, "Süreyya, you were always the smartest one among us. You know you're going to get out of here fit and healthy. Now I understand why you're worried, you don't want to go and leave everything behind. Your life is here, your past, your dreams. It pains you to think of leaving all that behind."

"It's really hard," said Süreyya, "leaving Mom, Dad, you..."

"If only everyone was as sensitive as you," said Reyhan, nervously running her eyes over the people in the garden. "Just look at them, they have no idea they're living in hell. The moment they do the pain they are already suffering will only get worse, they don't even want to know the truth."

"Okay, then how are we supposed to feel about them? Should we feel sadness or anger toward them?"

"Both, sometimes I feel sad for them and then I feel angry."

Süreyya reached out and put her hand on her friend's stomach.

"How is the baby?" she said. "Don't worry about anything else, tell me about her."

"Look how quickly she's growing," said Reyhan.

"I noticed when you first came, she's clearly there under your dress."

"The more she grows the more she wears me out, I always want to sleep."

"Is she kicking?"

"Yes, and sometimes she makes me laugh."

"What a little rascal," said Süreyya, leaning back before she went on. "Reyhan, there's something you need to know. I had an argument with our friends about your baby."

"What kind of argument?"

"They think you should have the baby aborted. It was a mistake that you didn't, they say. The conversation got a little heated. Me and some other friends defended you, or I should say the baby. We said, if there's anyone who has the right to speak on her behalf, it's you, her mother, and only you."

Reyhan lowered her head. There was a feeling running through her mind, not an idea: a love for her child that spread from her womb and her heart and moved through every cell in her body, taking precedence over everything, even her own life.

Süreyya said, "I told you this because I didn't want you to be surprised if you heard it some day. It's one of the discussions we always have, but don't take it seriously. Does your baby know anything about it? No. There's a beautiful world waiting for her."

"This beautiful world. Maybe the only proof this isn't a living hell is this baby. Though this fear in me doesn't pass..."

"What fear?"

"Sometimes in my dreams that cop comes and takes her out of me. I can't stop having this nightmare."

"Reyhan, you can't live your life with that fear. Let's get you out of the country, too. Then that guy will never be able to find you."

"The fear's only in my mind. Avdo told me that he had died, that he would never bother me again."

Süreyya looked at her friend through narrowed eyes. "Are you sure?"

"That's what Avdo said and I believe him. That cop is no longer around and what's left is only my fear of him. I haven't learned how to deal with my fear yet, but you don't have to worry, everything is going to be all right. You don't need to worry about me after you have gone. I fear for you and it will make me feel so much better after you have made it out of the country safe and sound."

"I understand you," said Süreyya calmly. "I'm leaving this place, but I'll miss you and your baby. I want you to know that I feel like she is partly mine, too."

"I know," said Reyhan looking at her sadly.

Süreyya took a package out of her bag. "As I won't be with you when you give birth, I brought this present."

"A present?"

"Take it."

Reyhan opened the package and looked down at the shawl inside. She slowly ran her fingers over the strips of orange, yellow, and green. Feeling something hard under the soft shawl she looked Süreyya in the eye then unfolded each layer. In the middle was the comb with the Shahmaran design. Reyhan looked up with tears in her eyes. "I can't believe it," she said.

"When you were taken into custody by the police, I went straight over to your dorm room and gathered up your things. That's when I saw your comb. I know how precious it is to you, so I kept it safe. I couldn't wait to finally give it back to you."

"I can't tell you how happy this makes me..."

"Reyhan, one day you'll definitely see this Shahmaran smiling back at you."

"Süreyya, you're my Shahmaran."

They held hands and with the peace of mind of two older women with a shared troubled past they sat together in silence. The shadows grew longer and became more numerous; swallows landed on the branches of the tree across from them and then took flight; children were playing catch on the grass.

"We are such stupid romantics," said Reyhan. "When I was taken into custody the police beat me and made fun of me, they said I was a stupid romantic. It was the only thing they said that was true. You are going far away but keep this in your mind."

"Which part? Being stupid or romantic?"

With a happiness they shared in the old days, they broke out laughing.

Merkez Efendi Cemetery

Istanbul, 1985

When the Blond Sailor arrived, the fall had already draped the city in pale copper. Evenings came early and the wind blew the dust that the graves had gathered over the summer. Avdo fought back the weariness of the day with cigarettes and tea. Reyhan was putting her little boy to sleep after breastfeeding, seeing his face wherever she looked.

As a new wind blew through the trees Reyhan shivered, picked up her sweater from the divan, and wrapped it around her shoulders.

"It's getting cooler," said the Blond Sailor.

Avdo pointed to the western sky. "If the Pleiades are visible in the evening sky the shepherds wrap themselves up in their felt cloaks, or so Master Josef used to say."

"I haven't heard that saying before."

"On the sea you must have different meanings to the same stars we see in Mesopotamia."

"True," said the Blond Sailor. "When the Pleiades are in the sky the waves and winds that blow over them are more compassionate and we say it is time to unfurl the sails. It is there in the sky that my crew sees the seven sisters and they dream of being in the shoes of the old Greek gods that had eyes on those sisters."

"Master Josef never spoke to me of the seven sisters, he would call those stars a bunch of grapes and like a wolf he would howl at them, *mul-mul*."

"What sort of sound is that?" said the Blond Sailor.

"It supposedly means star-star in an ancient Babylonian language."

Reyhan came out and said, "Dad, is that why you sometimes say that to the baby when you're playing with him."

"Yes, he's my *mul-mul*," said Avdo, suddenly letting go of his laughter.

"Oh, I'm so silly, here I was thinking you had just come up with a random rhyme," she said, sitting down.

Then the baby started crying. Reyhan sprang to her feet, saying he was hungry on her way inside.

Avdo and the Blond Sailor turned their faces to the sky again. Wandering through the stars, they were considering days past.

"How long have we known each other now," said Avdo. "In those early years when you went away I knew you would be back within a few months, and I would wait for the day. But now you come to Istanbul so infrequently it feels like I might never see you again. I can't imagine the day you will come back and I make do with dipping into the memories of the days we spent together in the past."

"I wish I could come more often," said the Blond Sailor in a broken voice. "Since I sold my house in the neighborhood,

I no longer have ties to this place. I go off on a voyage then return to my home in Venice. When I miss Roberta and my son, I sometimes imagine them living in Istanbul, but soon enough my ship is already pulling into the harbor of Venice. The walls of our home are covered with pictures of Istanbul. Now it's my fault for having gone away again like this. But you are partly to blame, too, as you never come to visit no matter how much I insist. Roberta also complains about my coming to Istanbul to see you when you never come to see us in Venice."

"If I could only leave this place, I would be coming over to see you all the time. But it's out of my control, I can't leave Elif."

"We've talked about this time and again, and every time I empathize with you, but the situation is different. Now you have Reyhan, she can stay here with Elif in your place. If only for a few days..."

"Ah there you have it wrong, in the past I had one reason not to leave but now I have three. I have a daughter and a grandson not to mention Elif. What would they do without me?"

"All right then, I'll say it one more time and then stop. Then it's up to you. But you know now when I think about you, I don't have the same worries fluttering through my head. It gives me peace of mind to know that you aren't living alone and that you have a happy family."

"To our two happy families then," said Avdo, raising his glass. "Come on, my friend, it's not like we've come to pray in a mosque. Raise that glass of yours."

"Avdo, when you told me the plight of your daughter I was angry with myself, why didn't I come sooner? I could have helped you out of a terribly difficult situation. I could have put her on a ship and taken her to Venice where no one would ever have found her. Then you would have had no choice but to come and visit us."

"When she came to me, I was so desperate I didn't know what to do. In the end I thought of the çilehane and I heaved a sigh of relief when they issued her new ID."

"That's where you went wrong, Avdo, I left you my number in Venice. You should have called and talked with Roberta. She can get in touch with me even when I'm on the other side of the world."

"I know, it was a mistake. It never crossed my mind that I might need to call you in a time of need. The slip of paper with your number on it was on the table for a while and then I suppose it finally blew away in the wind. Who knew any of this was going to happen to me?"

"I'll write down my number again but this time I am going to give it to Reyhan. She'll know how to keep it safe."

"Do you know I only ever used a phone once in my life. It was around ten years ago when I was keen to learn about Reyhan. I had read in the paper that her mother and her father had been killed so I called the owner of the gazino to see if I could adopt their daughter. I was afraid that she would be left alone. But I couldn't figure out how to use the phone. That was when Eşref Hodja was around. I'm grateful that he helped. Don't be surprised, I never had to call anyone before that. When I was a child in Mardin I used watch the shop telephones from a distance and I used to think that they were more mysterious than radios. I thought I might be able to reach my mother if I talked on a phone, but Master Josef explained to me how they were used and that I shouldn't foster a false hope."

"So you only ever used a phone once in your life," said the Blond Sailor, tapping his fingers on the table as he thought something over. "Let's do this tomorrow. We'll call home and speak with Roberta. She'll be happy to hear your voice and she'll get to practice her Turkish a little. Okay? From now I'm giving Reyhan the responsibility of making sure that you call us once a month."

"Have Reyhan take care of it then. I don't understand these things. In any case she's the one who makes all the decisions. I told her I would rent a house in the neighborhood and that she could live there with her child. She wouldn't have it and insisted on staying with me. So I added an extra room for them. We're comfortable now."

"You must have spent so much on that and are struggling now. Let me leave you something."

"Thank you, it's the thought that counts, I am doing just fine. For years I didn't know what to do with the money I earned but now I am happy to have two people to look after."

"How pleasant it must be for you."

"When Reyhan gave birth to her boy she wanted me to name him. I can't tell you how excited it made me, I was speechless. Years ago, I had an apprentice who came to an unfortunate end, his name was Baki. I named the baby after him."

"Reyhan couldn't have found a better father in the world."

"She couldn't have, right?" said Avdo in all seriousness.

"Do you have doubts?"

"No doubts, no, but in the end here we are living in a cemetery. A mother and her child surely would be more comfortable somewhere else."

"More comfortable perhaps but not happier."

The tense look on Avdo's face softened, his eyes went misty. "Let's drink to that," he said.

"Yes, let's," said the Blond Sailor and raising his glass he added, "and to Toteve."

Avdo took a sip then put his glass down on the table. He ran his eyes over the cemetery from one end to the other, pricked up his ears as if he might hear the dog's rough breathing in the darkness, as if Toteve might appear and come to him. If Reyhan and her child, Baki, had not come into his life Avdo would not have been able to bear the absence of Toteve. Almost a year had passed and whenever he heard the sound of a dog when he was sleeping, he still got up and looked out the window.

"If only you had seen him give his last breath, the poor thing, so hopeless. I didn't have the strength to save him. Can a person really bear a grudge against his own self? I bear one against myself for Toteve's death."

"It's not right to beat yourself up about it, you did the best you could. And you saved Reyhan's life."

"I did, right? But she still can't get rid of the fear. She mumbles in her sleep, calls out to me for help, and then wakes up screaming."

"She has endured so much, it isn't easy, she needs time."

Gazing into empty space, Avdo remembered another dog. "How is Apostle?" he asked.

"She got sick last month, and we took her to the vet who told us that we needed to prepare ourselves for her passing. We are doing all right but my son, Ali Andrea, isn't going to take this well. Think about it, he's now ten and he has spent his entire life with Apostle."

"Well my friend of the highs seas, there is a cure for all woes but no pity that comes with death. Enduring the pain of Apostle's passing will only prove to fortify Ali Andrea. I don't know of any other way to prepare for a long life."

"Master Avdo, you are a man of the earth and you have buried Toteve in the ground here. I have spoken to Roberta about this and if our son agrees we are going to bury Apostle at sea. She is of seas, too, she has been on many journeys with me."

"When you lay her to rest in the sea there will be a gravestone for her here, like the one I made for Toteve."

"You made him a gravestone?"

"I did. Or I should say I added a piece to a gravestone I had already made. When I found Toteve and Apostle, their mother and six siblings had already died. You might remember how I buried them in an old grave site and put up a gravestone on which I drew a dog tooth for each one of them. When Toteve died I put in one more. I'll make a sharp tooth for Apostle so her spirit will still be with the spirit of her mother and brothers and sisters even though she isn't buried here."

"Well said, this will bring the family together."

Merkez Efendi Cemetery

Istanbul, 1985

Avdo was unable to fall asleep after the Blond Sailor had left at midnight. He was troubled again by the problem he had not been able to solve for months: What kind of gravestone was he going to make for the Man with Seven Names? As he mulled over the possibilities, he slipped in and out of childhood memories, dreaming with the hope of stumbling into the light of inspiration. But none of the ideas that came to mind were satisfying. He was not merely going to shape a stone, he was going to forge a soul, he was waiting for that soul to appear before his eyes. He knew how to be patient. Patient with time, he watched the stars, counting the ones that continued to stream off in four different directions. There was another shooting star. The last seagulls flew over the cemetery cawing into the night. Avdo poured himself a glass of water from the pitcher on the table and drank. He lit a cigarette. Then taking the bag off the divan, he pulled out the journal the

Man with Seven Names had left behind. Reading through passages he had read so many times before might give him an idea and bring the shape of the gravestone he was going to make before his eyes.

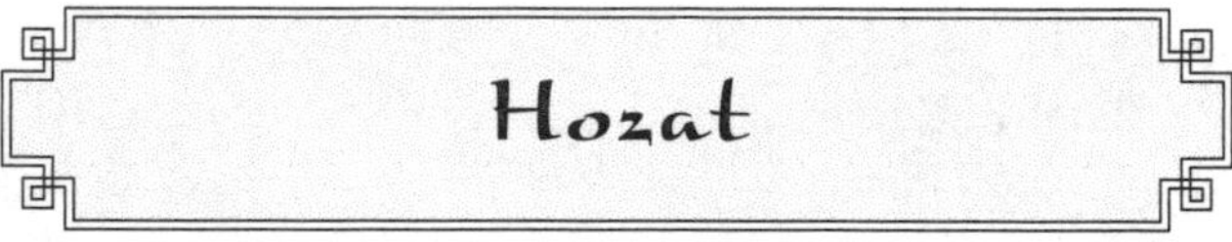

Hozat

Dersim, 1938

This journal belongs to Third Lieutenant Adem Giritli. I kindly request anyone who finds this notebook to mail it to the address of my fiancée, Miskal Durusu. What I have recorded here was intended for her and I would like to express my gratitude in advance for your respecting the intimate nature of what I have written down. The address of my fiancée: Salkımlı Street, Cevher Mansion, Emirgan, Istanbul.

WEDNESDAY, JUNE 1, 1938

My beloved Miskal, the first word is always for you, and the last will be yours as well. At the assembly this morning it was announced we would set out for the country early in the morning and that we had to be fully prepared before the day was out. We have been here a week since our unit left Izmir, the letter I already sent from here probably hasn't reached you yet. Tonight, I plan to write you another letter to give you the latest as we are going to be out of touch for a while. When I asked the field officer how long this mission was going to last, he said a few weeks. I won't be able to send you any letters or receive any from you for a while. I figured I could bring this empty notebook along with me. I can keep a journal in place of letters and when I come back from our mission I can mail you the notebook for you to see that I carried you with me wherever I went and that I never lost touch with you although we were apart. In the papers we read that the Dersim Operation was successfully completed last year and that ringleaders of the rebellion had been rounded up and hanged. But the truth is a restive spirit still remains. The fire may have been put out, but the embers are still burning, now we go in to put them out for good. Or so says Captain Tan, our commanding officer. The captain is a refined and knowledgeable man. He was interested in me when he heard that I was a history teacher and he invited me to his tent for tea. During our conversation, he told me that the town of Hozat was a military base in the past, during Byzantine times; you know when I say in the past, I mean thousands of years ago. There are mountains all around us, covered with acorns. Captain Tan laughed at me when I described the region as mountainous and he told me the real mountains were to the north of Dersim and that this place was a plain in comparison. Then he stopped and grew serious and corrected himself: But we call the area Tunceli, he said, not Dersim. Although the name was officially changed three years ago, we always slip and use the old name, Dersim, which is who knows how many thousands of years old—you can't wipe out a name like that at the drop of a hat. However, I couldn't care less for the mountains, all those acorns, or the right name for the place now when all I want to do is walk with you along the Bosphorus shore from Emirgan to İstinye. Now I'm trying to remember what it was we were doing together this time last year. Did we see each other that day? Was it the day we stopped along the coast to watch that waterfront mansion go up in flames on the opposite shore in Kanlıca? Or the day we talked about the German Zeppelin that came down in America? It feels easy to talk about what happened thousands of years ago but so hard to remember what happened last year. I suppose time is that much more important when you are separated from a loved one; we know each other when we are together, not time. When I was with you in Istanbul there was only you and we were outside of time, but now a thousand miles away from you I find myself inside it. Every moment spent without you is spent watching the minute hand on the clock, the sharp tip tilling the soil in my heart like a plow drawing lines in a field. Someone has just called out to me from a distance. I am writing this to you on my break, I need to go now.

NIGHT

We pass our day in intense preparation, spending a lot of time racing from here to there. But now we are finally in our tents and stretched out on our beds. I have finished your letter and sealed it in an envelope, tomorrow I'll hand it to the officer on duty. The lights will go out soon. I didn't fall sleep straightaway and opened up my journal, which I no longer call a notebook, so that I could spend these last minutes of light with you. In just a day I have grown used to the idea of keeping a journal, it feels as if you are right there in front of me when I open it. We are chatting in the Yeniköy tea garden at a table by the sea. I am talking about the repairs we are going to have done at the house on the coast in Bebek where we plan to live after we get married, and you are telling me about your aunt who is coming to visit us from Athens. But what happened to her? Now I remember you didn't mention her in your last letter. Then I am saying that I want to get married right away and you remind me how your father is insisting I should finish my military service first. A cold wind is blowing through the open flap of our tent and a soldier gets up to close it. How the cold wind picks up suddenly when night falls in the summer. A soldier from Konya starts singing a folk song. I have grown used to hearing them, I no longer stop up my ears, I shouldn't expect to hear European songs from anyone around here. These kids have come from all four corners of Anatolia, soldiers speaking with different accents, sometimes I have a hard time understanding what they are saying. As we are in a conflict zone we are staying in tents, I am the lieutenant on duty in this one, and they call me the Istanbulite. We are called by the name of the province we hail from. The soldiers here are curious to know more about Istanbul, most have never seen the sea, and when I tell them about its ancient walls, the Maiden's Tower, and the stylish women who come out to shop on the brightly lit streets they are all ears, listening to me as if a movie is running before their eyes. They ask me strange questions. Is the water really blue? Do stars come up in the night sky? How strange, isn't it? That they perceive Istanbul as another planet. For them the people of Istanbul have abandoned their religions and never go to mosques. What is it that they worship? Apart from me everyone is married, some with children. If your dad had let us, I could have been a married soldier now. In my pocket I would have carried a picture of you and our child. Mentioning children, something comes to mind, let me tell you what happened yesterday.

YESTERDAY

During lunch I heard shouting between soldiers not far away from me. Fights often break out here and I figured this had to be another. Then a foot soldier covered in blood was carried into the infirmary tent. Before lunch the solider had received a letter from home. Tears filled his eyes when he read it and he was silent in the face of questions from those around him. He was recently married and the news of his wife giving birth had come as a shock. For she had died in childbirth and the baby had died a day later. When the soldier finished the letter, he began hitting himself and then he pulled out a knife and cut his wrist. Who would ever want to be in a situation like that? People were angry at whoever wrote that letter to the soldier, it turns out it was a cousin, and they claimed that he was either mentally ill or an enemy of that soldier. There is an unsaid rule that a soldier should never receive bad news from home, even we Istanbulites know that. The situation for our soldier is serious and they weren't able to help him, so they transferred him to the hospital in Dersim.

Euphrates River

Dersim, 1938

TUESDAY, JUNE 14, 1938

My dear Miskal, let people say what they will say about time but now I know the answer: Time is a bottomless well. When I lean over and look down, I see only you. I have fallen in and am drinking of its waters, feeling the absence of the world outside the well. Knowing is one thing but feeling is another. In this world knowing is easy enough in an age when problems are solved by science and technology, now we need to come upon the secrets of feeling. New science should pave the way and seek to explain not only the meaning of existence but the meaning of nonexistence. Otherwise so many will remain tangled in the web of superstition and religion, the people of our country must shake off their old habits. We know how they work for they have followed us insistently for thousands of years. Habit is ready-made information that prevents us from learning. I have seen it here: Our people don't even know the time. Except the officers I have not seen a single first-rank soldier with a watch. Sometimes when they ask me about it, they don't even understand my answer; for them, there is no difference between three and nine o'clock. They merely look up at the sun or the moon every time, they have no idea why I carry a watch. They take it for some kind of symbol. Some ask me if it's a magic amulet as they have heard that people in Istanbul believe in a new religion—and they assume the amulet is a part of that belief. They might not say it to my face, but it isn't hard for me figure this out from what they are saying to each other. In the same way they are curious about what I am writing in this journal. Now we are in a village of thirty homes. We arrived two hours ago. No one was around, they must have left and taken everything with them. They even took their livestock, leaving not a single sheep or cow for us to slaughter. It's not easy feeding ninety soldiers. Today we are going to have to make do with what rations we have carried with us. Our local guide has been talking about caves outside the village. Most likely that's where the villagers are hiding. Now night is falling, it would be dangerous going there now and coming under direct fire. We will go have a look tomorrow morning. But the only thing on my mind is the Euphrates River, supposedly you can see it once you are past the caves. We have been marching over mountains and ridges for the past two weeks and now the only thing I want to see is the river. All the folk songs in this area are about the Euphrates. I heard the first one three days ago.

THREE DAYS AGO, SATURDAY

Again, we went into an empty village that was as still as a photograph. Not even the sound of a dog barking. One by one we searched every house. We had heard that the villagers in the north around Munzur Mountain were especially restive, killing soldiers in ambushes. We have already engaged in two different skirmishes, but we have suffered no casualties, it was easy enough to go up against people who are so poor. Some of our soldiers wanted to bury the enemy but Captain Tan forbade it. Their bodies were left for the birds and the worms. We were clearing the village when we were stopped suddenly at the sound of someone screaming, the voice ripping through the silence, and we looked around trying to find out where it was coming from. We saw the old woman sitting on a rock on the upper half of the village. With a dirty shawl wrapped around her shoulders, she was singing a lament in her powerful voice that echoed off the stones like a bell. We were rooted to the spot and could only watch. When she finished, she slowly rose to her feet and undid her shawl. Standing naked she looked a hundred years old, two hundred years old, maybe two thousand years old, as if she had stepped straight out of history. There was hardly any flesh on her frail body, nothing but skin and bones. Then she shouted. Speaking the language of the dead, not the living. We couldn't understand. Then she let herself fall off the edge of the cliff. Her courage was astonishing. We asked our guide what she was saying, and it seems she had told the other villagers that she refused to flee with them, saying she would die where she was born. As for the lament, it was about the Euphrates. They say the river absorbs our pain. For forty thousand years, it has embraced these lands. These days, too, will pass, the flood will recede, the old winds will return. Flowers will bloom again in the mountains, and the Euphrates will flow again with the songs of young girls. But I wasn't interested in these uninspiring words, I was fascinated by the river I had told my students about. I said that I wanted to go have a look if it was nearby. Before the guide could answer, Captain Tan told me the river was a day's walk away but that it would take us three or four days as we were taking a circuitous route. Captain Tan had been in this area for two years and had learned the language of the Kurds. Following his lead, I began learning the language, too. He tells me the Kurds are actually the Mountain Turks that have been living in these lands since ancient times—for at least a thousand years—and that, being cut off from the rest of the world, their language deteriorated over time. Seeing the villagers here I understood how the soldiers in our unit are more civilized. You have to teach these people the most basic things before teaching them time. I even doubt that they know how to count. They have no names for days and months. They know but two seasons: the one with sun and the other with snow. They resemble tribes in Africa. They have fallen far behind, have no sight of the horizon. They make mistakes because they don't know what they want. Primitive and poor, how could they ever make a future for themselves?

TODAY, NIGHT

We haven't washed for two weeks and I itch so much I can't sleep. I got up and now I am sitting by the watchman's fire. The others laugh and carry on while I try to put down these few lines here. My beloved, Miskal! I realize we have been neglecting nights in Istanbul. After our wedding, we should sit around a fire in our garden at home. Together we can take in the beautiful starry night in the sky above Istanbul. When I think of your eyes here, I think of Istanbul. The blue is the same blue of the sea and now I am drifting into that blue dream.

Euphrates River

Dersim, 1938

MONDAY, JUNE 20, 1938

My dearest Miskal, I saw the Euphrates today. After three days of skirmishes we finally cleared the area and heaved a sigh of relief. Our plan is to spend the night here before setting out tomorrow, but I was in no mood to wait. I was so eager to see the Euphrates from the rock on the opposite hill that I asked Captain Tan for permission to go. He is the only one who understands my enthusiasm. Looking at his watch he pointed to the sun setting in the west and told me I had to be back in two hours and that I would lose my way if I stayed out after dark. Though I was tired and hungry my legs worked like springs and I was up on top of the rock in no time, looking down from the edge of a steep cliff where a strong wind was blowing. My dear Miskal, I remembered how excited I was when I first saw you at a party. It was enchanting, seductive. The Euphrates stretched out like a copper-colored snake in the evening sun. There was no end in sight. Through binoculars I looked carefully for the other end of the river three thousand kilometers away. It felt like that view brought time, not space, closer to me; right there before my eyes lay thousands of years of history. These lands spreading along the Mesopotamian Plain and winding from the Persian Gulf to the Mediterranean Sea have been the mother to agriculture, the wheel, the written word. Homer, father to the Greeks, was not yet born when the legend of Gilgamesh was written here. They made irrigation canals, they forged trade routes, and they built not seven but seventeen wonders of the world. The names were Sumerian, Babylonian, and Assyrian and yet somehow over time their place would be taken by these bare, poor, ignorant people. I patiently moved my binoculars to the right and then to the left, I looked both near and far. Where had these makers of history gone, who were these people that now lived here in run-down, mud-brick houses. I could swear on the mighty Purattu, a name given to the Euphrates by Akkadians, that the people who dwelled here five thousand years ago, those people who spread civilization over these lands, they were more advanced than the people who lived here now. As I trained my binoculars over the land and then on the mountains on the opposite shore, I was startled by a strange dark shape right under my nose. Lowering the binoculars, I looked with my naked eye straight at the deer standing ten meters ahead of me. She hadn't sensed my presence, taking me for another rock on top of the mountain. Rooted on the edge of the cliff, her long neck against the horizon, she was watching the river below. There you were again. Enchanting. If I'd had a camera instead binoculars, I would have taken a picture. Let me try and describe her for you instead. A strip of yellow shot up from her white chest and streaks of orange and brown ran down her back. I have seen many foxes, wolves, and mountain goats in these parts, but I had never before come across a deer. She bore a nobility like no other wild animal. Standing fearlessly on the edge of the cliff with no concern for me at all, she was the true possessor of the mountain. I would vow that she came here straight out of ancient times. Gilgamesh hunted for this very deer five thousand years ago, Nebuchadnezzar II built the Hanging Gardens of Babylon with the inspiration that grew from the legends of this deer, Alexander the Great turned the Mesopotamian Plain upside down in his passion to find her. Now this holy deer was standing right before me. I took a breath and then another and on my third I drew my gun. I hit her in the hind leg with one shot. She was standing at the top of the cliff, she could have fallen forward, I hit her in the hind leg so she would fall back and be our feast. But the deer did not fall. She bowed her head and steadied her gaze as if catching her reflection in the water and in one last jump she shot up off her hind quarters, leaping over the cliff.

Euphrates River

Dersim, 1938

THURSDAY, AUGUST 18, 1938

My dear Miskal, it is with certainty that I have come to believe in the existence of a soul, as my body runs down, my spirit is with you in Istanbul. My body is able to bear the hardships here thanks to the joy of my spirit. We are now in the third month of the operation that was supposed to last only a few weeks and it is unclear how long it will last. The soldiers are in terrible shape. After so many days dirty, dead-tired, and often without food, we have been stripped of our humanity. Sometimes while clearing a village house we catch a reflection in the mirror and draw our guns fearing we are facing the enemy, and then steeped in silence we manage to calm down and stay still. Looking at that face gripped in fear as if it belongs to someone else, our fingers on the trigger, we have no idea who we are. I don't complain about it, but I do worry about being apart from you. I have been exposed to everything here so maybe now I will taste of death, too, but my only wish before I die would be to see you one last time. When I was with you, I used to talk so much and you would laugh, but this time I would like to be with you without saying a word, feel your presence, feel you breathing at my side. The conflict mounts and more of our soldiers are killed. I am losing my composure. I think of death more often. Death is like a photograph print on one of those old postcards, turn it over and you see what is written down. On the back of my card I always see your name. When I die, I don't want to think of any other name but yours. Let the dark curtain that falls over my eyes be in the name of Miskal. I most enjoyed being a history teacher when I was able to research your name in various languages and various ages. I haven't shared these with you, I have been saving them for our wedding night. Now with death breathing all around us, I want to write them down here. If you are reading these for the first time, I am dead. Souls are light, they say they can fly, but your name is heavy, and my soul can carry the weight of your name. Miskal comes from the Arabic word *sikal*, which means weight. In ancient times, thousands of years ago, miskal was a measure they used for gold, silver, and medicine. Now I am close to the lands of the Akkadians where four thousand years ago they, too, used your name, but they said Meshkalu. If we had lived then you would have been my beloved Meshkalu. In the language of the holy Moses you would have been called Shekel, and in the language of Jesus, Shikla. For you, I would convert to the religion of Moses or the religion of Jesus. The Phoenicians know you as Mishkal, the Syriacs and the Greeks as Siklos, and the Armenians praise your beauty with the name Mispal. There isn't a language or a religion that overlooks the holy nature of your name. It appears eight times in the Koran. You are Miskal over the lands that spread from the Balkans to Anatolia, from Iran to India. None of this is strange. The strange thing is that despite the long stretch of time, the many languages, religions, and civilizations, I never heard of another soul with such a name. Until I heard it here ten days ago. Since then I haven't slept well, I haven't picked up my journal. Tonight, I forced myself to write. Slowly I am trying to put down these words with the hope that the voices that come to me at night will subside. If I survive, I will tear out the pages that follow, I won't ever tell you the story, I will keep it to myself. But if I die, I want you to know everything, I want you to carry the secret with you on my behalf, the historian in my soul asks this of you.

TEN DAYS AGO, TUESDAY

We were ninety all told when we set out. Making our way along the Euphrates, we met up with other units, and our number rose to three hundred, not counting those soldiers we lost. We marched on with around two hundred prisoners, their numbers rising, too, as we are taking more every day. No one knew why we were doing this when the enemy was being bombarded and gassed in the caves where they had sought shelter or beheaded if taken alive. Captain Tan only knew that the order had come from headquarters in Dersim, we were to keep all prisoners alive. But you could hardly say these people were still alive. Most were women and children and they went barefoot, devastated from hunger and the deprivation that had lasted months. There was no need to know their language as they could only moan, snivel, or plead. It was unlikely the majority of them would survive, who knew how much longer the journey would last. Both the mountain and the hillsides were covered in snow and a cold north wind blew throughout the night even in the middle of summer. In the cold those some two hundred prisoners huddled together like sheep in a pen, shriveled up as they slept one on top of the other. They smelled of pus and urine. Approaching them in the dark you might think they were a herd of animals. But a beautiful girl came out of the herd like a bright diamond from a heap of coal. Soldiers from the unit we had just met seized her and took her down to the ravine where the hopeless girl was raped by dozens of soldiers. They left her body in the ravine. In the morning a woman came over to me. She had the voice of someone who might have been forty but the face of an eighty-year-old woman. Her nose and her lips were caked in blood as she struggled to speak to me through her tears. I had been learning their language for two months but crying so profusely she wasn't really saying anything, her words were all jumbled. I called over the soldier who was now acting as our guide since the guide from our unit had been killed a month ago. When Haydar saw the woman, he snapped his whip and laughed at the woman, who lowered her head in fear. Rumor was that the woman had been to see all the lieutenants last night and received a slap from every one of them, and so when she noticed my uniform, she knew that I was a lieutenant even from a distance and hurried over to me. She was the mother of the girl and she didn't want her daughter's body to be left in the wild, she wanted her to be buried. She had tried to do it herself, but they had stopped her and now she had no choice but to beg. I laughed at her, too, and pointed out the headless bodies on the opposite ridge. What difference would it make, I said, in the end the birds or the worms will eat them, they are already dead and gone, you should look to saving your own life. But when I recognized a name among her entreaties my attention was caught, this was a familiar sound. But not born of my study of Kurdish, this came from somewhere else. I couldn't be sure. I told Haydar to translate for me, every single word. Cover my Miskal so she isn't cold, the woman said. Her daughter's name was Miskal. I leapt to my feet, taking her hands in mine, and told her that she didn't have to worry, that I would do what she asked. Haydar looked at me in astonishment. I repeated myself and ordered Haydar to translate. The woman was as disbelieving as Haydar, and she asked me again. I told Haydar to take her back to the other prisoners and then come see me. Haydar was a strange soldier. Last month he had been wounded in a skirmish, falling and losing his memory. For whatever reason they didn't send him home despite his condition. Whenever Haydar had a conversation about the past, he would waver as if he were remembering something, rummaging through his mind, searching for a clue. Then he would flash his vacant smile and snap his whip at the ground. Sometimes he would pull his flute out from his bag and play for the mountains and the forests in the distance, not for us. After he left the woman, he came back to see me and asked me if I was serious about what I had told her. I knew if I didn't win Haydar over he would report me to my superiors, and if I lied it would be easy enough for him to expose me. I had no other option but to take refuge in the truth. I told him my fiancée was also named Miskal and that I felt if I was disrespectful to the dead girl I would be disrespectful to my fiancée. Without blinking his eyes, Haydar listened and then he said that he would help. I didn't think it would be that easy. In the middle of the night when the world fell silent, I set out with him to search the area; no one would pay any attention to a lieutenant going out with a private so together we went down to the ravine. Haydar knew where to find the girl's body and it wasn't long before we found her. When I looked up at the full moon shimmering above us like a lamp that seemed to have been lit for me to see her, the gentle light of the stars made the night as bright as it could be. I leaned over and looked at her face. She seemed at rest, it was good that she had died and took of the peace that came with death in a world of such pain. On her left arm was a tattoo. Do you know what angers a soldier most of all? When he doesn't find a Koran in a village home. I don't think the villagers even consider taking such things away with them, but they would surely take the picture of Holy Ali that hangs in almost every one of their homes like a flag. Like all the other villagers we met, this young girl was also an Alevi. A tattoo stretched down the upper half of her left arm, Zulfiqar, Ali's double-headed sword. I looked at her arm, the blood on her legs, she was beautiful in the moonlight. I took off my coat and laid it over her. Three thousand years ago the Greeks crossed into Anatolia to attack the Trojans and the Greek hero Achilles and the Trojan prince Hector waged the greatest battle. In the hard struggle, Hector fell, and his final wish was to receive a respectful burial, but it was not granted. His father raved for days as he did all he could to reclaim the body of his son for a proper burial, he even kissed the hand of Achilles, but only after twelve long days would he be united with the body of his son. I took the spade from Haydar and shoveled the first heap of soil on her body. I was terribly confused. I felt like I was Hector's father, the Trojan king Priam, and a hopeless mother burying her daughter. For the first time I realized my spirit had been living with you far away in Istanbul, but now as I buried this young girl, I could feel it returning to my body. And my spirit whispered into my ear so that Haydar, who was beside me, would not hear. It told me to keep in mind everything I see, it wanted me to see the evil. Third Lieutenant Adem, my spirit said, people are not the same in every place, you have become someone else as a soldier, you have forgotten that once you were the teacher Adem. Now there is no difference between you and Private Haydar; he, too, has forgotten his past identity. He is struggling to remember who he was, and you should do the same, make the effort to remember who you were, struggle to remember how you were in the past.

Merkez Efendi Cemetery

Istanbul, 1994

A crescent moon was in the sky and a warm summer breeze was blowing through the trees as Avdo and Reyhan chatted on the porch. As if they were crops cut by the harvest scythe, the stars were scattered across the sky. Tonight, the program *Song Tunnel* was on the radio, featuring songs with heavy, poignant voices. They pricked up their ears when they both recognized the voice in the next song. This was Perihan Sultan's most famous song. When it finished, the program played another one from her. Reyhan took in the sound of her mother's voice that came to her from another time, breathing in as if smoke were filling her lungs.

Avdo said, "Dear, we haven't been able to hear your mother's voice on the radio like this until today. Arabesk used to be prohibited on radio and TV, but now they are playing one song after another."

"When I was in university, I was terribly embarrassed by mom's Arabesk songs. School friends would put down

Arabesk as emotional stuff from the ghetto and there was nothing I could do. Her tapes were sold everywhere but I was reluctant to buy them, afraid someone might see me. Sometimes when I heard one her songs playing at a tape shop, I'd stop and listen to the whole song, pretending I was looking at the shopwindow. At first, I thought it might make me cry but then slowly this feeling of joy came over me. Looking at my reflection in the window, I thought I could see Mom. I looked at her tenderly and smiled, and she smiled back at me."

"You really do look like her. You know when I was little, I used to think that every child resembled his mother. Once I was in the street market in Mardin when I saw a woman who looked like me. If she looked like me, she might be my mother, I thought. So I followed her. I watched her buy tomatoes and peppers in the market and have the tinsmith fix her pan. At one point she stumbled and dropped her shopping. A few people ran over to help her up, but she had hurt her foot and was limping as she walked on. I kept following her and now I kept a close eye on her because if she fell again with that bad foot, I'd be able to catch her. I felt such love for her feet, the night after that I dreamed of falling asleep with my head resting on one foot and then on the other. Dreams move faster than reality, but reality has a surprising way of catching up with dreams. A little later she arrived home and two children, a boy and a girl, greeted her at the door. They were about my age and they looked nothing like their mother, and so nothing like me. This was a family with no resemblances, I wasn't one of them. That was maybe the first time I thought that searching for my mother was pointless. Maybe she had died, and that was why she couldn't find me."

"Dad, I also sometimes think we are dead. We have been living in this cemetery for years. What if we have already died and we still think we're alive? What if we are no different than those spirits?"

"I have had the same feeling. When I first came here, I used to wander among the graves and stop and take hold of one of those gravestones that were centuries old and ask, 'Are you my witness?' The old masters called these old gravestones *şahide*, a female witness, both a gravestone and a woman. These gravestones are the witnesses to our lives. I believe I am alive today because of them."

When *Song Tunnel* came to an end the news bulletin started. The radio presenter was giving statements from various politicians on the first anniversary of the Sivas Massacre when Reyhan said, "Dad, why didn't you let me join the protest last year?" Avdo was silent. The news broadcast that hung heavy in the air seemed to justify the reproach in Reyhan's voice. Avdo lit another cigarette and took a sip of tea. When a living soul looks at a cemetery from a distance, he might have the feeling of one death. But coming closer and wandering over the heavy earth and around the stones, he would understand that every death was a singular death.

ONE YEAR AGO

The thirty-three poets, writers, and folk singers whose names were remembered on the radio came to be known as the Sivas Dead. They had spent their lives writing books or singing folk songs, but on this unexpected day death caught them off guard. They had traveled to the city of Sivas to join the Pir Sultan Abdal Festival where they were attacked by a crowd of ten thousand people coming out from Friday prayers. The crowd trapped them in their hotel and set the building on fire. Politicians in government blamed the intellectuals and artists who had died more than the crowd that had surrounded the hotel with canisters of gasoline. Some papers claimed that a newly constructed statue of Pir Sultan Abdal had provoked religious sensitivities. When images of people chanting "Long live sharia law!" at the blazing fire and others dragging the statue of Pir Sultan Abdal through the streets of Sivas came out in the papers and were broadcast on television, the entire country shivered as if in the grip of yellow fever.

FOUR HUNDRED AND THIRTY YEARS AGO

With every passing day the Ottoman Empire was ramping up the policy of eradication that it deployed against Alevi tribes who dwelled in central Anatolia. It was a politics that fed on religious strife stretching back to the roots of Islam and its founders. To spread influence and power across Anatolia, the Ottoman palace, which upheld Sunni beliefs, accused nomadic tribes of refusing to pay taxes and poor villages of blasphemy and disobeying their edicts, and both were duly punished. Religion was the sultan, the palace, and the state. For the poor who upheld Alevi beliefs, religion was considered the center of humanity, and heaven could be achieved through the purification of the human heart along the road of life. Pir

Sultan Abdal had become the mouthpiece of the Alevi who lived on the Anatolian steppes, known for his folk songs whose lyrics articulated the idea that salvation was found in this world, not in the world beyond. Harsh criticism aimed at state bureaucrats was spreading from tongue to tongue and finally made it to the governor's mansion in Sivas. The governor was the sharp tip of the spear the Ottomans held fast in Anatolia. Worried about the revolutionary spirit the folk songs of Pir Sultan Abdal might arouse in the masses, the governor had the man arrested and brought to Sivas where he was sent to the gallows before the eyes of the public. The words of Pir Sultan Abdal, "Do not look for God in the wild / Keep your heart clean for God is close," have spread until this day, along with the fear of his lasting influence.

TODAY, NIGHT

Avdo was silent in the face of Reyhan. Since she had come to live in the cemetery, several times she wanted to go back to her former life in reaction to something she had heard on the radio, but Avdo had managed to calm her down every time. What could she do? Evildoers were everywhere, they were legion. With a stone from the mountain they struck down the bird of the plain. The mountain stone wasn't theirs, neither was the bird of the plain, but they had their sights on everything all the same. For a hundred years, a thousand years they were the same. They had bad hearts; they were sly. In the end Reyhan had her share, what was left was for her child. It made Avdo and Reyhan sad to talk about these things. The sadness was heavy, and it would surely pass. The cemetery taught them that everything came and went. Together they would look at the sky and listen to the night and when they woke in the morning, they set out to do the same work again and again.

Avdo switched off the radio. In the stillness of the night he lent his ear to a rising muffled sound. As if it was coming from among the stars, he turned his head to the sky. One by one, he ran his eyes over the constellations. Was the last zodiacal sign to be found there, the sign of the dead? The sound came to him again. Misty, distant, the familiar sound of the owl. The cry came to him from the infinite. Flying over the cemetery for ages, she was calling out to spirits, although he heard her, too, reminding him of the fleeting nature of life, which was painful, and showing him the eternal nature of death, which was wonderful. Her cry came down in waves, clinging to the trees, the stones, the earth. Touching the color of the water that ran from the fountain. The color of the night changed from blue to red, and then from green to black. The moon was a crescent moon, the wind a summer breeze, and one by one the stars broke off as if cut by a scythe in the harvest of the sky. The door opened onto the darkness. Baki appeared in his striped pajamas. Sleepily he walked over and climbed onto his granddad's lap. Curling up in his broad arms, Baki drifted back to sleep, murmuring that a bad dream had woken him and that he was afraid.

Avdo caressed his hair. "Shall I tell you a fairy tale? To help you sleep..."

"Tell me, Granddad," said Baki.

Village of Konak Görmez

Haymana Plain, 1958

The sun was falling behind the hill and the sky was nearly dark as the herd of cattle was returning to the village. Every cow knew the way home. Elif's two white cows moved slowly toward the indigo-painted house after the herdsman had left them at the entrance of the village. The last girls who had come to fill their copper kettles with water stepped away. The village was wrapped in a cool silence as the first shimmering stars were preparing to come out in the sky.

Avdo said, "Baki, I first heard this fairy tale when I was your age and learning how to make gravestones from a master."

Baki likened his past to the past of Master Avdo; he was now listening to the same fairy tale and learning how to make gravestones from this master. He was content. While he ate a cheese wrap, he listened to his master.

"Baki, you know how the wolves, the rabbits, and the foxes all live together in the wild. Well there once was an old Granny who lived out there among them, too, but she lived all on her own. The time she had left in this world was maybe long, maybe short, her home was maybe close, maybe far away. After her daughter married and left for a village on the plain, the Granny was lonely and decided to pay her daughter a visit before the coming of winter. She filled one basket with butter and another with cheese and the next day she set out in the cool, early morning. She crossed the river and made her way over the rocks and set her basket down when she arrived at the woods. There she drank water and rested. It wasn't long before a fox with an orange-red tail appeared among the trees. 'Sweet, blond Granny,' he said to the old woman, 'what are you looking for here?' When the Granny said she was on her way to see her daughter, the fox began to whimper and complain about his lot in life. He was alone, he had no one in the world, he said, if only he had a mother who would come to see him like this. Rambling on like this for a while, he finally said, 'Granny, take me with you, I can be your son.' Without a moment's hesitation, the Granny accepted the fox's offer. Ever since her daughter had left she had struggled with the idea of living alone but now she would have a son to accompany her on her journey, he was like a gift. They set out together. Now the Granny was old and weak and the baskets she carried were packed to the brim so the fox offered his help. After all, he was now her son so of course he would lighten her load. The Granny gave him a basket, and this took the strain off her muscles and bones. And they set off on their way chatting to each other. Leaving the woods, they came to a rocky meadow and the fox said that he needed to heed the call of nature. He told the Granny to keep going, in any event she walked slowly so he would have no trouble catching up to her. The Granny had taken no more than few steps when the fox disappeared behind a rock. He was so hungry that he threw open the lid of the basket and gobbled up all the butter. Then filling the basket with stones, he hurried off to catch up with the Granny. On his next break the fox secretly switched baskets and when they set out again, he played the same trick, slipping behind another rock. By now he was already full, but he was a greedy fox, and he gobbled up all the cheese in one go. When night was falling, they came to the village. At the home of the Granny's daughter the fox asked if he could go. 'Granny,' he said, 'you go in and see my sister and I will visit a few friends in the village.' 'Fine,' said the Granny and she went in through the courtyard gate and hugged her daughter with a passionate longing. As she handed her daughter the baskets, she gave her the good news, telling her all about how she had met a fox along the way and how she took him in as her own son. When the girl opened the basket lid and found nothing but stones, she said, 'Mother, this son of yours the fox has tricked you. He set you up then made a run for it, who can find him now.' The Granny stayed with her daughter for a week and full of love from her daughter she set out for home before the rains began to fall. Outside her house was a great black stone. That evening the fox came out and sat on the stone and started teasing the Granny, singing: *Blond Granny, blond Granny, what did you put in your basket? Blond Granny, hah hah hah!* He giggled as he sang. For two nights the fox came and had a grand old time singing the same song. The Granny decided to play a trick on him. During the day she prepared some tar and covered the black stone with it before going back inside to wait for her sly guest to appear. As soon as night fell the fox came back and sat down on his usual spot without noticing a thing, as the rock was now as dark as the sky. He started to sing. *Blond Granny, blond Granny, what did you put in your basket? Blond Granny, hah hah hah!* And just as he was getting up to go, he realized his tail was stuck to the rock. When the Granny flung open the door and raced out to him, the fox finally broke free but his tail remained glued to the rock as he darted away. Delighted to have seen him in such a panic, the Granny plucked his tail from the stone and took it inside where she braided it as if it were the hair of a young girl, then she decorated it with colorful beads and hung it on her wall. The next day the fox came early in the morning to beg the Granny for his tail. 'Gentle blond Granny,' he called out, 'give me back my tail. All my friends are making fun of me. You know how embarrassing it is for a fox to go about with no tail. Now they shout out rhymes behind my back: *No tail on his behind. Nothing in his mind.*' The Granny laughed when she heard this. 'So that's what they're saying then, *No tail on his behind. Nothing in his mind.*' And she laughed even more."

Finishing his cheese wrap, Baki happily jumped into the story.

"So the fox got what he deserved, well done, Granny," he cried.

"The Granny was both smarter than the fox and more merciful. Taking pity on the creature, she said she would give him back his tail on one condition. The fox said he would do anything. 'What I will ask of you is easy,' said the Granny, 'go to that goat in the mountain and bring me some of her milk. Do that and I will give you back your tail.' Happily, the fox dashed over to the goat. 'Hello, goat,' he said, 'I am in a hurry so could I please have a little milk? I will take it to the Granny, and she'll give me back my tail, and then I can join my friends again.' Now the goat was hungry and tired after spending the whole day grazing on grass in the mountains and on the hillsides. 'Brother fox,' she said, 'if you bring me some leaves from that tree down there, I will give you some milk.' The fox went over to the tree. 'Great tree,' he said, 'would you allow me to take a few of your leaves so that I can give them to the goat. I am going to bring her milk to the Granny who will give me back my tail so that I can rejoin my friends.' Rustling her long branches, the tree stretched and then told the fox to go down to the spring to fetch her some water. The fox arrived at the spring out of breath and said, 'Please could I have some of your water? I will bring it to the tree who will give me some leaves for the goat who will give me some milk and the sooner I give the milk to the Granny the sooner I'll get back my tail and rejoin my friends.' 'Oh, today I am feeling down,' said the spring, 'go and call over the girls. Have them come and sing me a song and dance and leap about in my waters. When my good cheer returns, I will give you some water.' The fox found the girls and tried to enliven them. 'Come on now, girls,' he said, 'come sing a song and dance around in the spring. I'm going to take some of her water to pour over the earth around the tree. Then I will give her leaves to the goat, and when I bring the goat's milk to the Granny, I will get my tail back and finally join my friends again.' The girls spoke as sadly as the spring. 'Our shoes are all worn out,' they said, 'bring them to the cobbler and have him fix them.' So the fox went and begged the cobbler. 'Look at the state I am in,' he cried, 'I'm all worn out from racing around. Please fix these shoes for the girls. They will sing and dance at the spring and I will take spring water to the tree. I'll give her leaves to the goat and bring her milk to the Granny. When she gets the milk, she'll give me back my tail and then I'll be able to play with my friends again. With no tail they make fun of me.' The cobbler was a poor old man. 'I am hungry,' he said, 'fetch me a few eggs from the chickens, I haven't had a bite to eat since morning.' The fox politely approached the chickens and said, 'Dear chickens, my friends, I have a task at hand and so here I am at your feet. For the first time I must ask you a favor. Would you grant me a pair of your glorious eggs, not for me but for the cobbler? He will repair the shoes of the girls and they will sing and leap about in the spring. I will take her water and water the earth around the tree and then I will take her leaves to the goat. When I bring her milk to the Granny, she will give me back my tail and at long last I will be able to play with my friends again.' The chickens pecked on the ground and then told him what they wanted. 'Go to the harvest,' they said, 'and ask the farmers for a little wheat. You have been very kind to us so don't forget to be kind to them.' Now the fox was truly tired, and out of breath. 'Esteemed farmers,' he panted, 'could I ask you for a little bit of wheat, not for me, as you know I don't eat wheat, for the chickens, I am trying to do what they have asked of me. In return they will give me eggs, not for me, they will go to the cobbler and he will fix the shoes of the girls who will dance around the fountain and sing. With water from the fountain, I will quench the tree's thirst and then I will fill the goat's belly with her leaves and take the goat's wonderful milk to the Granny. When she gives me back my tail, I will be the happiest fox in the meadow, and I will be able to join my friends again like it once was.' But the farmers were not having a good day and were not very friendly with the fox, they chased him away. 'What a wily fox,' they said, 'he takes us for fools, he comes right up to us to play his trick, who knows what he had in mind.' They threw rocks after the fox as he ran away."

Baki was saddened to hear about the Granny's fate but now equally saddened to hear what had happened to the fox.

"Look at what the poor fox has been through. The trickster deserves something, but this is surely too much. Who will help him?"

"Don't worry about him, Baki. The fox doesn't need anyone, he always finds a way out. That's just what happened this time. After the farmers chased him away, he hid behind a hill and waited for night to fall. Then when everything was dark, he came out. 'Help, help, a wolf is on the way. He's going to eat your sheep and your donkeys, save your animals,' he cried out, stirring everyone to action. Hearing his piercing cry, the farmers reached for their axes and pitchforks and raced over to their herds. The fox then quietly slipped into the harvest. 'What am I to do,' he said, 'this is the language you understand.' In one fell swoop, he scattered before the chickens the wheat he had collected, and he brought their eggs to the cobbler. After feasting on the eggs, the cobbler fixed the shoes for the girls who sang their merry songs and leapt in the waters of the spring. The fox then watered the roots of the tree with crystal-clear water and gave her leaves to the goat. But when he came to the Granny's house with her milk, the Granny was nowhere to be seen. For she had gone to the forest to look after a cow who was about to give birth. The fox climbed through an open window and took his tail down from the wall where it was hanging. In wonder he gazed at the plaits and all the colorful beads, his tail looked spectacular. He thanked the Granny for this, and he drank half the milk he had brought, leaving the other half for her.

"Then merrily singing he put on his tail and went to see his friends. They looked at him in astonishment and said he looked like the Fox Prince in the fairy tales and then they asked him where he got such a fancy tail. 'Oh, my friends,' said the fox, 'you made fun of me when you sang *No tail on his behind. Nothing in his mind* and I was hurt, but I will do you a favor all the same. Do you know where I got this tail? The lake right down there, that's where. At the bottom are many beautiful tails. Oh, if only I could have swum down to the very bottom as that's where you will find the most beautiful one. You know me, I'm a little lazy and I didn't want to go down that deep.' The other foxes then raced to the lake and jumped in and tried swimming down to the very bottom. But they nearly drowned as they didn't really know how to swim. And when they finally surfaced they were full of regret. Seeing them like that the fox let out a hearty laugh and from that day on he was a little wiser and kinder, and he went on to live a happier life. And many an old woman got her share of the happiness, too."

Merkez Efendi Cemetery

Istanbul, 1995

Reyhan spent the evening rereading a letter she had received from Süreyya. Then closing herself up in her room, she began to write her back. Since Süreyya had left for France they had been corresponding regularly. Avdo sat alone on the porch while she worked on her letter. With a cigarette in his hand, he lent his ears to the sound of the night as he waited for the sleep fairy to come to him on her way through the neighborhood.

As a yellow star shot west from the southern sky Avdo tried to make out its sound, like when he was little. From his master in Mardin, he had learned how to imagine the sound of a star. The sound came to him in waves and through the layers of the sky to mingle with the water of the fountain. So those who drank this water because they believed it was holy and healed them or led them to enlightenment were right. The Redbud Fountain was nourished by the tears of people and was cleansed with the purity of souls that forgot evil when they died. Avdo saw the yellow star fade without leaving a single flash of lighted dust, and when it was gone, he made a wish.

Today he had completed a monumental task. He had finished the gravestone he had been working on for years. He brought it to the Man with Seven Names and mounted it above his head. While reading the man's journal or losing himself in memory, Avdo sometimes thought he might not find the spirit of the stone and this led him into hopelessness. After giving shape to many different stones over the seasons and imagining new designs on sleepless nights, he had finally come back to the beginning, understanding that the stone he had considered on the first day was the stone that reflected the soul of this man. Knowing was one thing, understanding was another. He knew the first stone he made was right for the soul of the Man with Seven Names, but he could not understand. For that he would have to give up the stone in hand and set out on a journey, crossing seven valleys, giving shape to a new stone in every valley; and only then would he come to the startling realization that the stone in hand was the stone he had first imagined. Like it was told in the legends. The gravestone was black and in the darkness were white spots like the stars of the Milky Way. In the center was a small hole that drew in all the stars and swallowed them. Bring your eye closer to the hole and you fall into that vast abyss; and in the tumult, you might think that God has seen you. And looking at the hole from the other side you see but nothing. In the dark hole that had swallowed all the stars was either God or nothingness. As he wandered from city to city throughout his life, the Man with the Seven Names remained suspended between these two.

Since Avdo had finished the task that had so occupied his mind, he was now free to start working on his own gravestone.

Had it been thirty years? When he came here to find Elif's grave, he had set aside the empty plot beside her for himself, throwing a little extra soil on the ground and mounting a plain stone above it. Even on that night he knew he would spend the rest of his life here, and that he would die here. When visitors passed by that plot, they assumed a body lay there in the earth, they had no idea that indeed in that ground lay a living spirit. The white marble that had come down through the ages stood plainly at the head of the grave. Perhaps there was no need for Avdo to make himself a new gravestone. This stone fit his death. Smooth, simple. No need for any script. As white as mother's milk. Every morning the shadow of Elif's gravestone rose up like a cypress tree, falling over the white marble, it was enough, it was all Avdo needed.

As he turned the radio dial, he felt the need for tea. He opened the lid of the pot that had been resting on the table for hours and looked inside: a little tea left on the bottom. He filled his glass. He knew the cold tea wouldn't melt sugar but tossed three cubes into his glass all the same. He turned his attention to the news running on the radio: With the dissolution of the coalition government a political crisis was rocking the markets; businessman Vahit Koçsanlı was calling for the administration to calmly overcome the crisis in a period of economic growth; according to reports the crisis might very well lead to the collapse of the government; nearly half of the governorships in the country were opposing the republic in an outward expression of religious fundamentalism; more than one hundred and fifty thousand workers were now on strike; in an uprising at the Buca Prison three political convicts had died; the value of the American dollar had surpassed forty-eight thousand lira.

Avdo peered into the darkness and murmured a song he used to sing in Elif's village.

Oh beloved, on the journey to your heart,
A journey lasts as long as a lifetime,
Oh beloved, I am an orphaned bird after your cart,
A lifetime lasts as long as a journey.

It wasn't for naught that he loved the darkness. There he sang to the souls, pouring out his heart and listening to their sorrows. As they went down to a sinless place beneath the earth, they still had ears on the world above and they nurtured the hope of coming back again. Like new convicts in prison, they moaned and wailed at nightfall. They assumed they would see God when they died so they begged Him, but He simply would not come, they waited and waited and finally came to believe they had never died and that God would not come, they had merely slipped into a dream from which they would soon wake. They counted mornings, nights, months, seasons, but they could not wake up. Our God, they cried, have You forsaken us in this moist earth? If You do exist, then come and show us mercy. If You do not exist, then where have we come and where are we going? Our God.

Sitting through these thoughts, Avdo forgot all about his tea. He picked up his glass, drank half, breathed, and then finished the rest. He decided to get up and go for a walk. Passing among the frogs hopping in all directions at the sound of his footsteps, he went to the fountain and took a handful of water. He splashed it over his hair and beard. He slowly walked to Elif's grave. He stood at her side. "Elif, it seems the sleep fairy has forgotten about me tonight." He turned and walked past his workshop and stood in front of a grave in the back. On the stone at the head of the grave were nine drawings of dog teeth. One was for Toteve, one for Apostle, and the others were for their mother and her other puppies. Avdo placed his palm on the engraving that represented Toteve's tooth. To give the dog his scent. If he waited there any longer tears would well up in his eyes. He pulled back his hand and walked west in the direction of the mosque. Before he came to the wall on that side of the cemetery, he stopped in front of a little grave where the two-year-old daughter of the Registry Office manager Selim Bey lay. If she had lived, she would be turning twelve, maybe she would have gone to the same school as his grandson, Baki. There they would only have seen each other at the breaks, would never really get to know each other. Growing older they would move to different neighborhoods, go to different schools, find different jobs, and they would forget each other altogether. Then one day they would happen to run into each other and looking into each other's eyes they would have the sense that they knew each from somewhere but could not be sure where. Catching the sweet fragrance left from childhood, they would ask each other questions about their past, their memories coming back to life. Under the spell of that fragrance, they would find the connection of their shared past to the present and vow to never part for the rest of their lives. They would move into a house together, visit places they had marked on a map together, get old and gray together. Then one day after walking slowly through a park they would sit down for a rest and the daughter of the Registry Office manager would take Baki's bony hand and say, "Do you know I died when I was two years old, if I hadn't I would have had a beautiful life with you."

Avdo walked to the southern half of the cemetery. A cool night breeze blew in from the sea. Maybe it was the sleep fairy that brought the coolness. Avdo knelt beside a grave where the Blond Sailor's father lay. "Hello, Old Sailor," he said. "It's been quite some time since I last came to you. The world's the same as you left it. Maybe worse, I can't say, but clearly not getting any better. You bonded with the past as you knew that the future would only get worse. All your life you carried in you the sweetheart of your youth. Your son tells me that I'm like you. If that's what he says, then it must be true." Taking a handful of soil, Avdo looked to the west. Even in the dark he knew the cemetery like the back of his hand, his foot never caught a stone, he never took a wrong step. Blindfolded, he could walk with the same ease. He came to Madlen's grave and stopped. He did the math. "You have been here for eighty years," he said, casting the soil from his hand. "Have this, I brought it to you from the Old Sailor. He was your young sailor when you loved him. Later you died and remained eternally young, and he had to bear the great burden of old age without you. Don't think it's easy, I know myself, man is like that god from the Greek legend, tied to a rock and the wild birds come to eat out his liver. You sleep and you think the pain will subside but the next morning you find yourself bound to the same rock." With Madlen, Avdo always spoke Armenian. He put his hand on her gravestone, he ran his fingers over the Arabic letter *mim* and the engraving of a broken rose. "My Armenian is really quite rusty," he said. "If not for you, I would have forgotten it altogether. I'll be going now but the next time I come I'll take a handful of this soil for the Old Sailor."

Avdo remembered he had left the radio playing on the porch. Fearing it might wake Reyhan, he hurried inside. When he got there, he saw it had already been switched off. When had he done that? He couldn't remember. Everywhere was silence. All around was the stardust sprinkled by the sleep fairy. So, the fairy had come when Avdo stepped away. When she could not find him, she scattered blue dust everywhere. Avdo turned off the light on the porch. He took off his shoes, his coat. Throwing a blanket over his body, he stretched out on the divan. His eyelids grew heavy, and, as they were falling, he thought of the beauty of the gravestone he had finished that day and slowly he slipped into a dream where he approached the hole in the black gravestone of the Man with Seven Names. He slid through like a shooting star.

Mardin

Mesopotamian Plain, 1939

WEDNESDAY, SEPTEMBER 20, 1939

This journal has been in my possession for the past year. Its true owner, Third Lieutenant Adem Giritli, died last year in a skirmish on the bank of the river Euphrates. When the shooting suddenly started that night, we immediately took cover behind a stone. The conflict didn't last long but when it was over, I saw Adem Giritli stretched out on the ground. He had taken a bullet in the back. Was the real enemy behind us as we fired ahead into the darkness? I leaned over and took his hand. I could make out only two words as he whispered to me before he took his last breath. "Miskal" and "journal." I took his journal from his bag and tucked it away in my coat. For the past year I have been reading what he had written here nearly every day. In the quiet corners and shadowy recesses of these pages, I have been struggling to find those sides of Third Lieutenant Adem he would not share with others, and among those shadows I am searching for some trace of my own self, some kind of a sign. You see they played a trick on me when I was in the military: All the lieutenants—save Third Lieutenant Adem—were friendly enough to my face but the moment I was gone they teased me behind my back. They kept my true identity a secret from me when they knew who I really was. I had lost my memory and I needed help. Just one word would have been enough for me to find my way, and that word was my real name, but they wouldn't tell me that truth. They told me my name was Haydar but later I came across an old villager who said that I was Ali. A name was more than just a word, it meant another past, it meant an entirely different person. Haydar was a soldier who carried a whip while Ali was a poor villager. Which one was I? Was I one of them? Was I both? Neither? I had no idea how to find myself, so I fled, scaling mountains and fording rivers until I came to the city of Mardin. But I am leaving this place, too. I am leaving before the war that has broken out in Europe comes here. Now I am on the road to Damascus, making my way to Jerusalem. Will the war come that far? If it does, I will find somewhere else to go.

Miskal Hanım! Over the past year I tried everything I possibly could to remember my past. I went to the shrines of saints, I tied cloth to holy trees, I prayed in the mosques and churches. When the medicine the doctors gave me made no difference, I banged my head against the wall. I could remember nothing of either Ali or Haydar so I figured I could only try to become someone else. In a church one day I lit a candle and gave myself the name İsa. One's name is given by others. But I am a poor soul with the ill-fate of having to choose his own name, it is the source of my poverty. My head filled with a thousand thoughts, sometimes I say to myself: If I cannot remember my past then who is to say that I am not Third Lieutenant Adem. Maybe it's why I carry this journal with me. When I was wounded in a conflict, maybe my brain was shaken, and I couldn't be sure of the man shot dead beside me. Was he Haydar or Third Lieutenant Adem? Who was I? Forgetting my real name, I deserted my unit. Now it is night. By the light of a gas lamp, I am writing these words in a cemetery. The sky above me is filled with stars. We all have our own star in the sky, or so they say here. Only my star is lost; out of place, it is wandering through the void. I am searching for my own star. Dear Miskal Hanım, am I your fiancé? If I am, wait for me. Wait until I find the place of my star in the sky. I will come back to you. We will have our wedding. And move into our house with a large garden on the coast of Bebek. We will have the most beautiful children. And give each one a version of your own name as it appeared over the ages. Now as I write these lines, I can see it all coming to life before my eyes, except your face. If I cannot recognize you when I get there, how will I know that I love you? In place of struggling to remember who I am perhaps I should try remembering your face. For the moment I do, I will be sure of myself, and of you, and I will come running. Wait for me until that day.

Damascus

French Mandated Syria, 1940

WEDNESDAY, MAY 22, 1940

Miskal Hanım, the lady who is anticipating my arrival in Istanbul! I am now eight months into my journey to Jerusalem, a journey I thought would last only three months. From Aleppo, I passed through Hama and Homs on the Asi River and winter was upon us when I arrived in Damascus. I was so thin, nothing but flesh and bones. I fell on the street and when I opened my eyes, I found myself in a French military hospital, there were doctors and nuns racing everywhere. For weeks I lay in bed recovering as Sister Rakel tended to me; she was expecting me to die, as was I. The interest Sister Rakel and the doctors showed in me was born of their belief that I was a Syrian who had fled from Hatay Province. The province had once belonged to Syria and when it became a part of Turkey last summer many fled, and they took for me for one of the refugees. When I left the hospital, the many flags I saw were symbols of

Hatay's persistence, an indirect expression of a longing for independence from the French mandate. Even I, who was very much a stranger to these parts, could sense France's waning power in Syria, for at home they were under attack by the Germans. I could no longer stay in the hospital, for if I did, I would have surely died. Lying in bed and listening to those loud radio broadcasts of the growing war in Europe every day was like listening to the voice of an angel of death. One day we heard that Hitler and Mussolini had formed a pact which meant the war would spread; on another day we heard that Hitler had taken Denmark and Norway. Whenever we heard his rising voice, we knew that the German army was on a new path, to France, to Holland, to Belgium, to Luxembourg. One morning I woke up fearing I might see German soldiers marching on the street outside the hospital. But keeping my faith in my journey, I set out for Jerusalem yesterday and felt such relief the moment I did. Now I have regained my strength, my breathing is strong, and my legs are like steel. I should reach Jerusalem within the month. I am walking faster than the soldiers. My load is light, my goal is clear. My hope is to find myself on this journey. Saint Paul found himself along the same road. While I was in the hospital, I heard the story again from Sister Rakel, the story I had first heard from Master Dikran.

ONE THOUSAND NINE HUNDRED AND FIVE YEARS AGO Paul was born and raised in the city of Tarsus, one of the most important Roman cities in the region. In his youth, he traveled to Jerusalem where he received a Judaic education, and when he joined the Pharisee movement his talents quickly drew attention. Jerusalem had been under Roman control for many years and with every passing day the Jewish community was assimilating Roman culture. While the Pharisees opposed this growing tendency, the Sadducean sect accepted this cultural shift. Sadducees found support among the elite segment of society, while the Pharisees were broadly accepted by the lower classes; on many issues both political and religious the two sects were set apart. Although the Sadducees' beliefs were based on the first written Torah, the Pharisees also adopted scriptures that were written down after being passed on orally for generations. While the Pharisees emphasized immortality, the Sadducees did not believe in resurrection after death. Conflicting interpretations of holy scripture also distinguished the two groups. While the Sadducees interpreted "an eye for an eye" as the measure for punishment, the Pharisees felt it was sufficient to pay a fee for the compensation of a crime. In a time when the Jewish community was wrestling with such fervent issues that were deeply impacting daily life, they would also have to reckon with a new and emerging prophet by the name of Jesus and his followers. As the Sadducees and the Pharisees argued with each other on the matter of how to punish those who chose to follow Jesus, a judge by the name of Paul rose to prominence as he traveled from city to city bestowing punishment on sinners. Two years after Jesus had been put on the cross it was time for the Christians in Damascus to be punished. Paul set out from Jerusalem. While he was on the road to Damascus he was blinded by a light and then heard a voice. It was the light and voice of the Holy Jesus. For three days Paul was in darkness, and when he opened his eyes, he saw the truth and claimed that he had found himself through divine enlightenment. His decision was to carry on living as one of the most devout followers of Christianity. Once renowned for the way he punished sinners, he was now known for his bond to Jesus, indeed some even said he was the apostle to come after the first twelve. Sister Rakel also told me that everyone has their own road to Damascus, she said that I would find myself there, that one day I would no doubt be enlightened with the light of truth. She believed in the miracle of Saint Paul, she believed in my suffering.

TODAY, EVENING

As I think of myself now I can see how Third Lieutenant Adem Giritli found his own road to Damascus. In a place so rife with blood and death, he came to his senses when he knew that he had to bury the body of a village girl who went by the name Miskal to protect her from the cold wrath of the world, only then did he remember who he was. From that day on, he treated me well, he protected me from the others. I started to feel better. If he had lived maybe I would have succeeded in reaching my own light with his help. My work was left undone. I grew increasingly confused. I truly lost myself. And maybe now here in these pages, I will find the memory I lost on the shore of the Euphrates, I will remember that I am Third Lieutenant Adem Giritli. Dear Miskal, I do not wish to be blinded by light on this journey I have undertaken and hear the holy voice of Jesus, I only wish to see your face. Then I would come running to

Istanbul, no matter how many people the city might contain, for I would recognize you in the crowd and step over to those blue eyes that are as blue as the sea of Istanbul and take you in my arms. We would embrace. And then holding hands, we would set out for the coast. In İstinye we would walk along the promenade we used to take and watch ships on the Bosphorus and look over at Kanlıca on the opposite shore. You would hum the words to a popular European song, and I would tell you everything that happened to me.

Jerusalem

British Mandated Palestine, 1945

TUESDAY, JUNE 12, 1945

Light of my eyes, Miskal Hanım! The Jewish cemetery I can see through my window is treeless and bare. In such a cemetery you can sense the restlessness of its souls. I long for those trees in the cemetery in Mardin and their shadows that lay over souls. Today I played the flute on the street and wandered through neighborhoods that are hostile to each other, but I am an enemy to no one, and I made good money. These days the evening sun sets late. When it fell this evening, I came here to the Akdeniz Hotel where I am staying. Now I am sitting at the window and looking out over the cemetery. When I introduce myself as Musa—meaning Moses—Jews, Christians, Muslims from all corners of the city show kindness toward me and tell me how much they love the name. Everyone greets me with holy words, and I return the greeting with plain and pure layman speech. For I do not know God's place in language.

How can I know where God lies when I do not know my own self? That day will come, too. The day when I find my own old self, the day I will find the God I once believed in. For the two are connected. God should name me. He should give me a sign that points to that name. I have no other expectation. We should have no other expectations from God. But the people of Jerusalem think otherwise. As followers of different religions, they fight and bicker and forbid each other from passing through their streets. Hitler has died, Mussolini, too, the war in Europe has ended, and yet Jerusalem, a city that has managed to stay far from the fire of war for six long years, is still in the grips of this internal conflict. This city, which has had to endure countless wars over the long run of history under Assyrian, Roman, and Ottoman rule, has now fallen into British control and it does not seem as if the struggles will end. While each section of Jerusalem claims sovereignty, the claims are not put forward with words but with guns, each party insisting that this page in history will take their side. I avoided the world war here in relative safety but now I feel that everything is coming to an unforeseen obstacle, and I have my sights on the road again. I want to keep far away from trouble and think only of the search for myself. I am reading in the evening but recently I have also taken to pouring over maps. In the atlas of the world, I am searching for a new city and a new name. I will send you a beautiful postcard from wherever that place may be, Miskal Hanım.

After religion the most talked about subject here is history. Thinking it might help me find myself, I am reading along with everyone else and joining in their discussions. I am considering the next religion I will choose. I am learning so much but still fear that I might never discover who I really am. What if I never remember my past? What will I do, Miskal Hanım? What will you do there without me? Time is as fast as a stone falling from the sky and it will not stop, it will not wait for us. Should I think of this in another way? In ancient times the crusading soldiers that came to Jerusalem would stay away from home for ten, twenty years, and over such a length of time their families would lose all hope. Often when a soldier returned home, his loved ones would not even recognize his face, finding nothing of the young man who had left for the war so many years ago, and as his opinions and manners had changed so much over the journey, it took time for them to get used to each other again. With this in mind, some crusaders chose to return to their home countries in a surprisingly different way. Instead of returning to his village and his life that was poor, a soldier might return to the family of a soldier who had died who'd had a better lot in life. Before the expecting family, he would present himself with the name of the dead soldier. Astonished, they would say, how much you have changed over time, we hardly recognize you, and he would say the same. The soldier would then go to bed with a woman who had waited for him for all those years. More than anyone, she wanted to believe it was him, indeed she was afraid not to believe so much. Feelings of doubt, hesitation, and then acceptance of the family would move along a fine line but then would settle over time and everyone became convinced. Pleased that the great warrior had finally returned, they would have a celebration. It was better to change a little and form a bond with a man who had come to them than to grieve the loss of a man who had been away for so long and was never to return. This was life, weaving a web in myriad ways. It is the same today as it was a thousand years ago. I have been struggling to remember my past for years, Miskal Hanım, imagining that I am your fiancé, Adem Giritli, who is dreaming of a shared future that we will weave together. How much more will I imagine? Why will I not rise now and come to you? What if indeed I came and could not recognize you, like a Crusader who had not seen his wife in years, and if you, as a woman waiting all those years for the return of her beloved, struggled to know me. In little time we would understand the difficulty came not from ourselves but from the dust sprinkled on us from the breeze we know as time, isn't that so? We look into each other's eyes on the first day and sit together on the day after that and on the third day there will be no strangeness between us, and we will smile. Like it was in the old days.

Cairo

British Occupied Egypt, 1952

THURSDAY, JULY 24, 1952

My dearest Miskal Hanım, I managed to escape from Egypt on a ship that set out this morning. I have been fine over the last six years in Cairo where I made many friends—thanks to them I made it out of the city. I was planning to stay in Cairo for longer until everything took a dramatic turn yesterday. A group of soldiers rose up to challenge both King Farouk and the British. They are demanding the king's resignation and an end to the British occupation. While I am fearful there will be bloodshed, everyone here is welcoming the uprising as a holiday, flooding out onto the streets, including my friends. They have no reservations about the pain that will come with war; indeed, they don't seem to care. Who knows what tomorrow will bring? I searched for the quickest way to leave the country and found this ship at the port in Alexandria. Her name is *White Wind* and as she drew out of the harbor, I watched the receding shore from the deck and only when I was quite sure that we were on our way did I come down to my cabin where I now write these lines. The ship will make several ports of call in the Mediterranean, and in one—I have not decided yet which one—I will disembark. But first this restless feeling in me must pass. Yesterday I was overcome by the strangest thought when I was out among all those people racing through the streets. What if such chaos caused a similar disturbance in my mind and suddenly I remembered my past? It was a beautiful thought but with it rose another idea: What if in remembering my past, I came to see that I was not Third Lieutenant Adem Giritli but someone else? What if I am not the person I am dreaming to be? The thought struck me as I was walking past a garden. Despite the crowd that surged around me, I stopped and leaned against a wall. No, I said, I can't be anyone else. Miskal Hanım! My soul belongs to you, and I will accept no other past but the one in which I am your Adem. Remembering is meaningful if it is remembering you. I want to remember nothing else. Without you I am a stranger to myself. My dream of being a part of your life is enough, and it is better that I stay the way I am. Like this I could spend a lifetime. I could think of you every night and fall asleep with the hope that I might see your face in my dreams.

Merkez Efendi Cemetery

Istanbul, 2002

On the day Baki went to register at the Department of Economics at Bosphorus University, the weather was oppressively hot and humid. The sun seemed to grow larger and larger in the sky. Avdo had been spending the day chiseling marble in his workshop when he felt dizzy and suddenly his nose started bleeding. He called out to Reyhan who helped him onto the porch where she had him lie down on the divan. The bleeding stopped but Avdo still felt dizzy and he closed his eyes as if he were going to take an afternoon nap. Reyhan raced over to the clinic across from the cemetery and hurried back with the doctor she had been consulting over the years. When he heard their voices, Avdo looked up at them blankly as if he didn't recognize them. He briefly answered the doctor's questions.

The doctor took Avdo's blood pressure, he checked his eyes, ears, and throat, he listened to his heart. He took a syringe out of his bag and prepared an injection. He said

Avdo was having problems with his blood pressure and that he needed to go to a hospital where he could have a compete checkup.

“I’m not going to a hospital,” Avdo grumbled, “I had a nosebleed, that’s all, no need to make a fuss over that. The summer has been especially hot this year. When I was little, I always used to get nosebleeds in the heat.”

Reyhan was familiar with her father’s bad temper. If he had a backache or cramps in his stomach, he would under no circumstances go to a doctor, Reyhan having to make do with any medicine she could find at a pharmacy, and even then Avdo would stop taking it after a couple of days.

“Doctor, don’t mind my dad,” said Reyhan, “just tell me the medicine he needs, and I’ll go pick it up.”

“I’ll write you a prescription, but you mustn’t neglect going for a full checkup. Have them look at his heart and his brain.”

“My dad’s been forgetful recently, mixing up names. In fact, last week he forgot whose gravestone he was making.”

“Now that’s another reason to go to the hospital, our health is no joke.”

“Could you also write a prescription for his absentmindedness?”

“How long has he had such a problem?”

“It used to happen now and then, but it’s become more common over the last two months. I insist on going to the doctor and then he always says it’s just the summer heat and that he’ll pull himself together once the season passes.”

“All right then, I’m writing down four different prescriptions, but he has to remember to take them all.”

Baki arrived not long after the doctor had left. His face beaming with a smile, he held out his new university student card.

Reyhan hugged him and said, “Congratulations, son.”

Baki sensed something was off. “What’s up, Mom?”

“I’m fine, but your granddad’s feeling a little uncomfortable. He’s sleeping inside.”

“What’s wrong?” said Baki anxiously. “Let’s take him to the hospital.”

Reyhan asked him to sit on the divan and told him what had happened.

Men Avdo’s age usually only ever left home to go to a mosque, and when even that would have proved difficult Avdo spent the whole day in his workshop, figuring his vigorous body was no different than marble. He looked healthy and strong, but lately his body was showing new signs. An hour after eating, he would forget and go eat again, coming to his senses only when Reyhan had noticed. He sometimes took a nap in the daytime, something he had never done before.

“Mom, I’ll be leaving you with Granddad when I move into the dorm. You shouldn’t stay here either, it wouldn’t be right for Granddad. Let’s rent a place in the neighborhood, and you can move there. If Granddad really wants to, he can come here and work. I realize he’ll never give up on his gravestones.”

“You can talk to him about it if you want,” said Reyhan. “He doesn’t listen to me. Whenever I suggest moving out, he gives me the same answer. He says, okay, girl, let’s do it, you can move, and I’ll come and visit you, but I won’t leave the cemetery.”

“Can I go in and check on him?”

"He'll be happy to see you when he wakes up. Go and sit with him and I'll go to the pharmacy and get his medicine."

Baki went inside and sat down. Despite the heat outside, the room was cool. There was no other sound except Avdo's deep breathing.

Baki looked at his grandfather's right hand that lay on his chest. The large bony hand was covered in wrinkles and veins. Baki had never noticed so many wrinkles on his skin before. He leaned closer and looked at the lines on his face. There were layers of wrinkles on the edge of his brow and at corners of his eyes. Baki had the impression his grandfather would soon wake up and go to his workshop, as he always did without paying heed to any warnings. He put his hand on his grandfather's hand. Like he used to do when he was little. Some nights he woke up his grandfather instead of his mother and, embracing him, Baki found a sense of security in his presence. When kids in the neighborhood school talked about family heroes, Baki always spoke of his grandfather.

"My lion," said Avdo, opening his eyes, "so you're here. Did you register at school?"

"Yes, Granddad."

Baki took out his ID and held it up for him to see. Avdo studied the front and the back of the card. Admiring Baki's sharp gaze, Avdo kissed the photograph as tears filled his eyes.

"I'm proud of you," he said. "There's no need for me to worry about you anymore. I was afraid your mother would always be alone, but you grew up to be a strapping young lad. You can look after each other."

"Granddad," said Baki with some reproach in his voice. "What kind of talk is that, as if you are going to leave us . . ."

"I'm not going to do that, my health is just fine. You're a university student now, that's all I'm saying."

"Your health is fine, but I think you now know that you have to be careful about the way you live."

"In fact, you are the one who needs to be careful," said Avdo. "Don't go and get wrapped up in politics at the university. You're the only one your mother has. We listen to the news every day on the radio, and there are incidents one after the other. Look to your schoolwork and keep a good relationship with your teachers."

"Don't worry, Granddad, I always follow your advice."

"In this life I have always been a *gavsono*, Baki, and your mother has lived a hard life here. I don't want you to turn out like us."

"What does *gavsono* mean, Granddad?"

"It's a word that comes from my childhood. It means 'refugee' in Syriac. Lose your footing once and you are blown near and far, full of sadness wherever you might find yourself. That's how I lived, and I'm telling you not to live the same way."

"Granddad, wouldn't it be better if you and Mom lived in healthier conditions? The summer is almost over and soon I'll be moving into the dorm at the university. If only you would move out of this place. What if we rented a house on the other side of the mosque, a house with central heating that's cool in the summer, how nice, you could live there with Mom."

"We've already talked about this. You know I can't leave the cemetery."

"You need to break from this place, Granddad, you can come here a couple of times a week to work, but you can't keep up your old pace, it's bad for your health."

“Is your mother giving you these ideas?” Avdo smiled at the worried look on Baki’s face.

“These are my ideas. Is it really that hard to take a suggestion?”

“Where’s your mother? Why doesn’t she tell me this herself?”

“She went to the pharmacy to get your medicine. The doctor gave us four different prescriptions. Please stick to the schedule, Granddad, or you’ll upset Mom.”

“Pour me a glass of water.”

Baki filled a glass and brought it over to Avdo, who drank and then stretched out again. He was feeling tired. He closed his eyes. His breathing deepened.

“Are you all right, Granddad?” asked Baki.

“I am fine,” said Avdo, opening his eyes. “There’s a bag under the bed, would you give it to me.”

Baki leaned over and pulled out the bag.

“What’s in here?” he asked.

“Photographs, of you and your mother, some newspaper clippings, and a notebook that was a journal. Could you take that out?”

“Do you keep a journal, Granddad?”

“I don’t have the talent for that,” said Avdo, “it belonged to an old friend. In fact, before that, it belonged to someone else. It’s a little complicated.”

“I’m curious.”

“It’s a strange journal, how can I put this, there’s a beginning but no end. Or it might be better to say just the opposite, that would be more correct, there is an end but no beginning.”

Baki started flipping through the pages.

Emirgan

Istanbul, 2002

Baki was wandering the streets of Emirgan, asking people where he could find Salkımlı Street, but no one knew. No one had ever heard of the Cevher Mansion either. In a city where addresses rarely stayed the same for as long as sixty or seventy years, Baki decided his last hope was to find the post office. But the civil servants there could find no record of either the street or a manor that went by the name of Cevher Mansion. But there was an apartment building on Fatih Street that was registered as Cevher. Making the decision to try whatever information he had at hand, Baki dove back into the streets and soon he found the building with the words Cevher Apartments written over an iron gate with a flowery design. Maybe the mansion once stood on this spot before it was torn down and replaced with this four-story building with the eponymous name. Baki stepped into the garden and walked to the front door where he read the names written over the doorbells, no sign of Miskal Hanım's family name, Durusu. Indeed, it would have been surprising to find the same family still living here after the street name had changed, the mansion demolished and replaced with a modem apartment building, after a lifetime had gone by.

The wide garden that belonged to the building was still green despite the cold north wind of October. Beside redbuds and tall cedars, a silvery linden stretched up into the sky. Freshly cut grass covered the ground. After taking in the beauty of the garden, Baki was just turning around when someone called out to him from among the trees.

"Were you looking for someone?"

"I was looking for the home of Miskal Hanım, but it seems I have come to the wrong address."

"You have come to the right place."

"Really?" said Baki with an amazement that came at the end of a tiring day.

"Yes, Miskal Hanım lives on the top floor. What have you come to see her about? I am the caretaker of the building. I keep an eye on who comes and goes, neighborhood crime has been on the rise recently."

"I see, I have a journal that belongs to Miskal Hanım, I was hoping to give it to her."

"Come in then, they are home today."

It was a Saturday and Baki had decided to spend the weekend in Emirgan on a trail inspired by the journal he had read so often over the past two months that he had practically memorized its contents. So instead of going off to see his mother and grandfather that morning he left his dorm for Emirgan. Now he carried the journal with him wherever he went, as if it were one of his primary course books of the school he had just started, and over time he came to believe the journal belonged not to Third Lieutenant Adem Giritli nor the Man with Seven Names, but that its true owner was Miskal Hanım, and she needed to see it.

Not long after he pressed the doorbell, which twittered in birdsong, a middle-aged woman appeared on the threshold.

Baki smiled at her respectfully.

"Good day, I'm sorry to disturb you like this, but I was hoping to see Miskal Hanım," he said.

"Is that so?" said the woman with a light, attentive smile. Looking over her shoulder, she called inside. "Miskal Hanım! You have a guest, can you come over to the door?"

How old could she be? Considering the dates in the journal, the woman had to be well over eighty. How strange then that the woman who had opened the door had called her over instead of inviting Baki to come inside.

A young woman appeared at the door and said, "Yes?"

"I was hoping to see Miskal Hanım," Baki said, who was expecting to be greeted by an older woman.

"That's me," said the young woman.

"It seems . . ." said Baki, his voice trembling, "it seems there's been a mistake, I was looking for Miskal Durusu."

The two women looked at each other. "Oh, you're asking about my mother," said the older woman with a surprised look on her face. "She has been dead for some time now. What was the issue?"

The web of thoughts in Baki's mind was making new knots. "I have a journal that belongs to her, I brought it with me."

He took the old worn-out notebook from his bag and handed it to them. The older woman took it and opened to the first page. She read a few lines then looked up at Baki with frozen eyes.

"Please, come inside, we have kept you waiting at the door like this, forgive me."

"That's all right," said Baki.

In the living room they sat across from each other in armchairs. Through a broad window the blue waters of the Bosphorus and the green slopes on the opposite shore looked like a painting.

"When you said Miskal I assumed you were asking after my daughter, it never occurred to me you might be asking for my mother. She died the year my daughter was born, and I named my daughter after her."

Like a rare museum piece, the journal was resting on the glass coffee table between them.

"Let me explain," said Baki. "Your mother Miskal Hanım's fiancé died in 1938 when he was a soldier, well I actually don't know that, maybe he lost his memory after an accident. A soldier by the name of Adem Giritli kept a journal and his writings were dedicated to Miskal Hanım. In the note at the beginning he asks the finder of this journal to return it to Miskal Durusu and he provides an address. I came here looking for that address. When Adem Giritli died this journal supposedly fell into the hands of another soldier. Now that soldier was a little strange, it seems he was the one who had suffered a loss of memory, he remembered nothing of his past. After deserting the army, he traveled to many different cities, and he continued to write in this journal. There he hypothesized that he might very well be Adem Giritli and dreamed of the day his memory would return, the day he would remember everything. When he died, the journal was passed on to my grandfather, who gave it to me two months ago. Since then I can't stop thinking about it. Despite all the years since those words were written, I felt that Miskal Hanım had the right to see a journal that was after all addressed to her."

"We've made fresh tea," said the woman.

Young Miskal went into the kitchen and came back with tea glasses on a tray. She put down a glass for Baki and then one for her mother.

Baki tossed three cubes of sugar in his tea.

"Oh, and I haven't even introduced myself, I'm Baki."

"Zübeyde," said the woman, "and you already know my daughter. Are you a student?"

"Yes, studying economics at Bosphorus, I'm in my first year."

"What a coincidence, my daughter just started there this year, too."

"Really? Which department?"

"I'm studying mathematics," said Miskal, turning to her mother. "Mom, did grandma have a previous fiancé?"

"Yes," said Zübeyde Hanım. "Mom was engaged to a teacher who died during his military service. Back then there was a war in the East similar to the one now. Her fiancé was killed in a skirmish and was buried there, he didn't have a funeral here in Istanbul. Mom struggled to pull herself together and was dealing with the pain of her loss when she started receiving these strange letters.

Supposedly they were coming from her fiancé. The writer claimed that he had lost his memory and that once he remembered his past, he would come to Istanbul to marry her. She kept those letters in a box somewhere. There was an old mansion here before they built this apartment building on the same plot of land. When Mom married Dad, she moved to Büyükada, that's when they had this place built. When Dad died, Mom and I moved back here. But those letters—if they were still coming—would never have made it here as the name of the street had changed and the mansion destroyed."

"Mom, you've never talked about this before."

"How could I know. This was so many years ago, I even forgot all about it."

As Baki looked at the mother and daughter sitting across from him, he noticed that their eyes matched the color of the sea behind them. It reminded him of what Adem Giritli had written about Miskal's eyes. Baki was thinking of another past, one that had been lived by another man, and here it was unfolding right before his eyes.

"Mom," said Miskal, "do you know where those letters are?"

"They must be in the house in Büyükada, among the other things Mom left us."

They were speaking of a forgotten history.

"Shall we go to Büyükada tomorrow and have a look?"

"Slow down, let's read this journal first and get a sense of what's going on."

"How interesting," said Miskal, thrilled. "Grandma has led a life that seems right out of a movie."

Baki smiled as if he were speaking of something he knew well.

"Miskal Hanım, with such a wonderful name you are actually keeping alive the fascinating life she led."

"There's nothing interesting about my name," said Miskal, scrunching up her face. "Miskal was a measurement used to weigh things, that's all. They used to make fun of me for it when I was in primary school."

"What are you saying?" said Baki, sitting up in his chair. "It's the most beautiful of names."

"Miskal? Beautiful?"

"Don't you know? Four thousand years ago the Akkadians would have called you Meshkalu. In Aramaic you would be Shikla, in Hebrew they'd call you Shekel. In Syriac they would say Siklos, and the Armenians would praise you as Mispal. All the races and all the religions have adopted your name, drawing power from your presence. You are a Miskal, the one who gathers histories from new horizons, balancing ages and lands that are so very far from one another. No age in history would have meaning without you."

Bosphorus University

Istanbul, 2002

The downpour started when students were in the university garden protesting the education system at a forum they had organized. Despite the force of the rain, they were still shouting slogans and giving speeches, resolutely showing no sign of going anywhere. Although a large crowd had gathered most of them had quickly dispersed, leaving only a few people with raincoats or umbrellas; they were most likely plainclothes police officers. Baki was among those who were still standing. He would have long since taken shelter in the canteen if Miskal hadn't joined the protest. But luckily the next speaker announced that the forum had come to an end after crying out that new rallies would be organized every day.

Miskal and Baki went to the Central Canteen across from the garden where they ordered tea and sat down at a table by the window. They took off their raincoats and hung them on the back of their seats. They warmed up their hands on their hot glasses of tea.

"Do you always join the rallies?" asked Baki.

"Mom took me to the International Women's Day rally twice. This is third rally I've been to. When I saw the sign on the bulletin board the other day, I decided to come."

"Aren't you afraid?"

"I don't know."

"Wouldn't it be better to know?"

"Are you afraid?"

"I'm not afraid," said Baki, "but I don't want to get distracted from my lessons. I stay away from this sort of stuff."

"So many different things can distract you from your lessons: reading, going to the cinema, hunting down an address so that you can deliver an old journal to people you don't even know."

"You're right," said Baki, smiling and slightly blushing. "I do even more than all that."

"I'm like you," said Miskal, "I read, go to the movies, turn my grandmother's house upside down so I can find those letters mentioned in the journal."

"Did you go to the house in Büyükada?" asked Baki.

"I went with Mom and we found the letters in a cupboard. But after reading everything in the journal, those letters seemed strange, sad, and at the same time frightening."

"Did you read the whole journal?"

"Mom and I read it out loud," said Miskal. She stopped and narrowed her eyes. "We cried a lot. What sad lives they led."

"I couldn't stop myself from reading those pages over again and again."

"You're already distracted from your lessons then, or

am I wrong?" There wasn't a hint of teasing in her voice, she was serious.

"You're right, that's sort of what happened. Struggling to pull myself together, I understood it wasn't going to happen until I found the address in the journal and learned what happened next."

"Did it make you feel any better when you came and found us?"

Baki looked into Miskal's eyes. "It felt good knowing I wasn't alone wandering through the story in that journal, good knowing that you and your mom were there, too, I felt like it took a weight off me."

"Do you know what Mom said?"

Just then singing broke out in a corner. The song coming from a group of students flooded the canteen. Baki leaned in closer to hear Miskal. "What did she say?" he asked.

"She said, it's as if this young man is living among the people in that journal, as if the fragility in your voice belongs to that time."

"Is it that obvious?"

"It really is."

"It's like I've fallen down a well and I don't know how to get out and I don't actually want to."

"It's not that bad," said Miskal. "Now I'm down there, too, and I have no complaints at all."

"I'm happy to hear that."

"I brought you a few things you're really going to like."

Miskal took a schoolbook from her bag. She opened it, pulled out several postcards, and put them down in front of Baki.

"Letters that came to your grandmother..." said Baki, his eyes shimmering. He ran his fingers over the faded envelopes as if touching a rare work of art and looked at the random pictures on the front of the postcards. Streets, buildings, and the crimson twilights of cities he didn't know. Baki brought those postcards to his nose and tried to catch the scent they carried over all the years. He looked up at Miskal with a blend of sadness and joy that cast a strange color.

"Is this everything?" he asked.

"No," said Miskal, "there's more at home. I brought you these so you could have a look."

"Seeing that you read the journal, tell me what you think? Did Adem Giritli die a soldier or did he lose his mind and become a wanderer? Was it Adem Giritli who lost his memory or someone else?"

"I've been talking this over with my mom for days. On one page it seems like the journal was written by one person, but on another page we get the feeling it was written by two different people."

"I had the same feeling. I couldn't get it out of my mind for months."

"Mom carefully studied the handwriting. She said the pages written when he was a soldier look no different than the ones written years later. If this isn't the same person writing, then the other soldier who found the journal must have spent a long time perfecting Adem Giritli's handwriting, he had to have copied it."

"What you said the other day was true, this is something out of a movie."

"It makes you sad," said Miskal, "but in a strange way it gives you the desire to be a part of those lives in the journal. Every letter is full of passion and pain."

Baki turned over the card on top of the pile and looked at the date and the signature.

"You're right, Miskal," he said, "you're right... who knows on what kind of day this was written, with what hope or despair."

Rome

Italy, 1966

THURSDAY, OCTOBER 13, 1966

My dearest Miskal Hanım, I got up early today. I left my room on the second floor that overlooks the Piazza Navona and came to this café by the pool of the Fontana del Nettuno on the other side of the square. It is quiet here in the early hours of the morning. Now I am sitting at a table outside. While Fiammetta, who owns this café, brought me my customary coffee and croissant, I took out pen and paper and began writing these lines to you. Although she knows how fearful I am of war, she let me know that the Americans were bombing North Vietnam again. With a laugh, she added there was no need for me to be afraid, as Vietnam was still in the same place on the map, which meant very far away from us. I laughed with her and thanked her for putting me at ease. She asked me which post office I would use to send my letter today. I send every letter from a different post office, hoping one might bring me good luck and an answer from you. Today I plan to send this letter from the post office in Via Marmorata. I am always surprised to see people admiring such a strange building that seems to reject the history of Rome. What's to love of a building with nothing but smooth walls and simple, unadorned windows? Even from a distance you feel its lack of spirit. Maybe the envelope that carries your name in a whisper will inspirit the walls of a post office like this. Soon I will get up and walk for an hour along the Tiber on my way to the building. As I watch the broad current of the river, I will think about how changing my name over the years, from İsa to Musa to others and converting to new religions did nothing at all to help open the secret door in my life. The prophets were given the secrets of the universe, but I am only seeking my own. Why am I deprived of this? This is what I say to the Tiber. When no one else is around. Looking at the water and losing myself in its endless current can take away my troubles. We are enjoying the last beautiful days of autumn. Soon a sharp north wind will drive away these cool breezes, leaving rain and then snow. The winters in Rome are harsh. How is your Istanbul, my dear Miskal? Have the cold winds started to blow? Has the color of the Bosphorus turned from blue to gray? Fiammetta has come to me with my second coffee and one for herself and sits down across from me. She tells me her mother's health relapsed again yesterday. "If she comes down you should make a hasty retreat," she says. Fiammetta lives with her mother, Roza, on the top floor of the café. No longer able to carry the weight of her years, Roza is often lost and forgetful, and she gets confused. After a turn for the worse last week, she took me for her husband, who died years ago, she came over to give me a hug. An embrace full of such longing. She took my hand, put it on her head, and I stroked her gray hair. She looked as happy as a child. "Are you hungry? I'll boil you some potatoes," she said. "I'm not hungry," I said. Now this made her sad and a bitterness seemed to drive away the happy expression on her face, and tears filled her eyes. We tend to think that no one can relive the past, but with these tricks of the mind the elderly do. Toward the end of their lives, they come to the edge of a future where they are overtaken by the past, indeed finding a way to bring it back. Breaking the glass of this clock we call the brain they find themselves in a present between past and future. When Roza took me for her dead husband, it was not an expression of her malady but rather a victory achieved in the face of cruel time. A victory of happiness. When Roza brought my fingers to her lips and kissed them, she was the master her own time. The world before her eyes was different than the world before my eyes. While she was a stranger in mine, in hers I was her husband from the past. We were experiencing two distinct realities. Whose truth was more valid in that moment? I took a sip of coffee as I thought it over. Then I told Fiammetta I would stay when her mother came down. Let Roza come and see me. Let her think that I am her husband again. Let her embrace me, and I will embrace her. Taking her face in my hands, I will look into her eyes, caress her hair, and say, "I'm hungry, Roza, would you boil me some potatoes?"

Emirgan

Istanbul, 2002

On his second visit to the Cevher Apartments, Baki brought a bouquet of asters. Zübeyde Hanım took the flowers and arranged them in a vase, which she placed on the windowsill beside pots of violets and primrose.

"Thank you, Baki," she said, "these pink flowers make my purple and yellow ones look even better."

"I'm glad you like them."

"I have some things to do in the kitchen," said Zübeyde Hanım, leaving Baki and Miskal alone in the living room.

"Flowers mean everything to Mom," said Miskal, "the house is full of them."

Outside a light rain was beginning to fall.

Baki and Miskal stood at the broad window. In silence they looked at the windblown waters of the Bosphorus. The trees on the opposite shore were just disappearing from view as the rain began to fall more heavily. Soon it would be hard to make out the passing ships.

"Your home really is beautiful," said Baki, "you could spend the whole day here watching the world outside."

"Yes, it is," said Miskal, "but you forget when you are steeped in beauty. Sometimes I sit in this living room for days without ever looking out. That's the danger that comes with owning something."

"How so?"

"When you own something, you possess its beauty, and then it becomes ordinary."

Slowly Baki said, "But beauty like this has a different face every day. Look, it's raining today. That ferryboat there is swimming close to the shore. A red tanker is coming down from up there. The beauty is never the same, it's changing every moment. What I saw through this window last week was nothing like the beauty I am seeing now, it's both different and the same."

Miskal turned her head and looked at Baki who was a breath away.

"To always notice such beauty, you need an eye on the outside, and you need words."

"Come to our house one day," said Baki. "Maybe there you, too, will see beauty I fail to see."

They were interrupted by the sound of Zübeyde Hanım's voice. "Come sit down, kids."

Zübeyde Hanım put down a tray of teacups and sweets. As they sat around the table, she gave them each a plate and a glass of tea.

"You take three sugars, right?"

"Yes," said Baki, a little surprised, "thank you."

"Try this rice pudding, I hope you like it. Then we'll have cookies."

"My mother's really talented," said Miskal.

"Baki," said Zübeyde Hanım, "when you came here the other day, I was so overwhelmed by that journal that I didn't really get to know you. I asked Miskal to invite you back."

"The rice pudding is wonderful, hat's off to the chef," said Baki, swallowing another spoonful. "Thank you for inviting me."

"So kids," said Zübeyde Hanım, "tell me, how's school going? I'm asking both of you."

"I tell you that every day, Mom," said Miskal.

"Tell me again."

"As far as I can see," said Baki, "Miskal's doing well at school, and she easily fits in. I've had a hard time, because of that journal, it was difficult for me to focus on my studies."

"Baki, I was able to learn so much about my mother thanks to you. I started reading the journal again yesterday. I decided to visit her home in Büyükada and go through her things one more time. I'm sure that there's so much to discover among all that stuff. If you like you can join us next weekend, the three of us can go together."

"I'd like that very much."

"Why wait until the weekend?" said Miskal. "Let's go tomorrow."

"Miskal Hanım, tomorrow is Monday, don't you have school?"

"What's one day—"

"The house on the island isn't going anywhere, we can go on the weekend."

Thunder roared in the sky. When it passed, the sound of the rain was even more present. Istanbul was having a stormy day.

"It's a good thing we didn't get caught in the rain," said Baki.

"How's your mother?" asked Zübeyde Hanım. "Miskal told me that you live with her and your grandfather. Are they both well?"

"She's fine, but I can't say the same for Granddad."

"Is he ill?"

"He's actually really fit. He works from morning to night every day and he never complains. But lately he's been getting a little confused, and he is having memory slips. He'll have a brief episode and then come back to his senses."

"What do the doctors say?"

"Granddad refuses to go to the hospital. There's a doctor who comes to the house, but Granddad doesn't really use the medicine he prescribes. He fights about it with Mom."

"I know a good doctor, maybe he could see him."

"Thanks. If we can ever convince him to leave the cemetery, we'll bring him to see him."

"Leave the cemetery?"

Baki looked at her with a blank expression on his face. "Granddad is a master gravestone maker. For years he's been living in the cemetery where he has his workshop. My grandmother's grave is there, which is why he moved to the cemetery in the first place, and in the evening, he sits on the porch and talks to my grandma who rests in a grave under a redbud tree across from his house. It might seem strange, but he's happy, and I've never seen anyone happier—"

"How wonderful," said Miskal, interrupting him.

"Yes," said Zübeyde Hanım, "it seems wonderful from the outside."

Merkez Efendi Cemetery

Istanbul, 2002

The autumn wind made broad waves on the sea before it reached the cemetery, swirling over the earth and through the trees as the starry night slowly rotated like a sublime lamp casting light across the cemetery. Avdo looked up and found the stars he knew and drew the paths between them. It was a game he had played since childhood, where he would lose himself in the endless roads that were stretched across the sky. Time was passing and lives were ending but the stars were still the same. While the days dropped off one by one, stars were forever following the same route. In a wool sweater, Avdo walked slowly through the cool air as he looked up at the stars and at the passing gravestones. Which was on the earth and which was in the sky, on nights like these he was all turned around. He had the impression he was walking among the stars and, running his fingers over the stones, he thought he felt stardust. Startled by a noise, he stopped. He turned around to look. No one was there, but he heard footsteps. His own childhood, it was clear from how the footsteps fell on the grass, his childhood was gently coming after him. Avdo held his breath as he waited for the bare feet to come closer in the darkness. He waited, time passed, the night darkened, the sound of running water from the fountain circled the cemetery seven times. But his childhood had no way of returning. The footsteps kept the same distance. Was this what they call the past? Far away but close enough for you to hear it.

Lost in thought, Avdo continued to walk through the dried grass. He quietly passed the graves of the Old Sailor, Madlen, and Toteve and came to the grave of the Man with Seven Names. He looked down at the grave bed covered in leaves and up at the great stone that stood there. He leaned over and collected the dried leaves and cleared the ground. His hands still dirty and covered in leaves, he touched the gravestone. Black as the night and covered in white streaks that resembled the trails of stars. The autumn wind thrummed through the hole in the center of the stone. A life and a universe were entwined in that thrum. Avdo brought his head closer to the hole and whispered. "I know you," he said to the Man with Seven Names, "and you know me. But the Avdo you know is not this old man with a weary mind, he is a ten-year-old child. And that child who never left me over the course of a lifetime is right here watching us in the darkness." He turned to face the darkness. The darkness was a holy void. Not a beginning, not an end. Forever expanding. North was south in the darkness, and east was west, every direction in the same place. The center of darkness was wherever you stood.

There all truths became mystery. Spellbinding and terrifying enough to drive a man from his senses. The darkness deepened and the thrumming slowly grew. A wind aloft on broad wings blew through the cypress trees, rustling the branches. Somewhere an owl cried out. Again, there was the sound of footsteps coming from somewhere near the running water of the fountain. Who was watching whom? Was Avdo's childhood coming after him, or had he spent a lifetime searching for his childhood?

Merkez Efendi Cemetery

Istanbul, 2002

TODAY, EVENING

When the Blond Sailor arrived a wide-blowing southwester had already swept away the clouds, leaving a full moon shimmering in the sky. A cool evening breeze was picking up, but the Blond Sailor preferred to sit on the porch. Reyhan, Baki, and Miskal came and joined him around the table. They were all silent as they looked over at the fountain and the cypress trees. The Blond Sailor was thinking of something he had heard from Avdo years ago and events that Avdo had read to him from the journal. Fixing his glasses, he looked at the face of young Miskal who was sitting right across from him. From the hard lines in her face, he tried to get a sense of the other Miskal, whose name was evoked in the faded pages of that journal as if she were a goddess. He narrowed his eyes. He complained of how his glasses no longer helped him with his old eyes. Reyhan asked if he was hungry. "Don't mind that now," he said, "tell me about Avdo. He hasn't left my mind since you called."

A WEEK AGO

The sun was rising high in the sky when Reyhan grew restless. Although Avdo was in the habit of getting up early every morning to work, he was still asleep. After pacing around his bed several times, she finally decided to wake him and called out to him. Opening his eyes that seemed clouded over in mist, he looked up at her. It was not entirely clear if he was asleep or awake. "Where am I?" he said. Reyhan was at a loss for an answer. She sat down on his bed. Without changing his gaze, Avdo said, "Let me sleep a little more," and closing his eyes he began breathing hoarsely again as he drifted back to sleep. Reyhan wept in silence. She thought about what to do. If she tried bringing him to a hospital, her father would resist. If she brought a doctor, he wouldn't take the medicine. The only man old Avdo would listen to was still called the Blond Sailor, even though all his hair was gray. Reyhan hurried to the phone and called him in Venice and told him about her father.

TODAY, EVENING

"I miss this place," said the Blond Sailor, turning to the cemetery. "I love the sound of the waves in Venice and the voices that echo off the damp walls but with every passing day I really do miss the sound of the tinkling water of the fountain blending into the silent night here. Of course, I miss Avdo most of all. When I talk this way my wife,

Roberta, she tells me I am getting old." Reyhan smiled at the Blond Sailor. "My dad really misses you, too," she said. "If only he would accept his condition. He has such confidence in the power of his body that he can't come to grips with the weariness of his mind. He doesn't want to admit that his mind is aging faster than his body. Consider what he did today, a man who normally sits and listens to the radio into the wee hours of the night climbs straight into bed at twilight, and when he was so pleased that Miskal had come to visit."

TODAY, AFTERNOON

When Avdo heard the name of the girl who had arrived with Baki, he stopped what he was doing; the whole day he had been chiseling stone, engraving motifs for the souls. He went onto the porch and sat down with them. For the last week Baki had not been staying in his dorm, choosing to stay with his grandfather in case he took another bad turn. He hadn't told him he would be coming back with Miskal today as he wanted to surprise him. Miskal was full of excitement when she came into the cemetery and set her eyes on the shed among the graves. It looked like something from an old painting, she felt like she had stepped into the life she had read about in the journal. She drank some water from the fountain and looked carefully at the old trees and the crumbling stones. Sitting on the porch, she continued to take everything in with her eyes. When Avdo spoke, she listened to the way his voice rose and fell in waves. The way he jumped from one topic to another. At one point, Avdo stopped and looked at the young girl's face. "Miskal Hanım, did you once have long hair, the way you do now?" he asked. "I don't understand," she said, "do you mean when I was little?" Laughing, Avdo went on in a loud voice. "I mean well before that! Sixty or seventy years ago, when you were still engaged to Third Lieutenant Adem Giritli." Miskal was at a loss for words. A silence fell over them. They looked at each other. Avdo gathered himself, put on a serious face, and turned to the graves as he slipped into the distance. It wasn't long before he looked at the young girl again and said, "Miskal Hanım, let me tell you a fairy tale, the tale of the carpenter and the queen with the long hair." It was unusual for Avdo to tell stories like this in the daytime as he loved telling them around a fire on a dark night. "Once upon a time there was a carpenter," he began. "He was making furniture for the palace when he caught site of the queen and fell in love. She was sitting on a divan, looking at her face and her long hair in a mirror. When she saw the reflection of the carpenter, the mirror fell from her hand. Their eyes met as the glass shattered, and they both quickly looked away. After the carpenter left the palace and returned to his workshop, he knew he would not be able to give up on this love as it gnawed away at him throughout the night. He went and pulled a chest out of his storeroom. This was a keepsake left to him by his master. Inside he kept his magical mallet and his magical nails and with them he made a door, which he brought to the palace. After fixing it upon a wall, he stepped straight through it, disappearing into another world. A beggar watching him from a distance couldn't believe his eyes and called out to others as he raced over to the door. Although he swore that the man had gone through the door, not one of them would believe him. The beggar himself tried the door but to no avail—there was no passage through. When the crowd broke up, the beggar, who was terribly curious and fearful of the magic he had seen, hurried off to the soldiers who guarded the city. But where had the carpenter gone? Meanwhile the carpenter had slipped through the door into a lush green palace garden full of flowers. There he found the queen and told her of his love for her and his magic art. At that time, the glory of queens came not from their magnificence but from the depth of their hearts. The queen told the carpenter that she loved him, too. They embraced, they made love, they stayed together until the sun fell and finally left the sky. Promising the queen that he would come again, the carpenter left. He found his door and went through. But the moment he stepped outside, the beggar saw him again and cried out in excitement. The soldiers hurried over and seized the carpenter and brought him and his door before the king. The king asked the carpenter for his secret and then presented him with two choices: He could either speak of it or die. The carpenter said that every magic door was made for one person alone and that only he could pass through this door. Nevertheless, the king gave it a go. He stepped through and found himself on the other side but in exactly the same room. Make me a door, he ordered the carpenter, I will bring you the finest wood. But the carpenter refused, saying that all wood was the same, and that if the king wanted a door above and beyond all others, he would have to have one made from ice. Kings always deserved the very best of all things, he said. Back then, the greed of kings was astonishing. He ordered his men to bring ice down from the mountains. Straightaway the carpenter set out to work. The king waited and waited while the carpenter worked all night, not sleeping a wink, and before daybreak the king set his hand on the door made of ice. His eyes were flickering as he stepped through the ice door and was gone. The day dawned with the light of the sun streaming in through stained-glass windows, filling the palace rooms with light. So indeed, the ice was nothing like wood... as time slowly passed... the ice began to melt and melt... Meanwhile the queen was just rising from her sleep and speaking with her maids... the ice melting, melting..."

At this point in the story Avdo paused with absent eyes. If memory was a bird, he felt the bird of his mind had taken flight and was drifting away. For a little while he waited for it to return. But, flapping its wings, the bird of memory rose higher until it came to the clouds that laced the sky. Turning his gaze to the sky, Avdo laughed. Paying no mind to the strangeness of his laughter, he mumbled to himself, "You worked a lot today, your mind, too, let's go inside and sleep a little." With that heaviness particular to the elderly, he sat up, and as he stepped over to the door, he had the impression that, like the carpenter in the fairy tale, he would cross over into the world beyond.

TODAY, AFTERNOON

Reyhan brought tea, she poured a glass for Miskal and then one for Baki. She gave them each a slice of cake. As she spoke to Miskal she looked at her long hair, not her blue eyes. She thought of how her Shahmaran comb would suit hair like this and how the mythical creature would smile as she gently ran the bone tips through her hair.

TODAY, EVENING

After listening to Reyhan, the Blond Sailor said, "I never heard that before. So, there are stories Avdo never told me." In his voice was curiosity and concern. The story dropping off in the middle like that was cause for concern. Avdo's health was deteriorating. Without waiting any longer Avdo had to be persuaded to make a decision, and the job fell to the Blond Sailor. If he couldn't convince his friend then no one could. They heard the door open. As if he had come down from another world, Avdo stood on the threshold, a calm expression on his face. He turned his gaze to the darkness. He slowly walked over to the corner of the porch. He had no concern for those who were sitting there, his concern was either the graves or the old trees. He looked up and ran his eyes across the sky. He was expecting a broad-winged bird to appear and come to him. He could not see it, but he could feel it coasting in the dark sky. The Blond Sailor could wait no longer, and he stood up. "Avdo, my dear friend," he said. "We haven't seen each other in such a long time. I just arrived from Venice. I came to see you. My wife, Roberta, sends her greetings and her love." He waited for his words to jog Avdo's memory. Avdo waited, too; if he heard the flapping of the bird in the darkness he would come back to his senses, and so he simply stood there. The Blond Sailor embraced him. His arms around his shoulders, his nose close to his damp neck that smelled of sweat and longing. Like dry branches, Avdo's arms hung limply at his side as he waited. The sound of the wind licked the branches, the sound of time roused the spirits, but the whoosh of wings did not come. Slowly Avdo slipped out of the Blond Sailor's arms. One by one, he looked at the people around him. "You," he said sharply, "why didn't you wake me up? It's grown dark out!" He turned back to the cemetery. Sitting up in their graves, the spirits were looking at him. They were struggling to understand what was happening in his home tonight, curious to see what Avdo was going to do. As if these spirits were a part of the tale he had told. They had stepped through the ice door, crossing over into a totally different world, and now they were stuck. The door had melted. They could not go back to their former lives. They could only see and hear from a distance and endure the pain. They were leaning against gravestones that shone in the darkness as if freshly washed in the bronze light of the full moon. The water flowing from the fountain took its share of the light. Lifting his hand, Avdo gestured in that direction. "The almond trees," he said. "There are the almond trees!" Speaking in his softest voice, the Blond Sailor came closer. "Avdo, my dear friend, let's sit down and talk a little." Avdo looked at him with a worried expression on his face. "Sit down?" he said. "Sit down at a time like this? She is waiting for me over there." In the darkness they saw nothing but the graves and the cypress trees while Avdo looked out over a vast almond grove. In a commanding voice, he went on. "I can wait no longer. I have to get to the almond grove at once." He could no longer hear what those on the porch were saying. And suddenly he felt the talons of that broad-winged bird on his shoulder and he was lifted gently into the air and carried away.

Village of Konak Görmez

Haymana Plain, 1958

Since the meadows had turned green and the grass was more abundant, the cattle were being led back to the village late in the day. The young herdsman had planned to arrive before sunset, but the herd was taking its time, stopping at every patch of green they found along the way. When Elif saw that two white cows had left the herd and were grazing on the meadow beside the cemetery road, she left the girls who were still filling their buckets at the fountain and led the cows to the other side of the ravine. From there they could walk down to the indigo house on their own.

The next day when the herd was coming into the village there was no sign of those white cows. Considering that they hadn't made it to the meadow, they had to be idling somewhere among the almond trees. Elif went to find them as the sun was painting the sky red as it fell behind a hill. In the distance she spotted the white cows among the trees and quickened her step. If she left them there any longer, they would slip into the darkness. When she came closer, she saw someone sitting beneath a tree. She slowed down and then recognized the man.

Avdo rose to his feet.

"Don't be afraid, I only want to talk," he said.

"Did you keep the animals waiting here?" she asked.

"Would you believe me if I said no?"

"I'm engaged, stop following me."

"In my letter I told you I wouldn't, in the letter you never answered."

"I can't write back to someone I don't know. I sent word to you through Baki, I told you to forget me."

"Even Baki, who is still a child, understood that I will never be able to forget you."

Elif paused to think about how she might answer him. She did not want to make a mistake.

"You sent me a state-minted gold coin wrapped in a handkerchief."

"Yes, they gave it to me when I started work here, I gave it to you as a gift."

"I can't accept it. Tell Baki to come see me. I'll give it to him, and he can take it back to you."

It was Avdo's turn to pause. This was the first time he was speaking with Elif and perhaps he would never have another chance.

"Elif, I have nothing, all I had was that gold coin. I gave you what I own. From now on everything of mine is yours."

It was frightening to hear Avdo address her by name. She thought that suddenly the distance between them would disappear.

"You came to our village as a stranger. Finish your work, then go away as a stranger."

"Not unless you come with me."

Elif had nothing else to say. This was enough. She was about to forget that she had come to round up the cows. She moved to go fetch them.

Slowly Avdo stepped forward, trying not to frighten her. With two steps left between them, he stopped.

Standing her ground, Elif became firm, she furrowed her brow. "Go over there," she said, "I'll shout and the whole village will come running."

"There's no need for you to shout, I just want to talk, would you listen?"

"You said what you had to say. What else is there?"

"I still haven't said all that I have to say."

She ignored him and stepped over to the cows and took them by the neck to lead them to the village road. She assumed he would stop her. Then what was she going to do? She could hear the dogs barking in the distance. She looked at the houses on the far side of the village. She counted her footsteps, one, two, three, and then she stopped. She turned and looked at him.

"Fine then," she said, "tell me whatever it is you have to say. And make it quick, it's getting dark."

The red sky was turning dark blue. The wind was running through the trees, rustling the leaves. Almonds were trembling on their branches, and the skylarks were calling from a nearby hilltop. Night was quickly falling as she waited for Avdo to speak.

"The evening star has started to shine," he said, "can you see it?"

Elif looked at him in surprise. What he was saying? Were they going to linger here making idle small talk?

When the stars came out to light up the sky everyone in the village had to be at home. If she were just a little late, they would worry and go out to find her. When Elif saw Avdo still gazing up at the western sky, she became curious, too, and looked up from between the cows.

"Which one is the evening star?" she asked.

"It's there. Look, the one shining there right above the hill."

"That silver star?"

"Yes, that's it."

"How do you know?"

"It's easy to find, the silver one that is especially bright. It always follows the sun, in the evening it appears in the west, and in the morning we see it in the east. It never leaves the sun."

"How simple."

"Yes, it is simple," said Avdo. "In the same way I won't leave you either."

Elif held the cows tightly by the neck. She pulled them closer as if for protection, hiding her face.

"This goes nowhere," she said, "you have your road and I have mine."

Avdo took two steps back. He wanted to lessen the tension she was struggling to conceal.

"I am not going to take your hand and force you to come away with me. My wish is that you will understand me, that you will love me. Say whatever you like, but I will continue to wait until that day comes. In this life I have nothing else to wait for."

"Time will show that you waited in vain."

He looked at her with sorrow.

"Do you know when I was little and singing on the streets kids would pass me, holding their mother's hands. The mother had a name and when the child drifted off to sleep at night he knew her name, he knew her face. I never had the chance to fall asleep that way. I gave up on the idea of ever seeing my mother's face, but all the same, and if nothing else, I went from city to city on my little feet, looking for her name. I asked everyone I met, I looked for her in every language that I learned. I always said I would give up all the words in all the languages, I would sacrifice my speech, if only I could know my mother's name. The meaning of life was in that word, in sleeping with that word and forgetting life in doing so. I was a child. I could not manage to find that magical word. I grew desperate. With no other path before me, I decided to dedicate my life to gravestones, taking refuge in death. How could I have known that in a village on these steppes I would suddenly come upon the word I had sought all those years? It was an afternoon when I saw you at the fountain, I heard your name and slept so beautifully that night, I knew the word was you. The next day when I woke I was someone else altogether. You were the word that I was looking for, you were Elif, your face was Elif. The same fate that commanded me to live without a mother as a child has commanded me to live with you now. To my fate, I bowed my head."

The sharpness in Elif's voice softened. "Don't speak like that, you're a stranger who has come from far away. I am afraid of you."

"Don't be, Elif. Don't be afraid of me."

A silence came between them. These were hot days in the season, the evenings were warm. The wind was blowing more softly than usual. The silence made Elif feel even more confused, she didn't know what to say.

"They . . ." she scarcely said, "they will be worried about me at home."

"Can I ask you one last thing?" Avdo said.

"What's that?"

"Would you say my name?"

She was clinging on to the white necks of the cows. Amid the changing colors of earth and sky, it was only in their whiteness that she could hide. Slowly she looked up.

"Avdo," she said, whispering, "it's getting dark, I should go."

The End

Glossary

abla: Older sister, commonly used with a first name as a sign of respect.

agha: An honorific once used for landowners but now commonly used for those holding any position of power.

Alevi: A member of Muslim group, the followers of Ali, the cousin and son-in-law of the prophet Muhammed. Alevi is the term used for a large number of heterodox Muslim communities with different characteristics. Differing from Sunnism and other Twelver Shia, Alevis have no binding religious dogmas. They constitute the largest religious minority in Turkey and make up approximately fifteen percent of the population. Alevis believe in the unity of Allah, Muhammed, and Ali, since the true meaning of the Koran is considered to be taken as a secret by Ali and must be taught by a teacher, who transmits the teachings of Ali to his disciple.

Arabesk: A style of Arabic popular music created in Turkey that has become popular since the 1960s. The melancholy songs often focus on unrequited love.

ayran: A salty, frothy drink made from yogurt.

bey: An honorific title added to the first name to show respect.

bohça: A sack often made from a blanket or quilt.

çilehane: A windowless room where Sufis would spend forty days in complete isolation from the outside world, literally "a room of suffering."

Ferhat and Şirin: The legend of Ferhat and Şirin is a traditional, tragic love story. Ferhat is tasked with boring through a mountain with a sledgehammer in order to reach his beloved.

gözleme: A large savory crepe made with minced meat, cheese, mixed herbs, or spinach.

Halay: A communal folk dance common at Anatolian weddings and celebrations.

heyamola: A chantey or seaman's cry similar to "heave-ho."

Hıdırellez: A celebration of the advent of spring.

lahmacun: A thin-crust pizza made with minced meat and pepper.

meze: An appetizer typically made with seafood or vegetables in olive oil, often served with *rakı*.

misbaha: A rosary used to count the ninety-nine names of God in the Muslim faith, more commonly known as a *tespih* in Turkish.

muska: An amulet or charm used to ward off evil spirits.

nahit: A white stone prominently used in the architecture of southeastern Anatolia.

rakı: A strong alcoholic spirit that many people consider to be the national drink of Turkey.

Shahmaran: An intelligent and good-hearted creature with the body of a snake and the head of a human, common in Kurdish, Iraqi, Iranian, and Anatolian mythology. It was believed that the Shahmaran, whose spirit is passed on to girls when they die, never grow old.

Zaza: A Kurdish people who live in the heartland of eastern Turkey.

zemheri: The coldest time of the year, also used to express an intense feeling of cold that lasts forty days.

Zulfiqar: A double-edged sword that was used by Ali and which is a common symbol in Alevi culture.

THE SEVEN NAMES

Adem: The Turkish equivalent of Adam.

Ali: A cousin, son-in-law, and companion of the prophet Muhammed. Ali is the spiritual leader in Alevi culture.

Haydar: A title for Ali that means "lion."
İsa: The Turkish equivalent of Jesus.
Muhammed: The holy prophet of Islam.
Musa: The Turkish equivalent of Moses.
Yunus: The Turkish equivalent of Jonah.